S0-ESE-913

THE GIFT

BOOK I

ELEANOR

R. A. WILLIAMS

THE GIFT, Book 1. Eleanor.

Copyright © 2021 by R A Williams.

All rights reserved.

This is a work of fiction. The characters, organisations and occurrences in this novel are a product of the author's imagination or, where actual persons and events are presented, are done so fictitiously.

Library of Congress Registration No. : TXU 2-183-876
Service Request No.: 1-8417688381
Author Contact: HellfireCorner@iCloud.com

Cover design by BookBaby.
Maps by Uroš Pajić
Chapter heading artwork by David Pickford

Hardcover ISBN: 978-1-09837-8-578
eBook ISBN: 978-1-09837-8-585

Excerpt From: R. A Williams. THE GIFT, Book 2. Balthasar.
Available at all fine booksellers.

All my love to my wife, Daiana,
and our blinder, Tommy.

And for Mum,
for being the window to a world
long past, but never forgotten.

hic iacet: Balthasar Toule nicius huius ecclesie qui obiit año domini millesimo quingentesimo nono die mensis iunii, peat tibi deus.

Expecto resurrectionem mortuorum

Contents

14 April, 1912.
RMS Titanic, The North Atlantic 2

30 April 1912.
Banana, Belgian Congo 41

12 July 1915.
Cape Helles, Gallipoli 48

31 March 1929. St Dunstan's,
Bloomfield Hills, Michigan 81

4 April 1929.
Abaco Islands, Bahamas 103

8 April 1929.
Islas De La Bahia, Honduras 118

27 April 1929. St Dunstan's Prep,
Bloomfield Hills, Michigan 169

14 April 1912.
RMS Titanic, The North Atlantic 182

27 August 1936. St Dunstan's,
Bloomfield Hills, Michigan 200

26 August 1939. Tor Externsteine,
Teutoburger Wald, Germany 219

29 August 1939.
   The Strait of Dover   245

29 August 1939.
   Folkestone, Kent   252

10 April 1921.
   Kinuwai, Belgian Congo   284

30 August 1939.
   Folkestone, Kent   314

31 August 1939.
   Folkestone, Kent   334

Acknowledgment   387

Read an excerpt from
   The Gift, Book 2. Balthasar.   389

   9 September 1940. Highgate Cemetery

In 1925 a humble essay appeared in the French sociology journal *L'Année Sociologique*. Written by Dr Marcel Mauss, a French ethnologist and socialist, *The Gift* was considered by many in the field of sociology and anthropology to be groundbreaking. Mauss — like many of his contemporaries, — was deeply effected by the loss of both family and colleagues to the trenches of the Great War. As a result, he retreated from the known world, finding solace in research.

In *The Gift*, Mauss asked: 'What power resides in the gift that causes its recipient to pay it back?'

He believed the giver of the gift does not merely give a physical gift, but also the soul of themselves. As a result the gift indissolubly ties the giver to the recipient, creating a debt that must be repaid in kind. To not do so could have the gravest of consequences.

As a result of the horrifying mass slaughter Mauss bore witness to, he put forward a belief that sacrifice (some argue he in fact meant love) — more than anything else — was the gift compelling the recipient to "*Do ut des*. I give so that you may give".

In the end, nothing comes for free.

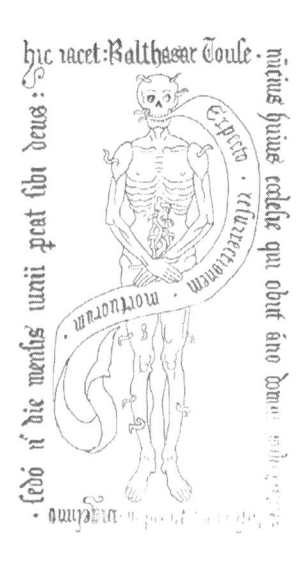

14 April, 1912.

RMS Titanic,
The North Atlantic

'Bollocks to Scotland Road,' grunted Podgy Higginbotham, waddling along the corridor named after the working-class thoroughfare he hailed from. Used by both steerage passengers and crew to traverse Titanic unseen, Scotland Road was poles apart from the stately First-Class corridors above. He paused. Something beyond the steady *thrum-thrum-thrum* of the ship's engines caught his attention. Straining his ear, he heard it again. Distant and peculiar, it sounded something like the sweet cantata of an Anglican boys' choir.

Titanic played tricks on him.

'Enough your mithering, Podgy,' he told himself. Further along the corridor, a steward emerged from the gentlemen's lavatory.

'Is that me auld fella Dougie?' Higginbotham asked, squinting through his spectacles. 'You heard something just now?'

Dougie Beedham put his mop and pail down onto the wood-planked floor before wiping his hands on his apron. Looking up and down the eight-hundred-foot passageway, he shook his head.

Higginbotham sighed, the strange choir going quiet. 'This ship is doin' me head in.'

'You want something to moan about, have a look in the loo. Atlantic's calm as a boat pond and some auld bastard manages to be sick all over it,' Beedham replied.

'You wouldn't be tidying up someone's horrible mess if you was a Second-Class steward.'

'You wouldn't be in a lot of bother about walking this great long passageway if you was better than a stores keeper.'

'I seen enough of Scotland Road in Liverpool. Didn't reckon I'd trudge up and down it on a White Star steamer thrice a bloody day,' replied Higginbotham, tugging at the peacoat prickling the back of his neck.

'You stout scouse,' Beedham pointed to the coat, buttoned tightly about Higginbotham's waist. The taut buttons looked as though they might shoot off at any moment. 'You look like a grease-filled sausage in that clobber. I reckon you only visited Scotland Road's pie shops.'

'Who you calling a scouse, you blert? You is from Liverpool an' all.'

'I ain't Titanic boiler-like, is I?'

Beedham wasn't wrong, "Podgy" wasn't just a term of endearment. He was four stone over regulation for seamen employed with White Star Line, but his decades at sea offered value beyond his weight. White Star Line had the pick of the best, ensuring Titanic's maiden voyage was without incident, and had been happy to overlook his ample girth.

'Have you a bifter?' Beedham asked.

Higginbotham retrieved a box of cigarettes, offering his friend one before sparking one up for himself.

'What time is it?'

Retrieving the watch attached to his ring of keys, he looked at the time. 'Quarter past eleven,' Higginbotham said. 'Bloody hell. I'm late on. Best get agate.'

'Crikey,' Steward Beedham said as he followed with his mop and pail. 'I was meant to be off duty at eleven. Where you off to, then?'

'Some First-Class berk taking his motorcar to the States. I've orders to inspect it thrice a day.'

'Ain't it your honest employment to inspect cargo?'

'Marching up and down Scotland Road to check a motorcar in these calm seas? Not a thing shifting down there.'

Stopping at a steward's staircase, he heard a melody flowing faintly up from the labyrinth of companionways below. It was different from the cantata he'd heard before.

'Right,' Higginbotham said, grasping the polished wood handrail. 'I'm off.'

'Me as well. Gagging for a pint. Come round the stewards' mess when you're done. The lads have a few fighting ales after duty.'

'I'm on the ghoster shift. Won't see my bunk 'til dawn,' he said. Descending a few stairs, he heard the singing more clearly. 'Sounds as though someone's holding up the bar down here.'

Pausing at F-Deck, Higginbotham gazed aftward. The singing came from the Third-Class saloon — far from the ears of the nobility in their opulent staterooms above. Recognising the tune, he hummed along, *My lady far away*. It brought a smile to Higginbotham's sea-worn face; he'd left home to the same tune, thirty-five years before.

Descending to G-Deck, he leant against the stair railing, catching his breath. He was too heavy, his hips ached from rheumatism and he needed the loo. From the moment he'd boarded Titanic, he had felt unsettled; the ship was unashamedly decadent. Too big. Too surly. Below decks, an ominous darkness concealed itself. A darkness more foreboding than the fathomless North Atlantic. It gave him the shivers.

Higginbotham tucked the clipboard of cargo manifests under his arm and knocked on the door to the mailroom. He wasn't surprised to find that the clerks weren't answering at such an hour. Removing the ring of keys attached to a button on his trousers, he unlocked the door. Brass racks filled with bags of post cluttered the room on all sides. Descending an iron stairway to the Orlop, a deck completely off-limits to passengers and nearly at the bottom of the ship, he waddled across the mail storage hold brimming with registered post from the Continent. An unpleasant blast of stale air filled his nose as he swung open the hatch on Watertight Bulkhead C. Securing the handles behind him, he entered the icy gloom of the No. 2 Hold. He felt a thousand nautical miles from the lights and gaiety of the First-Class decks far above. Down there, in the gloomy and dank holds, all that was left below was the keel, and the freezing blackness of the North Atlantic below it.

'Baltic in here,' he moaned quietly to himself, pulling his coat collar tight about his neck.

Mr Carter of Pennsylvania had insisted his new Renault motorcar be inspected three times a day. If it were up to Higginbotham, he'd give it a single looking over in the morning and be done with it. However, orders came down from the ship's captain, and nobody mucked about with Captain Smith.

The holds of Titanic were unheated and also sparsely lit. Making his way through the cargo stores, Higginbotham's Wellington boots squeaked against the iron floor. Carter's Renault sat in the centre of the hold, strapped tightly to a wooden pallet. As ever, all was in order. Slipping the cargo manifest out from under his arm, Higginbotham ran a gloved finger down the list: mink coats from Russia, leaded crystal from Venice, rugs from Persia, a Roentgen secretary — whatever that was — and one 1912 Renault.

'Odds and sods,' he muttered, looking forward to the end of his shift and a warm pot of tea.

The sound of a distant cantata broke the silence once more. Straining his ear, he heard it cease, then begin again. High-pitched and pure, a distant, sweet staccato ending in a curious fugue as other angelic voices joined in.

'You're hearing things, you daft apeth,' he mumbled.

Squinting through the thick lenses of his spectacles, he noticed the hatch on Watertight Bulkhead B was ajar. Certain he'd secured it at the start of his shift, he moved to inspect it more closely. Condensation dripped from the handles, and as he swung it open, a peculiar odour greeted him. Dry-rotted cloth, like old sails.

There was nothing like that in the hold.

'Wot niffs in here?' he muttered to himself as he peered into the forward hold, more curious than afraid. It was dark and silent within. He reached for the light knob and found it too wet with condensation. It clicked, but the hold remained in darkness. Dodgy circuit — a common failure. Nonetheless, Titanic's engineers had been clever enough to fit an oil lamp to a hook beside the hatch. Striking a match, Higginbotham lit the wick, and amorphous shadows began to undulate around him. Resting the lamp on a crate stamped *RF Downey & Co*, he glanced at the his cargo manifest: 'Eight dozen tennis balls.'

He scoffed, removing a tin of cigarettes from his peacoat. It wasn't the oddest thing he'd heard shipped transatlantic, but it seemed silly. Tennis balls. Couldn't the Americans make them themselves?

Opening the box of matches once more, he tutted; just a single match remained. He singed his finger as he struck it and dropped the glowing match to the floor. He found it, still lit, lying between the crates beside what looked like an odd pile of debris. Bending with a groan, his gut impeding his reach, he retrieved the match, sparked up his bifter and adjusted the lamp's wick to have a closer look.

It wasn't debris after all; it was a jumble of fresh rodent guts. 'Nay, damn and blast it,' he cursed. Squinting through steamed-up spectacles he swept the hold with the lamp, nervous now about what could have torn the rats to pieces since Titanic's mouser abandoned the ship in Southhampton with her litter of kittens.

From the bow came an echo sounding a bit like the flutter of wings — a sound unusual in a ship's hold. It travelled in one direction, got lost amongst the crates, ricocheted off the iron hull and found itself again, now moving in another direction.

'Who's there?' Higginbotham called, flickering shadows rising and falling before the lamp. The disturbance came again. Fear leeched through his peacoat and, not for the first time that evening, a shiver ran down his spine.

'You ain't meant to be down here,' he said and paused, awaiting a response. None was forthcoming. 'I'm getting right knotted,' he boomed, more to fire his own courage than bait whoever was there. Then from the pocket of his coat he withdrew a cudgel, non-regulation, but in his trade, he'd found it useful on the odd occasion.

Advancing warily, his eyes swept the crates. All remained secure. His fear subsided, only to be replaced with the urge to wee again. Resting the lantern upon a crate he unbuttoned his kecks, and pissed against the hull.

'Uff, that's all right, that,' he said, looking lazily about. At the forward end of the hold, he noticed an upturned crate. He buttoned his trousers and picked up the lamp. Shuffling towards the disturbed crate, he raised the lamp above his head and gazed four decks up the shaft to the underside of No. 1 Cargo Hatch. It remained sealed.

His wellies crunched down on something. By the lantern's flickering light he saw the deck ahead strewn with rough-hewn ingots.

'Wot's all this mess?'

As he approached the upturned crate, Higginbotham's lamplight revealed a pair of ornate stone sarcophagi, the ingots spilling from the shattered lid of one. Ornately chiselled into that lid was the form of a human body — a river of maggots flowing from its split gut, topped with a skull. An engraved phrase came from its mouth. '*Expecto resurrectionem mortuorum*,' he read slowly. There was also a name — Balthasar Toule.

Yet more condensation dripped from an iron beam above his head, landing on his spectacles. 'Bugger,' he cursed, wiping them clean. Replacing them on his face, he rested his hand on the sarcophagus. A chunk broke away. He held it to the light to look more closely and, as he did so, it crumbled in his hands. The sarcophagus wasn't stone at all, but chalk. Peering inside, he covered his nose. The fabric lining was dry-rotted and, save for the odd ingot, the sarcophagus was empty.

'Hang on,' he whispered, noticing something more. Reaching in, he fumbled with a railway spike. It was lustreless but heavy. Leaving it for for the moment on the sarcophagus edge, he flipped through his cargo manifest. Stopping on page eight, Higginbotham's thick finger slid down the list, coming to a last-minute addition, scribbled in pencil crayon:

27061965QI.
Item description - 1 Large Crate. Roentgen secretary
Notation - Excess weight. Charge levied.
Destination - New York
Port of Origin - Folkestone Harbour

Looking back to the upturned crate, he located a lading number stencilled in black on the side: *27061965QI.* QI denoted Queenstown, Ireland. Titanic's last stop. Podgy Higginbotham hadn't the first idea what a Roentgen secretary was, but he struggled to believe the shattered crate's contents were it.

Cadging a pry-bar from the hook on a hull support, he hung the lamp on the hook, and decided to prise loose the other sarcophagus lid. He knew perfectly well the penalty for tampering with White Star cargo was dismissal upon destination, but the contents of the crate didn't seem to match the manifest, and it wouldn't have been the first time he'd discovered smuggled goods.

The crate must have tipped on its side during loading and the second sarcophagus likely fell in, shattering the lid of the other. Chipping away at the intact lid's lip with the pry-bar, he used his stout middle as leverage to slide the lid away. Crashing to the floor, it shattered into three pieces.

Lying within was a trove of ingots, packed tightly around it, a mummified fiend swathed in an exquisite pearl frock. Higginbotham gagged. The remains stank like Liverpool's overflowing rendering pits prior to cooking. He tried breathing through his mouth, but the sticky rot coated his tongue. Unease caused bile to rise into his throat, his hands trembled slightly from a surge of adrenaline.

'Balls,' he muttered, spitting on the floor, his mind cooking up a scheme. Avarice elided caution. Each ingot was of a similar size, its rough-hewn shape their only variation. Although lustreless, the sharp edges were burnished. Shifting the contents of the sarcophagus, he held the last two in his greedy hands.

'Seaman Higginbotham, your ship's finally come in,' he told himself.

From the darkness came a sudden crackling sound, like the head of a carrot being twisted off.

'Oi!' he said with a start, staring into the maze of crates. First a boys' choir, now someone preparing a stew.

The hold was giving him the jumps. The sooner he finished shifting these ingots, the better. He looked to the corpse. No doubt it was a woman, its long, frazzled black hair touched with curls, thin nose and sunken lips the remnants of a seraphic siren. Laying his hands on the edge of the sarcophagus he took a deep breath. He inched closer, gazing at her narrow eyelids, long eyelashes still intact. 'Co', you must have been a right angelic bird.'

Her eyes flashed open.

Cataract-glazed pools of darkness stared back at him. Leaping away, Higginbotham heard the secular choir arise again, very close now. Foul breath licked the back of his neck. He turned.

'Spring-heeled Jack,' he gasped in terror, his trousers suddenly warm as he shat himself.

The fugue died away.

Eleanor Annenberg was just dozing off when the shudder awoke her. Gazing at the wainscoted ceiling of her stateroom, she watched the chandelier above her gently rattle. Elle ran her hand along the mahogany panelling behind the headboard and felt a distant shuddering through her fingertips. She rolled over and looked out of the window. The moon reflected off the sea, casting moonbeams through her window, which looked like countless tiny diamonds dancing across the ceiling. They vanished abruptly as a white mass swept by the window. When it passed — and the shuddering with it — the diamonds danced again. Elle rubbed the sleep from her eyes. Perhaps she wasn't quite awake. Why would a ship's sail be so close to Titanic?

She awaited an alarm. None came. Rolling onto her back, she stretched her willowy limbs almost regally, and looked around her First-Class accommodation: Queen Ann-style opulence, a grand brass bed, excessive polished wood and Chippendale furniture. So new was her B-Deck stateroom, the smell of paint and beeswax hung remotely in the air still. Her only bother had been to use the bath in her parents' room, as her own cabin had none.

Despite its luxury, there was something defiant about the ship she found unnerving. It wasn't the aristocratic passenger list; old money was nothing new, and the Annenbergs were red-letter members of Detroit's social follies. Perhaps it was the ship's arrogant reputation. "Unsinkable" flew straight into the face of God.

Elle was nearing the final leg of her journey home to Michigan. Her parents had enrolled her in a private school for girls in Highgate two-years ago. Although she passed out of sixth-form with top marks, her head of year hopelessly failed in her attempt to turn a maverick American schoolgirl into a dainty lady. In London, Elle glimpsed life beyond her own society, to a life filled with foreign intrigue and adventure. Getting out of trouble, as it turned out, was more interesting than getting into it.

And as she began to outgrow her gangly figure, it was no longer just her attitude that got her noticed. She'd been told her entire life she'd inherited her mother's beauty but suddenly, Elle became aware of it. Like her mother, Elle was bestowed with unruly chestnut hair and eyes neither brown nor green, but something in between. Her pouty lips — the cause of much scorn as a child — became an object of desire as she reached adulthood. She seduced merely by talking. Almost overnight, it seemed, men begun to fancy her. But she wanted nothing to do with coquettish schoolgirl games nor unwanted advances from odious geezers. Even in these supposedly "modern" times, a proper girl was relegated to courtship larks. Elle flouted convention and, as a result, was regarded as a troublesome suffragette — a seventeen-year old in a woman's body. But while her mother — a German Jew, whose family fled to Detroit years ago — had learnt caution in a world where *her* tribe was hated, her father, Franklyn Annenberg, was altogether quite different. Growing up privileged, he never found reason to worry. Yes, *he* had married outside his own tribe, and for that he was ostracised, but he never minded, nor had cause to. Love was the foundation of all things, and optimism was his strongest trait.

And so Elle, like him, was an optimist, although perhaps inheriting a little of her mother's caution. Even if she did not yet know what life had in store for her, she knew without doubt it wouldn't be a life tethered to a repressive, chinless wonder.

There came then voices from the companionway, followed by a knocking at her door. Elle climbed from her bed. Cabin Steward Swinburne had come round earlier in the evening to turn her bed down, but her electric heater was on the fritz; it was either freezing cold or sweltering. She'd opted for the latter, sleeping atop the eiderdown in her new French lingerie. Of course, her mother derided it as too risqué for a proper young lady, but the silk brassière with stitched-in pearls and scalloped, silk knickers were all the rage in Paris. A lady was meant to wear petticoats and corsets under an evening gown, like the one her mother forced her to wear to dinner and which was presently thrown over the back of a chair. Elle loathed the quaintness of ladylike attire.

She ran with the youth of London. Disinterested in the opinions of others, they were smart-mouthed, confident girls who smoked cigarettes without a holder, drank whisky in front of men and dressed in the *avec désinvolture* — free and easy — style of Parisians. Elle liked disguising her long limbs, and sensual body beneath jodhpurs, riding boots and Teddy Bear coats. Unrestrained. And at times, uninhibited.

She was every bourgeois gent's nightmare.

The knocking on her cabin door became more rapid and urgent. Passing the wardrobe, she grabbed the Teddy Bear coat she had liberated from Father years ago and tied its belt around her. She opened the door to Park Lane, the companionway named after London's fashionable thoroughfare. Mother pushed her way into her stateroom. She wore a worried look on her face and a lifebelt over her nightgown and mink coat.

'What is it, Mother?'

Steward Swinburne peeked in then, reading-glasses swinging like a pendulum on a chain about his neck. 'Miss Annenberg, please put on your lifebelt. We've been requested on deck.'

'Are we sinking?'

'Not to worry, it's just precautionary.' Hurriedly continuing his journey, he disappeared through the baized doors to the deck's reception area.

'He seems worried,' noted Elle, as Mother closed the stateroom door.

'Eleanor, I fear the incident is rather serious. You'd better get dressed and come to deck with me.'

Pulling on a pair of thick woollen trousers, Elle sat on a sofa in the corner of her cabin to lace up her motoring boots. She watched her mother pick up Elle's gold Cartier watch, diamond rings, and her sapphire necklace and stuff them into the concealed burglar pocket of her mink.

'You're taking my jewellery. It's *that* serious?'

Mother turned to her, looking over the Teddy Bear coat she put on. 'Why must you wear that moth-eaten coat of your father's?'

'It's warm.'

'You look like a dyke,' she scolded.

'Blame Father,' Elle replied.

Her mother sighed but pursued the matter no further. 'The steward banged on my door first. He said the ship has struck ice.'

'Is that what it was? Ice?' Elle said, taking up her lifebelt. 'I saw it through my window.'

'You *saw* it?' Her mother turned her round, tying the lifebelt over her Teddy Bear coat.

'I thought it was a ship's sail. It must have been an iceberg.'

Mother turned Elle to face her. 'We must find your father.'

❖ ❖ ❖

It was eleven forty-five by the time they made their way to the First-Class entranceway, joining a queue of regal, if not heavy-eyed, passengers proceeding to deck. Bundled up in a fur coat over a kimono and evening slippers, the pinched face Lady Cunard gave Elle's modern attire a scowl of disapproval, for which Elle was only too happy to reply with her biggest and most disingenuous American smile. Lady Cunard had married up. Lord Cunard kept fashionable addresses in both London's Belgravia and the Kent countryside. Rumour had it Lord Cunard found Her Ladyship dancing topless in Soho's Windmill Cabaret. It could be said she got the goldmine marrying an old duffer like Lord Cunard. And he got the shaft.

Following Mother up the staircase to A-Deck, Elle spotted Second Officer Lightoller walking briskly towards the Promenade Deck vestibule. He had given Elle and her father a tour of the ship the day they departed Southampton. She caught his eye. He offered an unconvincingly brave face.

She knew then the matter-at-hand was serious. How serious, Elle was as yet unsure.

Pushing through a revolving, bevelled-glass door, she followed Mother into the First-Class smoking room.

'I've not been in here before,' she said, squinting curiously through a blue haze of cigar smoke.

'I should hope not. This is a gentleman's lounge.'

Unashamedly tarted up with dark mahogany panelling and far too many leaded glass panels, it looked like a Pall Mall gentleman's club after a night in a bordello. Despite the seriousness of the moment, Elle couldn't help but smile. It was nice to see Mother breaking from convention now and again.

A foursome, including her father, sat calmly around a Chippendale table near the coal fire, playing bridge. On the mantelpiece stood a sculpture of Artemis of Versailles. The men in the company of her father, all side-whiskers and smoking jackets, Elle had known since she was a child. Hutton Armstrong and Artie Moorhead were Detroit royalty. Automobile money. Elle's father provided them with the steel they needed to build Henry Ford's Model Ts. The fourth, Ribs Wimbourne, stroked his greying Kitchener moustache as he studied his hand of cards. A commander in the British Royal Navy, he'd been dressed in full navy blues the first time Elle had clapped eyes on him. She was nine years old. And smitten. Ribs was the only gentleman, other than Father, whom she regarded as genuine.

Wobbling to the table in her lifebelt, Elle's mother swiftly admonished her Father. 'Franklyn, the ship is sinking and you're playing bridge.'

'Weezy, my dear, Titanic won't sink,' replied Father. He used Mother's pet name when he wanted her to do something she wasn't keen on.

'The engines have stopped,' she said.

'Routine,' Ribs told her, watching the legs of his port creep down a chunky Waterford tumbler in his hand. 'I've gone through this drill in the Royal Navy. They're just sounding the ship. Making certain there's no damage.'

'Franklyn,' Mother pushed a lifebelt into his lap. 'You shall put this on *at once* and accompany your daughter and I to the boat deck.'

The others smirked over their cards.

'Dearest, would *you* leave this comfort and warmth for the chill of an open deck?' He raised his cards for her to see. 'Particularly with this hand?'

'Piffle,' Armstrong scoffed. 'Titanic sink? What rot.'

Elle's father chuckled, tipping his cigar ash into the cuff of his trousers and resting his port glass on the card table. It slid straight across it, tumbling into Rib's lap. The ship listed towards the starboard bow.

Looking up to the Commander he said, 'Perhaps we ought to have a look?'

❖ ❖ ❖

Elle followed her parents onto A-Deck's enclosed promenade. Ribs accompanied them, chatting to her mother and father with little more concern than he might if he was simply taking a stroll along the seaside. Keeping themselves warm under their steamer rugs, other First-Class passengers sat in polished deck chairs, watching crewmen crank down the promenade windows. Pulling her collar tight from the frightfully cold night air they let in, Elle was left to wonder why. A clammy hand touched hers. Recoiling, she turned.

Brooks Thompson, a Detroit banker known as much for venality as for being a loathsome cad, crowded her.

'Aren't *you* sprightly,' he said.

Elle pulled her hand away. She'd done this dance. Men like Brooks Thompson made such advances only to women they held in low regard. Normally, she'd have given him a thump but, given the situation, she decided to try something else.

'I'm Eleanor Annenberg, Mr Thompson.'

He stared at her blankly through his boozy eyes.

'You're my father's banker.' She tossed in the smile, the very definition of mischief. Big and toothy, it filled her face, banishing her aloofness, replacing it with confidence. She found through experience it had a magical ability to light up rooms and defuse even the most uncomfortable of moments. It was equal parts androgynous and feminine. It accentuated the kindness in her eyes and stole away a man's resolve. It charmed even the most spiteful of women. Well, perhaps not Lady Cunard.

'Haven't you grown into a pretty young lady?' Dressed in pyjamas and carpet slippers, he bowed unsteadily. 'Call me Brooksie.'

Elle sighed, smile fading. 'Really, I'd rather not.'

'You're a very pretty girl.'

'You already said as much. Won't you let me alone?'

'Don't know about that bear-skin rug, though,' he said, looking over her Teddy Bear coat.

'Said the man wearing pyjamas and slippers,' she replied petulantly. 'You do realise the ship has struck an iceberg?'

'Do you think I could manage a chip off it for my drink?'

Snatching the glass from Mr Thompson's hand, she knocked it back. Vodka stung her throat.

'To hell with ice.'

The stewards beckoned for women and children to come forward and walk the plank that stretched from the deck to lifeboat. There weren't many takers. Most preferred the fear aboard Titanic to the uncertainty of a lifeboat at sea.

'I'll climb in if you do,' said Mr Thompson.

'Are you a woman or a child, Mr Thompson?' Irritated, Elle shoved the glass into his hands.

'My God, aren't you deliciously complicated.'

She stared at him, pursing her lips. 'In point of fact, I'm simply uncomplicated.'

'Oh now?' he asked, giving her a salacious grin. 'What am I then? Simply irresistible?'

'Simply stupid.' The vodka had pleasantly sharpened her tongue. 'Now get lost, you vulture, before I rat you out to your wife.'

A brash Molly Brown, the widowed American millionaire, barrelled across the promenade deck, knocking Thompson aside. Maids trailed behind, carrying her hatboxes.

'Hurry to it; they're uncovering the lifeboats up there.' Uttering curses so thick her words could be spread on bread, all watched in admiration of a woman unafraid to speak her mind. Lifting her skirt to her knees — and with the help of the stewards — Molly Brown "walked the plank" across the deck chair bridging the deck and the lifeboat. Her maids hurriedly passed over her hatboxes before joining her.

'Elle?'

Turning, Elle saw Titch Blaine-Howard, a minute socialite and sixth-form chum from girl's school, sitting in a deck chair drinking from a bottle of 1904 Taittinger. Titch was youthful, gay and pure British aristocracy. Elle often thought Titch was the very antithesis of her.

'Come and join the party.' Passing the champagne bottle to a fair-haired boy, she stumbled to her feet, still in her glad rags. 'Missed you in the Café Parisian tonight.'

'I was recovering from the champagne we swizzled there last night, actually,' replied Elle, a shiver making a mad dash up her spine. And not because she was cold. Lurking under the veneer of bravado and sharp words was fear. 'You do understand an iceberg has struck us?'

'Pfft.' Titch said and waved her Dunhill cigarette holder dismissively.

'Who's the bookend?' asked Elle, looking to the fair-haired young man in dinner jacket and white celluloid collar.

'An Austrian I met tonight in the Café. Come have a natter with us.'

Elle shook her head. 'I really should stay with Mother and Father.'

'Doesn't look as though they're going to miss you, darling,' she said, drawing Elle's attention to her parents, now sitting casually in deck chairs, chatting with Ribs.

'For a minute, then,' replied Elle, eyeing the Austrian as he guzzled champagne straight from the bottle. He had big ears, a long nose and a lascivious gaze.

Titch stepped back, taking stock. 'Sporting a bull-dagger look, are we? Chiltham School for Young Ladies was meant to turn you into a lady, not a *déclassé* lezzer.'

'"Teaching young ladies to behave in a manner conforming to one's position?"' Quoted Elle.

Titch shrugged.

'The Teddy Bear coat is practical.' Elle shivered. 'Especially tonight.'

'Strangely enough, I don't feel the cold one jot,' Titch replied.

'That's because you're drunk.'

'*Drunk?*' she asked as she staggered, taking Elle's arm in hers. 'I'm banjoed.' Then plonking down in a deck chair, she took Elle with her.

The young Austrian laughed, passing her the bottle. 'Fancy a sip, lovely?' Elle refused.

'Something more exotic, then?' he asked, tapping the side of his nose.

'You do realise this ship is taking on water?' she asked, matter of factly.

'Sinking? Poor poppet,' he said condescendingly, all grand manner and dapper clothes. 'Titanic is unsinkable.'

'Oh, you think so?' she chipped, sharply. 'Tell me why this deck is angling down to the head then?'

'I'm an officer in the German Navy.'

She looked to Titch. 'You said he was Austrian?'

'Who knew there was a difference?' Titch asked, blowing him a kiss.

'Titanic has nineteen watertight bulkheads,' said the German. 'She's down at the head because one of them has taken on water. But the watertight doors have sealed the rest of the bulkheads, and I can promise you Titanic isn't going to sink. We'll continue to New York under reduced steam.'

'Actually,' Elle corrected, 'there are sixteen watertight compartments on Titanic. Not nineteen.'

His chin shook. He looked unhappy at being shown to be wrong.

'See much action in the German Navy?'

'Pardon?'

'Had a few bombs thrown at you?'

'I do not understand.'

'Of course you don't,' Elle said. Then, taking the cigarette from his hand, she dropped it into the neck of his champagne bottle.

'When they spoke of "winter campaigns", you thought they meant the Cresta Run at St Moritz.'

Titch snorted out a laugh.

'I will not participate in this battle of wits,' said the German and stood, turning to Titch. '*Sie ist ein gemeines Stück.*'

'This is no battle of wits between you and me,' replied Elle, offering a cut-glass smile in response to being called a mean bitch. 'I never pick on an unarmed man. *Sprich bitte nicht mehr mit mir.*'

Realising Elle spoke his language, the German wisely chose to escape her scathing contumely. 'You will excuse me,' he said before stomping away.

'I'd say someone's got their mad up, haven't they?' Titch said to Elle as she watched him go. 'What did you say to him?'

'I merely explained he should probably stop talking.'

'Don't get your knickers in a twist when I say this, Elle, but sometimes you really are a stroppy bitch.' Titch shook her head, lighting a Baronfield before stuffing it into her cigarette holder. 'And, despite the attire, you're still a snob.'

Elle glanced towards her mother, who replied with a disapproving stare. 'Mother thought shipping me off to Highgate would turn me into a lady.'

'Do you mean like me?' Titch replied, coyly.

'Exactly like you. She hadn't a clue I'd hop the wag the moment I got there.'

Elle sat forward, taking the cigarette from Titch's holder, smoking it bare. 'Sorry, darling. Mother keeps flushing mine.'

'Why must you frighten away all the men?'

'Oh come now, Titch. We both drink from the same bottle of spite.'

'Don't we just?' Titch said, and laughed.

'Tell me, what could be worse than a man drunk on champagne? Snorting devil's dandruff? How *vulgar* boys like that are.'

'Matron would be pleased,' said Titch, lighting another Baronfield. '*All* the girls let their knickers down once, at the least. Even the hideous ones. You though? You were the prettiest girl in the school. And yet I never once heard you having a tryst.'

All of Elle's school chums had been in and out of love — or at least a man's bed — already. 'The British think I'm a cheeky, American gold-digger.'

'You aren't.'

'Whilst Americans think I'm a stuck-up Anglophile.'

'You are.'

'Thank you.'

Titch blew her a kiss in reply.

'We're just four days out of Southampton and I've had to dodge Titanic's homunculus squash pro, a dull-as-ditchwater doctor, a dead-from-the-neck-up yachtsman, a loathsome banker from Philadelphia, and that *ung-eschtupped-mit-gelt* Benji Guggenheim.'

'Hell's an *unge*—whatever you said?'

'Just something my Jewish grandmother used to say. Sort of means considerably wealthy. But not in a good way.'

'What's so bad about considerably wealthy? I'd happily *shtup* him for some of his loot.'

'Conformity is what's so bad about him. And the rest. I've no interest in becoming a trophy, paraded about for the amusement of my husband.'

'You've not had a shag yet, let alone a husband. Still, I can't fault your veracity, but aren't you taking *noblesse oblige* rather too far?' Titch took a long drag and exhaled slowly. 'If you don't take care, you'll end up a dowdy old maid painting landscapes in an atelier filled with mad cats.'

Elle watched the cigarette smoke above her head find its way to the open windows of the promenade, dissipating into the night sky. Her eyes wandered among the glittering parade of wealth. Lord and Lady Mucks, ordinarily confident, now unsettled by lifeboats and orders for women and children to take to them.

Her eyes were drawn to a passenger then: a man descending the narrow stairs from the Boat Deck. Crossing the deck, he stood alone by an open window, a feather of breath appearing with each exhale before his fresh, if not raffish, face. His eyes swept the promenade. Elle found his silently observant attitude chilling given the fervent activity all around him. Nobody apart from her paid him any attention as lifeboats were lowered from above. Nonchalantly, he brushed his mop of dark brown hair back, revealing eyes as dark as a the North Atlantic the lifeboats were lowering into. There was something ruthless about his eyes — all confident — and yet lacking in cruelty.

As he rubbed a hint of stubble on his chin, he appeared at first glance like any university boy gone to seed. From the heavy duffel coat draped over his un-starched collar to the Wellington boots on his feet, he was an unpretentiously bound book giving no inkling of what lay within its pages.

Instinctively, Elle knew better. This was someone not to be trifled with.

Her eyes were drawn again to his boots. They were wet.

When she looked up, he was staring directly at her. Her first instinct was to turn away — but to her surprise, she found she could not. The same could not be said for him as, after one last look around, he returned to the metal stairs. Grasping the stair rail, he ascended to the Boat Deck.

Just before he disappeared from view, Elle noticed something more. Something out of place. A shotgun muzzle poked out the bottom of his coat. Definite fuckery afoot. Glancing to her mother and father, Elle stood up. Now would be the moment for prudence. But the intriguing man offered her a most curious charge as she'd never felt before.

Engrossed in conversation, neither of her parents would even notice her go. Titch however.

'Where on earth are you going?' she asked, stubbing her cigarette end on the wood decking.

'Have a little yomp around up top on the Boat Deck,' Elle replied curtly, keen to follow the man quickly.

'Don't leave me.' There was earnestness in her friend's face she'd rarely seen before.

'I know you're being brave, Titch. But right now, a lifeboat is the great equaliser.'

'From fear?'

'From drowning. Promise you'll get in one?'

'It's serious, isn't it?'

Elle nodded.

'I promise,' Titch answered.

Elle smiled, giving her friend's arm a squeeze. 'I'll be back.'

Turning, she followed after the man up to the Boat Deck where seamen swarmed over Titanic's lifeboats, pulling up gripes and canvas covers. First Officer Murdoch ordered the men to the lifeboat davits. Pulleys squealed as lines paid out, and slowly, the little boats swung away from the deck. The chaos and this distraction cost Elle valuable seconds — she moved to continue her quest, but the man had gone. Crossing to starboard she caught a glimpse of him again, moving forward with some speed, the ship's list more apparent now.

Pushing through the throngs of passengers and crew, someone grabbed at her arm. 'Have you seen my husband?' Vera Dick shivered as she held onto her Pomeranian, a lifebelt about its furry little body. The same age as Elle, Vera had danced in the Café the night before without a care in the world.

'No, I'm sorry,' Elle replied distractedly, keeping an eye on the man as he moved quickly forward. 'But get yourself in a lifeboat.'

She spotted the Maître D' of the ship's restaurant, standing nearby in a top hat. 'Monsieur, kindly make sure Vera gets to a boat.'

'Oui, Madame,' he replied, doffing his cap before laying his shawl across Vera's shoulders.

A rocket shot into the sky, illuminating the deck. Passengers, stewards, chefs and stokers surged aft as Titanic continued to sink at the bow. Fighting her way through the crowd, she saw the man turn into the forward,

First-Class entrance. She couldn't articulate what it was, but something about the man quickened her pulse and piqued her curiosity. She followed.

Passengers in nightgowns and fur coats sleepily ascended the First-Class staircase. But not him. He descended.

Elle gazed at the wood engraved allegorical figures of Honour and Glory crowing a grandiose clock on the staircase landing, and made a mental note of the time.

Four minutes after midnight.

She descended the stairs after him and found herself alone at the reception landing on E-Deck. To her right stairs led to the Turkish bath and swimming pool. Next to it, a door — one she had been cautioned not to enter by Second Officer Lightoller during her tour of the ship. And yet, she opened it and peeked around. The long corridor nicknamed "Scotland Road" continued fore and aft, innumerable adjacent companionways and doors leading to cargo stores, Third-Class kitchens, cold storage and crew quarters. She knew that somewhere ahead, the ship must be flooding.

She continued forward, adrenaline surged through her now and was startled when a door suddenly opened beside her. A man and woman carrying a child spoke nervously to her in an Eastern language she didn't understand.

'Go that way,' she told them, pointing to the door she'd just come through. They stared at her blankly. Grasping the woman by her hand, she tugged them to the door. Opening it, she took off her lifebelt, tying it round the child.

'Go!'

They nodded, making their way up the stairs.

Returning to Scotland Road, the ship shifted beneath her feet. She hustled to the top of the passage. A steward's stairway led down. Following it to F-Deck, she paused on a landing near the ship's squash court, looking down a companionway towards a closed, watertight door at its end. She recalled the tour again, remembering Lightoller telling her the doors were designed so should a watertight compartment be breeched, a lever could be thrown from the bridge, automatically lowering the doors and sealing off the bulkhead to isolate the flooding and keep Titanic afloat. But while the watertight door on the aft bulkhead remained sealed, the forward one was bent upwards violently. It looked as if it weighed a tonne. No one man alone could have done such damage. Passing under it, she entered a companionway, its bare, riveted walls sparsely lit. To the right was a staircase.

An angelic staccato rose briefly from below and then ended as abruptly as it had begun. Something clearly was happening below. Checking herself, Elle realised she had been holding her breath in. Taking a few deep breaths she took stock. It would be wise for her to take caution, the nagging sense of fear she fought off told her nothing good was happening deep down in the bowels of Titanic. If she returned to deck she could easily enough hop a lifeboat with her parents. They had Ribs to look out for them.

She descended.

The stairway ended at G-Deck. On the planked floor was what looked like fresh droplets of blood. Cautiously following the trail, she turned a corner. The drops ended at cabin 247.

The ship lurched to port, hull groaning. Elle's heart threatened to escape her chest and she placed her hand against the wall to steady herself. The groaning ceased, but the floor was now askew. Mustering up her courage, she turned the door handle of the cabin, cracking the door. Inside was darkness.

Pushing it open just enough to squeeze through, she skidded on something wet, almost falling to the floor. The door swung closed behind her, leaving her in the dark. Feeling for the cabin door again, her hand landed upon the light knob. She twisted it, gasping at what she saw.

Mattresses thrown from the bunks had been torn to pieces. Arterial spray and bloody handprints were smeared across the white walls. The tinny taste of fresh blood filled the air. She was in a slaughterhouse.

Whatever happened here, she thankfully missed it. The arcs of spray and massive loss of blood saturating the mattresses suggested a ferocious attack. Her breath escaped in a rush as she finally exhaled. And she couldn't get it back such was her fright. Her hands trembled. She thought to flee, but her feet were cemented to floor, back flat against the wall. Brave as she might like to think she was, she fought to regain her calm.

Then she put it together. This couldn't be the work of the man she'd shadowed. Elle fired enough shotguns with her father to know the odour of gunpowder lingered in a confined space for hours. There was no such odour. Nor was there any splay from shotgun pellets in the walls, or blood congealed on the planked floor. Most disturbingly, there were no bodies. The question begged. What *could* do such a horrendous thing? And did she really want to find out?

Hesitantly, she nudged a mattress aside with her boot and something rattled across the floor. She picked it up. It was a tiny compass, like a prize from a Cracker Jack box. The dial vibrated, pulling in the direction of the cabin door. She gave it a shake, and the dial spun wildly as the melancholy treble of the choir now cracked the silence again. Echoing along the companionways, it ended at the other side of the cabin door.

'Balthasar!' A voice close-by shouted in warning. '*Wilderzeichen,*' she then heard.

Balthasar. Was this the name of the man she shadowed?

Just as she reached for the handle again, something landed against the door with a thump. Instinctively, she leapt back and, in doing so, fell onto the torn mattresses.

Boom. Clack-clack. Boom.

A shotgun fired five times in quick succession, the .33-calibre buckshot perforating the door. The man was clearly trained; holding the trigger back, he fired another five shots while pumping the action. Slamfiring was a special skill. Only someone practiced with a shotgun could pull it off. Elle had watched her father fire with such effect at his hunt club. Properly done, slamfiring was devastating.

'Where is she?' another voice demanded. British accent. Not posh. But educated. The curious singing became a bayonet-sharp howl. 'Where is Siobhan?' Iron clanged, followed closely by footfall frantically descending.

Rising to her feet, adrenaline coursing through her veins, Elle slowly opened the door. A haze of gunpowder hung lazily in the companionway and, with it, a fresh blood trail. To a girl like Elle, curious to what screamed "bugger right off", this was an invitation crying out for her to follow. She rounded a corner. An iron grating in the floor was thrown open, an emergency escape ladder beneath, leading to darkness.

Had the crew made their escape? And did this mean the deck below was flooding?

More gunshots, distant now. Climbing down the ladder with a vigour that surprised even herself, she descended to the Orlop Deck, the very bowels of Titanic. She could clearly identify the greasy smell of lubrication oil. But there was something more in the air — something filling her with dread — the unmistakable odour of cold brine.

The ladder below disappeared into rushing seawater.

Gripping a rung to steady herself against the listing of the ship, she considered her perilous situation. She was far below deck, alone, as the ship flooded. She dared not continue.

Lined with thick pipes, the narrow passage below sunk down towards the head of the ship. Sealed lights continued to burn beneath the flooding waters; it didn't *look* terribly deep.

She couldn't say where her nerve came from then, but without another thought she stepped off the ladder, landing waist-deep in freezing water. Stunned by the cold and before she could decide if she'd just made a terrible mistake, there came splashing from ahead, followed by another sharp treble. It sounded different this time: less adolescent choir, more wounded rage.

Pushing her way through the deepening water in her alpaca coat was slow going. It kept her warm, though — from the waist up. Coming to a watertight hatch forced back by the strain of murky seawater, Elle slipped inside. The rank odour of putrefaction greeted her sharply. Ahead, neatly lashed-down crates emerged from the gloom.

She found herself in one of Titanic's forward holds. Water rained down through cracked seams in the ship's starboard hull, splashing onto a motorcar lashed to a pallet.

The iceberg had dealt the ship a mortal blow. Strangely, aside from the invading torrent, there was a sepulchral silence to the hold.

Something bumped her numbing legs. Looking down, she stifled a scream. There, floating up from the dark waters was the body of a man. A ring of keys jingled just above the waterline as the corpse bobbed like a cork in the freezing waters. Vacant eyes stared at her through spectacles. A crewman. His chest and podgy stomach were ripped open. Keeping the scream down, she couldn't, however do the same with the vomit, and the First-Class dinner, she had eaten earlier that night, hurled up and out of her before she could do much to stop it. It was no never mind as a grinding groan from somewhere far aft took away the sound of her vomiting. Wiping her mouth on her sleeve, she stole a second glance, and realised the poor man bobbing in the flooding wasn't just grossly mutilated; he was gutted.

A stab of light and the desire to move as far away from the dead man as quickly as possible drew her to another hatch at the forward end of the hold. As she made her way towards it, a sudden increase in the floodwaters forced it open.

Bodies washed out towards her from inside. Scores of them. Some in their nightshirts, others in ships uniform. She put a hand over her mouth to keep in a scream. None of the dead looked drowned. They looked *eaten*.

Terror gripping her, she had just made up her mind to take flight when the flooding swung the forward hatch open fully, offering her an unobstructed view within.

Another hold, rapidly flooding. In the waist-deep water, Elle made out the forms of two men, leaning intently over an opened crate. It seemed suddenly clear to her that this was a conspiracy. One she herself had unwittingly entered into.

A bespectacled boffin in a bowler hat pointed a sawn-off, double-barrelled shotgun into the crate, a weapon incapable of slamfiring. Hood of his duffel coat up, the other man she knew now as Balthasar hunched over the sarcophagus, wielded something resembling a railway spike in his extended arm.

Curiosity getting the better of her, she edged closer. Inside the crate, she could just make out the shape of an open sarcophagus. Something quasi-human struggled within, held down at the neck by Balthasar's other hand. Ashen and ribby, the fiend's body wept fetid fluid from innumerable sores. Clumps of grizzled hair shed from its swollen head as it shrieked a secular knell. This was the boys' choir she'd heard. The strain became primal as Balthasar savagely rammed the spike into its chest. Viscous gunge purged from the beast as it went berserk, twisting into a seizure within the sarcophagus. A final thrust of the spike, and it went quiet. Skin bronzing with rot, its anaemic body caved in on itself.

Balthasar's assault on the beast was vile. And yet, strangely stately. An unholy banshee howl reverberated from somewhere behind her, causing Balthasar to suddenly turn towards her. She saw his face clearly from behind his raised hood. Despite the grotesqueness of the act, his disposition remained calm and dispassionate, his black eyes seeing through her.

Rivets popped, and the starboard hull plates heaved as a wave of water burst through. She knew she needed to get out of there. Pushing through the rapidly deepening flood, she only just managed to grasp the hatch handle before a thundering wall of seawater slammed into her. Gulping for air, she was sucked into a foaming cauldron, the weight of her coat pulling her under. Colliding with objects as she tumbled, she was dashed against something immovable, the air forced from her lungs. She reached out, grasping for anything she could hold on to in the pounding blackness. Fumbling against a smooth sided object, she took hold of it, finally able to raise her head from the foaming water.

It was a headlamp attached to the motorcar. Gasping for air at last, she managed to take one salty breath before another surge sucked her back into the maelstrom. She knew if she inhaled again her lungs would fill and she would drown. Tumbling, she crashed into a bulkhead. Her lungs almost burst as she gasped, seawater invading them. Panicked, she regurgitated the water from her lungs. Instinctively inhaling again, she prayed for air.

More water filled her lungs.

Then, something grasped the collar of her coat, twisting her against the current. Reaching out in desperation, she felt an arm bend at the elbow, drawing her close. Grasping to take hold, her hand fumbled across heavy, soaked clothing. She felt a fine chain slip through her freezing fingers, until a small, flat object came to rest in her palm, coming away just as her hand closed tightly about it. Her head became heavy as her body went limp with exhaustion, and she blacked out.

❖ ❖ ❖

Brief moments of consciousness. She felt herself ascending, hauled by strong arms. Then she choked, vomiting oily seawater. She tried to raise her hands to wipe away the stinging in her eyes, but her sodden coat felt like sacks of cement on her exhausted limbs. Blinking, Elle realised she was being carried up the escape ladder, away from the flooding.

Sapped in both mind and body, she was only vaguely aware of stairs and companionways until she was set down in a brightly lit, mercifully dry, corridor. Scotland Road. Balthasar stared down at her.

'You've a long, dark road ahead, Eleanor,' he said.

Then he was gone. And so was she.

❖ ❖ ❖

'Oi.'

Elle drifted back to consciousness. A crew of stokers stood above her, faces soot-covered from shovelling coal into the ship's boilers.

'Wot the hell are you doing here?'

Shivering and confused, she pleaded for their help.

A wavy-haired young man wearing a lifebelt over his uniform approached her then. It was not a White Star uniform.

'If I were you, I would turn out, you fellows,' he said as he pushed by. 'The ship is making water.'

'What? Planning on going down with the ship in your uniform, Frog?' a member of the ship's black gang said dismissively.

'*Viswijf, Ik heb echt geen zin om mijn uniform, noch mijn nationale trots met u te bespreken,*' the young officer replied. Even a semi-conscious Elle recognised the term *viswiif*. She'd been chased about London by enough Belgian men to know it was a derogatory Flemish term for a woman. When directed at another man, it normally preceded a fight. The soldier must be Belgian.

Pushing towards her, he grasped Elle by her coat lapels.

'You have the look of the vagabond, *mijn schatje*. I am Lieutenant Jean-René Gaele. With your permission or without, I must carry you for the moment.'

As she was heaved over his shoulder, her hand relaxed, and the chain she gripped in her cold fingers bounced along the planked floor.

A stoker lifted it, tucking it into a pocket of her wet coat. 'Don't forget your locket, luv.'

The next minutes were a blur. More stairs. More companionways. The stokers' endless profanity hammered the tin of proper English. The Belgian remained silent, the smell of sweat and *Gauloises* cigarettes his only contribution to the conversation.

'I will leave you now,' he said after a while, gently settling her in a deck chair on the boat deck before wrapping her in a steamer rug. 'I have my superiors to look after. Someone will be along to put you into a lifeboat. Good luck, *mijn schatje*.'

❖ ❖ ❖

She lay there for what seemed ages, her mind reeling from the horror of what she witnessed below deck. A whip of bracing Atlantic air caused some give in the rigging above. Glittering ice shavings danced around a deck light, drawing her tired gaze. She thought of Mother, practicing her out-of-tune violin in the conservatory of their home in Detroit.

The blanket over her was pulled back.

'Eleanor?'

Her father stood above her, lifebelt tied about his immaculate dinner suit, a worried expression on his face. Mother stood beside him, a cross look on hers.

'Where have you *been*, child?' Father asked, removing the steamer rug to stand her up.

'Shivers,' said Mother, 'You're soaking wet!'

Unscrewing a sterling silver flask, Ribs Wimborne passed it to her father. 'Give the wet hedgehog a nip.'

She pressed it to her lips, gulping from the flask, cognac warming her.

Before anyone had the chance to question her, a shudder caused the ship to list to starboard, the slant in the deck growing steeper as Titanic sank further at the head.

Women shrieked, their former quiet concern replaced by panic. An order called women and children to A-Deck to be put off in the lifeboats.

Second Officer Lightoller approached. 'Are you all right, Miss Annenberg?' Elle nodded, teeth rattling. 'Mr Annenberg, won't you take your wife and daughter down to A-Deck and put them in a lifeboat?'

'Why must we go down there?' Mother demanded to know. 'Can we not load in from up here?'

'Not any longer. Titanic's list has grown too great.'

Another rocket exploded in the air, revealing the second officer's concern. Looking along the deck to the passengers descending to A-Deck, he continued. 'The crew has lowered the windows on the enclosed promenade.

If you would take your wife and daughter down now, I promise they'll have a place in a boat.'

Elle's father turned to the commander. 'Getting to be rather a tight corner, Ribs.'

'Best put the ladies off, just in case.'

Taking Mother by the hand, Elle's father asked Ribs to carry Elle down to A-Deck. She was in no condition to protest. As she was carried down the stairs, Elle saw the deck chair where she and Titch sat an hour ago. It was empty. The sea was now rolling well over the sides of the ship and onto the decks.

Father turned to Elle, kissing her forehead. 'Keep an eye on your mother. She does put on a brave face, but she's not as strong as you.'

Panic-stricken, Mother turned to him. 'Franklyn, you aren't coming?'

'Ribs and I will get in a boat after the ladies and children are safely away.'

Seawater crept up the deck towards them. Titanic groaned under the weight of the flooding.

'I won't go,' said Elle's mother.

For once Elle agreed with her mother. 'Not without you, Father.'

An irritated seaman grasped her by the arm, frog-marching her across the deck to a lifeboat. Mother followed, with a bit of nudging. Elle struggled. She knew she had to leave the ship, but not without her father.

'I've had enough of you annoying birds tonight,' said the seaman as he lifted her up to pass her through a window frame. A lifeboat swung just below.

'No!' Elle resisted. Squirming in the seaman's arms she kicked her legs. Holding one of Mother's arms, Ribs took one of Elle's motoring boots to the chin. Dropping her arm, he teetered at an open window before toppling over the side and into the waiting lifeboat below.

'That's enough of that,' said the able-bodied seaman, picking her up and pushing her through the window.

She plummeted headfirst into the lifeboat, clobbering old Lady Cunard sitting squirrel-like in the stern.

'Mind yourself, you impertinent brat,' she snipped, all pinch-faced and superior. Elle's mother followed close behind, landing on both of them. Before Elle could untangle herself, Lifeboat 4 lowered away.

'How about putting a few more in that bloody boat?' a trimmer on deck shouted to Lightoller.

Dazed, Elle shifted Mother to the side, gazing around the half-empty lifeboat. A seaman at the tackles lowered the boat in jolting lunges. Ribs sat on the bow gunwale, giving Elle the evils and holding a handkerchief to his bleeding mouth. The trimmer who'd shouted at Lightoller slid down the fall from A-Deck, landing in the lifeboat beside her, stinking of brandy. Her father remained at the promenade window, staring down at them.

'Father, climb down the rope,' she pleaded.

'Not to worry,' he said with a reassuring wave. 'I'll climb in the next one—'

A devilish hiss of steam from a funnel drowned out her father's reply. The ship's list to port increased, causing the lifeboat's rubbing strake below the gunwale to snag on the hull rivets. Taking up oars from the bottom of the lifeboat, the seamen fended them from the side of the ship as seawater poured through the big square ports of C-Deck, sweeping around a stateroom's furniture.

The lifeboat landed in the water with a shudder. Ribs slid an oar into its lock.

'Take up an oar,' he yelled to a quartermaster shipping the rudder. 'Lean hard into it or we'll be drawn into Titanic's suction.' The quartermaster nodded, ordering his crewmen to do the same. Pulling an oar from under her feet, Elle's shaking hands struggled to slide it into an oar lock.

'What are you doing, Eleanor?'

Dropping the blade into the water, Elle pulled back hard before replying to her mother, 'Rowing.'

Turning to Lady Cunard, she suggested she do the same lest they let the three available men in the lifeboat try to row them away from the sinking ship.

'Certainly not,' Lady Cunard whinged. 'A Lady does not do a man's chore.'

ng a man's chore?' asked Elle, splashing Her Ladyship's fur wrap.

 ing sea crept past the ship's bridge and over the windows of Titanic's stern swung lazily upwards there came a strange sound like breaking china.

The trimmer beside Elle looked over his shoulder. 'Cripes, them boiler plates is packin' in.'

'We must get clear,' shouted the quartermaster. 'Or else be sucked down with the ship.'

'Row like galley slaves,' Ribs ordered. More ladies took up oars. Reluctantly, so did Lady Cunard.

A wave washed over the roof of the officer's quarters. More agile passengers made their way aft, while those less fortunate were washed from the deck. A man in striped pyjamas went overboard with the wave. Swimming towards them, he was hauled in by Ribs. 'Corker of a cannon-ball, old boy.'

'*If Your law had not been my delight, then I would have perished in my affliction*,' he muttered, teeth chattering as a lady wrapped her heavy fur coat about his soaking wet body.

'Psalm 119. Verse 92,' said Lady Cunard, between strokes.

'Aye.' He wore a clerical collar under his soaked pyjamas. Ribs offered his nip flask to the obliging vicar.

'God gave me a boot up the behind, so he did.'

He drained the flask. God must have smiled upon him. He was saved by one of the last lifeboats. There were hundreds, perhaps a thousand souls, who remained on deck. ed on deck.ed on deck.ed on deck.

Standing at the opened window on the Promenade Deck, Franklyn Annenberg watched the sea churn towards him as Titanic continued to sink bow first. With all lifeboats gone, an odd calm fell over the ship.

Removing his pocket watch, he looked at the time. It was a gift from Louise. She'd be ever so cross with him if it got wet.

'Have you the time?'

He turned. A man wearing a worn-in Hacking jacket stood beside him firing up a cigar.

'Five minutes after two,' Franklyn replied. The man reached into his jacket, retrieving a cigar case. A single cigar remained. He offered it to Franklyn.

'Oh, I couldn't possibly accept your last cigar.'

'Ah, go way outta that, of course you will—I'll not need it.' Sliding it from the leather case, Franklyn gave it a sniff. It wasn't Cuban, but who was he to complain? The man held a flame. A few puffs and a cloud of blue smoke arose above his head. Franklyn thanked him.

'I was saving it until I got a peek at the Statue of Liberty.'

From deep in the bowel of the ship, explosions shook the wood-planked deck. Titanic shifted violently under their feet.

'Should'a stayed put in Cork.'

The lights of the enclosed promenade, which had burned brightly until then, began glowing red as they dimmed.

'New York is full of Irish,' said Franklyn, face blanching as he realised the end was near. 'You would think you were still home.'

'American?'

Franklyn nodded.

The man offered his hand. 'Corky O'Shea.'

'Franklyn Annenberg.' Shaking hands with the Irishman, he returned his gaze to the sea. 'Like a mill pond.'

'Aw, sure look it. Twenty years I been at sea. I never seen it this flat calm.'

'Not so much as a ripple,' Franklyn replied, the biting night air chapping his face. 'Can't imagine how cold it must be.' In the distance, he made out the green bow lamps of the lifeboats. 'Suppose we'll find out.'

Corky nodded. 'Got a missus in one of them boats?'

'And a daughter.' He felt tears welling up.

'That's something, then. Ain't it?'

'You?'

'Me missus won't go to America 'til I find work.' The Irishman blew a smoke ring. It drifted away from the doomed ship. 'Suppose she won't see it neither, now it's all gone arseways on us.'

'Sailor?' asked Franklyn, similarly blowing a smoke ring.

'Aye. Mate on a fishing trawler.'

Looking down the deck as the dark swirling water crept closer, Franklyn asked, 'So you can swim?'

The Irishman laughed. 'Not a damn stroke.'

A steward appeared on deck, a young man with a bushy moustache. He nodded in their direction, adjusting the lifebelt around his waist.

'Best take our chances in the water. Titanic doesn't have long left,' he said climbing over the windowsill. He hesitated, looking back at Franklyn. 'God bless.'

Leaping clear, he landed feet first in the water. Franklyn watched the steward surface, expelling a quavering yelp. The water must have been freezing. He began swimming frantically in the direction of the lifeboats, now more than a hundred yards away.

Taking a last puff of his cigar, Franklyn tossed it overboard. It bounced off Titanic's hull before snuffing out in the churning sea. 'Shall we?'

'Sure, I might,' replied Corky, his cigar joining Franklyn's. 'I wish I'd known you.'

'If you come through this, call on us in Detroit.'

Franklyn had barely got a leg over the windowsill before he heard a peculiar whipping sound. Steel lines securing the forward funnel under tension began snapping one by one from the stress of Titanic going down at the head. The securing lines freed, they whipped across the deck, one slicing off the arm of a cabin steward with surgeon's precision. Knees buckling, he collapsed, the encroaching sea swallowing him up as Titanic's forward funnel broke away.

Tipping forward it crashed across the Boat Deck above in a cloud of smoke and sparks as it landed in the water, the massive funnel crushing swimmers.

The steward popped up in the sea, his white jacket visible under the lifebelt that brought him to the surface. He continued to stroke one-handed amidst the other human flotsam, left arm gone.

Stoically untying his lifebelt, Franklyn tossed it to the sea, adjusting his velvet smoking jacket. It didn't matter if he jumped or remained on deck. The end was now a *fait accompli*.

At that moment, a collapsible Englehardt lowered by. Stokers working the blocks desperately tried to iron out the flutter foots in the falls.

'Mr O'Shea.' A man stood in the bow looking at them. 'It's Cabin Steward Beedham, here.'

'Ahoy, Dougie,' replied Corky, the deck pitching down as Titanic began its death dive. 'You need nae make up my bunk in the morning.'

Beedham grasped a fall, leaning towards them. 'You two better jump in,' he called, even though the flimsy boat was stowed out beyond the plimsoll.

Franklyn looked to his new friend, feeling ungentlemanly about abandoning Titanic. 'Why not?'

Corky nodded.

Tucking away his pocket watch, he obliged the steward as he reached out a hand.

'I hope I don't miss. Louise will be cross if I get my watch wet.' Climbing over the windowsill he leapt from the ship, the fall secured to the Engelhardt's bow, just out of reach.

Silhouetted against the starlit night, Titanic gave up the fight. Those not fortunate enough to find a lifeboat held on dearly to deckhouses, ventilators, and winches as the downward angle of the deck increased. Explosions erupted below decks, the ship's lights winking before going out forever. A clutch of passengers held one another atop the poop deck, wailing for mercy as the stern reared up high above the sea, only to fall to their deaths amid a maelstrom of spinning ropes and deck chairs. Somewhere amongst it was Elle's father.

And Balthasar.

Groaning in its death throes, Titanic turned, the sea closing over the ship's stern with a final gasp.

'Those poor souls,' Mother sobbed, clutching Elle in her arms. She felt numb. And not just due to the cruel night air chapping against her exposed face.

A peal of suffering arose from the frigid sea. Amid the mass of debris, survivors wailed in anguish, desperate to be saved.

'Mustn't we help them?' a lady called out, voice strained from weeping.

Looking to the bow, Elle made eye contact with Ribs. He nodded before turning to the quartermaster, demanding he turn the lifeboat back for the unfortunates in the water.

'No, we shan't,' old Lady Cunard barked, all priggish and privilege. 'They'll swamp us. You'll have all of us drowned.'

'Turn about,' Ribs ordered, Quartermaster Perks before turning on Her Ladyship. 'And there will be room for one more in this blooming boat if you refuse the quartermaster.'

'Turning us round,' Perks confirmed, leaning against the tiller.

Pulling hard on the oars, they reached the swimmers. Lifeboat 4 rocked as Ribs and the quartermaster hauled in anyone they could find alive.

'Good God, man.' Elle heard Ribs gasp, his brow furrowing as he pulled a fifth man from the water.

Women shrieked as a cabin steward was dragged over the gunwale. Elle realised, with a certain faraway horror, that his left arm was ripped away nearly to the shoulder. As he was gently laid in the bottom of the boat, she took a scarf off a crewman to make a tourniquet.

To her surprise, the steward's wound didn't much bleed. Either he had bled out already or the frigid water slowed his heart. Tying the scarf tightly around the remains of his upper arm she looked to his ghost-white face, recognising it.

'Steward Swinburne,' she muttered.

His eyes moved lazily towards her. 'Is it Miss Annenberg?'

Incredibly, Steward Swinburne was not dead. She tried hard to offer a comforting smile. 'By now, you should call me Eleanor,' she replied gently.

'By now, you should call me Tony.'

'I'm setting a tourniquet for your arm.' Focused on keeping at least him alive, she searched for something to tighten it with. There weren't many sticks to be had in a lifeboat.

'Here, use this.'

Next to her, Mother tossed the handle of a parasol aside, handing her the shaft.

Sliding it into the scarf's knot, Elle began to twist, tightening the tourniquet. Swinburne didn't so much as wince. Having stemmed the bleeding, Elle knew he would die from exposure if she couldn't warm him. 'Mother, give me your coat.'

'What's wrong with yours?'

'It's not for me. It's for Steward Swinburne.'

'What's wrong with *yours*?' Mother repeated.

'It's wet. Now give me your coat.'

Slipping Mother out of her chevron mink, she wrapped it about the steward. The crewman, stinking of brandy, produced a flask. Unscrewing the cap he then pressed it to Swinburne's lips.

Returning to her seat next to her mother, she noticed her own hands. They were slick with blood. Leaning over the side of the lifeboat, she dipped them into the icy water, rubbing them together and washing them clean. Something bumped her hand. She took hold of it. A tennis ball. *RF Downey & Co* stamped into its white felt. Without thinking, she stuffed it into her pocket before retrieving a silk handkerchief to dry her hands. Something came with it, pinging between the feet of a woman cradling a baby next to her. The woman picked it up and handed it back to Elle.

Elle knew her. She was the woman Elle had directed up the stairs from E-Deck. 'Where is your husband?'

'Lost,' she replied bleakly, tears streaking her face as she held her baby close. 'Titanic lost. He lost.'

'Franklyn's lost,' Elle's mother sobbed.

Staring at the thin pall of coal smoke lingering over the strangely calm sea, Elle wondered if the horrors she'd witnessed in Titanic's hold had been real or imagined. She looked at what the woman had returned to her. A talisman. A talisman Elle inadvertently pulled off Balthasar. A skull atop a human form stared through her, and an apothegm in Latin springing from the death symbol's mouth.

'Expect the resurrection of the dead.'

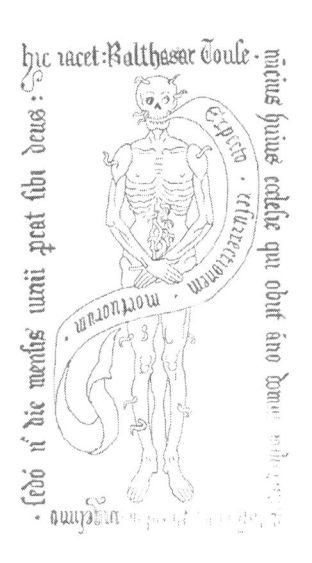

30 APRIL 1912.

BANANA, BELGIAN CONGO

*In short, the child, belonging to the mother's side,
is the channel through which the goods of
the maternal kin are exchanged against…*

—*Mauss,* The Gift

Moise Makombo wandered out from the steamy jungle canopy, fishing pole on his shoulder, his outsized shorts held up by a bit of twine. Congo's sun was merciless, but Moise was a smart lad. Though only twelve, he knew to keep to the shade of the corkwood and mangrove where the sand beneath his feet remained cool.

Wild waves pounded the beach, depositing all manner of debris each morning. Knotted together with the kelp and dead horseshoe crabs, he often found fishermen's nets and glass bottles, and even on one occasion, an unopened tin of Big John Tobacco from a place called Saint Louis. Walking parallel to the shoreline, he found a green rubber boot, its toe torn open. He'd found lots of lone boots before, but never a matching pair. He thought there must be many one-legged sailors.

This boot was of no use to him with a hole in it. Leaving it behind, Moise shifted the fishing pole the Belgian missionaries had given him to his opposite shoulder. It was they who had explained he was named after Moses. Moise didn't remember who Moses was exactly, only that he had the strength to part a red sea. Moise had only seen the Atlantic. It was blue, except where it met the River Congo. There, it was brown. A *red* sea must have been a long way away.

Following the contours of the shoreline, he continued north to the place his father had shown him — the rocky spit jutting far into the surf. At low tide he could stand at its point and snare fish for the orphans of the mission to eat. Mostly he hooked stumpnose. The missionaries liked rockcod. When he brought those, they gave him Belgian chocolate.

The shore north of Banana was sparsely populated, but Moise picked out the sound of someone groaning among the mangroves. He knew there was a Belgian rubber plantation not far inland. Leaving the fishing pole against a rock, he crept along the sand to peek through the twisting branches of mangroves.

A trap and donkey stood in a clearing. The donkey was still, munching on corkwood leaves. He heard the groaning again. Beside the trap, a big woman he recognised from the market square squatted on her hands and knees, her dress pulled down. A colonial, face orange like the sun, bumped her from behind, fat fingers fussing with her swaying breasts. With each bump the woman groaned. Moise watched for a little while. He knew what they were up to. Congo's natural resources weren't the only thing Belgian colonials took advantage of.

Schwalbe found abandoned April 30th 1912

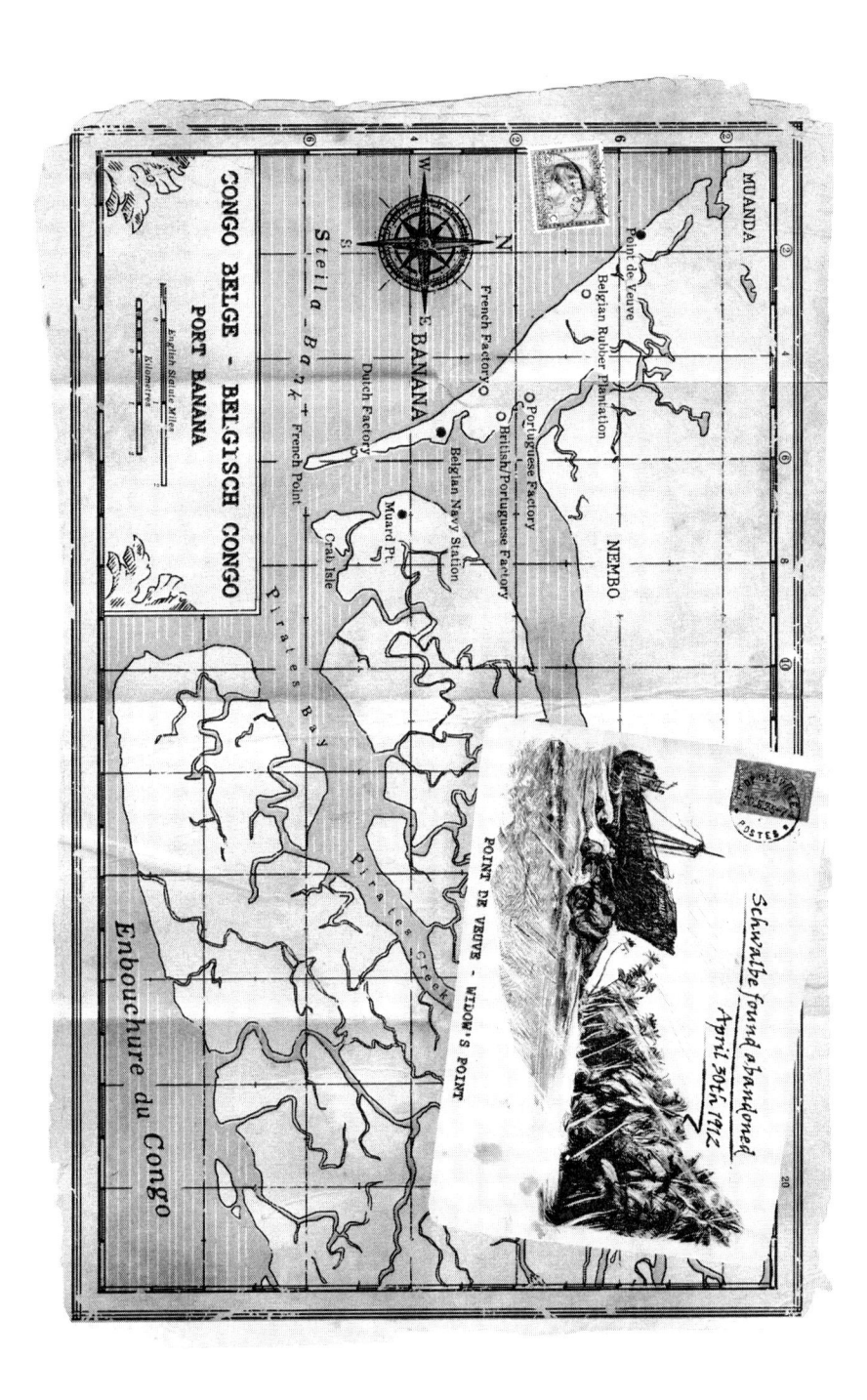

The woman looked up at him, her eyes resigned to her fate. In that moment, Moise decided she needed his help. Searching around, he found a stone and hurled it at the man. It struck him in the face. Toppling back, trousers about his ankles, he cursed.

'You little *zwarte*. I'll flay you alive.'

Moise ran and ran and ran. Even when he was out of puff, he ran some more. *Zwarte*, the Belgian called him. He knew what it meant. A horrible word. Moise remembered the first time he heard it, when the colonists cut off his father's hands and left him to bleed to death. Moise wished he could have thrown a larger stone. He would have crushed the colonist's huge, ugly head.

The Belgian's curses faded into nothingness, replaced by the squawking of seabirds. Moise slowed to a walk, sweat pouring down his shirtless body. After a little while, the landscape changed until it looked as if nobody ever ventured along that stretch of shoreline. He knew that wasn't true. A long time before the Belgians arrived, Arab slave traders had populated the region.

The Loango tribesmen ate them.

Then came the white missionaries; many of them were eaten too.

Soon, there were too many white men, and their guns drove the Loango into the interior. The colonists followed, the coastline now filled with white men carrying Bibles. Moise had never heard of Christianity before his father died. He never knew his mother. A Belgian mission in Banana opened an orphanage, and Moise got rounded up. Unlike the white men with guns, the missionaries brought beds, Bibles and fishing poles. He didn't understand how God could save him, nor why. He told the missionaries to give him a fishing pole; it was better than wading into the chaffing surf with a discarded net to catch fish.

Then he remembered: his fishing pole! The missionaries would punish him if he returned without it. He was about to turn round to fetch it when he stopped in his tracks.

A big iron ship sat beached on the spit of rocks the Belgians named 'Widow's Point'. Moise had seen large ships many times. They traversed the

River Congo en route to Matadi. Sometimes, the sailors would give boys a ride, sometimes even let them stand in the wheelhouse.

Cautiously, Moise approached the beached ship. It was not a pretty one like the passenger steamers bringing the Belgian colonists. This was an ugly cargo steamship with a single buff-coloured funnel. The ship's port side bow was staved in by the rocks and listing heavily. Above the damaged hull was a name: *Schwalbe*. Underneath, in smaller lettering, was the word *Hamburg*. He didn't have any inkling what it meant. All he did know was it was not there the day before.

Moise looked about pensively. As far as he could see along the shoreline in either direction, there was no one.

Cautiously he moved down the beach. The missionaries would have his balls for conkers for skiving off, but curiosity drew him towards the ship. Stopping in the shadow of the monstrous hull, he felt like a mere prawn to be swallowed by the beached whale above him. The front of the hull was already drying, spots of rust growing around the rivets of the exposed iron plates. He circled the ship from the safety of the sand, scared of venturing too close to the waves still battering the stern, lest he be dragged into the water.

He found a hatch on the hull ajar, and moved closer, keen to know what was inside. It was dark within; cool, dank air filtering out. Losing his nerve, he backed away. It would be wiser for him to run and tell the missionaries. But curiosity told him if there were riches inside he would have them before the Belgians — they were stealing quite enough already. Scrambling up the rocks with deftness only small boys knew, he climbed into the ship's belly.

Moise shivered as the cold air inside washed over him. It smelled of lubricating oil. Distant sunlight filtered down from a stairwell at the end of a companionway, and he couldn't resist climbing the stairs to the upper deck. Somewhere aft, through the maze of dark corridors, he heard the sloshing of waves against the hull. A hose lay uncoiled from its spool. He lifted the shiny brass nozzle, refracting sunlight from above, but gave up trying to pull it off after a few tries.

A cautionary shiver stabbed his spine. He did not like this place. Ahead, more stairs led into the light. Up the stairs he padded, re-joining bright sunlight as he arrived onto the main deck. He looked both forward and aft. It was strewn with debris, but there was no one about. Small boats remained lashed to the deck. One was different from the others. Larger. Its wood was splintered, white paint flaking away. It had a pretty red flag on its bow with a white star in the centre, and a word above it: *Titanic*. He looked inside the open boat. It was empty save for a coil of rope, bits of torn fabric and odd shoes. It was of no interest to him.

Beyond, he saw stairs leading up to the wheelhouse. He knew there was a lot of brass in a big ship's wheelhouse. Climbing the stairs, he found the room itself similarly abandoned. Bright sun poured in through its large windows. White signs with red lettering on them were attached neatly to the walls. Although he could read, the words were too long and strange. Another green rubber boot lay on the floor. Perhaps it was mate to the one he had found on the beach.

Intrigued by the ship's wheel, its brass-capped wooden handles worn from use, Moise tried to turn it. It held fast. In front stood the binnacle — another word he learnt from the Europeans — its wooden body polished, the brass compass housing glinting in the sunlight. He twiddled and fiddled with the clinometer inside it, fancying taking it with him, but was displeased when the housing wouldn't budge.

Next to it, he spied a brass telegraph used for communicating with the engine room. He grasped the handle, and found he could shift it with ease. A bell within the housing clanged. Leaping back, his bare feet slipped along the cock-eyed floor. He looked down, heart hammering.

Blood. It was smeared across the worn, green flooring. Something had been dragged across it.

He followed the blood trail to a door at the back of the wheelhouse, a bloody handprint smeared on the fascia. The missionaries would be cross with him if he found trouble. He gazed at the door handle. He couldn't resist.

The door creaked as he opened it. It was dark within. Pushing the door open a little more, he peered in. The round windows were smaller and fewer, curtains drawn across them, maps strewn about the floor, a chart table flipped onto its side. Moise pinched his nose. The room reeked. Beside the table lay the remains of white men. He was familiar with dead bodies — he had seen many in his short life — but never like these.

The remains looked like game carcasses hung out after being dressed. The head of one of the men was panned in, skin mummified, mouth locked in an agonised grimace. Its dark blue tunic was torn and its stomach cavity opened up and scooped out. It looked to Moise like a giant forest hog's kill.

Movement caused him to stop dead. He listened. It came again. Scraping. Hesitantly he pulled back the curtain over a porthole. A block and tackle hanging from its line slowly scraped along the glass. He sighed, relieved. Then, he heard something else: like the mission choir singing hymns.

He turned. Barely discernible in the semi-light, he saw a ghostly white woman standing in the far corner. He stared at her. For a long time. She stared back, eyes wide and unblinking.

Moise was beginning to wonder if his mind had gone when she moved. She came towards him, wraith-like, long, dark, hair filled with waves.

He thought her beautiful — until she moved closer. Ringed with crusted sores, her mouth parted, revealing teeth like the jaws of a goliath tigerfish. Frozen with fear, Moise thought of a story his father told him about these fish. Sometimes evil spirits entered them, making it attack people.

'*Mbenga!*' he yelped.

The hymn ended with a hyena-like howl.

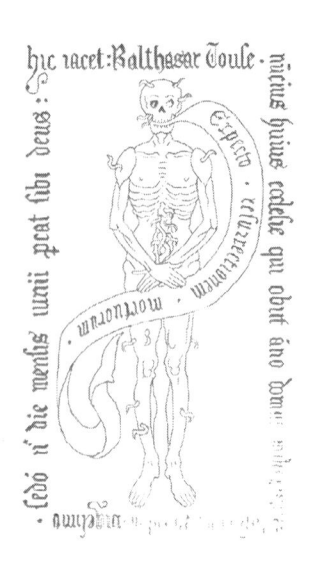

12 JULY 1915.
CAPE HELLES, GALLIPOLI

A parachute flare drifted from the night sky, casting the ravines of Cape Helles into quivering shadows of silver and green. The landscape flickered and went black as the flare waned. Shelling followed: highly explosive lyddite.

Harassing fire was aimed at the rabbit warren of British second-line trenches and rear areas. While Tommy sheltered in his dugouts, a head popped up from the Turkish lines, cautiously looking around as the shells whizzed overhead. An *onbaşı* crept from the safety of his trench. Here was Johnny Turk, defender of the Ottoman Empire. The arrogant British thought they would overcome him easily, but they could not. Rather than smashing his defences and banging on the gates of Constantinople in a matter of days, the Mediterranean Expeditionary Force still occupied a wretched scrap of the peninsula a mere 1,600 yards deep. Johnny Turk proved himself far more tenacious than the British reckoned.

Two *nefer* engineers timidly followed the corporal, worming their way stealthily towards a wire entanglement blown to bits by a British naval shell. A pioneer party, they dragged corkscrew pickets and a spool of concertina wire with them. Coming to the shell crater, they went to work screwing the iron pickets into the ground. They had learnt to cease work every little while and listen. Reassured the British were tucked away in their burrows, the engineers continued their chores, stringing the wire across the new pickets. The *onbaşı* ordered one of the *nefers* to go forward twenty yards with his rifle and keep a keen eye.

Although the artillery fire was deafening, the pioneers worked in silence. Attaching pull-rings, they tugged gently on the wire; it was important not to make it too taut nor too loose. Satisfied, they removed their gloves and began crawling back to their lines. The *onbaşı* paused. His private had not returned.

A rifle snapped, somewhere beyond Fur Tree Spur. The *onbaşı* looked into the darkness. It was of no concern. The shot was distant.

'*Imshi*,' he muttered, turning to his *nefer*.

Raw flesh glistened where the private's throat had just been slit.

The Turkish corporal looked frantically about. Nothing; only darkness and the *whooshing* overhead of shells from the Turkish batteries in the rear. He was a scant forty yards from his trench. Climbing to his feet, he ran. He had not gone twenty paces before a pile of souring corpses squirmed to life. Reaching for the engineer's hatchet in his belt, he yelled for this devil to go away.

'*Imshi yalla, şeytan!*'

A corpse, impossibly alive and impossibly vital, sprung on him. It smelled of earth and carrion. A blistering pain shot through the base of the *onbaşı*'s skull. Silence followed death's cold breath.

CAPE HELLES
THE OPPOSING TRENCHES
June, 1915.
(Only the main Turkish lines are shown)

① W Company Lines
② Y Company Lines & uncovered Roman Ruin
③ Gully Beach
④ Taggart's Dugout
⑤ 2nd Royal Fusiliers Positions

Disused Roman Necropolis excavated by Turkish Shelling

Hamish Taggart prowled beyond British lines. Creeping along Fur Tree Spur, the wiry second lieutenant watched the British naval shell fall short, blowing a section of Turkish barbed wire to bits. There was no chance the Turks would let a gap in their wire obstacles remain. Waiting for night, they would slip into no man's land again and patch it up.

A distant *thump* was followed by a whistle as enemy artillery sailed overhead, signalling the start of his nightly chores. Sliding over the parapet of an abandoned trench, he made his way into the land where no man dared go.

Taggart learnt quickly the enemy didn't waste their precious shells where there weren't any Tommies. He'd learnt all manner of other things too. His itch began on the troop ship from England. Nothing much at first — just a tickle in his brain. By the time the troop ship sailed by Alexandria, this son of a Pimlico actuary was suffering from endless pounding in his head. Then came dreadful urges. During the Fusilier Brigade's landing at Cape Helles, he brained his first enemy, and the pain immediately subsided — if only for a short while.

The landings were stillborn, the British ill-prepared for the Dardanelles expedition. His regiment — the 2nd Royal Fusiliers — was one part of the 29th Division led by Major General Hunter-Weston. The Butcher of Helles, as he came to be known, commanded the landings from his luxury steamship three miles offshore. He ordered the 2nd to land on the Aegean side of the Gallipoli peninsula, the first day's objective, a village called Krithia on the heights of Mount Achi Baba. Just four miles from the landing beaches, it loomed over the entire peninsula. From its heights, the Turkish effectively repelled the invaders with enfilade artillery fire. Achi Baba might just as well be the summit of Mount Everest.

Three months later, the allies had yet to conquer it.

Achi Baba was part of a plateau, like the palm of a giant's hand, called Kilitbahir. Its fingers, the gullies and ravines, the Turkish called *nullahs*. Cut into the hilly terrain by winter rains, these *nullahs* formed narrow stone-strewn beaches where they drained into the sea. The Butcher of Helles had chosen the least suitable terrain to land an offensive force. In the maze of scrub-covered ravines and ridges, Empire's youth were being annihilated by cleverly entrenched Turkish defences. Forcing the Dardanelles was nigh-on impossible.

Nobody expected Hamish Taggart. Particularly the *onbaşı* on whom he'd crept up. Leaping onto the terrified Turkish corporal, he wrapped an arm about his shoulder, covering his mouth and forcing the French Nail he held in his other hand into the back of his head where it met the neck. Just a slight crunch as the spike pierced the pioneer's skull, and a few wiggles. That was that.

Removing the French Nail, a welter of warm blood gushed over Taggart's hand. He left it there, as though cupping a hand beneath a spigot. Life in his hands. In no man's land, he felt himself a god, the wild savagery offering ephemeral relief from his pain.

Rolling over the *onbaşı*, his hand fell upon a wooden handle. Sliding the hatchet from the corpse's belt, he smiled, tossed the French Nail away and tucked the acquired melee weapon into his belt. Collecting the pioneer's identification discs, he began the journey across his personal slaughterhouse to W Company's trenches.

❖ ❖ ❖

Magnesium flares meandered across the sky, cradled by their parachute tethers. Taggart laid doggo, the piles of rotting bodies almost surreal under the flare's glow. No man's land was overlooked by knuckled ridges, bent wire piled in the *nullahs* to deny the British crossover points. Habitually, Taggart crossed lines in different places. Never did he return by the same route. At any moment, he could be under the eye of Turkish marksmen, but the blanket of night and his sodden khaki uniform offered protection. If there was a marksman looking for a snipe, all they could find in their crosshairs were ripening dead. Taggart, just another corpse.

His cutting blue eyes examined the terrain as the flares slowly sank to earth. The Turks had four machine gun positions enfiladed between Gully Spur and Fur Tree Spur, directing fire down on Gully Ravine — Taggart's section of the line. For the moment, there was naught he could do but linger among the stench of death — an odour to which he had long since grown accustomed.

Darkness finally fell as the last of the flares burned out. Taggart waited an extra minute. Too often he witnessed Turk machine guns wait until the flares extinguished before scything entire companies with brutal efficiency. Worming his way along a dry creek bed, he crawled to a point halfway between Turkish and British lines, where the Royal Navy's big guns had targeted a Turkish counter-attack across the meadow months earlier. Where once purple and yellow wildflowers bloomed, the shells had left a moonscape of deep crump holes in the tawny earth.

Staying to the lip of the bomb craters, he avoided the stew of decomposing bodies at the bottom.

Thunk.

A flare ignited where he had been only an hour before.

Remaining in the shadow of a crump hole, he waited for the light to sputter out. He was just about to move off when he heard distant, sweet voices carried by the breeze, like a hymnal choir.

Surveying the ground ahead, he saw nothing. The choir resumed, closer, innocent and adolescent, like a boys' choir.

Crawling to the crest of the crater, he heard it more clearly.

More flares popped. By their sullen glow, he saw it: a naked goblin, devoid of hair and brindle-coloured, it flopped about amidst the corpses. Membranous wings struck out from a stickleback spine. Spring-heeled Jack. Like in the *Penny Dreadfuls*. The pain in his head must be playing tricks on him now.

Sliding the hatchet from his belt, he watched the little goblin crane its neck, the flickering of the flares revealed a ghoulish face. A pudding-like rash covered its head, festering sores surrounding its chewing mouth. As the light waned, the goblin turned away.

Taggart moved closer to observe its doings. It dove headlong into a mash of decomposing bodies.

'Black shit and buggery,' he whispered.

Spring-heeled Jack was necrophilous. Adjusting the hatchet in his sweaty hand, he scraped it against his belt buckle. The goblin thrust its head up, chirping. The boys' choir sang out again. The fiend stared directly at him now, eyes black. The music ceased, replaced by a wretched howl as its spindly wings batted against the earth. Stumbling across the uneven terrain, it came at Taggart.

With wraith-like movement, something collided with the goblin, a glint in its hand. The pair tumbled down the far side of a crater and out of sight. A miserable quark was heard, like a seagull in distress.

Then silence.

Thump. A lazy whistle — from Turkish mortar bombs. An impact showered him in clods of dirt and human muck. More *thumps*. The air rent with incoming bombs. Climbing to his feet, he made a mad dash for a crump hole to his right. Leaping forward, he landed on its lip as a hot whirlwind rushed down upon him. A stray leg bludgeoned him in the back of his head as he rolled down the side of the crater.

Regaining his senses, he slunk up the crater's edge, squinting through the burning cordite vapour for another glimpse of the goblin.

'Oi!' A voice rang out.

Taggart went still.

'Is that a Tommy there?' the voice did then ask.

After a moment's pause Taggart replied, 'Oi.'

'Johnny Turk has you ranged. There's an abandoned communication trench fifty feet ahead. For God's sake, come towards our line.'

Taggart wondered who on earth could be madder than him to be so far out in no man's land. Making for the abandoned trench, he squirmed through a break in the bullet-riddled sandbag line. A sure hand pulled him through.

'Who's that then?' Taggart asked.

A shadowed figure crouched on a fire step, pistol drawn. 'A British officer.'

'What you doing this far from our lines?'

'I could just as easily ask you the same.'

'Sorting Johnny Turk,' replied Taggart, regaining his puff.

'You nearly bought it out there.'

Trying to work out what he just witnessed, he asked, 'Did you see anything odd just now?'

'Besides a daft Englishman dodging mortar bombs?'

The officer had brave balls, he had to admit. 'There's nothing out here,' replied Taggart. 'I've established a sap at the top of Gully Ravine already.'

'With a pair of corporals brewing up their tea in it.' The officer tucked his Webley away. 'Inspecting no man's land gives me an idea of what the enemy is up to.'

Taggart nodded, but he wasn't listening. 'I think I must be going barmy.'

'Oh?'

'Vagaries of battle,' he decided to say. 'I don't fancy being questioned.'

Crouching on the fire step, Taggart looked out across no man's land. 'Which company you looking after?'

'Y Company.'

'I'm W Company,' said Taggart. 'You're on my right.'

'Captain Hadley,' said the officer. 'Balthasar Hadley. The lads call me Buster.'

'Unless you want to be dead, Buster, I recommend you regain our lines. It'll be dawn shortly.'

Taggart moved off, still troubled by what he'd seen.

❖ ❖ ❖

Dawn blushed at half past four on the peninsula. Approaching British lines, a volley of rifle fire zipped over Taggart's head.

'Hold your fire, you useless gits.'

'That you, Mr Taggart?' came a distant voice ahead.

Crawling under a gap in the wire entanglement, he slipped over the sap, his most advanced listening post in the line. Manning it were Corporals Dodds and Davies, fusiliers of W Company whom Taggart shepherded like children. They stood on the fire step, rifles smoking on the sandbag parapet.

'Cor blimey,' muttered Davies. 'We could've slotted ya. Why did ya not give us the password?'

'We still do that, do we?'

The corporals stared blankly at Taggart. Looking down at his khaki drill jacket, he realised he was caked with a slurry of earth, decomposed flesh and squashed bluebottle flies.

'Johnny Turk didn't half give me a bad time of it,' he said nonchalantly. 'I'd kill for a gasper. Dodds,' he added, eyeing Dodds's tobacco tin. 'Dig us a shag, eh?'

The corporal obliged, rolling him a cigarette. Taggart put it to his lips, his hatchet shown in the flame Davies held for him.

'What's that 'orrible thing?'

'Pioneer hatchet,' he said, admiring the blade and its flat-backed head. 'Johnny Turk's engineers carry them. Perfect melee weapon. Brutally simple.'

'What's it for?' Dodds asked.

'Doing bloody murder,' chimed in Davies.

Taggart shot them a sour look. 'Murder is death without purpose. There is purpose to my butchery, so it can't very well be murder, can it?'

Taggart made his way from Gully Ravine, dodging heavily laden mules carrying the wounded down winding dirt trails to the regiment's narrow beachhead. Dugouts honeycombed the hillside. Something between a cave and a grave, dugouts were used as command posts, casualty-clearing stations and lower-ranks bunk houses. Every inch of bloodied ground was taken up.

It looked like a brigade slum.

Below, the beach was littered with the squalor of war — crates, tents and bullock carts. In a slapdash corral, mules were fed before the day's hauling of ammunition and water to the front. A ship's hull lay abandoned, stripped of everything of any worth, while a collier tied up to a flimsy jetty brought in fresh troops. Stretchers with the night's wounded waited in the blistering sun to be evacuated. In the turquoise shallows bathed scarecrow-thin men. Further out to sea, the Royal Navy sat at anchor, the generals onboard awaking from their slumber with a cup of tea and a dollop of fresh cream.

Cape Helles was obscene.

Entering his dugout, Taggart stripped off his filthy clothing. Yesterday's khaki drill was laundered and folded on his cot, the gore washed clean from the uniform, if not his mind. Filling an enamel mug with brandy he drank it in one slurp. Naked, he turned to leave. First Lieutenant Cuthbert Muirhead stood before him.

Taggart's immediate superior, Muirhead was Staff Adjutant to W Company's commander. He benefitted, both in timbre and vernacular, from the privileged world of hunts and punting. Taggart had experienced none of this. He was of a class neither here nor there. The working class scorned him for attempting to escape, while Muirhead's ilk regarded him with derision and contempt. Taggart's relationship with him was akin to that of a pork butcher informing a rabbi of his intention to open a market stall next door to his temple.

'Quite the ragamuffin these days, Second Lieutenant,' said Muirhead, his eyes drawn to Taggart's naked body.

He did nothing to cover himself. He had not a clue which way Muirhead swung, but if blokes were his thing, there were hundreds of them bathing naked off the beach that very moment. 'It's unwise to swan around here like it's the South of bloody France,' Taggart replied bluntly, pointing out the First Lieutenant's polished tunic buttons. 'Makes a nice target for a Turkish sniper.'

'Captain Burrows asks for the pleasure of your company. He's not seen a written report from your section of the line in weeks.'

'I doubt Captain Burrows has the first idea where my section of the line *is*,' Taggart tut-tutted, crushing a buzzing bluebottle with his palm. 'Nor you, Muirhead.'

'*Lieutenant* Muirhead,' he snorted derisively.

Ignoring him, Taggart grasped an Enfield rifle, slinging it over his shoulder.

'Where are you going with that?' Muirhead asked.

'For a wash-up, *Lieutenant*.'

'An officer does not carry a rifle.'

'If they did, officers like yourself might get a bit more respect from roustabouts like me.'

Muirhead bridled with anger, but Taggart was halfway down the trail to the beach already.

❖ ❖ ❖

Leaning his Enfield against a rock, he waded into the Aegean, a dirty wake trailing behind him. Swimming to an outcrop exposed by the low tide, he climbed up, grasped a handful of sand from a crevice and began scrubbing his skin.

'You could scrub your skin raw doing that.' A slim fellow with a lean patrician face but with eyes as black as Newgate's knocker swam up. 'You never get all the filth off.'

'Know something about it, do you?'

'A bit.'

Mounting the rocks, he offered Taggart a block of coal tar soap.

Taggart was taken aback. Soap was hard to come by. Accepting it, he noted the colour of the man's skin. Pale for a veteran of the Dardanelles.

'Just arrived, have you?'

The fellow didn't so much as crack a smile, his flinty stare ruthless but lacking in cruelty. Even the likes of Taggart found it disquieting. 'Have we met before?'

'Both our companies transited from England on the same ship. You're the Second Lieutenant who goes about with a rifle.'

'Perhaps I like stroking my stock.'

'An officer carries a whistle and a Raj cane, and the ranks pray a sniper drops him. But an officer who carries an Enfield? Men give their lives for an officer like that.'

'Got me all worked out, have you?'

'Captain Hadley,' he said, extending his hand. 'Balthasar Hadley. 2nd Royal Fusiliers, Y Company.'

'Buster?' The penny dropped. Taggart shook his hand, his grip hard as marble. 'It was you.'

'I find myself in need of an officer with your abilities, Second Lieutenant.'

'And what abilities would they be?'

'A man who doesn't care for questions.'

It wasn't often Taggart was thrown for sixes, but Captain Hadley clearly concealed a secret. It was there, far back in the darkness of his eyes.

'You can keep that chip of soap.'

Diving into the shallows, Hadley swam away from him. Surfacing, he called back, 'In the meantime, keep scrubbing.'

❖ ❖ ❖

Lounging in twill shorts and chulpie sandals he bartered the Indian brigade in exchange for a German Luger, Taggart tried to make sense of what he'd witnessed in no man's land.

Dropping a dollop of spittle onto a whetstone, he distracted himself by sharpening the edge of his newly acquired hatchet. He had no intention of reporting any of what he saw to his superiors. Burrows was but a scab needing to be picked away and bled. His quaint thinking had caused the deaths of hundreds of Taggart's lads in ill-planned frontal attacks against fixed enemy machine guns. Killing Burrows would get him sent home and Taggart couldn't have that. So, instead he went native, deracinating himself from the foibles of a proper British soldier.

He picked at his meal. Lentils and oats from the Indian Brigade's mess. He could smell the British spitters preparing the meals each day: bully beef stew covered with swarms of bluebottle flies just in from feasting on the dead. Nearly all soldiers on the peninsula suffered from dysentery. Not the Indians, though; they wouldn't go near tinned beef and were all healthier for it.

Muirhead knocked on his door-frame, a stout Captain Burrows sauntering in ahead of him. Kitted out in a serge service jacket, riding breeches and ever-so-nicely polished riding boots, he was the very picture of colonial snobbery. Even his tie had the proper dimple.

Tucking his Wolseley helmet under his arm, he tweaked his perfect Kitchener moustache.

'Stand to attention,' Muirhead barked.

Leaving the hatchet on his cot, Taggart stood, arms akimbo, his stance slightly arrogant.

'Surprisingly correct,' remarked Burrows, inspecting the dugout. Knocking Taggart's half-eaten breakfast with his Raj cane, he asked, 'Issue with our messing?'

'The beef smells like dead man. I prefer the Indian Brigade's *petit déjeuner*. Keeps the enteric away.'

Burrows' moustache twitched.

'I have received nary a report from you for weeks,' said the captain, voice highly bred and prudent.

'I've been busy.'

'Doing *what*?' Burrows asked, his cane tapping a glass jar filled with identification discs.

'Giving Johnny Turk a bit of dreadful.'

Burrows turned to his adjutant. Muirhead responded with a slight nod, his gaze then darting to Taggart to gauge whether or not it had been seen.

'No sniping. No reconnaissance. No enemy saps occupied. Yet, in all the 29th Division, your four sections cause the most casualties to the Turks.'

'I really cannot imagine how that information comes your way.' He gave Muirhead a look of daggers. 'It certainly couldn't be from you, First Lieutenant. I've yet to see you up the ravine once.'

'I've duties here.' He waved away a bluebottle snapping at his ear. 'You would do well to remember that.'

'I wish I had half a crown every time one of them bloated brutes buzzed about my face at the front. You'd understand if you ever came round.'

'Taggart, you are a rascal,' Burrows replied, his disgust evident. 'The most disreputable officer in the division.'

Taggart responded to this reprimand by taking up his newly acquired hatchet and testing its sharpened edge with his thumb, opening it up so cleanly it didn't sprout a drop of blood. Pressing against the slice with the knuckle of his index finger, his thumb began to bleed. Muirhead winced.

'My sections have advanced one hundred yards in a fortnight. We occupy two of the Turks' frontline trenches, have taken a hundred and fifty prisoners and killed twice that. We sent down only thirty-nine of our own — all with squitty bottom from eating that rubbish beef.'

'How on earth can you claim such a remarkable figure when the rest of my line is stalled?' asked Burrows, sitting his neatly pressed backside upon Taggart's campaign chair.

'I don't send my sections out.'

'I beg your pardon?'

'I don't send my lads over the top. The Turk has four machine gun posts commanding the heights beyond the ravine. As you know, they're marvellously accurate. Your order for our aborted push on Krithia gave the chop to a hundred and forty of my lads, with no ground gained.'

'I find it impossible to accept your report.'

'Such high enemy casualties are beyond belief,' snapped Muirhead. 'Whom are we meant to congratulate, the ruddy Easter Bunny?'

'Since you ask,' Taggart replied, relaxing on his cot, 'you may congratulate *me*.'

'You?' Muirhead scoffed. 'You have taken a hundred-odd prisoners and killed twice that, single-handedly?'

'The Turks surrender of their own accord.'

'And the enemy casualties?'

'Personally, I don't take prisoners.'

Taggart passed a Cross & Blackwell jar to Muirhead.

'A fortnight's action. Last I counted, there were one hundred and sixty nine identification discs in there.'

Captain Burrows rolled the jar in Muirhead's hands, the discs jingling.

'You suggest you alone caused the death of all these Turks?'

Taggart nodded.

'Rubbish,' Muirhead snorted.

'Perhaps you would come round for a visit, Lieutenant?' Taggart asked in reply.

'And how exactly have you done this?' asked the captain.

'Sorting Johnny Turk,' Taggart said and stood, hatchet in hand. A strong seven inches taller than Burrows, he watched his captain back away. 'I can't imagine a more terrible place than right here and right now. As I am right here and now, I aim to win.'

Laying the hatchet on his bunk, he then directed his words towards Muirhead.

'The only road to victory is by going into bandit country and slaughtering those poor Turks before they slaughter me. As it is, they've got four enfiladed Maxim machine guns emplaced and I'll keep going out until I've found them.'

'It's ruddy impossible.' Muirhead shook his head cynically. 'One man, an undisciplined officer no less, causing such a disruption.'

'I must agree with the lieutenant; it's utter flannel,' Captain Burrows said as he dusted off his breeches. 'We're to make a consolidated push on Krithia, part of a big offensive to open the line and advance on Achi Baba. What I require is officers who follow orders. Your men will be sent across. I don't care if you sacrifice every last one, you'll do as ordered.'

Taking the jar from Muirhead's hand, Burrows gave it shake. 'Discipline.'

Letting the jar fall, it smashed on the hard dirt floor, scattering the discs. 'If there were not a shortage of officers, I'd have you on charge.'

He turned to step outside, putting on his pith helmet. 'Am I making myself understood, *Second Lieutenant*?'

'You are, indeed.'

Burrows gave him an authoritative glare before going off in a dust of poor leadership. Muirhead followed, slinging Taggart a mocking wink.

He looked at his thumb as blood ran down his arm.

❖ ❖ ❖

Red stabs of flame lit the darkness. Salvo after salvo from the nightly Turkish barrage whistled overhead. The breeze shifted on-shore, carrying with it a thick odour of putrefied flesh. Lieutenant Muirhead raised his head above the sandbagged sap, his shoulder pips proud in the new moon.

Taking hold of his collar, Taggart yanked him down.

'You want your bloody head shot off?'

Muirhead looked to Corporals Davies and Dodds as they chuckled quietly. Taggart snarled at the lieutenant's kit.

'Take your shoulder pips off. A Turk marksman will slot you before you're over the parapet.'

As the lieutenant fumbled to rip them off, Taggart surveyed the void ahead with a trench periscope.

'And remove your hose-tops. They get fouled in the barbed wire.'

Obediently, Muirhead began to unwind the standard battle-dress stockings.

'And leave behind your flat cap and Sam Browne belt as well.'

Turk parachute flares began to pop, revealing Muirhead's worried face as he fiddled with his wristwatch for the umpteenth time. Captain Burrows had sent him to the front to witness Taggart's claims. From the first shell-burst, Muirhead's arrogance faded faster than he could dodge a Saville Row tailor's bill. Taggart had no intention of shepherding him. There were chores to do, and the inexperienced lieutenant might lose his nerve before Taggart got to his work.

Muirhead swallowed dryly.

'Been out there before, have you, sir?' Corporal Davies asked.

'No,' he replied. 'I've meant to.'

'Down here, out of sight of Johnny Turk, there's a bit of safety.' Dodds passed him his periscope.

'Out in that darkness...' Davies crawled up next to Muirhead. 'Up them gullies and over them ridges, is a slaughterhouse.' Muirhead lowered the periscope.

'Corporal Davies is right,' said Dodds, enjoying this chance to unnerve a superior. 'Stay close to Lt Taggart.'

Taggart watched the last of the flares go to ground.

'Ready for a bit of fun?'

Muirhead replied with a nod, his eyes saucers.

'Do us a favour, Lieutenant,' said Davies. 'Tuck in them peepers. Johnny Turk will spot the whites of your eyes clear across no man's land and put a bullet between them.'

Taggart had a little chuckle as Muirhead actually squinted. Edging over the parapet, he wriggled under the barbed wire entanglement. Muirhead followed.

'God almighty,' he whispered as he was hit by the odour of putrefaction.

'Enjoy the fresh air whilst you can,' said Taggart, tucking the hatchet into his service belt at the small of his back. His revolver remained holstered. Firing it would attract every Turkish marksman atop the spurs ahead.

They crawled in front of the first wire entanglement, propelling themselves by toes and forearms, drenched in sweat and covered in earth within minutes. Making his way through a morass of rotting corpses, clouds of bluebottles took to the air, sticking to his gore-stained uniform, Taggart had become almost invisible.

'My heart is beating nineteen to the dozen,' whinged Muirhead, a sprung branch whipping across his face, cutting the bridge of his nose. 'How on earth are we meant to make way through this?'

'Shush,' whispered Taggart, angrily. 'We're in bandit country. I've already sussed out four Turk machine guns on the spurs ahead. But their marksman, he's a crafty one.'

Muirhead would be his witness if he managed to stay alive. He wasn't holding out high hopes though. Crawling under the last British entanglements, he directed Muirhead towards a split in the nullah. To the right, a goat's track ascended a barricaded ravine.

'We'll stay well away from "the Sunken Road",' Taggart whispered, drawing Muirhead's attention to a mass of barbed wire wrapped around seven-foot prickly oaks.

'What are those bits hanging from the barbs?'

'Strips of flesh,' said Taggart. 'The nullah beyond is a meat grinder. Our lads were so desperate to free themselves from the entanglements they preferred pulling off their own skin to facing Turkish machine guns.'

A gust of wind howled down from the ravine, the odour of putrefaction causing Muirhead to retch.

'You've not smelled nothing yet,' Taggart made mention.

A flare popped beyond the ridge above, revealing a dreadful sight. Bodies. Heaps of them piled one upon another. Left where they'd fallen, the maggots had gone to work on them.

'During the first days of landings, the Lancashire Brigade got caught out by a fusillade of Turkish rifle and machine gun fire. The brigade ceased to exist.'

'How will we pass?'

'We push through them. Now be quiet, unless you wish to join them.'

❖   ❖   ❖

Taggart slid into a crump hole, pulling Muirhead in by the scruff of his collar. After an hour of crawling, they crested the ravine. Rolling down the side of the crater, Muirhead's hand went through the chest of a dead body. Whatever little was left in the First Lieutenant's stomach swiftly surfaced.

Pulling his balaclava up over his nose, Taggart climbed over the dead for a look around. He was familiar with the terrain, having crossed the meadow innumerable times. There was another gully on the far side. Using the holes as cover, he could reach it unseen. What concerned him, though, was the Turkish marksman. He could be anywhere.

Sliding back through the morass of corpses, he came to rest next to Muirhead.

'Right, Lieutenant. The stretch ahead is quiet. If we go up the gully to the left, I reckon we'll be able to flank the first machine-gun position.'

Muirhead stared vacantly at him, spittle running from his lower lip.

'Oi. You home?'

A soft huffing came from a corpse beside them, its head heaving. Straining for a better look, Taggart came eye to eye with a rat emerging from its mouth. Muirhead shrieked. Launching across the crump hole, hand cupping Muirhead's mouth, Taggart held his hatchet to his throat.

'Shut up! You want the Turk to rain mortars down on us?' Swinging the hatchet, he cleaved off the rodent's head. 'Never a moggie around when you need one.'

'What have you gotten me into?'

'I haven't gotten you into anything, Lieutenant.' Taggart wiped the hatchet on the corpse's uniform. 'You've Captain Bitterballs to thank.'

'You're out of your box. You dragged me here to kill me.'

'If Burrows had let me be, it wouldn't be necessary for you to be here at all. You're hampering my fun.'

'*Fun*? For God's sake, we're in a crater full of corpses.'

Taggart leaned close.

'Don't lumber me with your tosh.'

Turkish artillery whizzed overhead.

'I'll knock out those four Maxims and open this section of the line. Then the 29th Division can pour up Achi Baba, taking the Turkish big guns.'

Muirhead was shaking now. 'I'll tell Burrows anything you want. Don't let me catch a packet.'

Taggart wagged his hatchet in Muirhead's face, a drop of rodent blood pattering his cheek.

'I don't suffer fools gladly. Be still. Keep schtum. When this night is over, you can make your way down to the sap. Ring Brigade and inform them we've breached the Turk lines. You can take credit. I don't give a damn.'

Muirhead nodded in agreement, clearly verging on mental paralysis. Taggart had seen it many times before.

'Good man. Now be still.'

In an instant, Taggart vanished into the dark maw of no man's land.

❖ ❖ ❖

Festering corpses, rifles, spades and discarded overcoats littered the nullah ahead. Grasping bushes and roots, Taggart pulled himself up the ravine and onto the ridge, all the while set upon by buzzing flies. He easily flanked the Turkish machine gun nest, slipping into a sandbagged communication trench. So confident were they of their advantage, the Turks had not bothered with barbed wire about their position.

Keeping to the shadows, Taggart got closer. Although heavy water cooled machine guns normally had a crew of four, including a spotter and ammunition porter, at night the Turkish machine gun posts were manned only by a gunner and loader.

Perfectly situated on the edge of a crest and hidden in a thick overgrowth of camel thorn, the machine gun crew had a clear field of fire sweeping the gully below. They had not the first idea of how Taggart had stolen away their advantage. It was all he could do to keep his impulses in check and race the last ten yards downhill and lace into them.

Wiping his sweat-soaked hands on his sleeves, he reached for his hatchet. He was about to move when he saw the loader climb over a raised, earthen parados. Approaching, he unbuttoned his kecks.

Taggart shoved his face into the dirt. The snap of a twig under the loader's boot came just a yard from Taggart's head as the Turk began to wee on him. Rearing up, Taggart pulled him to ground by his wank, slashing his throat with the sharpened hatchet blade.

Soaked in blood and urine, he moved downhill silently. Even if the gunner heard him, he'd presume Taggart was just his loader returning. Stoving in the gunner's head with the flat of the hatchet, he left him slumped over his Maxim. Pulling the belt of ammunition away, he tossed it down the ravine. One less machine gun to harvest his lads.

It had just gone midnight as he slunk away from the position, blood soaking through the bread bag he had buttoned to his belt. He felt euphoric, thankful to have learnt of this new world where he could butcher men without fear of recompense. Already, he dreaded the day it would end. In the meantime, there were three other machine gun posts and a marksman to be sorted.

❖ ❖ ❖

Taggart watched the crescent moon reach its highest point in the sky from his eyrie on the ridge. Locating the third machine gun position under a tree, he dispatched the gunner and loader with vim, wiped his hatchet on the gunner's ragged uniform and tucked it away again.

He crossed the Turkish rear, passing through meadows of cornflowers and poppies, his movements drowned out by the unending racket of cicadas. How beautiful a place the peninsula was before the British arrived. He made for the height on the opposite side of the plateau and sat, picking through Turkish rations: olives, figs and grape leaves. He quite liked Turkish fare. Just not the Turks themselves, killing his lads by the score, as they were. Why wouldn't they, though? This was their country. The British had no business here.

He surveyed a section of the enemy line below. Since learning how to quench his desires, Taggart had become curious as to what was over the next hillock. The next spur. The next ridge.

Lifting a set of binoculars he'd liberated from a dead officer, he surveyed the terrain below. He knew there remained a machine gun crew somewhere — and a marksman to run to ground.

He was about to move on when he picked out movement. Adjusting the focus of his glasses, a wire entanglement sharpened before his eyes. A figure writhed. It was Muirhead. The lieutenant must have scuttled, attempting to regain brigade lines, and got himself in a muddle.

Shadowy figures crawled over the broken no man's land towards Muirhead. Lowering the glasses, Taggart grinned. Unknowingly, the lieutenant was acting as a beater, drawing game to Taggart. Finishing off the last of the grape leaves, he moved.

❖ ❖ ❖

Four Turks crept towards Muirhead. Hopelessly mired in a web of concertina wire, he twisted and thrashed, crying out for mercy. Moving downhill, Taggart spotted the remaining machine gun crew poking their heads above a parapet. Further along the trench crouched the marksman Taggart sought.

Edging forward silently, Taggart blindsided the sniper. Pulling back his helmet, he exposed the marksman's neck, severing his carotid artery and windpipe with a single blow from his hatchet. The marksman fell to the ground without a sound. Releasing his helmet strap, Taggart exposed the top of his head. Another instant and he had completed his bloody business.

The machine gunner turned just as Taggart bashed him with the blunt side of the hatchet, crushing his young face.

The loader was next. Taggart swung and split his face open from forehead to jaw. Forcing him down, he chopped his neck, dousing himself with arterial spray.

With no time spare to enjoy the mess, Taggart turned his desires to no man's land. The four Turks were now upon the lieutenant. Taggart knew he could chop the lot of them down with a single burst from the Turkish Maxim, but he wasn't an especially good shot. He'd most likely cut Muirhead in half as well.

There came a scream. The Turks were tearing strips of Muirhead's flesh away with the barbed wire. Laughing, they shook it further, eliciting despairing moans of agony from the lieutenant. His pain must have been exquisite.

Leaving the trench, Taggart closed in on the Turks, invisible amongst the churned-up earth. He drew close. So close that even in the darkness he recognised the terror on the Lieutenant's face. Drawing a curved sabre, a Turk pricked Muirhead's chest with the tip, peeling off a strip of his flesh and eliciting another cry for mercy.

It was answered.

Launching to his feet, Taggart heaved his hatchet, burying it in the Turk's upper back. Fleet of foot, Taggart had it out of him again before his knees buckled, braining him with the blunt end of the weapon.

Turning, he kicked a second Turk in the balls before bludgeoning him, shattering his skull.

Two now remained, tormenting Muirhead with the wire. They made the mistake of moving too quickly, hopelessly ensnarling themselves with him.

Removing his Webley, Taggart shot both of them in the head. The echoing gunfire meant it wouldn't be long before the Turks poured from their dugouts.

'Half a mo', Mr Muirhead,' Taggart shouted, regaining his breath. 'Gotten yourself well arseholed in there haven't you?'

'Taggart,' Muirhead bleated, face liverish. 'Drive the beggars away!'

He fired three quick shots into the air. From the direction of Gully Ravine came a sound of whistles. Flares popped and the sky filled with light. W Company's fusiliers, awaiting Taggart's signal, started their attack, now without opposition.

❖ ❖ ❖

Taggart accompanied the stretcher party down the ravine, his hair a tangle of sweat and congealing gore. Men of 2nd Brigade were rushing up the ravine towards no man's land.

Returning to lines, Davies gave him a Craven A — his preferred tobacco. He took a drag, the caked blood in his fingernails adding a tinny tang.

'Taggart,' Muirhead muttered, gripping his hand tightly. All arrogance was gone thanks to the unpleasantries he had seen. 'You've done it. You've opened the line.'

Taggart tipped his ash. 'We gave Johnny Turk a good drubbing.'

'*You* did.'

Muirhead winced from the wire barbs still embedded in his flesh. An orderly dispensed a tot of rum from a grey hen. Muirhead gulped it back.

'I was done up like a kipper. Then you were there,' he squeezed out. 'Tossing your hatchet like a ruddy *Mohawk*. You saved my life.'

A stretcher-bearer looked to Taggart. 'Mohawk, eh?'

'You will look after him?'

The stretcher-bearer gave a nod. 'Yes, Second Lieutenant Mohawk.'

Taggart's feelings towards Muirhead had not changed, but he was glad the lieutenant had borne witness to his proclivities. Patting his arm, Taggart said, 'I'll give the captain your regards,' and left.

The Mohawk had arrived on the peninsula.

❖ ❖ ❖

Captain Burrows slumbered soundly. His Indian mess waiter, preparing to awaken him, was startled by the sight of Taggart so covered in blood and dirt.

Dismissing him, Taggart parted Burrows' mosquito netting and went in.

The quarters were sumptuous in comparison with the lad's bolt-holes: entirely sealed with mosquito netting, there was a proper bed and matching mahogany desk and a jug of rum sat beside a silver-framed photograph of Mrs Burrows.

Taggart loosened his bread bag, and sat down in the first proper chair he had seen in months. Sinking into the soft leather club chair, he leaned back, before giving the captain's bed a kick. Burrows' eyelids parted.

'Morning,' Taggart said congenially.

Wiping sleep from his eyes, the captain squinted, clearly surprised by the state of Taggart, head to toe wetted in human gore and sweat, and stinking like a dead man. 'Second Lieutenant? What are you doing in my quarters? And where is Muirhead?'

'Your lieutenant is knackered.' Taggart rose and walked towards the dugout entrance, tossing the bread bag between Burrows' legs, leaving a bloody smear on the sheets.

'We've broken the Turks back beyond Gully Ravine. Whilst you were sleeping, W Company occupied the enemy's front-line trench. And as your tea goes cold we are pressing into their rear.'

Burrows sat up and kicked the stinking bread bag off the bed. It fell to the floor, spilling its contents. He reeled.

Fifteen scalps lay before him.

'Fifteen.' Taggart turned to leave. 'Fifteen in remembrance of 1915. The year you died here at Cape Helles. That is, if you don't fuck right off and leave me to practice my trade.'

Burrows stared at the Turkish scalps, trembling.

Saluting smartly, the Mohawk excused himself.

❖ ❖ ❖

The shelling began anew after dark, the precious few days of relative quiet now over. The Mohawk watched from above Gully Beach as a steady stream of mules brought the wounded down from the new front. On his way up, he received nods from the ranks, followed by whispers of the Mohawk's exploits. Climbing the trail to Y Company's post headquarters, he watched Turkish shells randomly explode amongst the 29th Division's trenches. His advance was squandered by ineffective officers, useless gits lacking an ounce of nous, again wasting Empire's youth.

The Turkish artillery seemed especially fierce that night, intent on retribution.

Y Company's HQ was tucked into an unusual location. Rather than sitting behind the front, it was right on it. A monstrous shell crater exposed a ruin of some such, with picks and shovels dotting the mounds of disturbed earth. At the end of the trench, a *foreign* looking boffin in a bowler hat and round spectacles stood guard with a trench sweeper. Shotguns were uncommon in the Dardanelles.

Turning down a communicating trench, its walls reinforced with earth-filled ammunition boxes, Taggart passed guards on stand-to. Bayonets fixed, they stood on the firing step, keenly watching no man's land, while a corporal peered through a trench periscope. Y Company had a discipline to which he was unaccustomed.

'Where can I find your commanding officer?'

'Who's askin'?'

'The Mohawk.'

'Christ almighty.' Hopping from the firing step the corporal snapped to attention without saluting, showing respect of rank without risking his superior being sniped.

'It's an honour, sir.'

'Where is Captain Hadley?'

'Carry on ahead. Pass the command dugout, you'll find a dump of sandbags. That's the captain's quarters.'

'At the front?'

'That's the sort our commander is.'

Taggart found him in his dugout, studying documents from a leather Gladstone bag. Balthasar filled his uniform like a soldier, not like entitled nobility playing dress-up. A commanding officer who situated not only his HQ, but also his quarters at the front, was a superior officer Taggart could respect.

'Oi, Buster.'

Balthasar looked up and gave a nod of recognition. 'Lieutenant Mohawk.'

'I've considered your offer.'

Balthasar stood. 'I understand you've been up to all manner of mischief.'

'Perils of the peninsula.'

Taggart looked about the captain's bolt-hole. It was cramped, the roof reinforced with ship's timber, safe from artillery. A civilian trunk with a curved lid sat in the corner, the name in red letters stamped on the front all but faded away — he could only just make out "Balthasar". The Captain most certainly was a traveller. On a chart table beside it were all manner of historical curiosities: broken vases, vivid mosaic tiles and statue fragments. A cup with long handles caught Taggart's eye. They were ethereal in their delicacy, like palpitating wings. It reminded him of the goblin.

A brass bicycle lamp on an upturned crate illuminated the opened attaché. By the dim light Taggart could see what Hadley was reading: "Externsteine Wilderzeichen. By Eleanor Annenberg. PhD Ethnology". Brushing by him, the captain blocked his view.

'Light bedtime reading?'

'I am willing to give you free rein in the field,' he said, closing the documents wallet. 'But not in my quarters.'

Raising his braces over his grey field shirt, he slipped a Webley into the holster on his belt. He wore no collar badges or shoulder titles, carrying himself with authority rather than pomp.

'What's Wilderzeichen?'

'There are many ways to butter a parsnip,' he replied elusively. 'Brought your hatchet?'

Taggart was confused by the question.

'I'm off for a stroll round the manor,' Hadley continued. 'Expect the Turks to counter-attack at any time.'

They made their way along a communication trench, the ranks nodding to them as they passed.

'The attrition rate of your company exceeds forty percent,' Balthasar said.

'It's not due to the Turks. Not any more. My lads are dropping from illness.'

'The same holds true for Y Company. Our superiors have decided to amalgamate us into a single full-strength company.'

'Another offensive?' Taggart asked.

Balthasar listened as a Turkish shell screamed overhead, landing not far from the rear.

'I suspect we're going on the defensive.'

Taggart was shown along the communicating trench leading to the ruin. The shotgun-wielding civilian remained on post.

'This is my colleague, Mahmoud Hajian.'

Mahmoud doffed his hat, tough black hair tumbling over his forehead. 'The Mohawk, eh? Heard all about your audacious exploits.'

'Hajian?' Taggart asked, looking to the captain. 'You've got a Turk here?'

'Persian, actually,' came a dry reply from Mahmoud.

'This is not a soldier's matter,' said Balthasar, tickling a pair of oil lanterns until they gave off a low flame, 'but one of personal importance. Mr Hajian is the right man for his task, as you are the right man for yours.'

'What's the task?'

The Persian stepped aside, allowing them to pass.

'Keep sharpish,' the Captain instructed the Persian.

After going down a flight of ancient stairs cut into the rock, they stood in a subterranean passage, recently excavated. Taggart shivered in the cold air below ground. Adjusting the lantern's flame, Hadley handed him one.

'We're in a long-forgotten hollow unearthed by a shell from Asiatic Annie.'

'Hollow?'

Shining the lantern down the narrow passage, Taggart's light picked out deep gouges in the floor. Something very heavy had gone that way a long time ago.

'This was Johnny Turk's front line before your one-man offensive. A round from Asiatic Annie, the Turkish siege gun on the Asian side of the Dardanelles Straits fell here three nights ago creating quite a crater.'

'And thus uncovered this?'

The captain nodded. They arrived at a massive slab of stone, blown aside. Scrawled into the bare rock above it, Taggart recognised runes:

ᛁᛁᚱ

What it meant he had not the first idea.

'They clearly didn't want anyone getting in and finding whatever was sealed behind this blocking stone.'

'Or getting out,' replied Balthasar. 'Turkish conscripts are not paid well, you see. They wasted little time in cracking the entrance's seal using explosives.'

'All of this to loot a lot of old trinkets?'

The captain shone his lantern ahead to reveal a low arcade supported by a double row of columns.

'Bloody hell,' Taggart gasped, slowly making his way across a mosaic floor depicting panthers and leopards stalking flocks of goats. 'What is this place?'

'An old Roman bath,' Hadley replied, fragments of plaster crunching under his boots. 'Long ago, in another epoch, a Roman trading settlement existed here.'

He looked around. The bath had been looted. Tiles were pried up, vases smashed. Only feet remained where a statue once stood on a pedestal.

'Bit pranged, isn't it?'

'Johnny Turk opened a sarcophagus,' said Hadley, pointing to six plain sarcophagi tucked between the columns.

Taggart approached. 'Looks sealed up to me.'

'They are *now*.'

He touched one, the surface rough against his hand. 'What is this? It's not limestone.'

'It's chalk.'

In the lid, an engraved figure with a skull for a head grimaced at him. An apothegm sprung from its gritting teeth.

'*Expecto resurrectionem mortuorum.*'

He turned to the captain. 'Expect the resurrection of the dead.'

'You're an educated man, Taggart.'

'Read Latin as a schoolboy. Now, what's this all about? I'm a soldier.'

'With a hatchet.' Balthasar's steady gaze met his. 'A soldier you shall be permitted to be. What I am, though, is none of your concern.'

'Permission to speak freely?' Taggart felt unsure lest Captain Hadley think him mad and pack him off to England. He didn't want to leave this place.

'That night,' he continued.

'In the no man's?'

'You saw it too, didn't you?'

Balthasar gave him a look like a lion gave a gazelle before the dinner bell. 'Got a few scalps on your belt now, Mohawk. So, why don't you say what you really want to say.'

'A goblin…'

Balthasar nodded. 'Indeed.'

'It came from here, didn't it?'

'From its deviant burial in this hollow, yes.'

'Whatever have you gotten yourself into, Buster?'

'They are called Crimen.'

'Latin again, right?'

Balthasar nodded.

'It means Guilty.'

'That goblin, as you called it,' said Balthasar. 'It *is* Guilty.'

'It was feeding on the dead. On human flesh.'

Balthasar sat his lantern on the lid. '*Wilderzeichen.*'

'Yeah. What does it mean?'

'You witnessed a wild sign and lived to tell of it. The Turkish conscripts who opened these sarcophagi were not so fortunate.'

'I see,' said Taggart.

'No, I don't think you do.' Lifting the lantern, he turned towards the hollow's entrance. 'You are seeing without looking. It's not for the Mohawk to be concerned with.'

Even far below the lines, the *whoosh* of incoming artillery overhead was unmistakable.

'What concerns me,' Taggart said, 'is losing this Dardanelles business.'

'All of us are but six-shilling-a-day tourists.'

Taggart shrugged.

'You understand our holiday here nears its end.'

The truth of his aphorism gave Taggart a dash of reality. *His* holiday was near its end.

'You won't rein me in?' he asked, questioning Balthasar's intent. 'You'll let me do my doings?'

'I earned my quality a long, long time ago, Lieutenant Taggart. And you're messy. You kill without elegance.'

The blackness in Balthasar's eyes terrified even him.

'But your primeval instincts are useful to me. Here. Now.'

A shell *plomped* above, bits of plaster from the vaulted ceiling crashing to the floor. Neither of them ducked.

'You just keep Johnny Turk away from this line long enough for me to bury this hollow so deep it'll never be opened again, and you'll get nil complaint from me.'

'In for a penny,' said Taggart.

The floor shook violently. Turkish artillery was now targeting the British frontlines. Balthasar shepherded him from the hollow. As they emerged, he saw the Persian standing upon a firing step, his trench-sweeper pointing towards Turkish lines.

'Is it on?' asked Balthasar.

'Expecting a counter-attack at any moment.'

Balthasar hurried along the sandbag traverse, Taggart following as he turned into the front-line trench. Men prepped bombs made of old jam tins, useful only in close action. Taggart felt his urges build within him.

'This section of the line is ticklish,' said Balthasar. 'The Turkish are a cricket pitch away, industrious in throwing bombs into our trenches. W Company haven't any.'

Taggart looked to the W Company lads readying jam tins.

'So. We make our own bombs.'

Cautiously, Taggart peeked over the parapet. On the other side of no man's land, Turkish bayonets glinted in the moonlight as they waited orders to attack.

'Reciprocity, Lieutenant Mohawk.'

The artillery ceased.

'Keep the Turk off me,' Balthasar continued. 'Do that, and no man's land is your abattoir.'

Taggart's surprise kept him silent.

The shrill sound of a whistle from the Turkish trenches signalled the counterattack. Unbuckling his holster, Balthasar handed over his service revolver.

Looking at the pistol he handed him, Taggart asked, 'Won't you be needing this?'

'I don't need a gun.' A nod and he was gone over the parapet, rushing towards the enemy lines before they counter-attacked.

Climbing over the parapet the Mohawk crept into the no man's land as his head began to pound. What was to become of his proclivities when he left the Dardanelles?

It was early days.

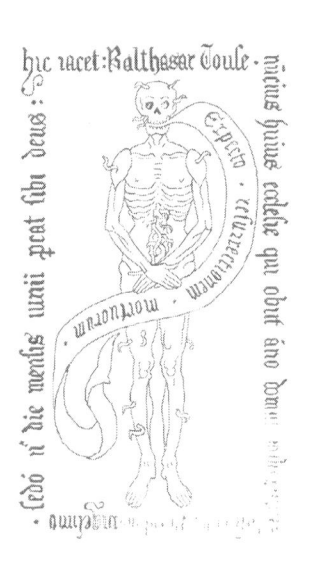

31 March 1929.
St Dunstan's,
Bloomfield Hills, Michigan

They are whole 'entities', entire social systems,
the functioning of which
we have attempted to describe.
We have looked at societies in their dynamic or physiological state.
We have not studied them as if they were motionless,
or as if they were corpses.
Even less have we decomposed and dissected them…

—Mauss, 'The Gift.'

'*Expecto resurrectionem mortuorum.*'

Elle's voice echoed through the church's nave. The congregation of students, masters, administrators and colleagues in Brooks Brothers suits and Vitalis-slicked hair hung onto her every word.

'Expect the resurrection of the dead.'

Verbalising it made her smile. Made what motivated her every waking moment more real.

Seventeen years had got behind her. A degree from the University of Michigan and a PhD in ethnology hanging from her belt, the once incorrigible Elle had become a broad-minded and optimistic Dr Eleanor Annenberg. Like Father, cautious and captivating, like Mother, witty and gritty. Since the night Titanic sank, her passion had remained unchanged: to find the truth of the horror she'd witnessed, and in doing so, to learn the identity of the man who had saved her.

Steel — a material more precious than gold in Detroit — made the Annenbergs wealthy. But after Titanic, the noise and chaos of the growing city lost its charm for Father. Selling off his steel mills to Henry Ford, he moved the family twenty miles north to the forests and farms of Bloomfield Hills. On a dilapidated apple farm, he built the first great house outside the city, filling it with artwork and furniture the family brought back from their many Grand Tours of Europe.

Franklyn Annenberg had no interest in buying respectability. Instead, he built St Dunstan's, a preparatory school named after the English village from which his grandparents had emigrated. To design the campus Father envisioned — Arts & Crafts with a Bauhaus flair — he retained a renowned Finnish architect. St Dunstan's would be the most inspiring prep school in the Midwest.

Not satisfied with preparing only boys for university, Mother saw to it that a girls school was built on the opposing shore of St Dunstan's lake. There followed an art museum, and finally a science institute, the ethnology department now directed by Elle. Prestigious universities came calling, due in no small measure to the Great War's slaughter of a generation of men. But as was oft true in a capitalist society, nothing came without a price. Elle could almost see those Ivy League chancellors licking their chops at the prospect of getting their mitts on some of her father's money.

St Dunstan's offered her what no university could guarantee: funding. This allowed her to search for proof of her theory: to expect the resurrection of the dead.

She tolerated the patronising masters who resented a woman in their Old Boys Club; she would have accepted funding from Detroit's Hebrew mafia if it got her closer to the truth of what she had witnessed on Titanic.

There had never really been any doubt in her mind that she would end up back home.

'*Expecto resurrectionem mortuorum*,' she repeated, the excited susurrus of her audience fading. 'Lurking out of sight in every epoch of civilisation.'

She took in the packed-out stalls and side aisles of the nave. Earlier in her career, at least half her students would ditch her final lecture before the Easter holidays. No longer. She had learnt a good mystery with lurid lashings kept her audience glued to their seats.

Word spread fast that Dr Annenberg's vivid tales were better than any *Penny Dreadful*. Soon enough, the lecture was moved from her classroom to the school's two-hundred seat assembly hall. By the time Elle tenured, requests to attend her lecture were coming from as far away as California. It was moved again, this time to the only building capable of seating five hundred—the newly completed and, fortunately for her, as yet unconsecrated, St Dunstan's church.

More carnival barker than professor, she juggled ethnological tennis balls for university administrators, students and masters. Her lips tightened at the sight of colleagues already shaking their heads at her. Old dogs, confined by convention and unwilling to risk their precious tenure on unconventional theories, they were quick to lob opprobrium at her. Yet all were vying for a seat to the big show, wanting to know if they should indeed '*Expecto resurrectionem mortuorum.*'

She nodded to an upperclassman in a bow tie and a stupid smile as he perched behind a Viewlex slide projector.

'As they appear, so they vanish.'

Charlie Burkhammer simply stared at her, same old guileless smile on his face.

'As they appear, so they vanish,' she repeated.

Nothing.

'Unless you too want to vanish too, Charlie, I recommend you make my slides appear.'

There were a few titters from the seats. Snapping out of his enchantment, he glanced at the maintenance man waiting by the church's narthex, and the lights dimmed.

A strategically placed spotlight threw Elle into a dramatic pool of light. It also served to wash out the naysayers rolling their eyes.

She took a breath before beginning. 'From the rainforests of Honduras to the mysterious Tor Externsteine in Germany, and as far away as a salt waste in the Persian Empire, there is a myth. Written in ancient languages, in different epochs and without any possibility of interaction, these developed but remote civilisations all have the same myth to tell. Tantalising clues to predation events. Wicked seraphs coveting the flesh of man. Hints of blood frenzies of such savagery and on such a scale entire cultures were consumed by these fiends. These Spring-heeled Jacks. These boogeymen. The anthropophagi — eaters of human flesh.' She paused as the audience whispered excitedly. They always did.

'During this last Christmas break, I participated in an archaeological investigation, co-funded by the University of Michigan.'

The projector *clicked* as Charlie inserted a slide. A screen in front of the high altar beside to Elle came to life, showing a step pyramid obscured by rainforest.

'Copán, in Honduras,' Elle explained. 'The capital city of the ancient Maya civilisation. Archaeologists from the University of Michigan discovered a hidden chamber beneath a previously explored pyramid.'

The screen went momentarily dark as Charlie swapped out slides. An inconspicuous and empty chamber then appeared.

'Something was once here — but later, was taken. My colleagues from U of M believe it was a stela, a sculptured stone, containing Mayan hieroglyphs that explain the exact purpose of the chamber.'

Another slide. Stepping closer to the screen, she almost became part of the photograph, pointing out rough-hewn marks in the walls and empty altars of the chamber.

'These are chisel marks. The stelae, as you can see, were not removed with great care.'

Stepping away, she nodded towards Charlie.

'I don't believe this was a temple. I think it was an abattoir,' Elle said.

The next slide revealed a stucco frieze and, within it, a winged Mayan God.

'This is in the chamber's ceiling. You can clearly see Camazotz — an ancient Mayan God associated with night, death and sacrifice. Camazotz is quite common: found in nearly every site throughout the ancient Mayan empire. But there's something unusual about this particular frieze.'

With her long, practiced fingers, she pointed out a symbol below the mask, representing Camazotz's face.

'I'm by no means an authority in Mayan semiotics, but this is clearly the symbol for *matan*. It is neither unusual nor uncommon. But finding it on a frieze of the God Camazotz? That's a royal flush.'

An adolescent voice punctured the darkness. 'What does it mean?'

'That's a good question.' She took a few, slow paces away from the screen, enjoying so much the moment in which she had total control. 'It means "Gift".'

Murmuring followed her revelation.

'My colleagues have never seen this symbol together with the Mayan bat god,' she said and paused again, leaving an extra beat for more dramatic effect. 'But I have.'

Charlie changed the slides again, and a relief of a black-winged creature appeared.

'Camazotz looks an awful lot like Hel. To a Germanic pagan, Hel was the undead demigod of the underworld. I took this photograph in a chamber high up in one of the Externsteine's natural sandstone towers in Germany's Teutoburg Forest. Germanic clans didn't preserve much evidence of their gifting, but look here,' she said as she pointed out some apparent gibberish fringing the relief.

'*Angebinde*. It's Germanic for the strength of the bond, which makes up an exchange. It doesn't specifically translate to "Gift" but rather the *binding* of gifts to a person. The drift is pretty clear: the stronger the binding of the Gift, the stronger the bond.'

The next slide showed the profile of a winged creature with claw-like talons carved into stone.

'Now. This is from a tomb along an old spice route in Iran. This charming fellow is Ahriman, Persian god of pretty much all things that go bump in the night.'

Her captive audience chuckled nervously.

Tapping her finger against the screen, she directed the audience's attention to a cluster of rigid lines below the carving. '*Atâ*.'

The slide projector fell silent, and the screen went black. The lights in the nave rising.

'In old Persian, "*Atâ*" means "Gift".'

A gasp filled the nave.

'When I was working towards my doctorate at the University of Michigan back in 1915, I first presented a dissertation titled "Externsteine's Wilderzeichen". In it, I theorised that something was taken from all of these civilisations. The *same thing*.'

She paused. Her theory had evolved as she herself evolved, from ingénue to a woman of academic authority.

'Since then, however, I have changed my mind,' she admitted. 'As I theorise in my recent paper "Mayan Wild Signs" published in the most recent *St Dunstan's Journal of Science*, I am convinced not only was something taken but also offered back in exchange.'

This, finally, was her *pièce de* theoretical *résistance*. Delivered cold and bold.

'Well?' a plump master quipped, as the lights came up. 'What then was it?'

The old dog cut short her hubris.

'I'm not absolutely sure. I speak of clues, historical breadcrumbs on a path long overgrown. Theoretically speaking — '

'So that's all this is. A mere *theory*,' interrupted another member of the Old Boys Club.

'*Mea culpa*,' Elle smiled through gritted teeth. She hated to agree, but agree she must. 'Theoretically speaking, the use of the word "Gift" is in itself telling. Gifts are seldom free.'

A student wearing a Letterman sweater and a clever smirk spoke up.

'So if I give my sweetie a gift, say my football Letterman pin, you mean to say it's not free?'

'Gift exchange leads to interdependence between giver and receiver. You expect recompense for your Letterman pin,' she said and with confident sarcasm, she added, 'And considering St Dustan's football season, I would have chosen a better gift.'

A wave of laughter filled the church.

'What if the Gift were not reciprocated?' someone asked.

'A contradiction would ensue,' replied Elle. 'Gift exchange creates deep social ties. Or, in the case of this young gentleman, a slap in the mug from his sweetie in the backseat of Daddy's Pierce-Arrow.'

Gales of laughter followed. When they finally ebbed, she continued, enjoying herself immensely now.

'Shall we get back to business?' she asked.

With the exception of a few unamused expressions, the audience nodded almost as one.

'I don't pretend to have all the answers. I don't know where these Spring-heeled Jacks came from. I don't have a name for them. Not yet. I do know they appear prior to a devastating predation event — in some cases, causing regional extinction. Then they're gone.'

A thought came to her.

'Charlie, would you show us the slide of Camazotz again?'

The screen lit up.

'The Mayan bat god here is worth a second look.' She turned to the image and sighed. 'The Mayan bat god — upside down.'

'Sorry.' Charlie fumbled clumsily with the slide, turning it round. The Copán frieze reappeared, right way round this time.

Turning to the photograph, her eyes were drawn to the corner of the frieze. Moving closer, her nose almost touched the screen as she stared at the chisel marks. Or what she had assumed were chisel marks.

'Charlie, would you please turn the slide the wrong way round again.'

'Dr Annenberg?'

'Just do it, please.'

The slide was re-inserted, upside down again.

She stared at the screen. At the image. And what she had missed.

'Shit,' she breathed, as the nave filled with giggles and a few tut-tuts. She touched the screen and could almost feel the grooves in the stone. Right way round, the deep gouges made no sense. Upside down, she recognised them immediately.

'These are runes,' she said at last, turning to her audience.

Silence filled the nave; the mere mention of the word was utterly captivating. It took a long moment for her to regain her thoughts.

'Some of you know my emphasis has always been pagan Germania and the Tor Externsteine in Germany's Teutoburg forest.'

She pointed back to the photograph on the screen.

'These are runes. Proto-Germanic runes to be precise. The very definition of which is *something hidden*. Here, in plain sight, something *was* hidden. How could I have missed it?'

She shook her head, stealing a little smile at her stupidity.

'My fellow archaeologists date the frieze in this photograph to approximately AD 900. Soon after this frieze was completed, the ancient Maya vanished from Copán.'

'This rune, you can translate it?' a French voice asked.

'Yes,' she replied. 'It means "Sekr".'

Every face in the audience looked blank.

All, that is, but one.

'It contains several meanings,' Elle continued. 'The most common is outlaw, but Sekr can also mean — '

'Crimen,' blurted the French voice again. All eyes fell upon a little man with an unremarkable beard and a remarkable nose. 'In Latin, of course. Or "Guilty", in English.'

He stood, a wily smile appearing.

'Yes,' said Elle, flummoxed. 'That would be a more precise translation.'

He nodded. 'Introductions, oui?'

'Please,' she replied.

'I admit to being a quiet man. My work usually speaks on my behalf,' he said, his manner slow, yet erudite. 'Marcel Mauss.'

She gave a little laugh as the air left her lungs. Dr Mauss stood before her. And the fiend she'd witnessed on Titanic finally had a name.

Crimen.

❖ ❖ ❖

The world went white, sky and earth merging as the snowfall became a blizzard; soft, fluffy flakes piled one upon another, weighing down the bows of the oaks along Lone Pine Road. A trap and pony used by the gardening staff slowly plodded up the road passing parked-up motorcars that looked like sleeping polar bears. A throng of students and administrators toiled along the unploughed sidewalk. The pony came to a halt, struggling masters hoisting themselves up into the trap, sparing them the slog back to main campus.

Elle was considering whether or not to forget returning to her office and instead make the short walk home, when her assistant let the door to the church porch slam behind him.

'Have a nice Easter holiday,' he said.

'I ought to thank you,' she replied, raising the collar of her old Teddy Bear coat, warding off the cold.

'Oh?'

'Were it not for you dropping that slide in the wrong way round we might never have discovered that rune.' She shook her head with a smile, reflecting, 'A Germanic rune on a Mayan frieze. That's going to shake the Old Boys Club up.'

'Thank you.' He smiled, his teenage crush unmistakable. Elle tucked away her broad grin in an attempt to fend him off.

Fortunately, another voice joined them in the cold air.

'Dr Annenberg?'

She turned. Marcel Mauss emerged from the church, doffing the pork pie hat on his head.

'Dr Mauss.'

'I do hope you can forgive me for interrupting the presentation of your paper,' he said, wrapping his greatcoat around himself more tightly and buttoning it.

'There is nothing to forgive,' she said. If she hadn't been so cold she would have blushed. 'It's just, I'm — '

She stumbled to find her words. 'How are you here?'

'A morning of surprises.' The twinkle in his steel-grey eyes suggested there were more to come.

'That a sociologist of your acclaim should bother to attend my lecture leaves me at a loss for words,' Elle said.

'That's a first,' Charlie blurted out, a dumb look on his young face.

'Dr Mauss's theory on the matter of gifting was published in *L'Année Sociologique*. It influenced me to the point I have come to embrace it, reconsidering my own theory.'

Charlie looked blank.

'*L'Année Sociologique*? France's most respected journal of sociology?'

'"The Gift!"' Charlie finally realised, turning to Mauss. 'Dr Annenberg had our French class translate all of it.'

'Honoured, I'm sure,' Dr Mauss replied with a slight bow.

'Your essay has become the guidepost to all my ethnographic work,' she gushed — something she almost never did. 'Charlie, return the expedition slides to my office. And please ask Hattie to put the kettle on.'

He nodded, excusing himself.

Stomping her fur-lined boots to keep her feet from going numb, Elle turned back to Dr Mauss.

'It's freezing out here and it's a ten-minute walk to my office. I'm afraid that in these times of prohibition, a warming nip of giggle-juice is hard to come by. But my secretary will have hot tea waiting.'

'I find the air quite fresh. I will not mind to walk.'

'Are you sure? It's Baltic.'

'I have lived in the deserts of Arizona for some months. I am accustomed to such cold temperatures at night.'

Shoving her hands into the deep pockets of her coat, Elle showed him across Lone Pine Road and through a pair of wrought-iron gates. A guard peered out of his gatehouse, waving. She waved back.

'Shortcut,' she explained. 'This is the gate to my family's home.'

'*C'est magnifique*,' he complimented as he looked up the winding drive to the manor house, which peeked through the snow-laden trees. 'It is something extraordinary you have established here, Dr Annenberg.'

'My father and mother deserve all credit. They're firm believers in obligation, not privilege.'

'Their patronage is a beautiful example of the American *noblesse obligé*, I'm sure.'

'Something I wouldn't expect to hear from the mouth of a socialist,' said Elle.

'I am socialist, it's true. However, even I can respect the generosity of the American *bourgeoisie*,' said Dr Mauss.

'The motorcar business afforded my father the possibility of such philanthropy. But we're new money,' Elle replied.

Turning onto a path through the forest between the manor and St Dunstan's campus, she added, 'Respect is not *ours* to have.'

'But there is no class system in America, oui?'

'My father once said, "We have a famous name and a Jewish banker".'

Mauss tilted his head to the side.

'To a Protestant family, Father committed an unforgivable sin; my mother was part of the diaspora fleeing Germany. There's a large Jewish community in Detroit. Her family, bankers.'

'Ah, anti-Semitism. A complicated problem.'

'There are two things the establishment in America despises: taxes and Jews. Marrying outside his faith mattered to everyone but my father. He left Philadelphia before I was born, slamming shut every door his family name opened, to join Mother in Detroit. The infant motorcar industry was making millionaires out of mortal men.'

'Capitalism,' Mauss replied, with spite.

'Please tell me you've not come all this way to hear about my pedigree?' Elle added.

Producing a well-worn leather cigar holder, he asked if he might smoke. Removing her own from a silver cigarette case in return, she lit a Dunhill. Mauss smiled.

'It's something I adore about Americans. Even a lady of high breeding can behave in a manner not conforming to her position.'

Exhaling, she smiled. A great, big American one. 'Is it the Teddy Bear coat?'

'It is neither the coat nor an absent cigarette holder. It is evident in your straight back and your confidence when speaking about your Crimen theory.'

A pair of masters carrying stacks of books passed on the path, hats peaked with snow.

They greeted Elle politely, if not curtly. Dr Mauss watched them go before turning to her.

'A theory your colleagues see as piffle, no?'

She pulled a face. 'To them, I'm an interloper spouting gobbledygook.'

'Eleanor, you have the very thing they can never possess.'

'Disingenuous and cloying methods of deduction?'

Mauss chuckled and shook his head, adding, 'The feminine intuition, of course.'

She laughed at herself. 'A friend of mine, back in sixth-form, put it another way.'

'Oh?'

'She called me a bitch.'

'At the Chiltham School for Young Ladies in Highgate?'

Elle stopped laughing. 'I don't mean to come across as churlish, but how is it — *why* is it — you know this much about me? I am nobody important.'

'You are more important than you can know Eleanor,' he replied, walking again.

Elle watched him go, his tracks leaving fresh footprints in the snow. Optimism won out over caution, and she quickly caught up with him again.

'I have been studying a Native American tribe for some months. But my work is done for now. I was on my way to New York by train. In three days' time, I return to France, by steamer. My train made a scheduled stop in Detroit. It would have been irresponsible not to call on you.'

'But why? I'm just a professor at a prep school,' Elle said, almost repeating what she'd said earlier.

'Great oaks once were acorns,' he reminded her, raising his eyes to the snow-laden trees. '*St Dustan's Journal of Science* found its way to me.'

Elle dismissed the mention of her school's journal. 'Not exactly *L'Année Sociologique*, is it?'

'A tribe of *anthropophagi* lurking at the fringes of society emerges from the night, committing predation upon ancient civilisations? *Mon Dieu*,' he said with a chuckle, blowing blue cigar smoke into the air. 'Your theory is still à *ses débuts*, but you are closer than you yet realise.'

She awaited an explanation, for him saying her theory was in its infancy, but none was forthcoming.

Leaving the wood behind, Mauss paused before a three-tiered reflecting pool, lined with oaks. 'These are the Triton Pools,' Elle thought she should explain. 'My favourite place on campus. I often take a sack lunch here.'

Looking across the dry fountain bed, its bronze statues cloaked in snow, Dr Mauss nodded silently.

'It's prettier in the fine weather,' she continued. 'Triton dancing in the fountain spray amidst fish, swimming mermaids and all.'

'I can see it perfectly in my mind.' Then, abruptly, he added, 'But, you asked me if I travelled here to debate the merits of capitalism with you. I did not. Is there somewhere we might sit?'

'Of course. Come with me.' Mounting freshly shovelled stairs, she directed him under the school's Marquis Arch and into St Dustan's Quadrangle, the heart of the campus. Already, the flagstones had been dusted with salt to keep the snow at bay.

Dr Mauss looked about the quad.

'What a unique environment for study. Both monastic and collegiate.'

'It is a bit neither here nor there,' she remarked. 'Medieval meets Finnish Bauhaus.'

Mauss's steel-grey eyes fell upon her. 'Would you not agree things seen are mightier than those heard?'

She paused, thinking.

'I would.'

Wiping the snow from a bench, he sat, resting his gloved hands neatly on his lap. 'We drink of the same apéritif.' Leaning towards her and with voice hushed, he added, 'Tell me of your *Wilderzeichen* and I will tell you of my own wild sign.'

A shiver rocketed down her spine.

'You have also had a wild sign?'

'As I said, we drink of the same *apéritif* — only from different cups. I've been studying a small group of Pueblo Indians living within a Reservation in Arizona. Unlike your ancient Maya, who left evidence of their existence in hieroglyphic form, the Pueblo pass down their stories orally.

'They tell of Crimen predation?'

'You are familiar with the Pueblo?'

She shook her head.

'Well, they are descendants of an earlier nation — the Anasazis. Their dwellings were built in caves, high up the side of cliff faces, accessible only by retractable ladders.'

She listened, attentive to his every word, but didn't quite understand what he was getting at.

'Do you not see? They tried to protect themselves.'

'*Tried*?' Elle asked.

'And failed,' replied Dr Mauss.

'They vanished?'

He nodded. 'Like the Maya of Copán. You can imagine my surprise when a Pueblo Elder uttered a word as foreign as a Frenchy in Arizona.'

'*Wilderzeichen?*'

He nodded. 'You can be sure of the resurrection of the dead.'

Staring at him, she was hit by a sudden overwhelming wave of emotion. Jaw quivering, she tried desperately to keep her tears back, but it was no use. Tears came, fat and warm, thawing her cold cheeks where they fell. Leaning against Dr Mauss, she was suddenly a vulnerable child who desperately needed a protective arm.

Dr Mauss comforted her. 'There, there now.'

She was gripped by the need to explain herself to him.

'Seventeen years ago, I witnessed something I couldn't accept,' she said, grasping hold of the thick sleeve of his greatcoat. 'It awakened a curiosity in me I've never lost. I left the path chosen for me, took my own. But I resigned myself to keeping the details of what I saw a secret. That secret is my private salvation.'

A gang of students carrying ice hockey sticks heaved snowballs at one another. Spotting her, their fight came to an abrupt end. She leaned back against the bench, wiping her tears away before they passed.

'Move along, boys. And Happy Easter,' she called out to them.

'Happy Easter,' they replied as one, doffing their hats before scurrying off.

She turned back to Mauss.

'I'm not usually a weepy old maid. It's just I thought nobody ever could understand the things I saw.'

'I do understand.'

'Do you really?' she asked, the thought making her feel uncomfortable, almost. 'A vestige of that terrifying night remains with me. But with the passing years, that vestige bleeds away. I have long given up trying to deny what I know within my soul to be true. But I am alone in this knowledge, Dr Mauss. I shun friends, and my colleagues mock me. Only my research is cathartic. For Chrissake, I haven't had a close friend or lover since boarding school.'

Mauss tipped cigar ash into the cuff of his trousers, and then turned towards her.

'My dear, I am a sociologist. I cannot help you. What you require is a psychiatrist.' He paused, and then he looked straight into her eyes with a smile. 'Or three nights in a hotel in Havana.'

She laughed. It was much needed. Taking a deep breath and wiping away the last of her tears, she asked about his wild sign.

'The Pueblo are suspicious of outsiders. It took me three years to earn the trust of their Elders. Last week, in the dead of night, I was taken to a hollow, deep within their spirit mountain. At its entrance I did see these same runes.

'Sekr?'

He nodded. 'Here, they showed me something both extraordinary and terrifying. The place where Crimen are entombed.'

He went quiet, puffing away at his cigar and watching the snow fall around them. Elle was impatient for him to continue. Having spent seventeen years desperately searching for answers, she felt she couldn't wait an instant longer. Just as she was about to give him a poke, he returned from wherever his mind had taken him.

'Among chalk sarcophagi of ancient origin, the medicine man passed a pipe. A long, wooden thing packed with a sacred medicine they call *peyote* — a fascinating desert plant, brimming with psychoactive alkaloids. When smoked, it permitted me to see clearly those things lurking in the twilight realm.'

'Sarcophagi? You suggest there were more than one?'

'There were many. More than I could count. Inhumed within were terrible, terrible fiends.'

She almost laughed. Finally, someone who understood. 'They are elusive.'

He agreed. 'Yet, I have seen them clearly.'

'Tell me.'

'You have seen these Crimen, oui?'

'Just one,' she admitted.

He shook his head. 'You have seen many.' She looked at him perplexed, and without reply.

'Camazotz. Hel. Ahriman.'

'The gods?' she replied, confused and excited at the same time.

'Sentinels.'

'Sentinels?' she repeated.

'*La Reine Blanche.*'

'The White Queen? Really? Next you're going to tell me there are seven dwarfs.'

'I assure you there are no dwarfs. But the White Queen is very real.'

'Siobhan?'

It was his turn to look flabbergasted. 'How could you know this name?'

'I heard it. On Titanic.'

'She is a banshee,' Mauss declared, almost spitting into the snow.

'Tell me. Please.'

'She is predatory. Opportunistic. Appearing when her prey is vulnerable, at times of upheaval: war, famine, pestilence. In this instance, the predation event caused the extinction of an entire Native American nation already under stress from disease. Upon arrival, she turns a mortal.'

'The Sentinel,' Elle repeated. 'Like a guard?'

'Far more than this — a partner to her awful lusts.'

'And then?'

'You must understand the stories the medicine man tells are passed down over many, many generations. Hundreds of years. Critical details are lost. My vision is incomplete, but an important fact *is* preserved; before she vanishes, she endows a gift upon her victims,' Dr Mauss continued.

'A gift? You're suggesting there is truth to my theory?'

'Your theory is *fact*.'

'Shit,' she mumbled, as any self-doubt melted away like the snowflakes now landing softly on her cheeks.

'And this "gift". What is it?'

He exhaled. A cloud of blue cigar smoke drifted slowly amidst the falling snow as he seemed to contemplate his words.

'What is it all old men want?'

She stared at him incredulously. 'Not—immortality?'

He nodded.

'I'll be damned. This really is a *Penny Dreadful*.'

'There is more truth to your Spring-heeled Jack than you suppose.'

'What form does the Gift take?' she asked.

'For this, you need look into the etymology of the word itself,' he replied.

'Latin, right?'

He nodded again.

She had a think. '*Dosis*?'

'From the Greek word — '

' — Dose.'

He nodded and then added, 'Dose of what?'

'Dose of what?' she repeated. 'Dose of…I don't know.'

'*Matan. Angebinde. Atâ.* You hypothesise these hollows were abattoirs; slaughterhouses, where the predation occurred. A dose of — '

'*Venenum*,' she realised. 'Venom.'

'*Venenum*,' he repeated. 'And in Sanskrit?'

'I'm afraid you've totally exhausted my knowledge of foreign tongues.'

'Pleasure.'

She looked away, her mind pushing through the blizzard within her head, sorting through all that he had said. Finally, it clicked.

'Siobhan.' She turned back to him. 'The banshee takes a Sentinel through seduction.'

He nodded. 'By giving pleasure.'

'*Venenum*. She injects them.'

'Once she has turned them, they begin to feed.'

Elle's mind took her back to Titanic. To a berth splattered with blood, half-devoured corpses bobbing in an awash hold.

'I witnessed a predation event.'

'And lived to tell of it. That, in and of itself, is remarkable.'

At last, she told him of her wild sign. He listened.

❖ ❖ ❖

Elle had never shared what she had witnessed with anyone. Finally doing so flooded her with a sense of bliss she hadn't felt ever. She lit a cigarette, savouring the moment.

A question came to her.

'My theory of a subculture of Crimen lurking at society's fringe was born from what I witnessed. You have also witnessed them?'

'Crimen have structure.'

'They are not mindless fiends?'

'They are not,' he confirmed. 'They exist in a distinctive hierarchy. The fiend you witnessed was merely prey. Not consumed, it was infected, turned Guilty and began to scavenge. This lowest caste, these are Huntians. Feeble feeders.'

'The one I witnessed wasn't feeble.'

'*Pardonnez-moi*?'

'It tore through a cabin full of men as if they were sides of beef.'

'*Mon Dieu*. Your Wilderzeichen was a Sentinel.'

Leaning back against the bench, she took a good long drag from her cigarette. 'Strange.'

'What is?'

'Hearing you say it. *Wilderzeichen*. When I hear it outside my head, it makes me realise these Crimen are real and not just a crazy theory of mine.'

'They are real.'

She blew the smoke out into the cold morning air.

'I heard it on Titanic. *Wilderzeichen*. From a man carrying a shotgun. I thought it strange at the time. I mean, why would anyone carry a shotgun on a sinking ship?'

'Tell me of this man.'

'Titanic was going down at the head. Hold awash. Pitch dark. This fiend, this Sentinel, was in its sarcophagus. The man killed it.'

'How?'

'With a spike. He thrust it into the beast's chest.'

'*Merde*,' said Mauss, leaning back against the bench. 'You were witness to the Nephilim.'

'Nephilim?'

'The Nephilim is a mortal, taken by the banshee.'

'Is that not a Sentinel?'

'He was to be more than a Sentinel. More than her guard. The Nephilim is chosen for special privileges — to be Siobhan's *lover*.'

Elle felt an unexpected stab of spite. She tried her best to hide it behind her cigarette as she took another hit.

Mauss continued. 'But this man you saw is unique. Rebellious. He cast aside the heinous addiction of being Guilty. And it is only he who prevents mortal man from becoming a *festin de reine*.'

She knew French and understood: a queen's feast.

Mauss continued. 'The medicine man called him Balthasar the Good. He is Nephilim. It is he who saved the Pueblo from Crimen infestation.'

Loosening the collar of her alpaca coat, Elle removed the fine chain tucked in under her woolly jumper. On its end swung the silver talisman she had worn around her neck since Titanic. 'Balthasar saved me.'

Pulling on a pair of *pince-nez*, Mauss inspected the death symbol. 'From where did you get this?'

'You've seen this before?'

Dr Mauss nodded.

The snow continued to fall, as they sat in silence.

102

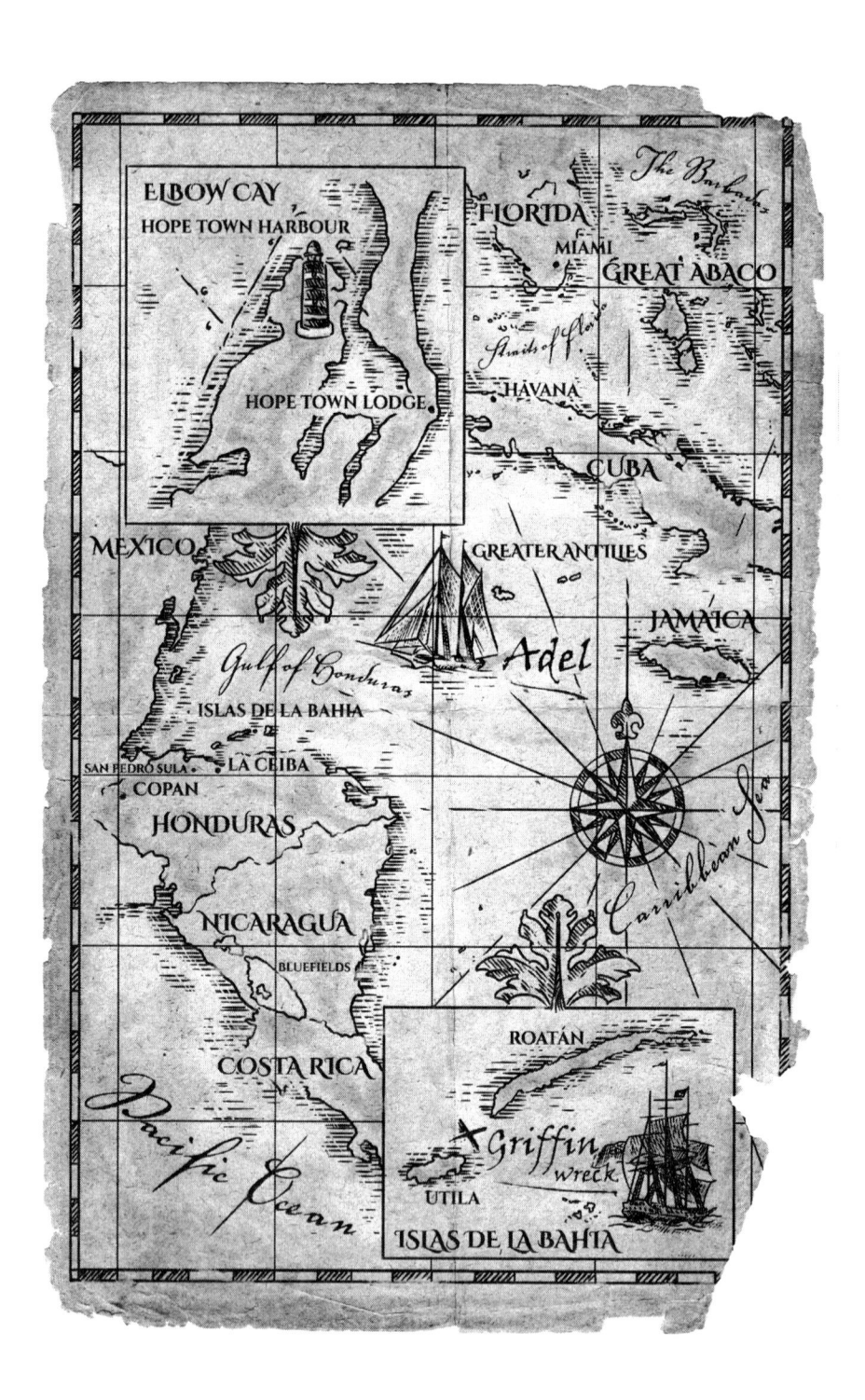

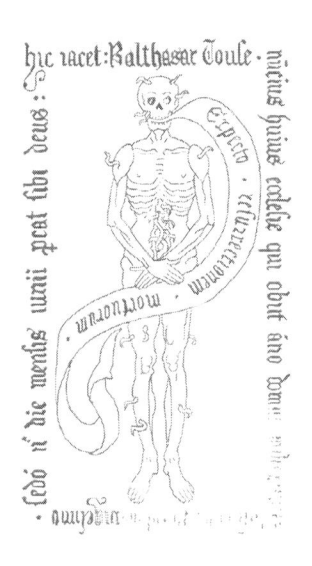

4 APRIL 1929.

ABACO ISLANDS, BAHAMAS

Elle grasped the talisman swinging about her neck, sun prickly on her bare shoulders, sea spray splashing her legs dangling over Weezy's bow.

Hope renewed, she watched her shadow dancing in the curling waves, her thumb pressing against the talisman's face. Balthasar Toule. The name etched into the periphery of the death symbol. Balthasar the Good. One and the same. Both her lingering vestige.

'*Expecto resurrectionem mortuorum*,' she whispered to herself. There was no need to look at the talisman; she'd worn it every day for the last seventeen years. Etched into it was a human figure, cleaved stomach releasing a river of maggots, a *Totenkopf* proclaiming the peculiar apothegm, '*expect the resurrection of the dead*.'

Balthasar Toule had been resurrected.

Mauss thought so. He recognised the death symbol from the sarcophagi lids. And, like the passel of Crimen buried deep in a mountain hollow in Arizona, Elle kept the terrible things she'd witnessed buried within herself. Until Mauss.

Now, she was not alone in her adamantine belief in Balthasar's existence. And not in the past tense.

It gave her hope.

Raising her head, she followed the sun's path across Bahamian shallows to distant, palm-dotted cays. Spending Easter holiday on the family yacht was tradition. Father had named her Weezy — Mother's nickname. Mother hated it. She also hated ships. Elle couldn't really blame her.

Elle had arrived late to the yacht, the crew already asleep in their bunks. Coming aboard, she'd gone directly to her cabin and fell asleep. Awakened by the thrum of engines, the gentle sloshing against the hull told her Weezy was making way. She climbed to deck. There was nothing quite as spectacular as a first morning: shimmering sea, warm sun turning winter skin a golden brown. The most ordinary of things, the most extraordinary of all.

'Don't go falling in the drink, now.'

Snapped out of her daydreaming, she turned her head. On the foredeck, skin like leather, stood Corky O'Shea.

'Not to worry, Cork. My crawl is pretty fair.'

'I still swim for shite.'

The Irishman and her father had leapt from Titanic together. As promised, he looked up her father in Detroit. And in return, Father made him skipper of the family yacht. Elle returned to the sun lounger, pulling a silk Hermès stole around her shoulders before giving Corky a kiss on his stubbly cheek.

'Ain't you a sight for these tired lamps,' he said, his brogue punctuated by the Bahamian drawl he acquired over his seventeen years in the Abacos. 'Proper lady, you is.'

'Every year you say that, Cork,' she reminded him, squeezing his rough old hands. 'You know perfectly well, I'm no proper anything.'

They shared a laugh. 'Lord's image of Eve.'

'Bilge,' she dismissed with a wave. 'Mrs O'Shea better not hear you say that.'

'Mrs O'Shea took a launch to Hope Town, lobster provisioning.' Reaching back through an opened bridge window he took up his pipe. 'Birthday coming up, haven't ya?'

'You really needed to remind me?'

'How many candles?'

'Better not ask a proper lady that.'

'You're no proper anything, remember?'

'Touché,' she laughed. 'Thirty-four.'

'Thirty-four,' he repeated, dragging a match along the deck rail before sparking up his pipe. 'Haven't seen your da' in a few years. How's he gettin' on?'

'Well enough.' She sank into her sun lounger. 'St Dunstan's keeps my parents occupied. Neither of them have the pot for open water anymore.'

'No keeping you away from the briny deep, though.'

'They wish to forget Titanic,' she replied, lighting a cigarette. 'I *never* want to forget.'

'I can't understand your fascination with that night, Eleanor. I been trying to forget it for seventeen years.'

'Yet here you are, a ship's captain.'

'It ain't the same.' Looking across the sun-drenched calm he added, 'Sea is all I know.'

Her gaze joined his. 'On days like this, it's not a bad place,' Elle said.

'Ain't found yourself a yeoman?'

She screwed up her face.

'Why not?' he asked. 'Swell girl like you. Must be boxing them off with a bullwhip.'

'Something happened that night,' she blurted without meaning to. Leaning back in her lounger, she pulled on her sunglasses, hoping he would let go of her admission. Corky acknowledged her with a nod, but made no comment. 'You're the uncle I never had, Cork. You know I don't hold bellicose men in high esteem.'

'Window-lickers, the lot.'

'I don't know. Maybe I'm too cynical,' she said, taking a drag from her cigarette. 'Mother and Father fostered in me an appreciation of the world. And I dove headlong into it. But, Titanic.' Normally, this is where she would end the conversation. But not only was Corky like family to her, he was there that night. 'Titanic hit me like a brick wall. What I was witness to is the reason I became an ethnographer.'

Corky fitted his pipe between tightly clenched teeth. 'Crikey. Sound like a proper doctor as well, dun ya?'

'I'm no society dame sitting around in pumps quoting Mauss. I'm true to my words. My wanderlust is a practical application of my degree — '

She bent to pull a stack of ungraded term papers from her valise, and gave them a shake.

' — not this pedagogy.'

He nodded. 'Well then, what do you and your pedagogy hanker for?'

'Hanker for?' She sighed wistfully, thumb touching the only trace of Balthasar she had. '"You've a long dark road ahead," Balthasar said to me.'

The statement's opaqueness had drawn her in.

'I've been on that road since Titanic sank. I've faltered more times than I want to admit, praying for an end to my nihilism.'

She looked up at Cork, a smile crossing her face.

'But not today. Today I'm confident, and that road is considerably brighter.' She looked to the distance, the red-and-white-striped lighthouse of Hope Town just visible off the starboard bow.

'I never shall forget the morning after the night before.' Cork drifted away with his own thoughts now. 'When we was picked up by the steamer Carpathia, your ma' and da' were right shaken.'

He turned to her. She hung on his every word. Never did she hear him speak directly about that terrible night.

'When a man is pulled out a lifeboat after they been through something terrible, you see it in their eyes. Like some kind of shroud has been pulled over them, never to be taken off again. When I looked into yours — '

He paused, clearly muddling with what he was trying to say to her.

' — *Go dtitfidh an oíche ort.*'

Elle raised her eyebrows, awaiting explanation.

'It's Gaelic. Sorta means that night will befall ya.'

She shrugged.

'Sort out what you witnessed, Eleanor. Sort it out before it sorts you out. I think you witnessed something terrible. More terrible than the rest us seen.'

'You see a lot, Corky.'

He did. He seemed to see right through her.

Standing from the lounger at last, Elle went to the bow rail, not wanting to look Cork in the eye. Fearful he would work out she wasn't quite the hard-as-you-like character she oft portrayed.

'Who was he?'

'My vestige,' she said, losing herself amongst the shimmering shallows. 'I seek a world far bleaker than the one our awakened eye sees.'

For the longest time, she stood in silence, reverently watching the sea ebb and flow.

'Suppose my inwardness is a by-product of my vestige. In a hiding place in my mind is a light that never goes out. "You've a long dark road ahead of you." What is that even meant to mean?'

She was whispering now.

'A long dark road before the reveal? Or to uncover his identity? Or perhaps he simply meant I had a long walk below Titanic's decks ahead of me?'

She recalled his gaunt face, skin pale, and those fascinating, empty eyes. Her heart beat with what he had given to her. And it caused her no end of frustration that she couldn't work out why the briefest of moments left such an indelible mark upon her very soul. Maybe it was for that reason. A briefest of moments was not nearly enough.

'My vestige caused a rift in my life, impossible to fill. So much changed in one night. Here I am. I walk alone. Yet never say goodbye.'

She turned to Corky. He sat in her lounger, head seesawing to the side as he softly snored.

❖ ❖ ❖

Weezy was the bee's knees. Built by Bahamian chippies, the yacht's sixty feet of decks and railings were accented with teak, while her interior was fitted out in cherry. Twin three-fifty engines and a five hundred gallon diesel tank gave the ship enough range to ply the Abacos a week at a go. Sitting in her lounger on the bow, Elle had nothing more to do than watch Corky navigate into Hope Town harbour at half a knot. It wasn't too tricky, but Elle had seen plenty of boats stray from the red channel markers, beaching on shifting sandbars.

Inhabited by anglers, transient breakers and a few pirates, Hope Town had not ripened much since British loyalists, fleeing the newly independent United States, founded a trading station there in 1784. Some of the cays added tarmacadam airstrips, electricity and even telephones. Others remained uninhabited. A two-week holiday here offered Elle exactly the seclusion she required to reconsider the theory Dr Mauss had proclaimed à *ses débuts*. In its infancy.

She'd had two days on the train to mull over his revelations. The truth felt ever closer, with her wild sign explained. But where did Balthasar Toule fit into her theory?

À *ses débuts.*

Letting off the engines, Corky helmed over, allowing the yacht to pass the lighthouse warning ships of the thorny reef to the windward side of the island.

'Hasn't changed titch nor tittle,' he shouted through the open bridge windows.

Elle smiled. 'You say the same thing every year.'

'Reflector come from Manchester a hundred years ago. Imagine the locals' surprise the first time it lit up the night?'

'You say that every year as well.'

'Slips are chock-full.'

Weezy slowed to a drift. Anchor dropping, she joined other pleasure craft anchored between smack boats and sponge schooners.

Tucking her ungraded papers into her clunky Gladstone bag, Elle hefted it over her shoulder, lowering the brim of a straw hat over her eyes. She found Cork and an able-body seaman making ready the launch. Tossing her bag into the little boat, she sat at the bow.

'That long dark road — ' said Corky, knocking his pipe against the rail emptying its tobacco into the water ' — Can you make a detour?'

'You were actually listening?'

He nodded. 'Ain't much I miss. So listen then, there's an old ship captain in Hope Town.'

'There's a lot of old ship captains in Hope Town, Corky.'

'This one lives in a blue painted cottage, bit down the path from the ferry dock. Can't miss it. His schooner is tied up round the back. Adel, she's called. Ask for Captain Henrikson.'

She didn't recognise the name. 'Thanks. Perhaps I shall.'

'No perhapsing,' he replied with an authority she wasn't used to. 'See him directly.'

'What's this about?'

'It'll be worth your while, Eleanor. I can promise you.'

'All right, then. I'll stop round and see him,' she replied, firing the launch's outboard. It puttered more than roared. Engaging the prop, she pulled away from Weezy, Corky waving her off. She waved back, trusting him without reservation.

She hadn't the first idea why visiting an old sea dog was important, but it couldn't be any less so than her alternative plan of sitting under a coconut palm soaking up the Bahamian sun.

❖ ❖ ❖

Making for the rickety ferry dock, she moored alongside a dozen tied-off launches, straining in the current. Grabbing her bag, she ambled barefoot off the dock's creaking wood planks, following a narrow dirt path edged with roses, spilling sweetness into the air.

Sure to Corky's word, a modest Bahamian-blue cottage appeared. A battered Model T, back seat piled high with seafaring jumble, hissed and pinged beside a boathouse. She felt the hood. It was still hot. Someone had just returned from a supply run. Tipping the brim of her straw hat, she looked over the cottage's shingled roof. Twin masts jutted above.

A tow-path led to an impressive schooner, its teak handrails and boom gleaming from a fresh application of marine spar. Stores of every description sat on the dock. Supplies for keeping a working ship at sea for weeks.

Touching a hand-cranked air pump, Elle's fingers came away sticky with red paint. She wiped them on an old, discarded rag before inspecting copper diving helmets and coils of air hose, piled on a sea chest. Bare-chested crewmen manhandled a clunky winch onto the schooner's quarterdeck.

A racket arose below-decks — a flurry of effing and blinding. Someone evidently wasn't happy. A moment later, a tousled character, skin weathered from adventure, appeared from an aft stairwell, his white General Kitchener moustache twitching as he carried a dead rodent to the rail. Tossing it overboard, he removed his brimless porkpie hat, wiping the sweat from his brow. Replacing his hat, he noticed Elle standing on the dock looking at him.

'Rats eating holes in the wirework.' She noted his accent. It wasn't quite American, nor English. Removing a rag from his pocket he rubbed his greasy hands once over. 'All right there, missy?'

'Looking for a Captain Henrikson.'

Sauntering down the brow, he met her on the dock.

'That's me.'

'Lovely schooner.'

'Adel's been round the horn a few times, but I wouldn't dare change a jot of her,' he replied proudly. 'Found her in a knacker's yard. Shame to see a lady stripped and sold off in bits. She's fast, but at two hundred and fifty feet she's a big girl for the sort of racing done these days.'

Tossing the rag aside, he took a half-smoked stogy from his shirt pocket, clenched it in his teeth.

'A bit sharp with her cod's head and mackerel tail, but Adel's spry enough to run when there's good blow.'

Distracted by his crew manhandling the red pumps up the brow to deck, he yelled out, 'Careful with those, lads! Make doubly sure they're well lashed down. If we lose 'em in a squall we'll have a devil of a time replacing them.'

Henrikson turned back to her. 'You got me at a disadvantage.'

She gave him her quizzical look.

'We're not yet acquainted.'

'Elle Annenberg,' she said thrusting out her hand.

'Dr Eleanor Annenberg?'

Caution. She never liked when anyone knew more about her, then she them. She nodded.

'Aren't I a berk?' Grasping her hand he shook it gladly. 'Half-expected you to look like Eleanor Roosevelt, not Greta Garbo.'

She nearly blushed. 'You're too kind.'

'Thank goodness you arrived before we made way.'

'I'm not entirely sure why I've come.'

'Cork didn't tell you?'

She shook her head. He smiled. There was wisdom in it.

'I've a kettle on, Doc.'

'I'd not refuse a cuppa, Captain Henrikson.'

'Skip,' he said, showing her towards his cottage. 'We're not much on formality in these cays.'

Settling into a bleached wicker chair, she watched as he disappeared through the kitchen door. He reappeared some moments later with a tea service.

'Detroit, eh?' he said, laying out cups and saucers. 'Lake-effect winters — that wind coming off Lake Michigan, turning a snow flurry into an arctic blizzard — I wish to forget being that cold.'

'Dreary this time of the year.'

'I sailed the Great Lakes as a young man. I come from Halifax.'

That explained the accent. 'How did you come to know Corky?'

'Weezy's skipper. Fine ship, she is. And he's a fine chap.' Pouring her tea, he returned the pot to the service, sat down and smiled again, his lean face bunched with wrinkles he had surely earned. 'He lent me an interesting read… "Mayan Wild Signs".'

Elle felt a small pang of caution again.

'Whatever am I to make of a skipper who reads a mundane paper, published in a prep school magazine?'

'An imaginative paper,' he replied, offering her the sugar bowl. 'Ethnology and *Penny Dreadful* all in one.'

'Thank you, I prefer my tea bitter. Like me.'

'Can't imagine why,' he replied, pouring half of the bowl into his cup. 'I admit to having found the grizzlier details of your paper disturbing for such a presentable young lady.'

'Now, I'm the one at a disadvantage.'

'I hardly think you would permit yourself to be at a disadvantage,' he said with a sureness Elle admired.

'It's just I don't know a thing about *you*,' she replied.

Henrikson wiped his moustache with a linen napkin. 'Some months back, I had a dab at a shipwreck lying on the reef off Man-O-War Cay. A squall came up and swamped my launch. I was left bobbing about in an angry sea without so much as a lifebelt. Cork was transiting between cays on Weezy — if he hadn't happened upon me, I'd be a sea sponge on the reef by this time.'

Lifting a plate of sandwiches, he offered one to Elle.

'I'm fond of him too,' she said, accepting a sandwich gladly. She hadn't eaten since the train in Miami. She took a grateful bite, thinking it was potato and cheese, but the texture was all wrong.

'It's breadfruit,' he offered, before she could ask. 'I brought a couple of saplings back from my first trip to Honduras.'

'Honduras?' Now she was intrigued.

'Heard of Henry Morgan?'

'Great rum. Silly hat.'

'A man who wore many hats,' Henrikson replied. 'One as a nobleman, another as Brethren of the Coast.'

'You mean piracy.'

'That's his other hat. Buccaneering was a respectable trade, you know. Morgan had a habit of raiding fat Spanish gold fleets on their return from the Central Americas.'

As Henrikson twined on, Elle's eyes were drawn to Adel just as crewmen carried copper diving helmets up the brow.

'You appear to be provisioning.'

'Replenishing,' he corrected. 'I returned from Honduras two days ago. I'll heave anchor soon enough and head back.'

'All right, Skip,' she said, putting down her sandwich. 'Now, you have my full attention.'

Henrikson leaned forward in his chair and gave her his in return.

'Back in 1519, conquistadors were looting and razing what remained of the ancient Maya. Copán in particular.'

'You're talking about Cortez?'

'I am.'

She nodded, game for the conversation. 'Copán wasn't merely a treasure chest of Aztec gold,' Elle said. 'It contained a trove of Mayan stelae, lost by time.'

'No, they're not lost.'

'How do you mean?'

'The Spanish discovered the Copán trove.' He had a dainty sip of his tea. 'And took it.'

'I'm no expert, Captain Henrikson, but—'

'Skip.'

'Okay, "Skip". If those spokes were put into the wheel of history, we'd know all about it.'

'I'm not talking guff, Elle. Hear out my sea yarn.'

'Surrender another one of those sandwiches, then.'

Passing her the entire plate, he continued.

'Spain's gold fleets were in constant danger of attack, be it from French corsairs or British buccaneers. So concerned was Cortez, he formed a *flota* for his plunder.'

'*Flota?*'

'Like the American navy convoys, to protect merchant ships crossing the Atlantic, from German submarines in the Great War. Cortez's convoy consisted of two very heavily armed galleons — *Capitana* and *Almirante* — protecting nine merchant *naos*. But Cortez made a fatal mistake: he consigned the Copán haul to the fleet's fastest ship, *Señora de Marisol*.'

'With all due respect, where exactly *is* this supposed great haul?' Elle asked between chews.

'Henry Morgan,' he replied, matter-of-factly. 'His buccaneers intercepted the *flota* off Islas de la Bahia, mere specks of land off the Honduran coast. His ships bombarded the galleons, separating them from *de Marisol*. Morgan, on his own flagship — *Griffin* — boarded her, and with sword and rapier he overpowered the Spanish crew, transferred the haul to his vessel and sank *de Marisol* with enfilade fire.'

Elle continued chewing. 'Enfilade?'

'A volley from multiple guns.'

She shrugged.

'You're not convinced,' he said, resting his teacup on its saucer. Henrikson stood and invited her to inspect his schooner.

Taking one more sandwich to keep her going, they boarded Adel.

'She's a big sucker. Must be three times the length of Weezy,' Elle remarked.

'Won the America's Cup in 1879.'

'She's beautiful, Skip. Why would anyone break her?'

'Adel's too heavy for the racing style nowadays.'

'It's a fantastic sea yarn, Skip,' she finally said about his tale. 'I really liked it. But you speak of a haul of vast historical importance, never mind millions of dollars in gold. The missing stelae of Copán could crack the mystery of what caused the Classical Maya to vanish.'

'And turn your theory into fact.'

He had her there.

'Doesn't change the fact that none of the nine missing stelae have reappeared.'

'The sea took 'em,' he said. 'Morgan's own ship was sunk in a hurricane between the islands of Roatán and Utila. All hands lost.'

The crew struggled by, carrying a load of diving apparatus. She suddenly realised what Henrikson's expedition was all about.

'You found Morgan's ship.'

He directed her towards the foredeck.

'Couple weeks ago, I had just made sail from Utila Island. In the channel between the islands, we struck a sounding in ten fathoms - unexpectedly shallow for that part. The sounding lead snagged something. Took half my crew to drag it up, and when the lead finally broke the surface we realised we'd snagged an old ship rib.'

Henrikson pulled back a paint-splattered tarp lying on the forecastle hatch. A blackened arc of wood, partially disguised with coral encrustation, lay underneath.

'You think this is from Griffin?'

Lifting one end, he pointed out a wooden peg screwed into a joint. 'This is a treenail. It's been shaped by hand, not turned on a lathe.'

'I assume that's significant?'

'After 1825, treenails were all turned on lathes.'

Fishing a shiv from his dungarees, he dug into the blackened wood with its blade. 'British ships were coppered, to retard barnacles. They used tar as a bonding agent.'

Prying a fragment of wood from the rib, he pointed out a residue on the knife's blade. 'Do you see those particles in the tar?'

She nodded.

'It's birch pulp. Only the British mixed birch pulp into their tar.'

'So you think you may have found a British wreck?'

'You don't miss a trick, Dr Annenberg. I'll be making sail before first light,' he said, resting the rib back on the hatch. 'With a good blow, Adel can make Honduras in under five days. What I lack onboard is someone familiar with the Maya.'

'I'm flattered, of course. But sea yarns and shipwrecks? Skipper, this isn't my field of study at all. If this were pagan Germania, I'd gladly be your Huckleberry. But this? No. There are a hundred professors more qualified than I am. A hundred.'

'Before you make up your mind. There's something more.'

Following him into the galley stack, she passed a kitchen crew stocking provisions. Beside an unlit oven stood a row of fresh-water casks. One separated from the others.

'I made a hard-hat dive on the reef where we found the rib.' Henrikson pried the lid from the cask. The stink of stagnant seawater caused her to gag. 'There was an anomaly.'

'Anomaly?'

'Something man-made. I kept it soaking in seawater so as not to destabilise it.'

Reaching into the barrel with both arms, he lifted it out.

Elle stopped chewing.

'*Expecto resurrectionem mortuorum.*'

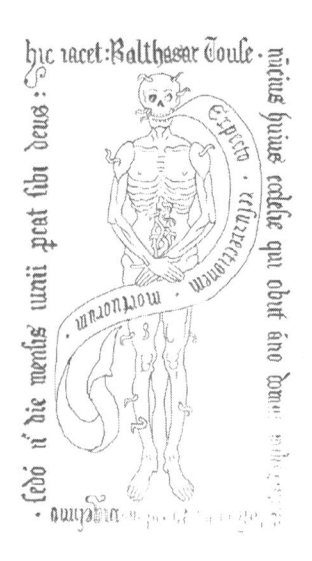

8 April 1929.

Islas de la Bahia, Honduras

Masts creaked as Adel's boom lazily turned, tacking into the wind, under the command of the master of the helm. The first watch kept an eye out for close reefs, as celestial moonbeams fell across the sea in the ashen-pale pre-dawn. True to Skip's word, the schooner pressed effortlessly through the Bahama Channel and into the Florida Strait, crew keeping the blow in the ship's sails day and night, completing the eight hundred nautical mile journey by the start of the fourth day.

'Morning,' Henrikson said as he appeared from the galley stack, two tin cups of coffee in hand.

'Morning, Skip,' Elle replied, taking one gladly.

'Slept on deck again?'

'It's stuffy in my cabin.' She sipped her coffee. 'The night air helps me process my thoughts.'

'It'll get hotter.' Henrikson looked up to the sails before shouting to the crew. 'Take in the top sails. Catch her on the foresail.' Turning to the helmsman, he gave an order to keep Adel scudding along.

Having now lived on Adel for three days, Elle had got to know the crew, their seamanship meticulous yet at ease. Hoisting courses on tackles, the crew drove the courses through blocks on the jackyard, heads coming to attention as Adel's power winches pulled the jackyard taught. Effortlessly, the sail came home to the yard. Secured to catheads, the forecourse canted, and the foresails fluffed as an abrupt gust filled them out, scudding the schooner along at an impressive seventeen knots.

She had little understanding of the complexity of their seamanship. But that wasn't the point. It was for the crew to know. And do. She was a passenger. And what she knew, they couldn't understand much.

Correcting the helm by a degree, Henrikson returned to his coffee. 'Sorted 'em out yet?'

'What's that?'

'Your thoughts.'

She offered him an unsure smile - crooked lip with a slight upturned snarl. In other circumstances, she would sweetly wrinkle her nose and make men go weak in their knees. 'Do you know how Cork and my father came to be friends?'

'On Titanic, wasn't it?'

'Yes. That's where my life changed, and my story really begins.'

Moving across from the helm to the row of deck chairs Elle reclined in, Henrikson settled in a chair beside her. She was about to tell him her own sea yarn, when he spoke up.

'Do you not recognise them?'

'Recognise what?'

'The deckchairs.'

She leaned forward for a better look. They'd certainly seen better days.

Henrikson didn't wait for her to deduce their origin. 'They came off Titanic.'

Elle nearly leapt from her chair. For all she knew, it was the very chair where she first clapped eyes on Balthasar Toule. 'But... how can that be?'

'Found 'em.'

'You *found* them?'

'Cork didn't tell you?'

She shook her head.

'He really didn't tell you anything, did he?' Sparking up a chewed stogie, he leaned back in his own deckchair. It creaked, taking his weight. 'You know, I've met yachtsmen over my many years at sea who thought drinking grog and chewing tobacco were the only requisites for making a seaman. But a *wise* seaman knows different. We accept the sea for what it is.'

'Which is what?'

'A beholder of death.'

'I know a little something about death,' she replied. Seventeen-year old girls were not meant to witness the things she did on Titanic. In fact, considering the talisman she wore about her neck, it could be said death had her by the throat.

He took a few puffs from his stogie before turning to Elle.

'So it was, for Griffin. And Titanic. The hardships and privations of a seaman's life are greater than those of any other. It's a life I love. I was captain of the Mackay-Bennett, you know.'

Elle shrugged indifferently.

'She was a cable-laying vessel. Not a pretty ship, but a sturdy, working-class girl. We were in a Halifax port when news of Titanic arrived. We sailed the same morning for the wreck site.'

She stared at him, mouth agape now.

'What did you see?'

'A floating graveyard. I stationed my ship outside the recovery area so as not to disturb the dead, and sent my crew out in skiffs. Fished out all manner of flotsam: mouldings from staterooms, Gladstone bags, deckchairs. Loads of deckchairs. I think Titanic must have broken her back when she went down.'

'How could you know that?'

'A lot of wardrobe trunks and stores came up from her holds. Then there were the bodies. There were so many of them. Hundreds. All in their lifebelts, mostly floating upright. The maritime embalmers onboard our ship found very few of the dead had any water in their lungs: the cold killed almost all of them.'

'I heard their cries from our lifeboat.' Elle reached out, gripping his hand, offering him a bereaved smile. 'They pleaded to be saved. It wasn't too long before it got quiet.'

'When the sea is that cold, death comes quick. Minutes. We surely did find the damnedest things in their pockets - from biscuits to diamond necklaces. One of my sailors found $2,500 in John Jacob Astor's coat pocket. We handed it all over to White Star Line when we returned to Halifax. Nobody had much interest in the deckchairs.'

Falling silent, he puffed away on his cigar.

Elle stared out to sea, the night's shade giving way to the cheerful blues and greens of morning. Already the heat of day was coming up.

'I sat in these chairs with my friend Titch, swigging a bottle of Taittinger.' She looked down, rubbing the armrest. 'Could've been this very one.'

Henrikson said nothing. A wise old smile finally appeared on his face before he said finally, 'I didn't make a mistake insisting you come, did I?'

Elle returned her gaze to sea, discerning a distant toehold of land. A bank of clouds hovered over blue, saw-toothed masses of mountains looming solemnly in the distance.

Honduras.

'You couldn't have picked a better person for the job.'

❖ ❖ ❖

An island appeared off the port beam.

Utila.

Adel glided into its emerald shallows, mingling with chebaccos and banana boats sheltering from the trade winds. Sails slackening as they turned from the wind, the schooner drifted towards a regatta of sailing sloops at anchor, their sterns in close formation. A familiar flag flapped in the breeze above the thatch palms and trumpet trees.

'Is that the Stars and Stripes?'

'American fruit companies run the customs office,' Henrikson explained, instructing a crewman to prepare a launch. 'They don't like delays. The fruit spoils. Bad for business. It's better for us to clear customs out here than suffer the mess on the Honduran mainland.'

Elle climbed into the launch. Skip joined her, nodding for his crewman to fire the outboard and take them to the wharf jutting from the shore.

'God, it's hot,' she sighed, linen shirt sticking to her damp skin.

'Not so bad here. The humidity on the mainland makes the Abacos feel like Newfoundland.'

In less than a minute, the launch's rubbing strake scraped against the wharf's wood pilings. Climbing a ladder, Elle was surrounded by sweating labourers shifting heaps of pineapple, bananas and guava. Parked up beside the customs shed flying the Stars and Stripes was a pair of olive-drab Ford Model T Tourers, their convertible tops stowed. A platoon of soldiers sweat through their khaki uniforms and wide-brimmed campaign caps, separating fruit for themselves.

One of the soldiers, stripes on his sleeve, approached Henrikson. They shook hands firmly.

'Gunny Schadowski, this is Dr Eleanor Annenberg.'

'Oh, Doc.' He clasped a hand to his chest. 'I got a terrible pain in my heart. Can ya take a look at it?'

'Not that kind of doctor,' she replied, spotting the eagle, globe and anchor emblem on his cap. A marine. 'I'm an ethnologist, leatherneck.'

'Call me Joe,' replied Gunny, as he pushed his way between her and Henrikson. Taking off his hat, he adjusted his "high and tight" clipped hair. 'We don't get many American gals down here, see.' He looked close at Elle's fingers. 'Least of all ones that ain't handcuffed.'

She realised he was looking for a wedding band on her finger. 'United States Marines?'

'Hoboken,' he replied. 'Actually, I'm a Pollock but what the hell. Where you from, Doc?'

'Detroit.'

'Tigers. I'm a more a Giants fan, but that southpaw, Ty Cobb…man oh man, can he swat a Spaulding.' Turning his attention to Henrikson, he asked, 'So Skipper, off on another treasure hunt?'

'Perhaps we'll find something this time,' he replied, glancing to Elle.

'Good luck with that. Umpteen chumps come out here looking for treasure.' Gunny waved out to sea. 'They always promise better luck next year. You're the first who actually came back.'

'Stubborn Canadians. Like our ice fishing: we get our hooks into something, we stick with it.'

'I'm guessing you anchored in our East Harbour hoping to jump the customs queue on the mainland?'

Henrikson nodded.

'Sorry to have to tell ya, but there's a day of fruit consignments ahead of ya.'

Gunny's eyes darted towards Elle. She gave him her hesitant smile. Including the wrinkled nose this time. The big brash marine crumbled.

'Tell you what; I'll do my damnedest to push you to the front.' He showed them to one of the Fords, throwing a guava at his corporal to attract his attention. 'Us Yankees don't suffer the *poco a poco* malaise of the local boys on the mainland, but things still take time.'

Crate of fruit under his arm, the corporal held the door for Elle and Henrikson. As they climbed into the back seat of the Tourer, Gunny added, 'It ain't all bad, though. No Prohibition here. And the giggle-juice is cheap.'

'*Poco a poco?*' she asked.

'Little by little,' replied Henrikson. 'Hondurans set the schedule.'

'Don't you worry,' interrupted Gunny, climbing into the front passenger seat. 'You're on the islands. Different ball-game out here. We'll have you on your way in two ticks off a hound's ass.'

Taking off his hat, he adjusted his hair before turning to the driver. 'Let's go, Marine.'

Gears grinding, the Ford parted the crowded dock. Leaning back in the seat, Elle raised her chin, trying to catch as much of the breeze as possible, a hot blast better than none at all. As the automobile gained speed on the macadamed road, she widened the collar of her linen shirt, letting air onto the sweat developing on her chest. She watched as the driver's eyes honed in on her from the rear-view mirror and he had to swerve to miss a trap full of bananas, hauled by a mule.

'Keep your eyes on the road, Corporal,' ordered Gunny. 'That's how accidents happen.'

Adjusting the mirror, Gunny gave her a nod and a wink. Elle thought better of leaving the top of her shirt open, sweat or no.

The Ford bounced along the narrow, coastal track, leaving East Harbour's *centre-ville* behind.

'Where we going?' Elle asked.

'Stopping round Scotland Road,' replied Henrikson.

'Titanic's crew nicknamed a passageway below decks Scotland Road.'

'Here, it's a hotel.'

'Not a good one,' added Gunny. 'Utila ain't exactly what you'd call cosmopolitan, like. There's a customs office, paid for by American companies buying up all the fruit from the locals on these here Bay Islands. Somebody with deep pockets got President Coolidge to send in us Marines. An entire company from the 4th Marine Division is quartered in La Ceiba.'

'The principal Caribbean port on the mainland,' explained Skip.

'Yeah. And where all the action is: officers' club, casino, ice cream, nurses. The whole tamale. Best we can muster here is a platoon.'

'And a gunnery sergeant,' said the driver.

'Yeah, and a gunnery sergeant. Utila is so small we don't even rate an officer. But, I make sure everything goes smooth, like.'

'There are two hotels on the island,' said Henrikson. 'The fruit companies built a posh one. All the comforts of home - even the Miami Herald delivered a couple times a month with the resupply.'

'Hotel Scotland Road ain't exactly the Waldorf.'

'We don't *want* to be at the Waldorf,' Henrikson replied. 'Too many nosy types.'

The car bounced over a bridge spanning a stagnant estuary, before turning onto an even narrower dirt track, finally coming to a halt under the blessed shade of a palm's feathery fronds. A faded sign nailed to its trunk read: *Hotel Scotland Road*. Climbing from the motorcar, Elle caught the scent of sea air. Henrikson closed the door behind her.

'You're not coming?' Elle asked him.

'Not directly,' he replied. 'I'll sort my bits with the customs boys while my crew gathers hogsheads of fresh water. Waste of a good day and tariff, if you ask me.'

Gunny raised his arms helplessly. 'I just follow orders.'

'What am I meant to do all day?' Elle asked petulantly, standing alone before the hotel, a mosquito already buzzing around her ears.

'Have a bath and breakfast. Ask for Dougie Beedham. He's the proprietor.'

'He's two sandwiches short of a picnic,' added Gunny.

'I'll be back by suppertime,' called Henrikson as the Ford pulled away. 'I hope.'

'So do I,' said Gunny with a wave, as they disappeared in a cloud of exhaust fumes and dust.

Elle turned to the hotel with a sigh. Obscured by verdant Lysiloma, the ageing, pink clapboard façade of Hotel Scotland Road peeked out at her. It was quaint. If quaint meant having a fresh coat of paint and new zinc roof.

Passing through a wooden gate hung by a broken hinge, she noticed sand replace dirt beneath her feet. Distantly, she heard the crash of waves.

Continuing inside, she found a little Honduran boy in a white waiter's jacket three sizes too big polishing the silver service, in a mahogany-panelled ante-room that smelled faintly of stale beer. The boy smiled, perfect teeth gleaming. She smiled back.

'*Dónde está Sr Beedham?*' she asked.

The boy pointed a spoon in the direction of reception. Giving him a smile and a pat on the head, she entered an open courtyard heavy with the scent of mango and orange blossom. At one end stood the aforementioned reception, its dark mahogany counter cracked by the humidity. A Papillon puppy coiled its line, whimpering at a coconut husk, just out of its reach. In a worn-out, flower-patterned lounge chair sat a rakish and rail-thin man in a wrinkled Panama suit, his gingery hair skew-whiffed. He pulled apart a green soursop with his fingers, the pulp falling onto his jacket lapel.

'Dougie Beedham?'

He looked up at her with a nod, stuffing the fruit into his mouth.

'I'm Dr Annenberg.'

'Somebody poorly?'

'Skipper Henrikson dropped me.'

'Ah,' he said, motioning for her to sit. 'I met a Franklyn Annenberg once. Years ago.'

'Funny enough, I have a father named Franklyn Annenberg.'

Ceasing his chewing, his eyes met hers, brightening. 'All grown-up now.'

She felt caution come knocking again. 'We've met?'

'Morning after the night before.'

'Titanic?'

Another nod. 'Steward. Second-Class.'

She smiled. 'Interesting name for a hotel.'

Tossing the loose skin of the soursop aside, he bit into the fruit. 'It was along Scotland Road I saw my best mate for the last time. On his rounds, inspecting the holds. Podgy old scouse.' Smacking his lips, he swallowed. 'Few hours later, I fled the ship in a collapsible lifeboat.'

'I remember you,' she said. 'The cabin steward in my lifeboat who lost his arm - he knew you.'

His brow furrowed. 'Tony Swinburne. First-Class Steward. Kentish boy. He survived. Gone back to Folkestone, last I heard.'

'You saved my father and Corky O'Shea.'

'That Irish fella?'

'Yeah. He's still around. Looks after my father's boat.'

Beedham looked away. 'I was once that sort, an' all. Disregarded fatigue and suffering for a life at sea.' He spat some pulp onto the packed sand floor. 'Navigated from the sixth degree South to the sixth degree North in vessels so exposed, entire crew were pallid with fever. I seen the oceans wreak havoc among men from Batavia to San Blas.'

Juice dribbled down his chin as he began chewing again.

'Last time I went to sea, I was a torpedo mate on a frigate in the Great War.'

He chuckled for the first time, as his Papillon puppy rolled onto its back, a palm husk in its paws.

'I hunted German underwater boats, until one torpedoed us off Uruguay.'

Leaning forward, he let the morning sun light his face through the courtyard palms.

'I got picked up by a Honduran banana boat returning to the Mosquito Coast. My nerves were broken. Never will I go to sea again.'

'You were a ship steward on Titanic?'

He nodded.

'I wonder if you remember a passenger?'

'Long time ago now, that is,' Beedham replied.

'His name was Balthasar Toule.'

'Pfft. I wouldn't forget *that* name if I'd heard it.'

'He was tall. Dark hair. Slender. Would have been in his mid-twenties back then.'

'Second-Class passenger?'

'I couldn't say.'

'If he wasn't Second-Class, I had nothing to do with him. White Star Line regulation forbade it. Unless, of course, the bloody ship sank. Did he perish?'

'I don't know.'

'You been looking for him all these years?'

She nodded.

'*Poco a poco*, eh?'

'Little by little,' she replied, sadly. 'I've heard that today already.'

'It comes in handy.'

'On the Mosquito Coast?'

'And in life.'

Beedham stood, toddling over to his puppy before unwinding the clothes-line tied around an old cannon, set on end, hibiscus flowering from the muzzle. Patting the Papillon on its head, he turned back to Elle.

'I'll fetch your room key. Why not wait in the bar? I've a few bits and bobs on display.'

She followed a dimly lit hallway from the courtyard towards the hotel bar. Open French doors across the other side of the club room faced scrub-grass, leading to a beach strewn with flotsam, most of which looked like the source of the bar's decoration. On the walls were tacked ship flags, dirty foul-weather jackets, a stuffed boar's head and various-sized shark jaws. In a corner was a collection of sponging harpoons, a walking stick and an umbrella, all shoved into a dinged-up spittoon. Deposited neither here nor there about the room were worn-out floral armchairs occupied by felicitously dressed Americans from the sailing regatta, slinging back glasses of rum and swapping stories with a pair of sponge fisherman.

On the well-varnished bar, a Victrola played *I Lost My Heart in Heidelberg*. Behind the counter a no-guff-looking Caribbean polished pint glasses. Stacked behind him were gloriously full bottles of spirits, the likes of which Elle hadn't seen since before Prohibition. Hotel Scotland Road was her kind of gin joint.

Feeling eyes on her, she took a circuitous route around the back of the clubroom, passing built-in bookcases stuffed with conch shells and Jack Daniel's bottles with half-melted candles shoved in the necks.

She stopped as her eye caught something familiar on a shelf. Pushing a yellowed copy of the Miami Herald to the side, she saw a tea-cup and saucer with a furrowing red banner on it. Beside it sat a chipped egg-cup, "White Star Line" inscribed on it. A small photograph of a ship leaned against a leather ledger, its cover falling to bits.

Delicately, she took the picture off the shelf. It was a postcard. A postcard of Titanic. She read the scribble on its back: "*Farewell and much love. From Dougie to Mum.*" As she went to put it back, she saw behind it a patinated frame holding a photograph of two men. She recognised them both.

Dougie Beedham as she remembered him, youthful and rail-straight in his white steward's jacket. Beside him, a man she knew but couldn't quite place.

A hand patted her arm. She jumped, nearly dropping the picture. Turning, she stood facing a fair-haired man with a strong neck and a stronger tan.

'*Wollen Sie etwas trinken, schöne Frau?*'

She gazed down at the hand upon her arm.

'Slam on your anchors, *Herr* Mack. I can buy myself a drink.'

He released her. '*Entschuldigung. Wir haben uns beim letzten Mal nicht miteinander richtig bekannt gemacht.*'

'*Scheisse*,' she mumbled. '*Der Deutsche.*'

Not just any German. It was *the* German. The German who had accompanied Titch and escaped her scathing remarks on the night to remember.

'Americans.' He laughed. 'Not ones for mincing words.'

'Also, not one for taking kindly to being manhandled.' She smiled. 'Never mind, I'm happy to see you survived.'

'Are you?' Extending his hand formally this time, he said, 'Erik Frisch.'

'Eleanor,' she said, shaking it. 'Eleanor Annenberg.'

'Your friend?'

'Titch Blaine-Howard?'

He nodded.

'She survived.'

'*Gottseidank*' he replied, eyeing the barman. 'We can raise a glass to those who did not?'

Grudgingly, she joined him as he ordered two glasses of rum. Two short glasses were dutifully filled. Passing one to her, Erik raised his.

'"*If death wait just off the bow, we need not answer to him now —* " To the poor souls lost.'

'"*We'll stand on and face the morning light without him —* " To the poor souls lost,' she replied, her glass clinking against his, guardedly. There had been rather too many coincidences for one morning. And she didn't believe in coincidences. She threw back the rum and put the empty glass down beside his.

Looking over towards the other Americans, the German asked, 'You are with the regatta?'

'No. Came in on a schooner. Planning on doing a bit of sport diving.'

'Ah, ja. On the reef.'

'Heard it's a treat.'

'The sea fans are remarkable,' he replied. 'Although this is not a place a woman goes alone. There are *Riesenhais*. Very big sharks.'

'Nice try, Herr Frisch. Give you points for originality, but even I know a basking shark eats only plankton.'

'You are as bright as you are lovely.' He laughed, nervously.

'You're a long way from home, Herr Frisch.'

'Erik,' he replied. 'You are very welcome to call me Erik.'

'What brings a German all the way to these islands, Erik?'

'I'm in command of a survey vessel.'

'Surveying what?'

'At this moment, the Gulf of Honduras. We seek to improve the navigational charts.'

'Who is "we"?' she asked. His explanation clearly intended to mystify.

'We?' The German stumbled. 'We are a German surveying contingent. This can be beneficial for all nations navigating through these waters.'

Watching him drop a few centavos onto the counter, presumably for another round, Elle decided it was time to take her leave. She scooted off her stool and turned to the door. He followed right after her.

'Way ya goin'?' the broad barman asked.

'To the reef,' said the German.

'Oh really?' she replied to him.

'Da reef? Watch out dem sharks now,' said the barman. 'Dem bull sharks rip the guts right out ya.'

'Guts,' repeated Elle. The mention of it stirred something long forgotten in her mind. The barman and Herr Frisch fell silent. 'Guts,' she said once more as she turned away from them, approaching Beedham's Titanic collection and spying the photograph on the shelf once more. The man beside Beedham… She remembered.

Ring of keys jingling on his belt as he bobbed like a cork in Titanic's flooding hold. Vacant eyes staring at her through cracked spectacle lenses, his body opened up. Guts scooped out. Unwittingly, Elle had met Beedham's friend.

But she had bigger fish to fry now. Ditching the German, she escaped through the open French doors, scurrying down a narrow towpath lined with lavishly blossoming poincianas. Nearing the end of the path, she saw Adel anchoring offshore.

'Your vessel?' Herr Frisch asked, catching up to her.

'Won the Americas Cup in 1879,' she replied dismissively, watching as a launch rowed to shore. A crewman waved for her. 'You'll have to excuse me, Herr Frisch.'

Before he could reply, she waded into the beach break towards the launch.

'Miss. Miss!' a crewman said excitedly. 'Skipper wants us on the wreck today.'

Pulled aboard, she asked, 'What's the hurry?'

'Someone been snooping round.'

'I wonder who that might be,' she replied, looking over her shoulder back to land, as the launch returned to Adel. The German stood forlornly on the beach.

She waved to him.

Adel hoved anchor, her crew hoisting the fore-topmost sail before turning into the wind. Elle found Henrikson in his cabin, peeling through a stack of charts.

'Gunny informed me of a ship carrying on some sort of inquiry in the area of our wreck,' he said.

'There was a German in Hotel Scotland Road. Captain of some research vessel or other. Surveying expedition.'

'Surveying expedition? Here?'

'It's a lot of phonus balonus, isn't it?'

He nodded. 'This area has been charted twice over by the fruit companies. How'd you come by this?'

'He told me,' Elle said.

'He *told* you?'

She nodded. 'Think he found Griffin?'

'Doubtful. To keep the wreck's location hush-hush, I didn't bother with salvage rights, nor did I leave dive markers behind.'

'How did you plan to find the wreck again?'

'Deduced reckoning. All I need is a compass and stopwatch.' He invited her to join him at the chart table as he hunched over a map of the Honduran coast.

'This is La Ceiba on the Mosquito Coast.'

He pointed out a port not far from the eastern border of Guatemala. Running his finger North across the sea, he passed a tiny island.

'Here we are. Utila. Thirty-seven nautical miles north-northeast of the mainland. Morgan's hide-away.'

His finger continued to a larger island on the other side of a channel. 'That's Roatán.'

Finally, his finger came to rest on a point between the islands. 'Griffin was just that close to safety.' Lifting a stopwatch, he checked the ticking seconds. 'Best we get a wiggle on.'

They returned to deck, and Elle settled into a deckchair by the stern, watching the crew tirelessly work Adel's enormous sails. Utila fell further and further into the ship's wake, until it was lost in a bank of cloud.

The sun grew oppressive. Even in the shade of a canvas awning, sweat soon dripped down her nose, pattering down her chest.

Henrikson stood at the helm, stripped to oil-stained shorts, his elderly frame surprisingly virile. He was eyeing a compass before the wheel. Checking his stop-watch, he pushed the wheel over a degree.

'Six nautical miles north-east of Utila,' he said to Elle. 'In eleven-and-a-half fathoms. That's where Griffin lies.'

Turning, he ordered the sails lowered, and Adel anchored by a four-point mooring. Crewmen gathered and began attaching air-lines to the pump receptacles.

'Lads are cracking on,' Henrikson said to her, retrieving a sounding line. 'With luck we can get a dive in before lunch.' He lowered the weighted line over the stern, the reel in his hand spinning as it descended. After what seemed like an age, the reel fell silent. Inspecting the line, he smiled.

'Eleven-and-a-half fathoms. Struck bottom.'

'That's good?' Elle asked.

'Seventy feet. It's good.'

Bringing up the sounding line he opened one of Adel's sea chests, tossing the line inside before retrieving a copper diving helmet.

'Fancy a go?'

Pursing her lip, she hesitated.

'Better I remain on deck and assist in stabilising anything you find down there.'

'Just a quick look over the wreck? There's but a quarter-knot current on the ebb tide as it flows through this part of the channel. It's nothing.'

'I'm better at sunbathing than diving, if I'm honest.'

'Can you inhale and exhale?'

Reluctantly she nodded.

'Well then. You can handle a John Brown rig.'

Elle offered up a gentle smile. It grew slowly until it filled her face with confidence.

'Okay.'

❖ ❖ ❖

'This a terrible idea,' Elle huffed as the watertight bolts that attached the diving bonnet to the copper ring corselet around her neck tightened.

Loosening the wing-nut securing her faceplate, Henrikson swung it open.

'These old John Brown rigs are awkward, I admit. But once we throw you in, they're quite weightless.'

Taking her hand, Henrikson raised it to the back of her helmet, letting her feel the connection point for the air hose, and a valve beside it.

'Give the valve a half-twist clockwise, the deeper you go. It'll regulate the flow of air so your suit doesn't grip you too tightly.' She looked at him nervously. 'Just nod.'

She nodded.

'Good. Now follow behind me. Our feet are weighted with lead, so walk slowly. Once you're down there, I promise you won't want to come back up.'

Before she could complain, he closed her faceplate and two crewmen spun the wheels on the pump to which her air hose was attached. Air whistled through her helmet, drowning out Henrikson's instructions.

'I'm not sure about this at all,' she shouted, her voice echoing inside the helmet.

Showing her a tightly twinned steel cable, he attached it to her weight belt and shouted back, 'You have any trouble, give this a good tug. The lads will reel you in like hooked marlin.'

Raising her to her feet, Henrikson duck-waddled Elle to a rope ladder strung over the side of Adel. Her suit was clumsy and, no matter how she tried, she couldn't get her heavy foot into the top rung.

Henrikson gave her a push.

She toppled helmet first into the drink and was instantly surrounded by surging bubbles. She felt panic rise immediately as the air hose coiled around her legs, suddenly claustrophobic, her vision restricted by the circular glass faceplates, air blew hot through the regulator making her feel sick. Before she could verge on sheer uncontrolled terror, a calming hand pat her on her shoulder. Henrikson smiled at her through his own faceplate, his hand gently rising and falling to simulate breathing.

She nodded. A few slow breaths and the panic began to ebb. He gave her an 'okay' gesture. She mirrored it.

Unclipping a weight belt from his waist, he secured it about hers. Immediately, she felt the pull as she began to descend, air hose and shot rope swirling up to Adel's keel, as the boat bobbed gracefully in the swells.

A mere twenty feet from the surface her boots thumped against the seabed. Pillar coral and sea sponges spread out on a glorious barrier reef. Clusters of crinoids and sea cucumbers crowded moose-antlered polyps and metre-high sea fans swaying in the gentle current.

Henrikson directed her attention to a dark-blue tear in the seafloor. Apprehensively, she followed him towards its edge. A thin trail of bubbles rose from a team of shipwright divers below, carrying red marker poles, their air hoses trailing to the surface like inverted jellyfish. Stepping off the side of the shelf, she began to descend the reef wall.

Tiny, goggle-eyed fish darted among mutant-looking brain coral, while lobster and turbot clung to clefts in the sheer wall. Her suit began to tighten like a vice. Remembering what Henrikson told her, she countered the pressure with a half turn of the valve on her hard hat. The pressure easing, her breathing relaxed.

As she continued to descend, the surface light began to fade and, with it, the world above. The jovial marine life vanished too, as inky-grey silt forced her to follow the twisting lines of ascending bubbles past her. A peacefulness she had never experienced before enveloped her.

All nervousness was now gone.

She felt an understanding of what those trapped within Titanic must have felt as the ship dove for the bottom. Noise and panic remained at the surface. Here, only quiet, and rest eternal.

Gracefully, she struck bottom, her lead boots stirring up a cloud of silt. Ahead, the other divers laid out their marker poles. Henrikson landed beside a coral formation, motioning for her to join him. Elle propelled herself towards what she thought was towering coral.

It was a ship's rib.

Griffin.

It was a strangely beautiful sight. Encrustations had formed over the entire wreck, jutting up from the bottom like Gaudi inspired towers. And all around silence but for the whine from the air hose.

Henrikson beamed at her, directing her towards the divers ahead.

Hovering over the coral, she picked out a cannon, its muzzle still sealed by its tampion. The shipwright divers squared their markers, the outline of a hull now apparent. The upper decks had long ago rotted away, but the keel remained. Even a few hull planks protruded from the encrustations. As she pulled herself up a crenelation, a great chunk of it broke off.

What stared out from underneath caused her blood to turn to ice.

❖ ❖ ❖

Out of the constrictive diving gear and once again on Adel's deck, Elle watched seawater flow over the wooden inspection tables on the stern deck. Pumped through hoses hung over the side of the ship, the excess water poured into open drains at the base of the tables and streamed off the stern, back into the sea. A steady flow was crucial — after centuries on the seabed, the artefacts were extremely fragile.

The canvas sunshade provided blessed relief from the scorching sun, but the heat did not abate, necessitating occasional plunges into the sea to cool off. Elle was just climbing onto the diving platform after a brief dip when she heard the crew cheer as a creaking winch brought the first haul to the surface. Leaning over the side, she waited eagerly for her discovery to surface, somewhat disappointed when a crab catch filled with lumps of encrustations appeared.

'Okay. Let's have a look,' she said as it was brought to the inspection tables, coral deposits spilling out.

Elle had trained a team of crewmen in conservation during the voyage from the Abacos. Apprehensively, she hung back as they went to work on the hard coatings with hammers, pry bars and chisels. She need not have worried. With precise and delicate taps, the encrustations came apart.

A silver decanter revealed itself. A boarding hatchet. Ivory dagger handle. And finally, a gold bowl engraved in Spanish.

Finer preservation work would be left until after returning to Hope Town, so Elle assigned each find a lot number, and jotted down a few details in a notebook before wrapping the artefacts in seaweed and transferring them to wood casks sailors referred to as hogsheads filled with sawdust soaked in seawater, for the return voyage.

The sound of the winch protesting drew her to the port side rail. Ropes strained and the surface churned as something heavy was brought up. A hard hat broke the surface. Holding onto his shot rope, Henrikson grinned at her through his faceplate. Raising a hand he gave a thumbs-up. Other divers appeared, accompanying another encrustation, this time enormous.

'That's the bee's knees,' she shouted excitedly.

The discovery was raised up and over the railing, swinging gently over the deck, seawater pouring from its fissures as fifteen strong backs manoeuvred it onto an inspection table. Its wooden legs groaned under the weight. The conservators descended like cats on a wounded bird.

'Go chase yourselves, boys.' Pushing her way through, Elle stood before the massive lump of coral. 'I got this one.'

'What do you reckon it is?'

Henrikson stood beside her now, still in his John Brown rig, helmet under one arm.

Taking up a hose, she washed the silt away from the coral she'd inadvertently broken off. Half a ghoulish face carved in stone scowled back. 'Camazotz.'

'I'm guessing he's Mayan.'

'Bat god of all things wicked.' Taking up a pry bar she shoved it under the coral growth, preparing to break it away. 'And a Sentinel.'

'A what-inel?'

'Never mind,' she replied.

'Can it be one of the missing stelae from Copán?'

'I can't say. It's Mayan. Of that I am certain.'

Something else was hidden. Another figure. She could just make out its shoulder, but before she could pry away the growth, a lookout hollered a warning, pointing south. Following his gaze, she spotted sails in the distance. A double-masted sloop, flag of the Weimar Republic flapping at the stern.

'Damn. Here comes trouble.'

Henrikson lifted a pair of glasses and peered silently through them.

'Your Hun?' he asked, passing them to her.

She raised the binoculars to her eyes. The sloop came into focus. On the bow, shirt off, Guatemalan straw hat perched haughtily on his head, stood Herr Frisch.

'What do you suppose he wants?' Elle asked pulling a white linen blouse over her wet swimsuit and closing two buttons.

Henrikson shrugged, the twinkle in his eye suggesting he knew precisely what the German was game for. 'Rather a fit chap, isn't he?'

'Don't suppose he's on his way to Roatán?' She watched the sloop lower its sails and drop anchor. She sighed. 'We're not so lucky.'

'I'd like to discourage visitors, Elle.'

'He'll get the icy mitt,' she replied, snatching a Springfield rifle from the hands of the shark watch.

'A what?'

'The cold shoulder.'

Chambering a thirty-aught-six round she made her way aft, watching as a little Chris-craft motorboat was short-lined to the stern of the sloop.

The motor roared to life and Herr Frisch crossed the distance between the two vessels with impressive speed.

'Ahoy,' he called out over the motor's whine.

'Elle.'

She turned to a nervous-looking Henrikson.

'We can't have that Hun boarding us,' he said.

'What do you want me to do, shoot him?'

'Not the worst idea,' he said and shrugged. 'Nah. Ink's barely dry on the Versailles Treaty. Let's just see what he wants.'

'We both know what he wants,' she said, as the small vessel glided alongside Adel's diving platform.

Killing the motor, Herr Frisch tossed a rope to a seaman on deck. 'You're not planning to take a shot at *me* are you?'

'For you to decide,' she replied, resting the rifle butt on her hip. 'What are you doing here?'

'I want to show you about Utila.'

He dove into the water and swam towards them. Elle fired. Herr Frisch ducked underwater as the bullet zipped overhead. Popping up again he shouted, '*Verdammt noch mal – Bist du verrückt geworden?*'

'No, I'm not the crazy one. A crazy person leaps into the sea when a shark is lurking.'

The German turned, the water behind him clouding crimson as a bull shark floated to the surface.

'It ain't no *Riesenhais* either,' she added.

'*Mein Gott*,' he said, shocked, swimming quickly to the diving platform.

'Lunch?'

'Ours or his?' Herr Frisch asked.

'Enough shark steak to feed the entire crew. What do you think?' she said to Henrikson.

He smiled. 'Wherever did you learn to shoot?'

'Shooting trap at the hunt club with my father when I was a kid. Fired thousands of rounds over the years.' Sliding back the Springfield's bolt, she ejected the spent cartridge. 'Never dreamt it would come in handy.'

The German began to scramble up the ladder.

'You ain't been piped aboard, Herr Frisch,' said Henrikson.

'Erik,' he replied, warily rising his hands in surrender. He turned to Elle. 'Utila is a nice little island. The windward side especially lovely.'

'Really now?' Elle questioned his intent. Arseing about with Herr Frisch was not her idea of a well-spent afternoon. She glanced at the inspection table, the stela under the encrustations so tantalisingly close. Then she turned to Henrikson.

'It is,' he replied.

Something had to be done to be rid of the German. And apparently, she was to be the sprat that caught the mackerel. Grabbing her silk stole, she turned to Herr Frisch.

'Let's go.'

❖ ❖ ❖

Pounding across the wind-raked crests, the Chris-craft thrust towards Utila. Sea spray soaked Elle as she leaned over the windscreen, permitting the German a peek at her bum under a pair of the crew's shorts she'd trimmed to fit, and rolled up just enough to keep him distracted.

She'd figured distraction would draw Herr Frisch's attention away from what Henrikson was up to. She wasn't wrong. And as the launch leapt over another crest, soaking her, she couldn't deny it was belting good fun.

Utila's shoreline appeared—a blanket of stunted palm trees dotted with white fisherman's cottages. Twin-masted ketches squatted low in the tide as lighters brought out fruit shipments from East Harbour. As the boat's rubbing rake bumped against the wharf's pilings, a hearty looking fellow in a frayed, palm-fronded hat with corned-beef legs waved to her.

'Toss a line.'

Taking a coiled rope from behind her seat, Elle heaved it up to the old man, who caught it and tied it off. Hopping from the launch, she caught his hand and he pulled her onto the landing dock. He smelled of brine and cheap tobacco. She looked around hopefully for Gunny. The marines were nowhere to be seen.

'Ey, Hun. Got yerself a mate this time?'

'Jeornagian Copper,' Herr Frisch replied. 'Still, you are alive.'

'Long as I got a whimper here,' he said, tapping a half-missing finger to his temple. 'I got a spring in me arse.' He coughed, depositing it off the end of the wharf.

'Have my launch short-lined. We're bicycling to the windward side for a swim.'

'Wot are ya doin' here?' Jeornagian asked.

Elle thought his peculiar accent sounded Cornish.

'I will show my friend Pumpkin Hill.'

'I mean all ya Hun mates running round the island.'

'We prepare more accurate navigational charts,' replied the German, dismissively. 'You have some bicycles for us?' he asked, shoving a fistful of lempira into the old man's overalls.

'End of the pier, Hun.'

Elle gave Herr Frisch a sideways glance as he hurried her along. 'Accurate navigational charts? Bum fodder.'

The German shrugged with a smile. Quite clearly, neither Herr Frisch nor his *Kameraden* were conducting a navigational mapping survey. It was down to her to figure out what he was up to. If twisting her lip and shaking her bum in his face got her the answers she needed, then so be it.

As they peddled along East Harbour's narrow lanes, they passed colonialist cottages tucked behind flowering hibiscus and trees heavy with breadfruit. Slowing to enter the town centre, Elle saw a policeman in tropical attire standing post before a tiny Bancasa bank. He waved.

'Afternoon, Herman the German,' said the policeman, tipping the brim on his pith helmet. 'Back again, eh?'

Herr Frisch waved back. Evidently, he was a much more frequent visitor to the island than he let on.

There were no motorcars. No Hondurans and only an occasional Caribbean. Considering Utila was just off the Mosquito Coast, it was all rather peculiar. East Harbour now left behind. Her grotty bicycle, its rubber tyres patchworked from repairs, rattled along the narrowing dirt track under a canopy of fever trees. 'Bit rum, this place. Strange the locals speak English with Cornish accents.'

'You do not know the island's history?'

'Captain Morgan's hideout, right?' Elle enquired in response.

'The islanders are descendants of his buccaneers. They hailed from Cornwall. For generations, the islanders spoke Cornish. They say Morgan's treasure is buried here somewhere. Nobody has found it.' Swerving to miss a crab scurrying for its hole, Herr Frisch gave her a quick glance. 'Not yet.'

They emerged from a copse of trees onto the windward side of the island, the track ending at a spit covered with broken coral and pink sand.

'So,' said the German, doffing his espadrilles as he walked barefoot to the sand. 'Will you tell me what your friends are doing out there on Adel?'

She joined him, sand hot underfoot.

'Just as soon as you tell me what the Reichsmarine is doing in Honduras?'

She smiled, feigning innocence.

❖ ❖ ❖

Sea grass tickled her feet, as the tide carried her over the jagged reef protecting the windward side of the island from huge waves crashing offshore. She eyed the pounding breakers.

'Fancy some body planing?'

'*Wahnsinn*,' the German called back, remaining on the shallow side. 'Those breakers would pulverise you.'

'Nah.'

Elle turned and swam beyond the safety of the reef, the undertow taking hold of her and pulling her towards the oncoming waves. She had body planed countless times in the Abacos. The key was to know when to turn for shore. The waves loomed large, forming walls of green the further she was carried into deeper waters. She felt their power lifting her as each wave crested. Another moment and she turned to face the shoreline. Kicking her flippers like mad, she planed out, arms ahead of her. She scooted along like a torpedo, riding the wave over the outer reef before tumbling under as the wave broke. Surfacing, she hollered in victory as adrenaline had her hankering for more. 'Yee haw!'

'You are quite mad,' shouted Erik, waving for her to come in from the surf.

Staying put, she waved for him to join her instead. After much dithering, he plunged in, swimming until he was beside her on the reef. A tall man, he was able to stand upright on the coral. '*Guter Junge*, Good boy,' she said, before turning to the waves and swimming away. Looking briefly over her shoulder, she smiled at Herr Frisch reluctantly following her. A few strokes more and she felt the pull of the waves again.

'Stay close,' she told him as he swam alongside her. 'When I tell you, turn round and flatten out. The wave will carry you in.'

Nodding nervously, he took a few more strokes as the wall of water grew, undertow pulling them in.

'Drowning is your idea of fun?' he asked.

'You won't drown,' she replied, treading water as the wave grew taller still.

'I've twice nearly drowned. I don't wish to tempt provenance.'

Before she could answer, the wave was on them.

'Turn,' she yelled. 'Swim as if your life depends on it.'

She continued treading water a second or two longer, watching the German turn and catch the wave perfectly. He planed out, and the wave's power carried him back over the reef.

But the extra moment cost Elle. Before she could get into position, the wave crashed down on her, rolling her over and pulling her under. Tossed about, she struck the reef, lacerating her back and knocking the wind from her. Her vision went white as her lungs screamed for air.

She was hauled up by her hair, spitting seawater. Herr Frisch stood bolt upright on the reef.

'*Mein Gott*,' he shouted, raising her up almost entirely free from the surf, the top of her swimsuit yanked down by the wave's suction, breasts in plain view. 'Will you have had enough once you've finally drowned yourself?'

Heart pounding, she reached for the talisman around her neck before worrying about covering up. It was still there, secured by its chain.

❖   ❖   ❖

Wrapped in a towel before a crackling fire, Elle felt sore and ashamed. As dusk approached, Herr Frisch's sloop appeared offshore, his crew landing the Chris-craft. With a few stitches, they mended her back then, digging a pit in the sand, they set a low fire alight. After it reduced to coals, wet seaweed was laid on, followed by clams, prawns and lobster. The smell of clambake pervaded the beach, making Elle's mouth water and her stomach twinge, despite her pain. She wolfed down the largest lobster she'd ever seen and a dozen or so clams; the meal did her good.

She did not fail to notice the crew slip away, leaving her alone on the beach with Herr Frisch, a new moon casting them in soft blue light. It was the perfect setting for a romantic interlude. There was no denying Herr Frisch was a handsome man. Interludes didn't interest her.

He set up a bar on a washed-up log, crushing cranberries and squeezing oranges. A bottle of vodka, gloriously cold, appeared from inside a rum cask, filled with chipped ice.

'You Germans do know how to organise an expedition,' she said taking a handful of ice and pressing it against her sun-kissed chest. 'Is that Russian vodka?'

'Of course.'

'That's better than the jag juice we got up in the U.S.A these days.'

'Prohibition, ja?'

'Ja.'

'I can't tell you how long I've saved this bottle,' he said, poking holes in a couple of oranges before squeezing the juice into tin cups. 'Waiting for the right occasion.'

'Don't spare the horses,' she told him, the pain of her wound throbbing. He smiled, cracking the waxen seal on the bottle cap and pouring a very generous glug of spirit into her cup, before handing it to her.

He sat on a blanket, not quite across the fire from her.

'You are better now?'

Sipping her drink, she felt a delicious burn down her throat. 'Ah yes. Better now,' she replied. 'Madras?'

'Ja. And there's plenty more,' he said, slinging his drink back.

The Madras was cold and refreshing, manna from heaven. She knocked hers back too, not in the least reluctant to ask the German to fix her another. He obliged.

'Thank you for pulling me out. It was a stupid stunt on my part. I'm really quite embarrassed.' She adjusted the blanket around her shoulders. Remembering he had gotten an eyeful of her, she added, 'For all sorts of reasons. Least of which was nearly drowning.'

'It was a poor decision. But do not worry. I won't tell.' He eyed her tanned legs as he returned to the bottle to fix them both a second round. His eyes met hers. 'About anything.'

She laughed.

'I had great fun today. Right up to the moment I nearly drowned. So, thank you, Herr Frisch.'

Returning to the fire with their cups, he sucked air like a bellhop cheated of a tip. 'Please, Elle, will you not call me by my given name?'

'All right,' she said, taking her drink. 'Thank you, Erik.'

He sat, closer this time. 'You didn't nearly drown.'

'You said something about that earlier,' she replied, sipping her drink.

He looked to the fire. 'About drowning?'

'Yeah.'

'In the Great War, at the Battle of Jutland, I was on a cruiser sunk by the British. A hundred of my men managed to take to the water alive. Until a shell detonated on the water.'

'Who fired it?'

'Does it matter?'

She said nothing.

'The explosion set the surface oil alight. I was one of only three of my crew who survived.'

'That's dreadful.'

'That's war. We knew what we let ourselves in for when we joined the navy.' Looking up from the fire, his eyes met hers. 'Titanic was another matter.'

'What happened to you?'

'I am not the strongest of swimmers.'

'A navy man not a strong swimmer?'

'Some of the finest seaman cannot swim a stroke. Incentive enough to ensure they are never so careless as to allow their vessel to go from under them.' Bending his elbow on another Madras, he topped up his cup and moved to sit close beside her.

'We stayed with Titanic until the last. I lost sight of my aid when we went into the water. Never saw him again.' Frowning at the fire, he took a long drink. 'The ship took me down with it. I held my breath. *Gott*. It felt like hours. The lifejacket I wore saved me, returning me to the surface.'

He drained the cup.

'I came up beside two men. They pulled me to a lot of floating debris knotted in cargo netting. I was so cold. Felt my life draining away. There were others in the water: *männer, frau, kinder*. Their wailing. I hear it still. Yet the two men clinging to the debris behaved as though they were on holiday at the seaside, passing a flask back and forth. They offered a nip to me. I managed it down. Don't remember what it was.' Wobbling to his feet, he retrieved a piece of driftwood, and laid it across the fire. Before sitting, he filled his cup yet again.

'I glimpsed a lifeboat in the distance. My companions wished to stay with their ersatz raft. They asked my name before wishing me good luck. I managed to crawl my way through the cold sea to the lifeboat. Thankfully, there was a German woman and her daughter onboard, or else I would have surely drowned.'

His shoulder brushed against hers as he tossed a twig onto the dancing flames.

'So many dead that night. Then, the Great War came. More dead. Spanish Influenza after the war. Twenty million dead. Our world devastated, and Germany destitute.'

He stared into the fire.

'Most of our Imperial navy was scuttled after the war. What was left was handed over to former enemies as reparation. The Versailles Treaty said nothing about civilian schooners. So… now I command at the pleasure of a new German navy.'

She stared at him. He was hammered, and she felt a pang of sadness for the man. But it was now or never, and as much as she empathised with Herr Frisch, she knew an opportunity when she saw one. She filled both their cups before asking, 'What are you really doing down here, Erik?'

He leaned towards her, his face shadowed by the crackling fire. 'What are *you* doing here, Elle?'

He was tougher than she'd thought. She pondered his question. 'On this beach? Or on Adel?'

'Both are good questions.'

'I'm on Adel looking for pirate treasure, obviously.' She took her time before answering the second question. Even she was not so callous as to wound him more. 'And I'm on this beach with you because I choose to be.'

The German gave her a boozy laugh. 'I've never met a woman like you. So full of life. Optimistic. Yet you are cautious. I think this is what it means to be American.'

She smiled, letting her hand rest on his. 'I have a lifelong philosophy: getting out of trouble is far more interesting than getting into it. I thought I was clever — cleverer than most, anyway. But… in the last few days, I've come to realise I'm not clever at all.'

The sozzled German stared into the bottom of his empty glass.

'You looking for answers in there, Erik?' She topped it up.

He looked up to her. Their eyes met. He was not a bad man.

'*Lichtmetal.*'

'Are you so pickled that you're talking gibberish?'

'Liquid metal.'

'Like mercury?' she asked.

'Ja, mercury.'

'What of it?'

'I'm not on a surveying expedition.' He took another long swig. 'I have orders. The Reichsmarine have orders.'

She nodded, moving closer to him, refilling his cup.

'What are those orders?'

'Not even I am so drunk as to tell you that. But — ' He drank.

'*But*?' She drank too.

'Your ship. It is on your ship.'

'What ship? On Adel?' She felt excitement bubbling up inside her, but was cautious to let it show.

'Nein,' he replied, his words slurring. '*Gott*. I feel poorly.'

'What ship?' she asked again.

'The wreck you have discovered. Griffin.'

She kept schtum, but in her head she cursed a storm. Seizing upon Herr Frisch's vulnerability she propped him up with an arm.

'Erik?' He managed to raise his head towards her. 'Those two men on the ersatz raft. The ones who found you after Titanic sank. You didn't catch their names, did you?'

'One of them was foreign,' he said, trying to remember. 'He was an Arab, I think. Perhaps Persian. His name — what was it? Mahmoud, that's it. The other? No, I cannot remember it.'

'Was he foreign as well?'

Herr Frisch lazily nodded his head. 'Ja. *Britisch*. What were they called, again?'

'Who?'

'Who did visit the *Jesuskind*.'

She stared at him in disbelief, and emptied her whole cup, straight down the hatch. 'The Three Kings?'

'Ja,' he replied. 'The Three Kings. Melchior. Gaspar. What was the other?'

She took a deep breath. 'Balthasar.'

'Ja, Balthasar.'

'Balthasar,' she repeated, climbing to her feet, a frisson of excitement shooting through her. It was all she could do not to jump up and down. Instead, she laughed. She laughed loud and she laughed deep.

'Balthasar,' she said again. Herr Frisch had seen him. After Titanic sank. He was real. Crouching down, she went to give Herr Frisch a kiss. She need not have bothered.

His head was already on the sand. Lights out.

❖ ❖ ❖

Adel's red mast light winked, a lonely picket in the sea. Elle felt a bit like that winking light. Alone. But also newly confident.

Balthasar Toule had survived Titanic. And, like Adel's masthead, he was out there somewhere in the darkness. She just had to find him.

Throttling up the Chris-craft, she hollered out a victory yawl as she crashed through the dark-maned waves. Henrikson must have heard her coming. By the time she let off the motor and drifted alongside Adel, he stood at the port-side rail staring down at her, a swirl of cigar smoke hovering above his straw hat.

'Gotten rid of Herman the German?'

'Couldn't handle his grog, so I took it on the arches,' she replied, climbing up to Adel's deck. 'He'll be wanting his launch back, I expect.'

'I'll buy him another. Hell, I'll buy him two.'

She noticed the two crewmen behind him shouldering rifles. 'Big day?'

'Big day,' he repeated.

'Me as well.'

'Fancy a wager who's had the bigger?' he asked, the moonlight revealing his jubilant grin.

'Show me,' she replied. He nodded towards the foredeck. Passing the empty inspection tables, Henrikson stopped her before a half-dozen wooden hogsheads leaking seawater. Two other crewmen sat in deckchairs, Springfield rifles across their laps.

'Expecting someone to rob the stagecoach, Sheriff?'

'Can't be too careful,' he replied, prying off the lid from one of the barrels. She looked inside. In the darkness, she couldn't see a thing. A bare bulb hung by a wire from the canvas awning above her head and when Henrikson pulled its cord, it cast the hogshead in a pallid glow. The barrel was brimming with seawater-sodden sawdust. He reached in, hands rummaged around before striking upon something with a *clink*. He brought his hands out and slowly opened them over one of the inspection tables. Gold coins gleamed in the barren light.

'Escudos.'

She took one in her hand, looking it over. Rough-cut, it was stamped with an anchor on one side and a fort with a 'G' stamped on the other.

'Spanish?'

He nodded. 'From their royal mints in Guatemala.'

'How many?'

'A shed-load.'

She looked up at him. 'Is that a scientific quantity?'

'Two long tonnes,' he blurted out with a laugh.

'That's the stuff,' she replied, before looking around for her own discovery. She couldn't see it anywhere.

'You've tapped Griffin's hold?'

He shook his head. 'A measly store in Griffin's bow,' he said walking among the wooden barrels, each brimming with Spanish gold coins.

'Value?'

'Millions,' he said, swallowing a laugh. 'Tens of millions.'

'Honduran lempira?'

'US Dollars.'

'What an apple,' she replied, unable to disguise her pleasure. 'You've become a tycoon overnight, Skip.'

He nodded. 'I imagine we can fill another twenty or thirty hogsheads with all the loot down there.'

'It's a wonderful haul but — '

'But?'

'None of it is Mayan.'

'Come,' he said, gesturing her to follow him to an inspection table at the starboard rail. A surplus sail was draped over something. 'I took the liberty of having my lads remove the encrustations.'

He drew back the fabric.

Elle shuddered, staring at what lay beneath.

'Remember the fragment?' she managed to squeak out. 'The artifact you showed me in the Abacos. The one you found on your previous visit here?'

'Still in the hogshead of water in the galley stack, I think.'

'Do you think it could be fetched and brought here?' Elle asked.

'Of course.'

After he had gone, Elle backed away from the inspection table. Leaning against the rail, she sparked up a cigarette, quickly taking a few puffs of tobacco to settle her nerves. While she was off larking about with the German, Henrikson's lads had removed all the encrustations, revealing a monolithic block within.

Henrikson returned.

'Here. I've got it.'

He lay a wet burlap bundle on the table, cutting off its twine binding. Tucking his pocket knife away, he unwrapped the burlap, removed the pinnacle of stone from within and laid it on the table. It joined perfectly to the crown of the monolithic stela.

Elle's hands hovered over it, the separated fragment aligning perfectly.

'Now then,' Henrikson said, looking up. 'Would you kindly tell me what this is all about?'

'Something more valuable than all the looted gold you found on Griffin,' Elle replied, eyes still fixed on what lay before her.

Taking a step back, she took in the carved, stone slab in its entirety. It was both beautiful and unsettling.

'How tall?' she asked.

'108 inches,' he replied. 'Precisely.'

She tried to do the maths in her head. 'Nine feet, right?'

Henrikson nodded. 'Is that significant?'

'Nine is a significant number. Divide it by three and you've got a Triple Trinity.'

Tossing the cigarette overboard, she lightly touched the intricate reliefs carved into the red sandstone.

'I've never seen one like this. There's a lot of variation in Mayan stelae, but normally they are of low-relief,' she said, inspecting the three-dimensional block packed with Mayan boxed hieroglyphs. 'The density of the epigraphy is wonderful.'

'Can you decipher them?'

'Hmm. If they were Proto-Germanic runes, then yes. But I'm no expert on these Mayan graphemes.'

She looked closer.

'Incredible detail. There must be all manner of information encrypted here. Red sandstone's correct for the region. I'm pretty confident this is one of the nine stelae raised from the chamber below the temple structure in Copán.'

'Pretty confident? Is that the scientific term?'

She glanced up at him with a smile.

'It's been an interesting day, Skip. Give me a minute with this, okay?'

Elle looked back to the stela before them, her hand running along the top, where the two broken halves met. It was indeed Camazotz, bat god of the underworld, dressed as a warrior. But he was not alone. There was another — a female with barbed fangs emanating from its sneering upper jaws.

'Awilix.'

'What?'

'A Mayan deity. Queen of the night. She is associated with sickness and death,' Elle said, inspecting the skilfully worked engravings. Awilix wore a necklace of skulls, hands and hearts about her neck, a skirt of writhing snakes and claws twinned about her feet.

'What's he doing with her?'

'Giving her the Saturday night holy water,' she said, her hands brushing away the drying sediment crusting the stela's detail. Camazotz stood behind the Queen of the night, his horn-shaped codpiece penetrating her.

Taking up the bucket that was catching excess water drips from the inspection table, she poured it over the stelae to reveal more hidden detail.

'Wings.'

'Wings?'

'Can't be,' she replied, voice hushed. 'This doesn't make any sense. Awilix is an earthbound god,' she said, looking closer. But there they were. Engraved in the stone and plain to see. Featherless. Like a bat's membranous wings.

'Camazotz, sure. He's the bat god, so I expect to see him with wings. But on a female god?'

'Is there a goddess with wings?'

'Can a woman really be behind all of it?' she muttered to herself. '*La Reine Blanche.*'

'A White Queen?' translated Skip. She looked up at him. 'I'm from Halifax. I speak French.'

'Dr Mauss saw her,' she said to herself. 'In his vision. A white woman appeared, bringing predation upon civilisation. Then vanished. Siobhan. She had wings.' Feeling the side of the slab, she asked, 'What's on the other side?'

'Ah, I think you'll find the other side especially interesting.'

Henrikson whistled for his crewmen. It required all their brawn to roll the stela over. Backing away from the table, Elle went quiet. Not because what she saw frightened her. It was familiar — all too.

'That's *not* Mayan,' Henrikson said.

'No,' she whispered.

Undoing a button on her linen shirt, she lifted the fine chain she had worn around her neck every day for the past seventeen years, revealing the silver talisman. Taking it in his calloused hand, Henrikson stared at it before looking back to this ancient monument.

'Well, then. Suppose I was right in picking you for this job.'

She nodded, staring at the back of the stela. A *Totenkopf* grimaced back at them, its lithe body eviscerated, a river of maggots flowing forth.

'*Expecto resurrectionem mortuorum,*' he said, slowly reading the Latin apothegm chiselled into the stone.

She pulled away, the talisman slipping from Henrikson's hand, and she stared at the life-sized death symbol. It was identical to hers, in every way but one.

'Is that gold?' she asked.

'Why do you think it's so heavy?'

She touched it. It was cool, the gold as lustrous as the day it was set into the sandstone. Her fingers ran along its skull, down its neck to the shoulder, and then down its arm to the hip before reaching its foot. It must have been six feet tall.

'Hollow?'

'Most certainly solid.'

She looked to him. '*Solid?*'

He nodded as she returned her gaze back to the stela, giving the symbol a knock. There was no deep echo.

'Do you yet realise the significance of this?'

He shrugged. 'I know its value.'

'To be clear, everything on Griffin came from the holds of *Señora de Marisol*?'

'Yes. Morgan transferred the lot of it from the Spanish flagship.'

'And everything on the flagship originated at Copán?'

He nodded.

'Where the Maya stelae were hidden?' she asked.

'Yes.'

'Then, by comparison to this, all your ill-gained lucre is worthless.'

She went to the rail, staring across the channel's calm waters. Henrikson joined her, offering a fat cigar.

'That stela is going to rewrite history.'

'Appears your theory is in fact…' he lit her cigar. '…fact.'

She turned to stare at the stela again. Balthasar Toule's death symbol stared back. 'Expect the resurrection of the dead.'

She began to chuckle. Henrikson joined in. A few more puffs from their cigars and the both of them burst out laughing. Throwing her arms around him, she gave him a big kiss.

'The old boys at St Dunstan's can *kush meyn tokhes!*' she joyfully hollered into the schooner's masts.

Henrikson choked on his cigar smoke. 'Something still confuzzles me about the wreck, though. Hardly important now.'

'Tell me,' she replied, her laughter dying away. 'Everything's important.'

'I've located fittings for twenty nine of Griffin's cannon. However, I can account for only twenty eight.'

He walked towards a mound of dripping seaweed piled on Adel's quarterdeck. Peeling away a handful of malodorous mess, he revealed a cannon breech and pointed out a crown stamped into it.

'This comes from the very best foundry in England. Made from brass. Only Griffin would have cannon of this quality.'

'How many did you say Griffin had?'

'Twenty nine.'

'One's missing?'

'Just one,' he replied, watching her throw her cigar into the sea. 'Hey, you just tossed a very fine Havana overboard.'

Elle didn't care. Her confidence was giving her a strength she'd not felt for a while.

'I know where your missing cannon is.'

❖ ❖ ❖

The Papillon puppy's tail thumped against the floor as Elle approached. Crouching down, she scratched his long snout as he raised his head to her. Dougie Beedham, who'd been sleeping in his chair in the hotel courtyard, languidly opened his eyes to the darkness.

'What's all this then?'

'Morning, Dougie,' said Henrikson, chewing on the remnants of his Havana. 'Excuse us calling at such an ungodly hour.'

'Skip?'

Rubbing the sleep from his eyes, he squinted at the crewmen standing behind Henrikson. 'What hour is it?'

'Gone two in the morning,' said Elle.

'Crikey.'

Beedham struggled to gain his feet. 'Can't have any rooms. We're packed out.'

'We don't want rooms.'

'Lord, don't tell me I owe you money?'

'We've come for your old cannon.'

'Old cannon?'

'It's over there.' Elle pointed to a moss-covered cannon buried end-up in the garden, a young hibiscus blooming from its muzzle.

'It's just old rubbish,' replied Beedham, waving a hand vaguely in the direction of the sea. 'A fisherman brought it up in his net.'

Henrikson scraped moss away from the barrel with his pocket shiv.

'Brass,' he said. 'Foundry stamp will be at the other end.' Turning to his crew, he instructed them to dig it up.

'Eh, you can't pull up my cannon. You'll kill the hibiscus.'

Removing a coin from his trouser pocket, Henrikson flicked it to him. 'That ought to cover both.'

'Probably a new hotel as well,' added Elle.

'What's this?' Beedham held the coin up to the reception counter's light.

'An eight-escudo coin,' said Henrikson. 'Gold.'

'Try not to kill the plant,' Beedham crowed, rubbing the coin with his thumb.

Spades in hand, the crewmen dug out the cannon. After a few good tugs, it slipped its sandy grasp.

'British cannonade,' Henrikson noted, pointing out the tell-tale foundry crown.

'Morgan's?' Elle asked.

'What's that you say?' Beedham was awake and interested now. 'You sayin' it's Captain Morgan's cannon?'

Grasping the base of the red hibiscus, Elle gave it a tug. It came out in a spray of flying earth.

'It's just an old cannon, Mr Beedham,' she said, handing him the plant.

'Hang on — you said Morgan.'

'Who did?' Henrikson winked at Elle.

'She did. The doctor.'

'Nonsense. Don't pay her no never mind.'

'You cheeky beggar. Trying to trick me with a gold coin. Have it back.'

'That coin's worth about thirty-nine thousand,' Henrikson said.

'Lempira?'

'Bucks.'

'You can have the cannon,' replied Beedham, tucking the gold coin deep into his trouser pocket. 'I'll toss in the hibiscus too.'

Taking the plant from his hands, Elle dropped it in the hole where the cannon had rested. 'Where do the chambermaids wash up the linen?' she asked, as the four crewmen heaved the cannon onto their shoulders.

'Behind the ablutions shed,' replied Beedham. 'You don't want to go there at this hour, though.'

Struggling with its weight, the crew took the cannon around the side of the hotel to a covered outbuilding. An old wash table and a spigot stood under the cover of its tin roof. Beedham pulled a string hanging over the table, and an exposed light bulb began to hum as its filament warmed.

Elle understood immediately why Beedham warned them away from the ablutions shed. Attracted by the light, giant blue damselflies dive-bombed them. Like dragonflies, they were really quite harmless, but their incessant buzzing was hard to ignore.

Watching as Henrikson's lads took chisel and hammer to the cannon now lying on the table, Elle turned to Beedham, touching his arm gently.

'Mr Beedham, I want to tell you something.'

'Gonna admit you said it was Morgan's cannon are you?'

'What? No. Never mind that. The photograph amongst your Titanic collection.'

'What of it?'

'The one of you with another chap. He was your friend, wasn't he?' she asked.

He nodded. 'Podgy Higginbotham.'

'He didn't die alone.'

'How do you mean?' he asked, clearly confused.

'I saw him.' She nodded. 'Rather roly-poly. Wore spectacles, thick ones with round lenses.'

'He did, yeah.'

'Kept a ring of keys on a chain clipped to his belt. I remember that because they jingled.'

'He was a stores-keeper,' replied Beedham. 'Always carrying a great ring of keys with him, he was. Always a moan about the slog up and down Scotland Road from the aft holds to the bow.'

He stopped and glared at her more closely.

'But how did *you* know him?'

'I told you. I saw him.'

'Where?' asked Beedham, his eyes brightening as she had not seen them before.

She couldn't bring herself to now break his spirit by telling him how she found his best friend eviscerated.

'He saved a lot of the passengers, your friend. He could have gotten away. He was already in a lifeboat — I saw him. He offered up his seat to several ladies.' She polished his memory further by adding, 'One of them had a baby.'

'He must have saved a great many passengers. Took up half a lifeboat, old Podgy did,' replied Beedham, sadness hushing his laugh. 'Podgy Higginbotham was not an important man. But he lived.'

Elle smiled. Taking his hand in hers, she gave it a comforting squeeze.

'It gives me solace knowing someone remembers him.'

'Where'd you get the cannon from, Dougie?' Henrikson interrupted.

Beedham turned to Henrikson, and after a small sniffle replied, 'I told you, fisherman brought it up in his net.'

'Yes, but where?'

'In the channel. Between Roatán and here.'

'This *is* our missing cannon,' confirmed Henrikson, examining the gun's breech.

'That's odd.' Elle moved towards the cannon for a look. 'Breech knob is sealed with iron slag.' Looking over the cannon's length, she added, 'How long would you say it is?'

'Bog standard seven-foot cannonade.'

Elle spied a broom leaning against the wall of the ablutions shed.

'Fetch me that, will you?' she asked one of the crewmen.

'Why?'

'Something I read when I was kid. Probably nothing.'

Taking the broom handle from the crewman, she poked it into the muzzle. With a bit of jiggling she punched the handle through the soil blocking up the barrel. It struck upon something with a thud. She looked up to Henrikson.

'If this is a seven-foot cannonade, why is the broom handle hitting bottom at only three?'

'Plugged with sediment, I expect,' said Beedham. 'It sat at the bottom of the sea for centuries.'

'Maybe,' she replied. Lifting a pry bar from the wash table, she whacked the slag bead a few times, cracking off a fragment.

'You think you're gonna find doubloons in there,' tut-tutted, Beedham. 'You think I didn't look down the barrel before I put a plant in it?'

'The knob end is sealed.'

Breaking away enough slag, she turned the pry bar around and, jamming the curved chisel under the slag bead, forced the bar down and wrenched off the knob.

'In a pinch, pirates sometimes sealed their most prized possessions in cannon and tossed them overboard, hoping they remained airtight,' said Elle.

'Where did you read that nonsense?' asked Henrikson.

'I was just a kid. I think it was a highly literary penny serial called *The Adventures of Bluebeard*.'

The knob end fell to the ground with a clang, muddy water pouring from inside the cannon's breech.

'So much for airtight.'

Undefeated, she crouched down and peered inside.

'What do you see?' Henrikson's thick moustache was twitching.

'Mud,' she replied, reaching in. Her hand rummaged around before striking upon something solid. Slowly withdrawing it, she held onto a thick glob of mud.

'What is it?' asked Henrikson.

With her hand now under the spigot, the water washed away centuries of mud and silt, revealing a small, intricately engraved gold box.

'Spanish,' she said, passing it to Henrikson.

'Valuable?' asked Beedham.

'Let's see.'

Cracking the lid revealed a huge diamond set in gold filigree.

Henrikson chuckled. 'Enough for a queen.'

'You crafty geezer,' said Beedham, trying to thrust the escudo back into Henrikson's palm.

'Take your coin back. I want my cannon.'

Elle had already retrieved another mud-covered artefact from inside, and was washing it under the spigot. A golden necklace covered in dense box glyphs was revealed.

'*That's* not Spanish,' choked out Henrikson.

'Most definitely Mayan,' she replied with a wink, her hand now back in the cannon and stumbling upon something substantial. She gave it a tug, but it held fast. Using the pull of both hands she was able to shift it, the mud's suction releasing it with a rude noise.

Everyone fell silent. Even covered with mud, it was plain to see what it was.

'Ain't that the bee's knees,' Henrikson was the first to mutter as she passed it to him. He held it under the stream of water. From under the mud emerged a prosthetic arm formed from gold.

Elle washed her hands and took a closer look at the arm. Around its wrist was a solid gold bracelet covered in box glyphs.

'Pilfered, from an armless Mayan royal, no doubt.'

While the others crowded around the wash table for a good look, she returned to the cannon breech, her hand pushing through the sludge, fingers finding something more. It slipped through her hands. Managing to get hold of it, she carefully pulled out an old bundle of leather, blackened and slimy from centuries underwater.

As she held it under the running water, the leather dissolved, revealing a gold phylactery bejewelled in jade and emerald. Popping open the oyster case, she stared in awe at what lay within.

'Now, that's the bee's knees.'

❖ ❖ ❖

A friendly game of poker. Skipper, Beedham, Gunny Schadowski and Elle. The celebration had started out over a bottle of rum, and by five in the morning, empty bottles rolled the length of the bar. Despite losing hand after hand, Henrikson remained in high spirits, using gold escudo coins as chips. Beedham and Gunny had already taken a small fortune off him, but there was no chance he'd run out.

Elle left the game early doors, propping the bar up, head muddled.

An idea had come to her. Fiddling with the phylactery, she popped open the oyster case, and removed the hand-blown, glass vial within, which was held in place by the finest of metal prongs. Without realising it, she must have wondered out loud what it was she could see rolling lazily around within the emerald-tinted glass because at that instant Henrikson launched up from the poker table, shouting for her to leave it be before swatting it away. The vial ricocheted off her cheek, its filigree cap drawing blood, before pinging across the bar counter and bouncing around the legs of her stool.

Smitten and drunk, Gunny took it upon himself to defend her honour, unholstering his .45 pistol and shoving it in Henrikson's face.

'Holster your weapon, for Chrissake!' Elle shouted, knocking aside Gunny's .45.

'Skipper hit you?'

'No, he just knocked this out my hand,' she replied, recovering the vial from the bar floor. 'It bounced off my cheek.'

Cooler heads prevailed.

'What did you say, Skipper?' she asked, as Gunny tucked his pistol away, mumbling some sort of apology.

'I said don't open it.'

'After that. What was it you said *after* that?'

'Was that before or after Schadowski shoved his mohaska in my face?'

'Before,' she and Gunny said as one.

'I said, it's *cwicseolfor*.'

Lifting the vial from the floor, she watched the aubergine-coloured globs inside rolling lazily from end to end. 'Quicksilver,' she said with a nod before securing the vial to the metal clips within the phylactery.

Silently, she stared at the now-familiar apothegm inscribed around the periphery of the oyster case. There could be no doubt of its connection to Balthasar Toule.

'*Expecto resurrectionem mortuorum*,' she said, so quietly that the others didn't hear.

'The hell is that?' asked Gunny.

'*Cwicseolfor*,' Henrikson repeated. 'It's what buccaneers called it, anyway.'

'Quicksilver,' said Beedham.

'*Lichtmetal*.' Elle stared at the globs again, captivated. 'Herr Frisch called it.'

'Hell's he got to do with it?' asked Henrikson.

'What the hell is *Lichtmetal*?'

'Mercury,' she told Gunny. 'In German.'

'Why would anyone in their right mind carry a vial of mercury?' Gunny asked, his face exhibiting confusion.

'It had importance to someone,' Henrikson replied, removing a handkerchief from his pocket and pressing it to Elle's bleeding cheek. 'The amulet containing it is of considerable value.'

Elle agreed. 'Important enough to seal it in a cannon's breech and chuck it overboard, hoping to recover it later.'

'But why would anyone wanna wear poisonous mercury round their neck?' asked Gunny again.

She turned to him. 'Say again?'

'Why would anyone wear a vial of mercury?' he repeated.

'You said poisonous.'

'Did I?'

'You did,' said Beedham, counting up his escudos, calling it a night.

'Shit,' said Gunny. 'I've forgotten what I'm forgetting.'

'Poison.'

Working her thoughts backwards, Elle thumped herself in the head with her closed hand. 'God, aren't *I* the fool?' She looked around the room at all of them. '*Venenum.*'

'Venom?' asked Henrikson.

'Yes.'

The cogs in her head now spinning madly, she turned to the shuttered French doors, spears of dusty moonlight seeping through the slats. Throwing them open, she let in the early morning breeze. Adel's mast light winked at her from offshore. She could just make out the glow of cigarette cherries on deck. Gunny's marines. Heavily armed. Just in case Herr Frisch's Huns got clever.

She inhaled deeply. It would be dawn in another hour, and the air was cool and sweet.

'Dose of poison,' she said, recollecting her conversation with Dr Mauss. She raised the phylactery she held in her hand, staring at it. '*Dosis.*'

She turned to the others, holding the amulet for all to see. They all looked at her with differing levels of confusion. 'It's Latin. For gift.' She laughed. 'Is it so simple?'

Henrikson shrugged.

'The Gift,' she continued. The vial contained poison for killing Siobhan. Going back to the bar counter, she had a sudden urge to get inelegantly shit-faced. She poured herself a glass of whatever was open. Port, by the legs of it. Raising the glass to the air, she said, 'To Dr Mauss. Genius.'

❖ ❖ ❖

Elle stood on the beach, waiting for the launch to take her to Adel. In the days since Henrikson cracked Griffin's hold, he had brought to the surface a haul too vast even for the schooner. Another visit would be required to recover the rest. Of more significance though, were the stelae. All nine had been recovered. A new chapter in history was about to be written. How it would fit in with her own theory was as yet unknown.

'You're off then?'

She turned. Dougie Beedham stood on the beach verge in his pyjamas.

'Morning, Mr. Beedham' she greeted. 'It's time I got back to my students.'

'Job's not done,' he said.

'It's a new day.' Looking to Adel, she saw the first hints of daylight unfolding behind the ship's masts. 'I'm a hired hand. My part in this adventure is over.'

'*All the world's a stage, and all the men and woman merely players: they have their exits and their entrances.*'

'Apropos,' she replied.

'*One man in his time plays many parts.*' He produced a black, leather-bound book from under his arm, offering it to her.

'My gift to you.'

Taking the book, she squinted in the pre-dawn to make out the gold lettering embossed on it: *US Commerce Committee Investigation into RMS Titanic*.

'Where did you get this?' she asked, immediately leafing through the pages.

'I was called to give testimony before a senate sub-committee in Washington D.C.'

He looked to Adel as the darkness fled.

'If I wanted to know something about a passenger,' he continued. 'I wouldn't go looking in his cabin.'

'Where, then?'

'Why in his baggage, of course.'

'Which is now, somewhat inconveniently, at the bottom of the North Atlantic.'

He shook his head.

'White Star kept meticulous records of every passenger's baggage. Both those delivered to staterooms, and those in cargo holds.'

She looked up at him from the ledger.

'Titanic's cargo manifest is itemised in its entirety. If Balthasar Toule had baggage or cargo, you'll find it in those pages.'

Elle closed the ledger slowly, stroking the cover almost intimately. 'I don't know how to thank you.'

'Just think of my friend Podgy now and again, as I do.'

'I shall.' She stepped towards him, planting a kiss on his cheek. 'I'll remember you too.'

'Ahoy!' Henrikson waved from the approaching launch. 'We've a good blow. Time to make sail.'

'Off you go,' said Beedham. 'My regards to Corky O'Shea and your pop.'

'I'll tell them.'

'Then there's nothing more to say. Farewell, Eleanor.'

She waded away through the beach break as the launch drifted towards her. Handing Henrikson the ledger, she climbed in as the boat turned around, and they started making for Adel.

'All right?' he asked.

She nodded, looking over her shoulder at Dougie Beedham standing on the beach. He waved. She waved back.

'Let's go home.'

- St. Dunstan's Prep. -
Bloomfield Hills, Michigan
Campus Map 1929.
ST DUNSTAN'S PREP
OMNIA
ITER ENIM
St Dunstan's Girls Upper School
Science Museum
Summer Cabin
INSTITUTE WAY
FACULTY WAY
Lake Jonah
Jonah and The Whale Fountain
St Dunstan's Lake
The Boathouse
Annenberg Estate
Brookside Lower School
ST DUNSTANS ROAD
Christ Church St. Dunstan's
LONE PINE ROAD
Greek Theatre and Annenberg Swimming Pool
St Dunstan's Theatre
St Dunstan's Art Museum
Triton Pools
ACADEMY WAY
Academic Hall (Elle's Office)
Peacock Gate
Thompson Oval
Elle's Bungalow
My Office
St Dunstan's Quad 1929

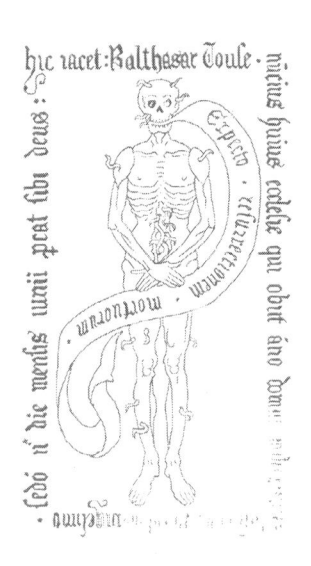

27 April 1929.

St Dunstan's Prep, Bloomfield Hills, Michigan

It had not yet begun raining when she alighted the Royal Palm streamliner from Miami, but the darkening skies were ominous. Transferring to the Interurban, she watched cracks of lightning arc in the angry skies, as the electric trolley crept north along Woodward Avenue.

At Bloomfield Centre station, one of St Dunstan's Ford Depot hacks waited for her. Piling her wardrobe trunks into the back seats, the driver dropped her at St Dunstan's Peacock Gate before carrying on to the main house with her trunks.

A choir of birdsong from the greening trees along Lone Pine Road welcomed her.

'Hope springs eternal,' Elle called back to the blue jays. No sooner did she close the wrought iron pedestrian gate, with its impressive peacock adorning the crown, than she felt the first spits of rain.

As she slung her bag over her shoulder, the escudos inside shifted with a clink. Passing the dining hall, she continued through the open cloister that was the heart of St Dunstan's, flowerbeds overflowing with spring daffodil blooms and forsythia. Water poured into a travertine basin in the quad's fountain, its gentle burping sound reminding her of the waves breaking on Utila's beaches.

The memory was short lived. The sky opened up and she made a dash for St Dunstan's academic building, pushing open the heavy door. She turned to pan the quad; she couldn't say why, but ever since leaving Adel, she felt as though was being watched. She didn't spot any threats now, only a lone student scurrying towards the dormitories, his shirt sleeves rolled back, optimistic for milder days.

Nothing much seemed to change in her absence. Although she was gone only a month, teaching seemed a lifetime ago.

Closing the lobby door behind her, she saw Charlie Burkhammer leaning over the reception counter, chatting up a female classmate volunteering at the school's switchboard. Elle couldn't hear the conversation, nor did she mind it, but by the look on the girl's face, it was clear she wanted Charlie to buzz off.

A fire in the north wall of the oak-panelled lobby crackled. Setting her bag down, Elle took off her coat and gave it a shake. Drops of rainwater sizzled as they landed in the flames. A clap of thunder caused the lobby's leaded windows to shake, raising Charlie's attention.

'Hey, Dr Annenberg. Welcome back.' He ambled across to her, all knees, elbows and ears, a dishearteningly thick pile of papers under his arm. 'Nice tan.'

'I'm guessing you received my Western Union from Miami?'

'Hattie sent word of your telegram,' he said, leaving the stack of papers on a side table. 'You've been gone nearly a month. We were about to send a rescue party looking for you. But by the look of your tan, I guess you didn't need rescuing.'

'I wasn't able to get a message out of Honduras.'

'Honduras? I thought you—'

'Long story,' she cut in, sitting on a sofa by the fire to unlace her patent leather daises, leaving them out to dry. Then she took a pair of white plimsolls from her bag, shaking out Honduran sand before pulling them over her bare feet.

'Three days ago, I was soaking up the sun.' A flash of lightning lit the room, followed by a not-so-distant crash of thunder. 'I see the weather has improved since I left.'

'Expecting a corker of a storm. Looks like it's coming now.'

Rising from the sofa, she pushed her bag into his skinny arms. He dropped it immediately.

'Golly. What you got in here, gold bars?'

'Gold coins, actually.'

The switchboard operator, who was clearly half-listening to the conversation, slid the headphone off her ear.

'You're kidding?'

Elle smiled. 'They're escudos. For the science institute.'

'You're *not* kidding,' Charlie said, sweat dotting his upper lip as he hefted the bag into both arms, its contents clinking. 'I could buy out the Dodge Boys with what's in here. I always wanted to be an automobile baron.'

'You're a good kid, Charlie,' she said. 'Don't make me shoot you.'

He laughed.

She didn't.

'Lock 'em in my safe until the science institute can slap together an exhibit.'

Charlie beetled along behind her as she mounted the spiral staircase to the second floor.

'What have I missed in my absence?'

'Well, Headmaster Bowie was pretty furious you ditched classes for almost a month.'

'That boiled owl. What can he do? Ask my father to fire me? That's a laugh.'

'No,' replied Charlie. 'He asked your mother to fire you.'

'Gotta give the headmaster credit,' she said with a smile. 'Mother *would* actually fire me.'

They passed under a sculpture of Diogenes projecting off the second-floor landing. She had walked under it a thousand times over the years without giving it a thought. He stood, lantern in hand, looking for an honest man. She couldn't say why, but in that moment, she thought of Beedham and what he had said to her in parting: 'One man in his time plays many parts.'

'Your Music Academy season tickets arrived.'

'Huh?' she said, jolted back from her reverie.

'I said your Music Academy tickets arrived. Are you all right, Doctor?'

'Yeah,' she said wistfully, a parting glance at Diogenes. 'Just looking for an honest man.'

She looked to Charlie.

'You ever look at something you've seen a thousand times and suddenly, you get it?'

He stared at her blankly.

'Yeah, I'm fine,' she said after an awkward silence. 'Anything else?'

'Oh. Well, the science institute asked for you to return their artefacts you borrowed for your European Ethnology course,' he replied, following her across the hallway.

'What *else*?'

'Your mother called.'

'She wants to fire me?'

'No. She wants you to teach more of the under fifteen-year-olds when fall term begins. The senior professors are too stodgy, in her opinion.'

'I'm Head of Department. How much more senior can she mean?'

'I think she means senior in age, not position.'

Elle stopped, mind still processing the last week's events.

'Of course. Sorry, my mind is still in the tropics. Anything more?'

'I graded all your general ethnology papers,' he said, dropping her bag to the floor, panting to catch his breath. 'I had to stay up all night — *all night* — but they're finished.'

Turning at the door to the ethnology vestibule, she looked at her student assistant. A lick of sweat dripped from his hairline and down the side of his face. She put her hand over his heart.

'How much coffee you drink today?'

'None.'

'Your heart's racing like you drank a pot full.'

'Your bag weighs a tonne.'

Giving his arm a conciliatory buffing as they entered the vestibule, she said with a sigh, 'At least you know what half a million weighs.'

'A half-million dollars?'

Elle nodded.

'Gee whiz.'

Behind a wooden desk sat a frumpish woman, pencils holding her coif in place.

'If either one of you were carrying around a half-million bucks, I'd rob you both and live the rest of my days by a swimming pool in Hollywood drinking rum-runners with Buster Keaton.'

'Hello, Hattie.' Elle gave an apologetic smile. 'I'm so sorry to be returning so last minute.'

'I expected you back weeks ago.'

'*We* expected you,' said Charlie.

'*I* expected you,' repeated Hattie, giving him the daggers.

'You did receive my telegram?'

'Two days ago.'

'Charlie, put my bag on Hattie's desk, will you?'

Hefting the Gladstone onto her desk, Charlie caught his breath as Elle removed the gold coins and stacked them into piles.

'I've been a little busy.'

Hattie stood, mouth agape. 'I should say you have.'

'Each coin's worth roughly thirty-nine grand.'

She could see Charlie doing the maths in his head.

'Lock them in my safe, Charlie.'

She turned to Hattie. 'Could you please put a call in to the conservators at the Science Institute?'

Looking up from the gold coins, Hattie replied, 'And Brink's.'

'This is just the start. There'll be more to come. Much more. We're going to have an exhibit any museum in America would be envious of.'

Between the three of them, they transferred the coins from Hattie's desk to Elle's office in one go. After locking the safe, inconspicuously set in the wall behind a shelf, Elle stacked textbooks in front of it. A tennis ball in the corner of the shelf rolled towards her. She caught it as it rolled off the edge. It had once been covered in felt, but floating in the North Atlantic, plus the effects of age and her constant squeezing of it during moments of introspection, had worn the fibre nearly bare.

'Anything more I can do for you, Doctor?' Charlie asked, standing in the doorway to the vestibule.

'Don't breathe a word of this,' she said, depositing her empty bag on an old red leather armchair she had taken from her father's den.

'Mum's the word. Promise.'

'Thank you, Charlie. I'd be in dire straits without you.'

She closed her office door, his silhouette peering motionlessly through the smoked-glass windowpane.

'You're welcome,' he said loudly with a sigh, before Elle watched him sulk away.

Drawing back her office curtains, she unlatched the window, lit a cigarette and watched the clouds boiling outside, flashes of lightning still cracking, lighting up the quad. Blowing her cigarette smoke outside, she turned to lean against the windowsill and tossed the old tennis ball into the air, caught it, then took stock of her office.

Books and papers were crammed into every available nook, untouched since she left. She wasn't disorganised; a little chaos helped her thought process. In that particular moment, her thoughts were on how hugely suffocating academic life was.

The intercom on her desk buzzed. 'It's five o'clock, Dr Annenberg.'

Elle looked to the clock high up on the wall. So it was. Putting the tennis ball back on the shelf beside the safe, she pressed the reception button.

'Go on home, Hattie. Take Charlie with you.'

'He already left,' she replied, and wished Elle a good evening.

Settling into her father's armchair, she opened her bag, removing the ledger Beedham had given her. Leaning back, she kicked off her plimsolls, sheltering her mind from the storms both outside and in her head by reexamining the ledger's contents. Nothing stood out. Not as yet.

❖ ❖ ❖

A clap of thunder woke her. It was dark outside. Rubbing her eyes, she leaned forward, and the ledger fell from her lap. As she stood to retrieve it, a lightning flash drew her attention to the windows.

Someone was there. Watching her through her second-floor window. Startled, she leapt back in the chair. Feet curled up under her, she had to force out her breath and take in a few more before working up the stones to cautiously stand up and approach the window. Rain pelted against the glass. Another flash of lightning lit the quad, causing amorphous shadows to rise and fall from behind trees and fountains. She was spooked. But she couldn't see anyone.

Suddenly, there was a whirl of movement beside the large bronze globe outside the bay windows of the library below. A student? They were known for doing sillier things than larking about in the pouring rain. Her eyes darted to the wall clock. It was one in the morning.

A shock of lightning came down close, followed by a *boom that rattled* the windows. She looked again, searching.

Whoever it was had disappeared.

Forcing caution from her mind, she hurried down the spiral stairs to the lobby, pushing open the door to the quad. It was chucking it down, wind howling through the courts and terraces. *Prudence be damned*, she thought and splashed through puddles on the wide flagstone terrace outside the hall, making her way towards the statue.

Lightning illuminated the quad once more. A clap of thunder rattled her teeth. Turning, she looked towards the archway leading away from the quad's North end. An upright form sank behind a pillar supporting the archway.

She squinted, wiping rainwater from her eyes. It was no student. It was a man.

'Who's there?' she shouted, voice lost to the wind. Another flash of lightning. No figure. Stepping under the arch for protection, the rain momentarily abating, she looked around.

The man was nowhere to be seen. The doors leading into the dormitory and Master's Hall were locked for the night. Instinctively, her eyes dropped to the concrete slab, as they always did when she passed this way. Carved into stone were the words "*Gateway of Friendship*". Then she saw them. On the dry slab: wet footprints.

Someone had crossed through a puddle and stood right here, before turning to make their exit from the quad.

A student would know better than to stand on the slab. It was tradition to avoid it. Upperclassmen took delight in punishing plebs who made such a mistake.

Cracks of lightning flashed through the tree-line beyond, revealing a figure running away. Elle hadn't bothered to put her shoes on before dashing out of her office, and she realised then a pursuit through blinding rain wasn't a wise idea. She shouted for him to stop, but he disappeared behind a fountain.

Shoes or no, her need to know if it was *he* who was watching her, overwhelmed her usually common sense. Running after him, she paused where Academy and Institute Way met. Prudence was needed, but curiosity and determination won out. She reached the fountain, only to find the man had already gone. Behind it, down a steep embankment, was Lake Jonah — really a concrete-lined pond shaped like a whale. Beyond it was nothing but dense forest, criss-crossed by trails. There was no earthly reason anyone would be there at such an hour.

Yet more lightning. At the foot of the tree-line across Lake Jonah she saw him, rain cape warding off the downpour. Bowler hat. Small, round spectacles over a gaunt face. Air of abstruseness.

Her voice echoed across the water and into the trees as she yelled, 'Crimen!'

He stared at her, unmoving, before shouting back, as the thunder rolled away, '*Expecto resurrectionem mortuorum.*'

A frisson of terror stabbed her. Turning, her bare feet slipping on the wet grass, she toppled down the embankment, rolling across a narrow grass verge before sliding down the concrete edge of the lake.

Suddenly, she was underwater. Cold, black, submerged, back in Titanic's flooding hold, the watertight door forced open by a sudden blast of seawater. Then she saw him. Balthasar's adjutant. Bowler hat, round wire-rimmed spectacles, sawn off shotgun in hand.

Surfacing, she twisted around to face the tree-line. He was gone. Swimming desperately to the edge of the lake, her bare feet tried to find purchase on the sloping, concrete sides. Twice she fell back into the water before dragging herself out on all fours to the grass verge.

Gaining her feet, head reeling from the onset of hypothermia, she forced her legs to carry her to the foot of the tall trees where she had seen him. Lightning revealed the entire length of the tree line. She was alone.

For a moment, she considered running blindly into the forest, hoping to pick up a trail in the darkness. But she needed to get out of the rain and dry off before she collapsed.

If the air got any colder, she could be dead by morning.

❖ ❖ ❖

Elle walked across the lobby, shivering. It was just as she put her foot on the stairs to her office she saw them on the limestone steps: wet shoe prints. Two sets.

Silently, she continued up the stairs, stopping abruptly when she heard a hollow thumping sound. From around the curve of the spiral bounced a little ball. She caught it. A tennis ball, with *RF Downey & Co* pressed into the worn felt. *Her* tennis ball. How had it come to find its way down the stairs?

At the second-floor landing, she quietly tried to open a fireman's provision box on the wall, her shaking hands causing the glass pane in the door to rattle. Retrieving the axe from inside, her attention was drawn along the landing, lightning streaks through the tall windows on the east wall revealing the door into the ethnology vestibule.

It was open.

She couldn't remember if she had closed it earlier. Gripping the axe handle tightly in her shaking hands, she tiptoed along the hallway, peeking carefully around the door-frame. In the darkness she saw Hattie's desk, askew. Reaching into the vestibule, her hand fell upon the light switch.

It clicked. Nothing happened. She tried again. Still nothing. Electricity was out.

Entering the room, she approached her office door. It was slightly ajar, the lockset bouncing gently against the frame.

Someone was in her office.

With the head of the axe she gently pushed the door. The windows were open, the wind causing her door to shudder.

A chaotic sight greeted her: the whole office tossed, the door to her safe ripped away and left lying beside her opened Gladstone on the floor. Taking a few cautious steps in, she tripped over her typewriter, which lay where it had been thrown.

As her hands broke her fall, she dropped the axe. It hit the typewriter's return arm, a *ding* breaking the silence.

Struggling to gain her feet, a hand tapped her shoulder. She shrieked.

'What on Earth is going on in here, Eleanor?'

Her father stood behind her in his pyjamas, umbrella in one hand and electric torch in the other.

'Father,' she gasped, relief flooding her. 'What are you doing here?'

'I was worried,' he replied. 'Mother and I expected you home yesterday. I was up at silly o'clock for a cigar and noticed you hadn't yet come in.'

'I fell asleep,' she replied. 'In the armchair from your office.'

'Always did like that chair,' he mumbled. 'Why are you all wet?'

'I saw someone out on the quad. I went to investigate.'

He looked around her ransacked office.

'Didn't we teach you to pick up after yourself? Here, sit down. You've had a bad dream, is all.'

'Father, I've been burgled,' she replied, shivering.

Taking her by the shoulder, her father stood the footed, brass lamp cock-eyed against the armchair before sitting her down in it. He went to the small water closet off her office and retrieved a towel for her to dry her hair with. Finding a woollen blanket amid the debris, he wrapped it around her before going to her bookcase, righting a fallen bottle of rye, normally hidden behind a stack of ungraded student papers, and poured a sniff into a pair of crystal tumblers.

'Here,' he said handing her a glass. 'Take a belt.'

'Thanks.' She took the glass tumbler in her shaking hands and knocked the liquid back, the rye's burn warming her.

Putting back his own drink, her father choked.

'Where did you get this coffin varnish from?'

'Where do we get any of our booze? Canada, of course.'

'It's not bad.' He put his glass down and went to the telephone on her desk. Lifting the receiver, he tapped the cradle several times. 'Lines are down. Was anything taken?'

'I don't know.'

Shining his torch around the room, the beam settled on the open safe.

'Anything valuable in there?' he asked

She nodded, looking inside. The escudos remained.

'Where have all those gold coins come from?'

'Services rendered. I assisted in the recovery of quite a treasure trove.'

'Looks like it. I had no idea St Dunstan's was participating in any expeditions just now. How much…'

'Gratis. In fact, St Dunstan's made a profit.' Before he could question her as to how, she said, 'I made a deal.'

'What kind of deal?'

'You know…a deal, deal. The science institute will be the first museum to display nine Mayan stelae recovered from the ocean floor.' Rubbing her hair over with the towel, she wrapped it around her shoulders.

'Those coins you're looking at are worth a half-million bucks.'

He turned back to the safe, whistling.

'Hang on. Someone goes to the trouble of prying off the door to your safe then doesn't make off with gold coins worth a half-million dollars?'

Contemplating this, she leaned over, lifted her bag from the floor and looked inside again.

'Unless they were looking for something more valuable to them.' Checking the interior pocket where she left Balthasar's talisman she'd kept since Titanic, she realised immediately. 'Shit. It's gone.'

'What is?'

'The talisman I've worn about my neck the past seventeen years.'

'It wasn't around your neck?'

Instinctively, she raised a hand to her chest, feeling the phylactery replacing it on the gold chain. 'I haven't worn it since Honduras.'

'You were in *Honduras*?'

'Long story, Father.'

She nearly leapt for the chair as the power kicked back on and the lamp suddenly flooded her office in soft light.

Opening her soaked shirt collar, she tugged on the chain around her neck, retrieving the small, oyster-cased amulet she had taken from the cannon. Had they been watching her all along?

On his way to try the telephone again, her father picked something up and put it on her desk. Her tennis ball. It rolled, and he caught it just as it fell off the end, offering it to her.

'Where did you find that?' she asked.

'It was right there, on the floor. It's yours.'

She rolled it around with her fingers. *RF Downey & Co*. It *was* hers.

Reaching into her pocket, she pulled out the one she'd caught bouncing down the stairs. 'So is this.'

They were identical. But she had saved only the one from Titanic.

Arms akimbo, her father asked, 'Eleanor, are you in some sort of trouble?'

Gripping the tennis balls from Titanic's hold, she looked out of the window, the lightning strikes distant now, the storm moving off. Through the parting clouds, she saw the whole of the moon.

'I think I am,' she replied, remembering what the phantom had proclaimed before vanishing into the forest behind Lake Jonah. 'Seems the dead have been resurrected.'

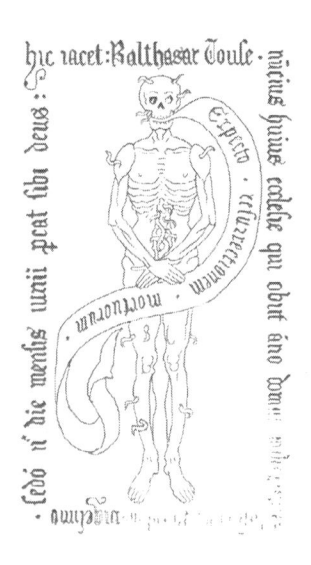

14 April 1912.

RMS Titanic, The North Atlantic

Mahmoud Hajian heard rivets popping an instant before a churning wall of water slammed him against the bulkhead separating No. 1 Hold from No. 2 Hold. Although he had managed the odd graceless crawl when splashing about off Folkestone's shingle beach, he'd never quite learnt to swim. There hadn't been much need for it in Persia.

His shotgun had been trained on the Sentinel while Balthasar impaled it with a spike when the foolish girl interrupted them. He hardly had a moment to wonder how she got there before the hold's hull plates fractured, his double barrelled Winchester taken by the icy cauldron. More bothersome though, was the loss of his bowler. It took months to fit it properly to his head, and there was no telling when he'd return to Turnbull & Asser for another. Pulled under by his heavy greatcoat, Mahmoud's lungs filled with seawater as he inhaled, the heaviness in his chest causing him momentary panic. Expelling the water, he inhaled again, lungs refilling. As odd a feeling as it was, he calmed himself. He had never drowned before — nor was he about to start now.

Striking a solid object, his eyes flashed open. Lights encased under glass still burned along a catwalk. Grabbing its rail, his body twirled in the maelstrom as mutilated corpses bumped him and were sucked away, their intestines trailing behind like a Portuguese man-o-war's tentacles. The Crimen had turned Titanic's forward hold into their abattoir.

None of them expected an iceberg.

Through stinging saltwater, Mahmoud glimpsed movement ahead. Abloom in the flooding, a faded pink gown offered a glimpse of perfection underneath.

The banshee Siobhan.

Flawless pale skin and long, lean muscled legs he could just imagine wrapped around Balthasar as he penetrated her. If the Persian were so inclined, he could fancy her carnal embrace. But he had no taste for what she had on offer.

She snarled, a submerged, primal howl muffled by the flooding and buckling bulkheads. She had consumed and was now whole. Given a chance, the wicked seraph would rip him to pieces, but in the cold chaos she was as helpless as he, and in the next instant was sucked through the hatch to No. 2 Hold and the rest of the ship.

The lights winked before Mahmoud was left in darkness. Grasping tightly to the handrail, the flooding unexpectedly changed direction, ensnaring him in some sort of netting. He knew how to reach deck via a Third-Class entrance, twists and turns through escape ladders, companionways and accommodation staircases under the forecastle head. But flooded and in total darkness, it would be impossible to muddle his way out. Before he could consider his next action, he found himself beginning to float.

The netting. A cargo net used for lowering stores from Titanic's deck to the hold; it was fringed with cork. Snared as he now was by the netting, he relaxed his grip on the rail, permitting the churning seawater to take him. He swirled and bumped against objects in the darkness, some solid, others malleable — the latter, surely corpses.

His ears popped. He was ascending rapidly and must have been forced into the cargo access shaft leading to the well deck. Far above, he picked out hints of light amidst churning water. No. 1 hatch had gone, probably blown off by back-pressure as the flooding forced the air from the hold. In another moment, he was purged from the ship's innards.

Bursting through the surface, expelling seawater from his lungs, he gasped for air at last. All around, the sea regurgitated crates and wardrobe trunks from the hold. He decided to remain attached to the net as the cork balls were keeping him afloat. Trunks, airtight and buoyant, became entangled in it as the escaping water from the cargo hatch thrust him against the ship's forward mast.

Shouts for mercy were drowned out by the deafening shriek of steam shooting from the foremost funnel as boilers blew off.

Although there were hundreds of passengers on deck, all the lifeboat ropes and blocks hung empty. Desperate passengers leapt from deck, reaching out to take hold of the ropes, like proverbial rats abandoning the doomed ship. Some slid down the ropes to the sea; others lost their grip, spinning helplessly into the water. Hopeless as it might be, abandoning Titanic was a wiser choice than hanging about waiting to be sucked down with the ship when she made her death plunge.

Silhouetted by one of the ship's enormous buff funnels, a man leapt confidently into a fall, slid down the rope and dropped elegantly into the sea, before swimming away from the ship. Mahmoud kicked his legs, disentangling his netting from the mast, already feeling the ship beginning to pull him down with it.

There were others alive in the water, kept afloat by their lifebelts.

'Spare me,' a small voice called to him in anguish. He turned. A woman, tangled wet hair over her face, flailed in the bitterly cold sea.

He grasped her lifebelt. 'I have you.'

Lifting her trembling arms one at a time, he rested them on his flotsam raft.

'Cold…taken the life…outta me,' she managed through chattering teeth.

'I know, darling,' he said with pity. 'Can you climb up onto the wardrobes? You'll be out of the water.'

'I can get air in ma lungs…just.'

She was Scottish. Not working class, nor a lady of high breeding, and she was neither young nor a grandmother. Already the cold had rendered her helpless and, like Titanic, she was doomed. Lowering his own stiffening arm underwater, he lifted her like a bear hauling salmon from a rushing river. Dropping her atop the crates caused them to sink momentarily, before they bobbed to the surface again. As the raft stabilised, she was just able to take hold of the rope netting.

'Bless you, sir. Bless you,' she whispered, face inches from his, her frosted breath clouding his spectacles.

'You'll be all right,' he said reassuringly, but as he took hold of her hand he felt her life ebb away.

Brushing her hair away from her face, he watched her grasp for the little bit of life she had left. But she could not hold on.

'Bless,' she repeated, voice a gentle rattle, before she went still.

'Death strikes when fate ordains,' he said, watching her eyes empty.

Already, she saw beyond the edge of mortal vision.

'I envy you. For you have arrived to a Paradise I shan't ever see.'

'Oi.'

Neck stiff, Mahmoud slowly turned to see Balthasar stroking towards him.

'All right, me old china?' he asked, oblivious to the misery all around him.

Swimming to the Persian's jumble of floating debris, Balthasar took hold of the netting, nose and ears bright red from the bitter cold. After a glance at the woman lying atop the crates, he gave her a poke.

'Don't do that,' snapped Mahmoud.

'She's on her way out,' Balthasar said, face wooden, voice devoid of anything at all.

'Let her be a little while.'

Balthasar looked back at him without response. Manoeuvring around the corpse until he was beside Mahmoud, he asked, 'However did you escape the hold?'

'Got belched out No. 1 Hatch,' he replied, his hand still tightly held the dead woman's hand. 'Where have *you* come from?'

'I bumped into our uninvited guest.'

'What, that silly girl?'

Balthasar nodded. 'Carried her up to Scotland Road. Strange as it might sound, I couldn't leave her to drown.'

Titanic groaned. Turning their gaze to the ship, they watched its stern raise entirely out of the sea.

'As opposed to her drowning when the ship sinks?'

Balthasar looked towards the now-distant lifeboats.

'There's hope she's on one of them. Strange, though.'

'What?'

'I half-expected to find terror in her eyes,' Balthasar replied, almost talking to himself. 'But she was having none of it.'

'I saw *her*,' Mahmoud said.

'Suppose she was just being a dopey girl.'

'No.' Clearly, Balthasar hadn't twigged on to what he meant. 'The banshee.'

'Siobhan?'

The Persian nodded.

'Where?'

'When we were swept up in the flooding. She must have been in the hold all along, Buster.'

'Bugger.'

'She's trapped below decks,' Mahmoud said, watching the wounded ship loll lazily from port to starboard.

'Titanic's lost her stability. Won't be long before she plunges.'

'Then the banshee is not going anywhere.'

'You managed, though,' Balthasar countered.

'Just dumb luck,' he replied, raising a hand swollen like a boxing glove. 'My extremities have frozen. Surely it's the same for her?'

'We ought not depend on dumb luck.'

Producing a nip flask from his pocket, Balthasar struggled to open the top, his own hands beginning to freeze. Taking a sip, he passed it across the netting to Mahmoud.

'It can't hurt.'

Mahmoud took a mouthful, his throat warming as brandy went down. A second gulp and he returned it. 'Sentinel?'

'He's done.' Balthasar took another swig. 'I spiked him right good. He'll go to the bottom with the ship.'

Terrific splashes abruptly drew their attention. Those left behind were leaping from the ship. They fell like bombs, six decks to the sea. Mahmoud looked to the distant lifeboats.

'For God's sake, why don't they come back?'

'They don't want to be pulled down by the ship's suction when she goes.'

He watched two men — two of perhaps a thousand left behind — light cigars.

'There ought to have been far more lifeboats.'

'There's one,' said Balthasar, pointing out a collapsible canvas boat being lowered just aft of the bridge.

'That flimsy thing?'

'Better than being in the water. But I don't expect it'll last long on the open sea.'

'Will we?' Mahmoud asked.

Prying a frozen hand from the netting, Balthasar's fingers cracked as he slowly unclenched them.

'We might freeze. But not to death.'

They watched as the two men smoking cigars tossed them aside and leapt into the descending collapsible.

'They're the lucky ones,' Balthasar added.

Turning the raft, he began to kick his feet, moving them away from the doomed ship. Nudging the dead woman's frost-covered body, he told Mahmoud she needed to be put off.

Mahmoud intensely disliked Balthasar's ruthlessness. 'Won't you let her be?'

'She's frozen stiff. We'll be better able to manoeuvre with her off.' Pitiless as the comment might be, it was a hard truth. The poor woman was dead weight, and only served to slow them down. Ashamed of himself for being unable to save her, Mahmoud begrudgingly helped shift the frozen body to the edge of the crates. Balthasar slid her into the water with as much interest as launching a toy boat.

'What a sad, bloody waste,' Mahmoud muttered.

A peculiar whipping sound drew his attention swiftly away. Steel lines securing the forward funnel under tension began snapping one by one, the freed ends whipping across the deck.

One of them whipped through the arm of a nearby cabin steward, slicing it off with surgeon's precision. Knees buckling, the steward collapsed, the encroaching sea swallowing him up.

'Kick!' Balthasar shouted, as the funnel leaned lazily towards them.

With all his might, Mahmoud forced his frozen legs into action, propelling the raft away as the funnel now bore down upon them. As it struck the sea mere feet away, the resulting wave pushed them further from the ship. The next moment an unearthly groan filled the night air as Titanic's back snapped.

'Jesus wept,' Mahmoud cursed, watching unfortunates sucked into the flooding cabins and public rooms. An explosion deep beneath Mahmoud reverberated through him, the bubbling sea growing strangely warm.

'Boilers brewing up,' Balthasar noted, without the slightest alarm. Titanic's stern rose high out of the water, its lights winking once, before plunging the ship into darkness.

'She's had it.'

An enormous air bubble belched from the bow as it disappeared beneath the waves. Small white balls surfaced all around the raft. Scores of them. Reaching out, the Persian took hold of one.

'Tennis balls.'

'A crate of 'em must have broken up.'

It was the stern's turn to plunge now. The shrieks of those remaining until the end filled the night, becoming a single hysterical wail. Abruptly they ceased as the fantail slipped beneath the sea.

Titanic was gone.

Silence.

Then screams from within the haze of coal smoke as hundreds of survivors bobbed to the surface, their cries for mercy dreadful.

Instinctively, Mahmoud kicked towards them — whether to save or watch them perish, he hadn't yet decided.

Balthasar reigned him back, towing the raft away from the survivors. Mahmoud knew there was naught to be done. Amidst the cries, he picked something out. A faint singular cry. Straining his water-logged ears, he heard nothing more of it.

Dearly he hoped he had imagined the banshee howl amidst the screams of the dying.

A man burst through the surface, vomiting up a lung-full of seawater. Even in the darkness, Mahmoud could see he was a gentleman in white tie and a fur-collared greatcoat. Despite Balthasar's frown, Mahmoud took hold of the man's life vest.

'All right then.'

'*Mein Gott,*' the man gasped. '*Mein Gott.*'

'*Alles in Ordnung ist,*' the Persian said the German would be all right now that he had hold of him. '*Ich habe dich.*'

The man pulled his face against the netting like a child to its mother's bosom.

'Is she gone?' he asked.

Mahmoud nodded grimly.

'I was at the stern,' said the German. 'I stayed until the end. The ship took me down with her when she went under.'

'Your life vest saved you.'

The German attempted to pull himself onto the flotsam, but he had not the strength. 'We must get out of the water.'

'There's nowhere to go,' Balthasar pointed out.

'It is freezing,' he said, shaking uncontrollably. 'We will be rendered helpless in minutes.'

Unscrewing the cap of his nip flask, Balthasar offered it to him.

'*Danke,*' said the German, looking to the distant lifeboats. 'They will come for us, ja?'

'We're to fend for ourselves,' Balthasar replied. 'It looks as though they're lying on their oars.'

'*Um Gottes Willen!*' replied the German. 'They are.'

He pointed to a single lifeboat, bow-lamp glowing in the darkness. It was closer than the others, perhaps only a tantalising hundred yards off.

'That boat nearer to us. Let us try for it.'

'We're quite happy here,' replied Balthasar, reserve habitually British.

'*Dann wirst du verschwinden,*' the German replied emphatically.

'Death would be welcomed.' Balthasar smirked at his comment. Mahmoud agreed. Neither of them would die. Not that night, anyway.

'*Wie ist ihr Name?*' Mahmoud asked.

'Erik Frisch.'

'I'm Mahmoud. My colleague is Balthasar.'

'We wish you luck, Herr Frisch.'

The German nodded before saying farewell. Slipping out of his lifebelt and coat, he began to stoke away from them.

Mahmoud watched in silence as Herr Frisch swam towards the nearest lifeboat. To his relief, he reached it and was hauled aboard. God only knew if he would survive the night. He stood a better chance than those remaining in the water. Already, the sea grew quiet. All around floated the dead. Mahmoud paid them no mind. He had long since grown accustomed to their company.

Looking to the diamond-clear sky, he imagined the faint changing hues of the Northern Lights were the shimmering souls of the dead, floating to heaven. The thought of it made him smile. Although he knew there was nothing noble about death, the horror of the night was magnificent.

❖ ❖ ❖

Morning gilded the sky in streaks of orange, along the sea's ridge to the east. Mahmoud followed Balthasar's lead. Kicking their legs, they were able to keep their pile of flotsam following the lifeboats. They weren't hard to follow: every so often a green flare arced into the sky. Although the sea remained relatively calm, they were surrounded by mile upon mile of icebergs.

Mahmoud quietly sang refrains from his favourite Gilbert and Sullivan song to pass the time.

'"*He is an Englishman.*
For he himself has said it.
And it's greatly to his credit.
That he is an Englishman".'

Balthasar repeated the chorus. '*That he is an Englishman.*'

Prying a frost-covered hand from the netting, Mahmoud held it up to Balthasar.

'I'm bloody useless. My limbs have frozen.'

'My feet have swelled so much they've burst the seams in my leathers,' Balthasar replied.

'Buster, let us pack it in and climb on one of those growlers,' he said, pointing out a substantial iceberg nearby. 'At the very least we'll thaw out in the light of day.'

'And look like a couple of wayward polar bears on an ice flow? By Jove, that won't look conspicuous.'

He said nothing. Arguing was pointless.

"For he might have been a Roosian.
A Frenchy, Turk or Proosian,
Or perhaps Italian!
But in spite of all temptations.
To belong to other nations".
"He remains an Englishman," sang Balthasar.

"He remains an Englishman". Mahmoud pried his frozen right hand from the netting. His knuckle joints cracked as he stretched out his frozen fingers.

'I'll never quite think of HMS Pinafore in the same way again.'

'Mahmoud,' Balthasar said with a sudden gleam in his eye. 'I've just realised what's keeping us afloat.'

Through the netting, he showed Mahmoud white lettering, stencilled on the crate: *Alberta Premium Canadian Rye.*

Plunging his fist through a gap, he smashed open the crate and retrieved a bottle from inside.

'Couldn't hurt, could it?' he said and smiled, breaking the seal on the bottle before cracking the top. Taking a long drink, he exhaled with grateful pleasure, 'That's not at all bad.'

Mahmoud swigged from the bottle too, the spirit tingling as it slid down his throat. 'It's quite shit as rye goes. But given our present circumstance, I'll not spit it out.' He drained the bottle and tossed it into the sea. 'Not likely we'll run low on our supply.'

Rummaging around in the crate, Balthasar retrieved another bottle. 'Depends how long we're adrift.'

The rye already made him feel better. 'Quite a night.'

Balthasar nodded, opening another bottle before putting it back. He looked at the ice field surrounding them.

'How could a captain let his ship steam at such speed through growlers and bergs?'

'Perhaps they were unawares?'

Balthasar shook his head. 'Do you see the oily sheen floating on the surface of the sea?'

The Persian lowered his hand to the water. It was viscous, its sheen similar to oil. 'Yes, what's all this then?'

'Spicules.'

'Sorry?'

'Frazil ice. The first stage in the formation of pack ice. A proper night watch would recognise such a thing.'

'How would you know?' Mahmoud asked.

'This isn't the first ship that's gone out under me in the North Atlantic.'

'Not that I find palaver dull…' Mahmoud took a long drink from the bottle. 'But what are we meant to do now?'

'I haven't made up my mind just yet,' Balthasar said and looked to the distant lifeboats. 'Neither have they.'

Joining his gaze, Mahmoud saw a green light in the distance, at first confusing it with the bowhead light of a lifeboat until he picked out a red sidelight and then a white masthead light.

It was a ship.

'Buster.'

'Let us linger a spell,' replied Balthasar.

The Persian became still, the pre-dawn glow revealing the outline of a single-funnel steamship. It was adrift, a blast from its horn all the proof they needed that the ship spotted the lifeboats ahead. Jacob's ladders and boatswains' chairs hung down its port side as crewmen began off-loading survivors.

The two of them waited amidst the pack ice until the survivors were all taken aboard. Crewmen from the steamer lassoed the lifeboats, a cargo crane raising them to the ship's forecastle deck.

'Crack on, Mahmoud,' said Balthasar, slowly kicking his legs. 'Can you help steer a course?'

He had a go, but it was no good; he had lost all feeling in his body and even his hands were frozen to the netting.

'I can't move, Buster. I have frozen solid.'

'I can kick my legs a bit. And the current is carrying us generally towards the ship.'

Slowly, they moved closer to the steamer until they were just yards from two crewmen preparing to raise the last two lifeboats. As the flotsam raft nudged the side of the lifeboat, the crewman with his back to the sea, leapt in fright.

'Would it be all right we come aboard?' asked Balthasar.

'Cripes,' the crewman shouted, latching onto their raft with a fending hook. 'There's two blokes down here in the water.'

'Can't be,' said the other, climbing from the lifeboat, blocked in against the hull of the steamer. 'Couldn't possibly survive in the sea all them hours.'

His eyes met Mahmoud's.

'Poor bastards. Must be nearly frozen solid.'

The seaman with the fending pole shouted up to deck. 'There's two more alive here!'

'By Jove,' yelled an officer, leaning over the side. 'Have them out the water this very instant.'

The second crewman grasped hold of Balthasar by the shoulders. 'Come on then, mate. Let's get you warmed up.'

'What's the name of this ship?' Balthasar asked as he was hauled out.

'This is the Carpathia.'

'Carpathia,' repeated Mahmoud as he too was pulled from the water. Ironic a ship so named was the deliverer of their salvation.

❖   ❖   ❖

'I haven't any sugar for you,' the cabin steward repeated as he sat the tray of tea and biscuits on the narrow table between their bunks. 'It's very unusual to serve steerage passengers in their berths. But the captain said we could make an exception for you two gents.'

The accommodation was cramped: two bunks separated by a narrow aisle with a tiny side table between. Mahmoud and Balthasar were the only occupants.

'I don't understand it.' The ship surgeon put a firm hand on the Persian's exposed arm. 'I'm having the devil of a time warming you two chaps.'

Mahmoud's eyes darted to Balthasar. Each had three blankets covering them. It wouldn't matter if a dozen more were heaped on top.

There was no warmth to raise.

'Who is ship captain?' asked Balthasar.

'That would be Captain Rostron,' replied the steward, as he poured tea into a pair of enamelled cups.

'He's eager to meet you both,' said the surgeon.

'Is that so?' Mahmoud replied, lifting a cup to his lips. The tea was bitter. 'Perhaps he can let us have a few lumps of sugar?'

'I'm afraid Carpathia's larder wasn't provisioned for an additional seven hundred passengers,' said the steward. 'The sugar is for First and Second-Class passengers.'

'Only seven hundred survived?' asked Balthasar.

'On Carpathia. There are other ships about. Surely others have been picked up.'

Mahmoud knew otherwise. Only the dead remained in the sea when they left the wreck site.

'That'll do,' interrupted the surgeon. 'No need to upset our guests. They've had a difficult enough time of it.'

'We're ever so grateful you're permitting us a two-bunk berth,' said Balthasar.

'Normally, we move immigrants to the States in Third-Class,' said the steward. 'We've filled the four and six-bunk berths with a lot of foreigners.'

'It's plain to see the both of you are gentlemen and haven't got measles,' the surgeon added.

Mahmoud reached for another shortbread. 'Perhaps we could have a bit more?'

'If you feel well enough, you can leave your cabin for the lunch messing. But it's all right if you don't. Titanic's Marconi operator is suffering from severe frostbite in his legs. The poor man can't walk,' explained the surgeon, before there was a knock at the cabin door. 'Do please enter,' he called.

The Captain entered, buttons on his double-breasted Cunard jacket perfectly polished, collar tight below his lean face and officer's cap perched atop his head.

'Surgeon McGee, how are our guests?'

'Not bad, Captain Rostron. Having a bit of trouble warming them, though.'

'Not surprising considering how long they were in the water.' He turned to Mahmoud and Balthasar. 'You're being well looked after?'

'Yes,' said Mahmoud. 'Though the steward is being a bit mean with the sugar.'

The Captain looked to his steward.

'We're having to ration sugar to First and Second-Class only, sir.'

'I think we could make an exception for these gentlemen.' The Captain said through a thin smile.

'Yes, sir. I'll fetch a sugar bowl.'

'What's become of our clothes?' Balthasar asked.

'On deck. Drying,' replied the Captain. 'Expect you'll have them before too long. Carpathia isn't crewed for this many passengers. Valeting takes a bit longer.'

He touched Balthasar's bare arm. Startled, he drew it away. 'Damn sorry about the cold. To make as much speed as possible we diverted the steam from heating. I've instructed the engineer to revert that now. Sorry to say, we're having trouble heating the steerage. It's a mild day on deck, though. If you're well enough, the sea air might do you good.'

'We're grateful,' said Mahmoud.

'Your survival is something of a miracle,' said the Captain.

'Slight frost nip on their fingertips and some swelling to their feet,' said the surgeon. 'Nothing more.'

'In all my years at sea, I never heard a man survive more than twenty minutes in these frigid waters. You chaps managed six hours.'

'They tell me they shared a bottle or so,' said the surgeon.

'Oh, indeed?'

'One of the crates we clung to,' said Mahmoud.

'Full of rye,' added Balthasar.

'We managed to get into it and drink our fill.'

'Good thinking, that,' Surgeon McGee replied. 'It may have saved your souls.'

'Have you requested a marconigram?' asked the Captain. Mahmoud shook his head, averting his eyes.

'Thank you, no,' replied Balthasar.

'Surely you have relations who would wish to know you're safe and well?'

'We have no one,' replied Balthasar, glancing back at Mahmoud. The Persian understood. Preserving their *omertà* was important above all else.

'I see,' said Captain Rostron. 'White Star has requested a survivor list. A purser will be round presently to collect your details.'

Sensing Balthasar's growing frustration, Mahmoud asked, 'What's our destination?'

'*Carpathia was* making for Gibraltar. But I've decided to turn round and return to New York.'

'When do you expect we'll make landfall?'

'We're in the midst of quite an ice field. We'll make half a knot until we get through it. Once we're clear, Carpathia can make fourteen knots. Expect we'll arrive in New York in three days' time.'

'So rest up,' said the surgeon, closing his medical bag.

'I'll look in again once you get your feet under the table.'

With a nod, they excused themselves.

Balthasar stood. Dressed only in a nightshirt, he propped open the porthole between their bunks, taking in the sea air. 'Seven hundred survivors,' he said, inhaling. 'There were more than two thousand aboard Titanic.'

'There will be hell to pay.'

Balthasar nodded. 'You heard the name of this ship?'

'Carpathia.'

Balthasar repeated the name, almost sadly.

Mahmoud watched him go away with his thoughts. He knew where they took him. To the place where the banshee turned him: to the hamlet at the foot of the Carpathian Mountains. Uličské. Mahmoud drank his tea, palmed the tennis ball, and waited for Balthasar to return.

'I've gotten us into the soup, haven't I?'

Mahmoud nodded, tossing the ball against the corner of the wall, trying to regain a sense of normality — whatever that meant, in men like they — after the night's events.

He caught it, the tingling sensation from frost nip subsiding at last.

'What are we to do, Buster? Our Jungfrau went to the bottom of the Atlantic with Titanic.'

'There's more.'

Mahmoud was genuinely surprised. 'More?'

'On a ship.'

'You're going to tell me it's at the bottom of the sea as well, aren't you?'

He nodded.

'Off the Honduran coast. Where the water is shallow and warm.'

'Griffin?'

Balthasar nodded again. 'What shall we do about Captain Rostron?'

'What about him?' asked Mahmoud.

'He's expecting our details for the survivor's list. We're attracting attention. I should have taken your advice and had us wait it out on a growler.'

'Two blokes sitting on an iceberg like lost polar bears?' the Persian replied. 'That's not going to attract attention?'

Balthasar's eyes zeroed in on something outside the porthole. Turning back to Mahmoud, he asked, 'Fancy going to California?'

Joining him at the porthole Mahmoud looked out. Amongst the growlers, another ship sat adrift. A freighter. SS Californian.

Looking away from the porthole, he asked, 'And what then?'

'We find *her*,' said Balthasar, turning back to the other ship. 'We find Siobhan.'

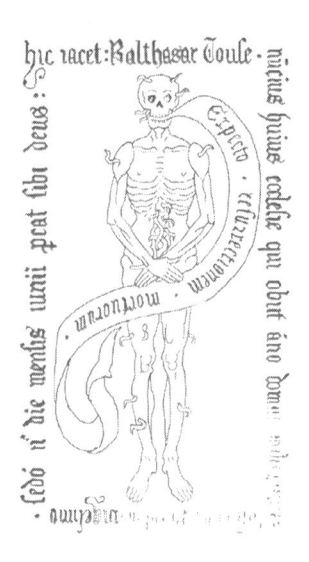

27 AUGUST 1936.

ST DUNSTAN'S, BLOOMFIELD HILLS, MICHIGAN

'The Gift is therefore at one and the same time what should be done, what should be received, and yet what is dangerous to take. This is because the thing that is given itself forges a bilateral, irrevocable bond…
The recipient is dependent upon the anger of the donor, and each is even dependent on the other. Thus, one must not eat in the home of one's enemy.'

—*Mauss*, The Gift

'**M**orning, Dr Annenberg.'

Elle looked across Thompson Oval, her morning walk interrupted by a huddle of preps in rolled-up chinos and oxfords, tossing a pigskin about the dew-covered football field. One of them waved.

'Morning,' she replied from the shade of a row of stately oaks, providing respite from the morning sun. Looking into the branches, she inhaled the pleasing odour of waning leaves.

She marvelled at those oaks. They had been planted after the completion of the athletic field sixteen years before, and she watched them grow — like her students grew — from saplings to adulthood. The sun drifted through the murmuring leaves, touching her face. She cherished her walks across campus during those ephemeral August mornings, before the tedium of a new semester.

Nothing compared with the calming rhythm of a Michigan summer's morning when the dew was heavy on the grass and the cicadas droned from perches high in the oak's summer foliage. Fall Semester wouldn't commence for another week, and with the exception of the football team, there were few students to interrupt her bliss.

'How was your summer?' asked a Varsity prep, as he ambled across the field grass to fetch his pigskin.

'Very fine, thank you,' she replied.

Picking up the football at her feet, she tossed it back to him before continuing her stroll to the academic hall.

She wished her statement was true. She had turned forty-two that summer. Although she was no longer to be confused with a co-ed, dressed in her Schiaparelli-print skirt and linen blouse, her breasts hadn't fallen, she had yet to find a grey hair amidst her unruly locks of chestnut and beguiling smile still caused young bucks and old dogs to give her the *come hither*.

It still didn't work on her, of course. But these days, she rejected with a smile. The years in academia turned her less flippant. More quotidian. Her old school chum, Titch Blaine-Howard, called her "Everest with willowy legs".

Not only did suitors suffer the humiliation of never summiting her icy peak, none of them even reached her base camp. She couldn't give up her private obsession with halcyon love. There was no antidote for the self-torment she kept locked inside.

America faired ever worse. In the midst of the Great Depression, family fortunes were wiped away. Bankers leapt from office windows. Farmers' fields dried up, forcing entire communities to move west in search of greener pastures. The exhibition of recovered artefacts from Skipper Henrikson's wreck, which had afforded St Dunstan's Science Institute international notoriety, was threatened with termination by a court injunction from the Fascist Spanish dictator, Franco. What began with such promise could now shutter the school and bankrupt the Annenberg family.

Worse yet, too many years had got behind her since she last found a lead to Balthasar's identity. It made her heart heavy, like the thick morning mist in Bloomfield Hills when it sunk down into the dales. 'Damn,' she groaned quietly. 'Yeah,' she continued with a sigh, reminding herself that, on the bright side, the Volstead Act had been repealed, and everyone was free to get as drunk as monkeys again.

Ascending the broad stairs leading away from the athletic field, she entered the south lobby of the academic building, the lights in its high ceiling all dimmed during the summer months. It wasn't until then she realised she had worked up quite a sweat.

Tucking her sunglasses into her valise, she climbed the spiral stairs up from the lobby, stopping beside Diogenes holding his lantern.

'Still looking for an honest man?' she asked him. He always remained quiet.

As too, did Balthasar Toule, his clues swallowed up as the years rolled into each other.

Entering the ethnology vestibule, she found Hattie humming a Cole Porter tune before a whirling table fan, windows cast wide, hoping for the slightest breeze.

'Morning, Hattie,' she puffed, beating a path to her office. It was as hot as Honduras inside, sallow, amber light filtering through curtains drawn over the windows. She wasted no time throwing them back and opening the windows.

'Tea?' offered Hattie.

'Iced this morning,' replied Elle eyeing the lofty stacks of unopened morning mail on her desk.

'Shall I get cracking on those?' Hattie asked, pausing from her retreat to the door.

'Nah. Until they're opened there's no more bad news.'

'I hope you'll find a student assistant to help me out during the new school year?'

'Slowing down, are we?'

'Absolutely not. I just need a little extra *assistance* these days.'

Elle smiled, thinking. 'Remember Charlie?'

'How could I forget him?'

'He was sort of nicely gormless. Would tackle any task assigned him, be it grading papers or shovelling the snow off my front porch.'

'Am I insufficient to your needs?' Hattie's tone suggested she was only half joking.

'Hattie,' Elle put her hands over her own heart, feigning adoration. 'You are my rock.'

'Uh-huh,' she replied. 'And Charlie's a man. Young and slightly feckless, but a man none-the-less. You only have to smile that great big smile of yours and men will join the Texas Rangers if you ask them. That's your gift. I have to promise to change a student's marks to get them to sharpen a pencil for me.'

'How long since Charlie graduated?'

'Must be six years now.'

'Six years,' Elle repeated, surprised by how many years had come and gone since her last clue to the enigma that was Balthasar Toule. 'Where does the time go?'

'The way of Prohibition.' Before Hattie closed the door she added, 'I'll get some ice for your tea.'

As she leaned against her desk, Elle's eyes shifted from the unopened mail to the tennis balls sitting in her stuffed bookcases. She took one off the shelf and twirled it in her fingers, long ago having lost track of which was which. Didn't much matter; both came from Titanic.

She browsed her shambolic collection of souvenirs: books on subjects of interest to nobody but her, a clay pot shaped like a breadfruit propping up a photograph of Elle with Skipper Henrikson on Adel, her doctorate degree in a cracked frame, Dr Mauss's *The Gift*, her Titanic lifebelt, a postcard of Utila Island from Gunny Schadowski, and the ledger Dougie Beedham gave her. Bits and bobs from a joyless life, displayed on dusty shelves.

You've a long, dark road ahead of you. Twenty-four years on that road had got her nowhere. Her salad days gone, with no more clues to Balthasar's whereabouts since a cold rainy night in 1929, when presumably he and his adjutant had paid her a visit to retrieve his talisman.

Putting the tennis ball back on the shelf, she lifted an envelope on top of the pile of morning mail; an official-looking letter from Headmaster Bowie, her nemesis. He was a clever sort. Biding his time, he tolerated Daddy's little girl's lectures on Spring-heeled Jack and endless papers on Crimen predation, awaiting the moment when being the daughter of Franklyn and Louise Annenberg was no longer relevant. She tossed the letter into her rubbish bin.

The intercom buzzed.

'Eleanor,' said Hattie from the vestibule. 'Your father is here.'

'Uh-oh.'

Shortly after, Hattie entered the room carrying a silver tray balancing two glasses, a crystal decanter of tea and a rattling ice bucket. Elle's father trailed behind.

'Hello, my darling daughter.'

The years had not diminished her father's *bonhomie*. At seventy-eight, he remained modest yet optimistic, dressed in a bespoke Panama suit. Unbuttoning his jacket, he slipped it off, and kissed her on the cheek.

'Hot today.'

'Thermometer heading north of ninety degrees, Father.'

He laid the jacket across the back of his old armchair, and mopped his brow with a hanky.

'Iced tea?' she asked, adding chipped ice to a tall glass.

'Delighted. I'm parched,' he replied.

Glancing through her shelves, he innocently took down the hardbound black ledger, reading the gold lettering stamped into the cover. '"US Commerce Committee Investigation into RMS Titanic." Wherever did you get this, Eleanor?'

'Dougie Beedham.'

Her father pulled a face suggesting he didn't immediately recollect him.

'Steward Beedham.'

'Ah, of course.'

After pouring tea into her own glass of ice, she took a sip. It was only then that her father drank from his. Ever the gentleman. 'You never thought to mention it before?'

'Life got in the way. Mr Beedham owned a hotel on an island off the Honduran mainland. I told you.'

Her father shrugged, before handing back the ledger.

'You know what's funny. He became so frightened of the sea he wouldn't so much as put a toe in.'

Removing his pocket watch, her father popped the clasp, revealing its face.

'I was wearing this *that* night. Checked the time just before I was going to leap overboard. Steward Beedham happened by, in a flimsy collapsible. Do you know what crossed my mind? "I hope it doesn't get wet".'

He smirked, winding it.

'Can you imagine a sillier thing before dying than saying, "I hope it doesn't get wet?"'

He choked out a sad, little laugh. 'I use it every day. Every day.'

He turned from her to look at her collection of knick-knacks.

'I don't look at it to remind me of Titanic. I look at it when I wonder what time it is. It's just a watch. A watch attached to a chain I tucked into my vest pocket one regrettable night.'

'Do you ever feel guilty our family survived unscathed, when so many others didn't?' she asked.

He turned to her. 'If you're asking me if I would feel less guilty if you or your mother had drowned, the answer is no.'

'Why *did* you stop by here so early?'

'Why? Your mother and I miss you, Eleanor. We worry about you,' he said, face austere. 'We've hardly seen you since you moved out of the main house and into your little pied-à-terre.'

'Father, are we going to have our annual "If you're not careful you'll end up a lonely drunk woman who gets eaten by her twenty-five cats" lecture?'

'Eleanor, I don't give a hoot if you die an eighty nine-year-old spinster.' Giving the knees of his trousers a tug to preserve their shape, he sat in his old armchair. 'My only want for my daughter is her happiness.'

She smiled. Sitting on the armchair's ottoman, she laid a hand on her father's. 'When I was a little girl, your hands swallowed me up. I knew so long as I held onto you, I was safe.'

Elle knew the purpose of her father's visit, and there was no sense rushing what would inevitably be a bad ending.

'I gave you and Mother a hard time when I was a teenager. In case you didn't already know, I love you both a lot.'

Her father smiled. 'Mother's greatest worry was that she was raising a Republican.'

Elle laughed, genuinely. It felt nice to let go for a moment.

'I have seen what wealth did to the children of my friends,' he continued. 'Running around all hours of the night drunk, injecting themselves with enough solution of cocaine to kill a horse. I'm pleased your mother and I raised a daughter of the world, and not a victim to it.'

Elle hugged him. She hadn't had a hug in ages.

'Have you begun the syllabus for your courses this term?' he asked.

'Not yet,' she said. Then standing, she pushed the stack of post to the side, perching herself on the edge of her desk, readying herself for the executioner's axe. 'Why?'

'This morning, I received a telegram from Ribs Wimbourne.'

'Ribs?' she replied, recalling how she had knocked him from Titanic's deck into a lifeboat. 'How is he?'

'Promoted to Commodore. On loan from the Royal Navy. Using his diplomacy skills to get us out of trouble.'

'Are we in trouble, Father?'

'Ah, the insular world of academia. We're in the depths of the Great Depression, its end nowhere in sight. St Dustan's has lost half its students.'

Elle stood, thinking it was time to have a last smoke before the axe fell. She removed a cigarette from a silver box on her desk and lit it. She held the box open by its hinged lid for her father, who took one, and gave it a sniff before putting it to his lips.

'There was once a five-year waiting list for a membership at my golf club. Now they can't give 'em away for five bucks. And five bucks isn't worth what two bucks was.' Lighting his cigarette and inhaling, he coughed.

'How long has it been since you had a gasper?' she asked, leaning against the windowsill, blowing her smoke outside.

'Had more than a few of late,' he said, breathing in deeply. 'I can name on each finger and toe the friends I prepped with, giants of industry, who've gone bankrupt and lost everything.' His smoke found its way lazily to the open window. 'Our problems don't amount to a hill of beans.'

'Is St Dunstan's in jeopardy?'

'Do you remember when I sold our steel mills to Henry Ford?' he asked, clearly dodging her question.

'Just after Titanic sank.'

'1912. Two months before the 16th Amendment was ratified, legalising income tax. Was just dumb luck I sold off my biggest assets before I would have to hand over the lion's share of the profit to Uncle Sam. As it was, we held on to a hundred per cent of the sale price.'

Elle almost dreaded to ask. 'And now?'

'Your mother.'

'Mother?' she replied. It wasn't the answer she had expected.

'The prudent one,' he said with a nod. 'Her family.'

'The bankers? I thought they caused this mess in the first place.'

'Bankers from the Old Country. They saw the warning signs before the rest of us. Mother saw to it that most of our assets were divested overseas before the crash. Diamond speculation in Amsterdam, whiskey distilleries in Londonderry, cork factories in Palafrugell.'

'Pala-through-hell?' she asked.

'Palafrugell. It's in Spain. Catalonia, technically. I've never been there.'

'Oh,' Elle, replied, knowing now where her father was steering the conversation. 'The Fascist dictator, Franco.'

'It's already been decided,' he said, his sober tone disheartening.

'No,' she said and stood from the sill, throwing her cigarette butt out the window. 'You can't do this to St Dunstan's.'

'If I don't, there won't *be* a St Dunstan's next semester.'

'The escudos from the exhibit? That's what Franco wants, isn't it? Gold.'

Father nodded. 'There's a civil war in Spain. Germany is siding with the fascists. Catalonia is Republican, and the Soviets are siding with them. Ribs struck a deal.'

'A deal?'

'I have a lot of Americans managing the cork factories. The Germans agreed not to bomb Palafrugell.'

'You're bribing them?'

'Bribery is such an ugly word. Ribs *negotiated a settlement*. A half-million in gold.'

'You're taking St Dustan's gold escudos?'

'Half, actually. Your escudos are worth a bit more these days.'

She stared at him, mouth agape. '*Half?*'

'Well, yes,' her father replied as if he was talking about the price of milk. 'I'd offer Franco the gold fillings from my teeth if he would accept them, but he wants the escudos. A matter of pride. He claims you committed predation in acquiring them.'

'Predation?' she replied. For her, it had an entirely different meaning.

'Plunder, if it makes you feel better. These escudos, they're Spanish. Therefore, they're property of Spain.'

'Never mind Spain committed predation themselves when they looted the Aztec empire.'

'I remain outside political intrigue. Gives me heartburn. Franco wants a half-million in gold. Your coins are worth a cool million these days. We hand half the coins to Franco's fascists, and Spain drops their court injunction against St Dunstan's. The Germans agree not to bomb our factories in Catalonia. The other half-million you keep.'

'And the exhibition that gave St Dunstan's respectability? Is it gone?'

'I'm afraid there is more to it.'

Before she could ask, her intercom buzzed again.

'Eleanor? Your mother is here.'

As her mother entered, Elle's father stood up. Mother's presence was a bit like watching Moses part the Red Sea.

'Louise.'

'Ah, shit,' Elle said. It was serious when her father didn't call her mother Weezy. It all made sense now. 'I'm to be struck off, aren't I?'

'Eleanor, you don't help your cause with that language,' her mother tut-tutted, sitting in the chair newly vacated by her father.

'It's true isn't it; I'm to be fired?'

'I've spoken at length with Headmaster Bowie—'

'I knew it,' Elle said and went to the window, the air in her office suddenly stifling. 'He bided his time well.'

'Shut up, Eleanor.'

When Mother said "shut up", you shut up.

'On the contrary; he was *against* firing you.'

'Then why?'

'This dealing with a fascist dictator,' said her father. 'President Roosevelt thinks it smells bad.'

'The President of the United States told you to fire me?'

'His Secretary of State, actually,' he replied to her.

'Wonderful. Who's going to hire me after this?'

'You've become notable.'

'Notable? A highly strung heiress with peculiar theories, making deals with fascists in the midst of a depression. "Notable" isn't the word I'd use.'

'Mother has an idea.'

She looked to her mother. 'Oh? I bet it's a doozy.'

'We have friends, many of whom owe us favours. Your aunt Anna is a patron of *das Klassische Archäologie Institut*, in Berlin,' her mother said.

Elle pushed the books and mail aside from her desk. 'I need to sit. My world is coming unstitched.'

'The museum assisted us greatly in acquiring artwork,' said her father.

'We have assurances that a position in their ethnology department is available to you,' her mother interrupted. 'You'll be able to continue your research. The Germans, no doubt, will be charmed by your oeuvre. Abstruse is all the rage in Germany these days.'

'So is bashing in Jew's heads.'

'We're rich Jews,' replied Mother. 'There will be no head bashing.'

'You're passing your daughter from one nationalistic dictator to another?'

'Roosevelt assures me America will remain isolationist. There is a significant American community in Berlin. You'll be offered diplomatic privileges and spared from public ignominy,' her father said. 'I'm sorry, Eleanor. I know you've worked very hard to make St Dunstan's Science Institute what it is today.'

'It's just for a few years,' said her mother.

Removing his pocket watch, her father checked the time. 'Secretary of State Hull will want this news right away.' Approaching Elle's mother, he kissed her on the cheek before turning to Elle. 'It's only temporary, Eleanor. Just until the dust settles over this deal with the fascists. Once this has died down, you can return to your position.'

Straightening her father's jacket lapels, she planted a kiss on his cheek. 'I know you've done what you think is best for St Dunstan's.'

Before disappearing out the door, he offered Elle a weak smile. 'I'm not sure my best is nearly enough.'

Passing through the vestibule, he thanked Hattie for the iced tea before disappearing into the hallway.

Her mother gave her a stern look before closing the office door behind him. Elle spoke up before she did.

'I'm to be exiled?'

'Call it a sabbatical.'

'Malarkey,' Elle said and lit another cigarette. 'You didn't raise me to be a sucker. You know it'll be impossible to fund research as "abstruse" as mine.'

Snatching the cigarette from Elle, her mother took an out-of-character drag from it. 'A half-million dollars buys a lot of philanthropy.'

'You're *buying* me a position?'

'I'm a German Jew, Eleanor,' she said with just a hint of hubris. 'You're buying it yourself.'

Elle huffed. 'I'm sure my sabbatical gives St Dustan's tenured professors plenty of reason to smile.'

'*Scheißdreck.*' Drawing close to Elle, Mother took up her hand and caressed it. 'I imagine at this moment you feel the only right you can do by those privileged professors, is suffocating in the *Kacke* of a crippled *Schwein* farmer?'

'Don't think I'm not appreciative of your colourful colloquialisms but—'

'Darling daughter, I once was a bright young thing like you. All legs and lush hair.'

'I'm forty-two years old now, Mother. I'm not as bright nor willowy as I once was.'

'Point being, I understand your wariness. Those men, vacuous and arrogant, honours up their hindquarters, not too proud to accept our benevolence yet too proud to break bread with us in a deli because we're Jews. What do they know? To them, Adam and Eve on a log is Bible verse.'

'Two runny eggs over kosher sausage,' Elle added and smiled, remembering. 'I miss those breakfasts at Hurwitz's Deli with you.'

'"The wisdom of the fool won't set you free". It's a truism you must never doubt.'

'You mean like "Mother knows best"?' Elle asked and sighed. 'Tell me the name of that museum, again?'

'*Das Klassische Archäologie Institut.*'

'God. It sounds like instructions for deploying a parachute in German.' She looked out the window, frowning incredulously and then burst into tears.

Her mother placed an arm around her shoulder, comforting her like only a mother could her own child. 'You'll be quite all right, Eleanor,' she said, her voice so soft and heartfelt Elle felt it must be truth. 'You think I bust balls? Spend a week with my sister. She'd laugh in the face of that frothing-at-the-mouth Hitler, simply for the fact he has only got one.'

'One what?'

'One ball, of course.'

Eleanor let go her frustrations with a laugh. 'Do you remember when I was a little girl and Father took me to the county fair every summer? I adored it. I'd sit at my bedroom window looking out at winter's gloom, counting the days until you let me sleep with my windows open. I knew then it was just a matter of weeks until the fair came to town. There was a hawker selling bags of hot popcorn for two cents. Father never understood why I always asked for salted popcorn when I never much fancied it.'

'Why did you?'

'Because there were always one or two sweet kernels mixed into the bag. I would eat so much I'd come home with a stomach ache.'

'I always thought you'd eaten too much candy floss.'

'Eating an entire bag of salted popcorn in the hope of a single kernel of sweet was so much more satisfying than an entire bag of sweet. Father never understood. He was born in America, into a great family. But you…you were born a Jew. In Germany.'

'And I was taught to savour the smallest of things.'

Releasing her, Elle's mother removed a pen from her purse, scratching a series of numbers onto a notepad on Elle's desk.

'You've a keen mental grasp.'

Tearing off the top sheet, she handed it to Elle.

'What is this?'

'A kernel of sweet amongst a bag of salty.'

❖ ❖ ❖

Elle examined the paper her mother had scribbled on: "*SI.3.524.1643.28.*" Call numbers. The Dewey Decimal System (DDS) was an ingenious scheme for categorising large collections of references into one of nine categories, using numbers and letters separated by decimal marks. The longer the DDS number, the more specific the instruction to the reference's location. St Dunstan's version was unique unto itself, for one reason and one reason only: Mother devised it.

The school library was housed in the same hall as Elle's office. Over the years, her family bought up vast collections of books on almost every subject. There wasn't space enough in the library, so books were housed wherever space was found. The more esoteric, the further from the library they were kept.

SI.3.524.1643.28.

The first two letters identified the building on campus. Whatever her mother wanted her to find, it was certainly esoteric. *SI*: science institute.

The lead took her deep into the bowels of the institute. She had visited the basement before and dreaded going again. They were deep, dank and dark.

The first call number referenced the level: *3*.

The lift lurched to a halt. Sliding back the cage gate, Elle hesitantly took a step onto the labyrinthine network of darkened catwalks hanging above the boilers. Beside the lift hung a white plaque. Block letters informed her: CATWALK LEVEL 3. LIGHT SWTICH BELOW. TURN OFF WHEN EXITING.

The knife switch was composed of a wooden handle with ominous positive and negative connection wires.

Pulling the handle up, she locked it into the positive position, a hum rolling along the catwalks. Light bulbs in hanging sockets burned dimly. Although she often found herself at the science institute, she seldom ventured down here.

In librarian-speak, archiving in a cellar was just above the refuse heap. Her finger cut through a thick layer of dust, as she trailed it along the rail. It had been ages since anyone ventured here.

Ahead, another sign. Another knife switch.

Throwing it cast a spiral staircase in spectral light. An arrow on the sign pointed down.

'500 to 550.'

She checked the next set of numbers on her DDS: *524*.

Peering over the edge of the walkway, she spied an enormous, idle boiler. Descending the latticed stairs she arrived at another level, edged by rows of bookcases packed with cardboard boxes. The familiar mildew odour of old books heavy in the air. She glanced at the bookcase numbers before she continued on.

The pressed cardboard boxes on all the shelves were marked with numbers. She found *524* halfway along the catwalk, and *1643* on a box stuffed into the third shelf. Sitting down on the iron, latticed floor, she pulled off the box's lid.

Books. And an open box of white powder.

The lights were too dim for her to inspect the books within, but at the end of the row stood a wood lectern, a reading lamp balanced atop.

Hefting the box into her arms she carried it there, clicked on the lamp, dust on the bulb burning as it heated. Sorting through the large cardboard box, she inspected the small box of white powder within first.

Church & Dwight 'Flu' Bicarbonate of Soda

Elle's mother had fed similar stuff to her; a preventative for warding off influenza during the pandemic of 1918. As she looked closer at the box, the penny dropped.

'Mother,' she whispered with a smile. She hadn't fed Elle from a similar box, but from this exact same one. Bicarbonate of soda also kept books mould-free. She took out all the books, becoming disheartened as the pile increased. With only two remaining, she found it.

SI3.524.1643.28. Book 28. Box 1643. Archive bookcase 524. Catwalk level 3. Science Institute physical plant.

It was an insignificantly small, leather-bound book with embossed borders. She had found it. Six inches in length, no more than four inches wide. The calf-leather folio binding cracked. Opening it, she felt its spine strain. It had not been read for a long time. The title page was delicate, paper yellowed and brittle.

"*A Brief Account of fome Travels in Germania with King Ferdinand von Hapsburg*".

It was hard to read, the pages stained with damp, but the hand-blocked writing was Old English; the date at the page's bottom confirmed it: *1634*.

Authored by a *William Harvey Folcanstan. Physician in Ordinary. His Majefty Charles I.*

'Who are you, William Harvey Folcanstan?'

There came a distant hum. She looked up and saw the lift going up.

Returning to the book, she flipped through its stiff, yellow pages. A chapter heading caught her eye: "*A vifit to the ftrange Tor Externsteine, cwicseolfor minef.*"

'A visit to the strange Mount Externsteine quicksilver mine,' she whispered aloud. She knew the Tor only too well, a mountain long worshiped by Germanic pagans. Elle spent a good amount of her academic life studying it. But a mercury mine? She had no knowledge of it.

The lift was on the move again. Someone was coming down. She hastily read through the page.

'At the foot of a strange tor, I did descend one hundred and thirty fathoms into the Pit of Hel.'

She read it again.

'Pit of Hel.'

Hel. The pagan demigod of the underworld. And a Sentinel.

'The Pit of Hel, where the most virgin cwicseolfor is found. Jungfräu. Dark in colour, mixed with violet, this strange cwicseolfor can be mined only through excessive labour, requiring extraction by fire.'

Elle gripped the phylactery under her blouse, the vial within containing globs of cwicseolfor she now knew to be Jungfräu, a German word whose meaning she knew.

'Virgin.'

This was pure, virgin cwicseolfor.

The lift came to a stop, its cage sliding open. Footfalls echoed along the catwalk above. Elle continued to read, quickly.

'Committed not presently to fire, the cinnabar ore is powdered grossly, and becomes once more solid. Then did I so take forty faumes of Jungfräu. Each faume containing three hundred and fifteen bushels. The pit exhausted,

I so carried away the cwicseolfor to the Church of St Emiliana, for Holy Anointment.'

'Jungfräu,' she said.

Finally, she had a clue after so many lacunary years.

The footfalls grew louder, descending the stairs to where Elle stood. Turning off the lamp, she tucked the book into the hip pocket of her blazer.

'Headmaster Bowie, you're just in time.'

St Dunstan's headmaster stood before her, the very image of an unimaginative prig, no doubt there to personally escort her from campus. 'I'm happy to see you,' she said, brushing past him, heading up the catwalk in the direction of the lift. 'I could use your help.'

Turning, she flashed her most mischievous smile. 'If I hurry, I can just catch the Graff Zeppelin before it departs for Berlin.'

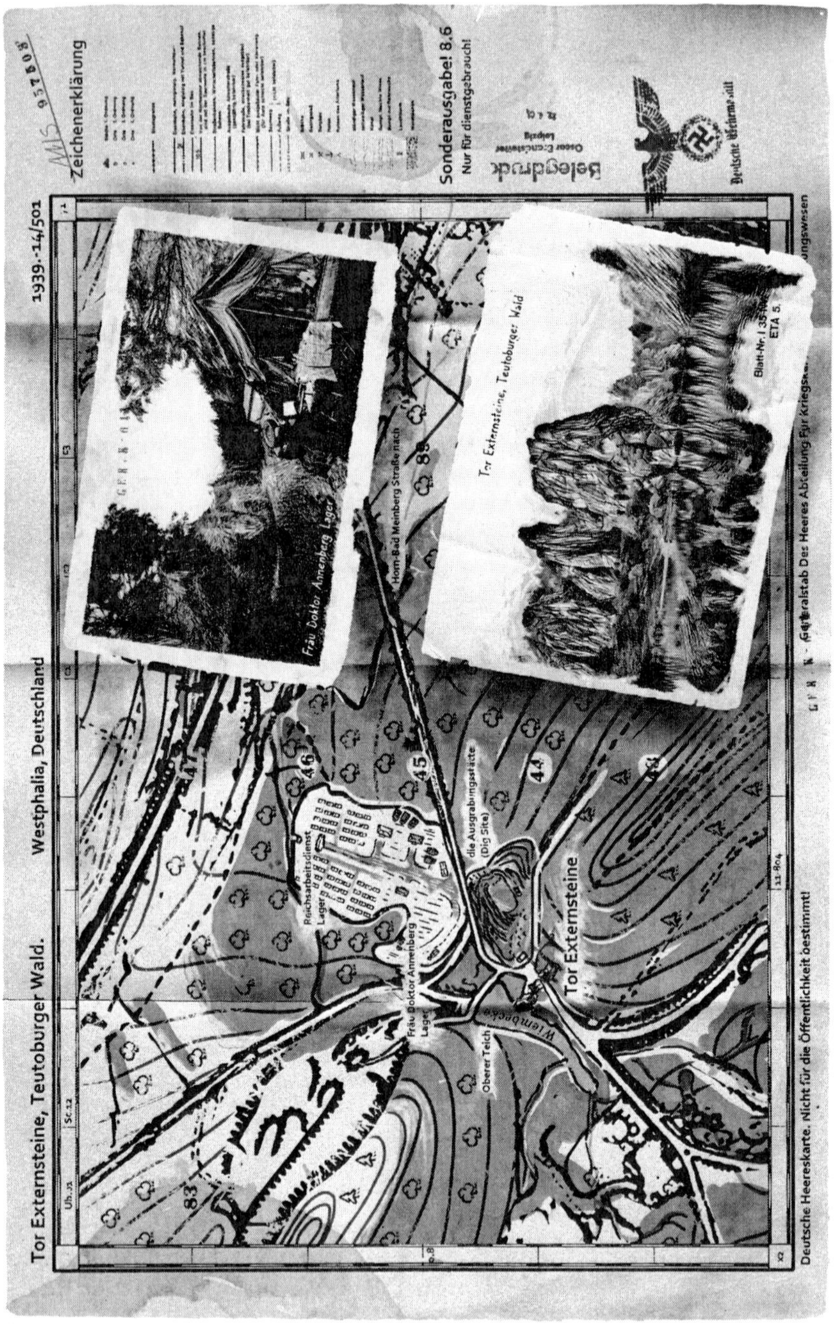

Tor Externsteine, Teutoburger Wald.
Westphalia, Deutschland
1939.-14/501
Zeichenerklärung
Sonderausgabe! 8.6
Nur für dienstgebrauch!
Belegdruck
Fräu Doktor Annenberg Lager
Tor Externsteine, Teutoburger Wald
Horn-Bad Meinberg Straße nach
Reichsarbeitsdienst Lager
die Ausgrabingsstätte (Dig Site)
Tor Externsteine
Fräu Doktor Annenberg Lager
Oberer Teich
Wiembecke
Deutsche Heereskarte. Nicht für die Öffentlichkeit bestimmt!

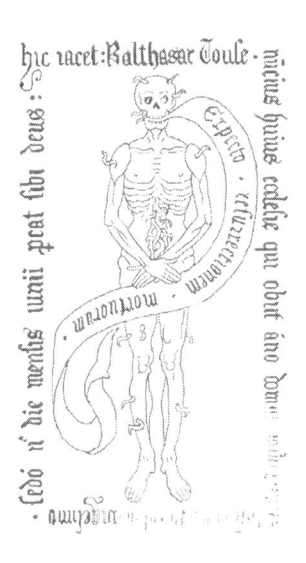

26 August 1939.

Tor Externsteine, Teutoburger Wald, Germany

The tree stump clung to the edge of the excavation site. Seven months earlier, it had been indistinguishable from the forest, fringing a meadow beneath a cluster of *tors*. For a thousand years, these towers were a place of worship for ancient Teutonic tribes. Rough-hewn staircases riddled the tower's fissures and crevices, leading to mysterious chambers.

As a young girl, Elle picnicked with her aunt on the gentle meadow beside the Externsteine, mesmerised by the tor's fantastical shape. Later, after the rise of the Third Reich and their fascination with mysticism, the Externsteine became known throughout Germany as a sacred place where Teutons once worshiped Aryan supremacy. Of course, the Germans lacked proof. But what did that matter to them?

The once-peaceful meadow now ploughed under, the sheer walls of the ever-deepening pit were lined with scaffolding to support precarious switchbacks, where endless *Reichsarbeitsdienst* labour-trains pushed wheelbarrows filled with spoil from below. It was back-breaking work, and the Reich Labour Korps were largely unskilled.

All available strong backs had taken up the Fatherland's calling and joined the armed forces. What remained were the stiff, greying country *Volk*, with little interest in Elle's discordant theories and none of the finesse of skilled diggers.

But time was of the essence, and she stuck with them. Germany descended into the frothing febrility of National Socialism and it was only a question of time before she was chucked out. Despite the protection of *das Klassische Archäologie Institut* and Elle's hard-as-you-like demeanour, she was a Yank. And everyone knew which side America would take up arms with when the balloon went up.

Each morning, she sat with a cup of tea and the day's first cigarette, overseeing the increasingly enormous hole in the ground. And each morning with each cubic metre displaced, she grew more disheartened.

A distant shout. Adjusting the threadbare brim of her Detroit Tigers ball cap, she shielded her eyes from the morning glare. At the bottom of the hole stood Herr Dietrich, the dig foreman. A slight man with fair hair, blue eyes and large, all-hearing ears, he spoke excellent English, smoked heavily and hummed American swing, despite it being *verboten* in the new Germany.

He didn't wear a party armband, but still Elle didn't trust him. She felt sure he reported everything going on — or, rather, not going on — to his boss in Berlin. She watched him make the arduous trip up the switchbacks to the rim of the pit. Even from a distance, she could see he wasn't pleased.

She took a final drag of her Enver Bey. After three years in Germany, she was yet to develop a taste for their *Zigaretten*. But watching her foreman make his way up to her perch, she knew the six *Pfennig* of bitter tobacco she'd smoked wasn't near as bad as the National Socialist *Scheisse* sandwich she was about to be served.

'*Fräulein-Doketor* Annenberg?' Dietrich approached, brown work shirt stained with sweat. It was August. Hot. And humid. She knew too well how brutal the climb from the bottom of the dig was.

'*Guten Morgen*, Herr Dietrich. Warm today, ja?' Why not start with pleasantries? She reckoned the conversation would deteriorate soon enough.

'We have excavated for seven months. There is nothing here.'

'Cup of tea?'

He shook his head, wiping his neck with a handkerchief. Civilities aside, he said, 'We have shifted fifteen thousand *Kubikmeter* of earth. The labourers are to the point of exhaustion.'

'Analysis of the soil?'

'The ground is undisturbed. There is no mine here.'

Dietrich had already been a foreman for three previous pseudo-science quacks seeking evidence of Aryan tribes sacrificing virgins, and goose-stepping about the Externsteine, so he knew the tors better than anyone. The expeditions had not found a thing.

But Elle had a new theory. A theory of Germanic tribes not only worshipping at the tors, but mining a most peculiar *Lichtmetal*: Jungfräu.

In the Third Reich, a mere mention of virgins and Teutonic tribes piqued interest. With her funding easily secured, she had organised a new dig. Her dig.

'There *is* a mine,' she said, more to reassure herself than Dietrich. 'Just not here.' She refused to accept defeat. Germans didn't react well to it. 'I need a minute.'

'We should—'

'*You* should,' she cut in. 'You should, at this moment, do nothing, Herr Dietrich.' Leaving her cup on the stump, she slung her rucksack over her shoulder. 'I'll take my ablutions now.'

She left the rim of the dig and followed a trail through a shallow wood. In one direction, it led to what the Germans called a *Reichsarbeitsdienst Lager*—a fancy term for an encampment, rather like summer camp at Interlochen on Lake Michigan, complete with tents smelling of mildew. She headed in the opposite direction, wandering between the Externsteine's rock towers and down to Lake Wiembecke, where she could bathe.

The lake wrapped itself around the tors. It was not dissimilar in shape to Lake Jonah back at St Dunstan's. The lake nearest the tors was assigned to the labourers for their evening bathing, the lower one for *Fräuleins* during the morning hours. As Elle was the only such *Fräulein* at the dig, she had the entire lake to herself.

Kicking off her work boots, she lowered her feet into the soothing water. From her rucksack, she retrieved the old journal she'd wagered her reputation on and thumbed through its pages.

'So, William Harvey Folcanstan, where you hidden this Pit of Hel?'

Raising her head to the dense forest on the far bank, she listened to the cooing of the mourning doves, unseen amid the leaves of the beech trees. It wasn't hard to imagine herself at St Dunstan's; August in the Northern Rhine region wasn't much different than Bloomfield Hills. It was hot and humid. She swatted at mosquitoes, buzzing at the back of her neck.

'Get away, damn mozzies.'

She unbuttoned her dungarees and slid out of them, pulling her work shirt off over her head before leaping into the water, instantly free of the marauding insects. Surfacing with a satisfying splash, she brushed her wet hair back to look along the lake's length. Save for bird song it was quiet, and her thoughts subconsciously took her back to a rainy spring night in '26, treading water in Lake Jonah, the lake built by her father.

A sudden frisson of excitement jolted her mind. *Man-made.*

Wading to the shallows, she climbed up the bank of the lake, scurrying naked across the wet grass and pulling her work shirt over her dripping wet body before slipping her dungarees back on.

'Dr Annenberg?'

She turned, momentarily startled.

Dietrich appeared along the path cutting through the trees back to the Externsteine. Upon seeing her dripping wet and half-dressed, he looked quickly away.

'Are you quite all right?' he asked.

'Yeah, what do you want?'

'Your permission to begin back-filling the dig site.'

Quickly tucking the journal into her rucksack and tying her wet hair back, she realised Dietrich was doing his very best to not look down her shirt at her breasts. Fastening two buttons, she asked if he knew how deep the lake was.

'Deep,' he replied, eyes still hesitant to look at her. 'For a long time, Lake Wiembecke was believed to be bottomless. A few years ago, a sounding line was dropped down.'

'And?'

'It is deep.'

'How deep?'

'As I recall, the line found bottom just short of two hundred and forty metres.'

Converting the depth to Imperial measurements in her head, she smiled. 'I'll be damned.'

'What is it?'

She took a breath, saying to her herself, 'Sometimes you gotta step outside the tornado.' She looked up at him. 'Seven hundred and eighty feet.'

'Is correct, I think. Why?'

She laughed. 'Because, Herr Dietrich, I'm an idiot.' She stood looking along the lake. 'In the seventeenth century, British measurement was conducted in fathoms. Much like nautical depth today. Opening her bag, she held up the journal of William Harvey Folcanstan.

"'*At the foot of strange tors, I did descend one hundred and thirty fathoms into the Pit of Hel*'." Turing to him she added, 'One hundred and thirty fathoms.'

Her foreman said nothing.

'It's seven hundred and eighty feet. It's at the bottom of the lake, Herr Dietrich. Lake Wiembecke *is* the Pit of Hel.'

'*Mein Gott.*'

'We have got to drain the lake.'

'*Was?*'

'The mine is under the lake. If we want to get at it, we must drain it,' she repeated.

'Do you have any idea how many litres of water would need to be transferred? It's impossible. Where would we transfer it to?'

'Oh, I don't know. Maybe we can transfer it that giant hole we've just spent the last seven months digging and you now want to fill in.'

'Lake Wiembecke is a part of the spiritual heart of the Externsteine. It cannot simply be drained.'

Slinging her bag onto her back, she replied with a confident smile, 'Fortunately, I don't require your permission.'

She headed back to the Lager to fetch some dry clothes. Dietrich did not cease his protestations until they heard shouts from the bottom of the dig. Approaching its rim, they peered below. Excited labourers waved back.

'They have finally found something,' Dietrich almost shouted with excitement.

Hurrying down the switchbacks, her wet feet squishing in her boots as she ran, Elle reached the foot of the pit before wading through labourers leaning on their shovels. As the last man moved aside, she saw what they had unearthed.

'It is a trench line,' Dietrich said, his voice suddenly quieter.

Elle turned to him.

'I was wounded at the *Dritte Flandernschlacht*,' he told her.

'In the Great War?'

He nodded. 'The Third Battle of Ypres. I hoped never to see a trench again.'

She stared down the trench's length. Several labourers dawdled, resting on their spades.

'Clear outta there, fellas,' Elle said. '*Lassen sie mich bitte vorbei.*'

Now cleared of men, the trench revealed itself fully.

'*Scheisse*,' she cursed. 'Dietrich, give me a gasper.'

She put the cigarette to her lip as her foreman held up a light.

'Is it the mine?'

Staring through the cigarette's pale blue smoke at the parallel gouges in the rock floor, she could hardly suppress her excitement. Something heavy had been dragged along the trench a long time ago.

'No,' she said, taking a fresh, deep drag. 'Something better.'

Leaping down into the trench, she followed the gouges as they descended towards the tors. The trench came to an end. As did the peculiar grooves.

Dietrich glared at her. 'What is it you do not tell me, Dr Annenberg?'

Wiping away the water dripping from her hair, she stared at the gouges' end, her mind trying to work it out.

'After all this time, you do not have trust in me?' he asked her.

'It's not a matter of trust,' she replied. Removing the trowel she kept tucked in her back pocket, she crouched down, gently shifting the soil at her feet. 'I just wouldn't want you to presume I was mad.'

The trowel clinked against something. She tapped it. Bare rock. Sandstone, like the tors.

With her hand, she uncovered a heap of sharp-edged fragments, tossing one no bigger than a softball out of the trench to Dietrich's feet. Sifting around in the loose soil she found more of different shapes and sizes, all similarly sharp-edged.

'What have you found?' he asked.

Holding up a shard, she blew the dirt from it.

'Scree.'

Dietrich knelt, picking up the fragment. 'There are a lot of these fragments around here. It is just the spoil, when solid rock was cut into.'

'We have yet to find any rock cuttings this distance from the tors.' Digging into the loose soil at her feet, it took mere seconds for her to expose the sharp edge of solid rock. 'But we have now.' Brushing the dirt away revealed a step. Removing more soil revealed another.

'The trench does not stop?' Dietrich asked.

'This isn't a trench.'

'What then?'

She looked to the tors towering above them. 'It's a way in.'

'*Wunderbar*,' he exclaimed, his grin almost viperish.

'Let us not send word to Berlin yet.'

'But this is monumental,' Dietrich said.

'We don't know what *this* is.'

Tucking her trowel away, she reached for the spade lying on the ground above her. She pushed the spade's head into the hard pack with her boot, prying out a clump of soil.

'Okay, Dietrich,' she said, tossing the loosened dirt over her shoulder. 'Get the boys back down here. We need to clear this out.' Returning to the step, she pushed the spade into the earth again.

'It is not correct for the dig director to work alongside labourers,' protested Dietrich.

'Oh, is that right?' she said and threw a spadeful of soil onto his boots. 'Roll up your sleeves and get down here.'

❖ ❖ ❖

Elle emerged sweaty and sticky from being confined in the subterranean passage with the labourers for hours. Inhaling a lungful of dusk's fresh air, she filled a tin cup from a water butt, pouring its contents over her head and neck, her sweat-stained work shirt covered in earth. Looking along the trench, flickering oil lamps showing the way below, she slowly removed her work gloves and clenched her aching fingers, the blisters on her palms bleeding after a day of digging.

A cold bottle touched the back of her neck. Craning her neck, she could not help but smile, wanting to wrap herself round the bottles of Vernors ginger ale Dietrich held in his hands.

'Brought out the good stuff?' she teased, gratefully accepting one. Putting the bottle against one edge of an upturned wheelbarrow, she thumped it with her fist. The bottle cap spun away.

She handed it to her foreman and repeated the action with the other.

'How did you get your hands on these?' she asked, holding it as if it were some kind of treasure in itself. Bottled in Detroit, it was a friendly reminder of home so far away.

'I have a contact in France who travels often to the States. He brings back cases for medicinal purposes. It is the most powerful of ginger ales, ja? Another American extravagance in which I occasionally partake.'

Pressing the cold glass against the back of her neck again, she sighed with satisfaction before taking a long drink. It was the most refreshingly effervescent, yet sharp-tasting thing she'd had in months. 'That's all kinds of all right.'

In Germany, beer practically flowed from water taps, but Vernors was a true luxury. She raised her bottle. 'I salute your bravura, Herr Dietrich.'

'And I yours, Dr Annenberg. Americans…' he said, before drinking. 'It's amazing what your countrymen can do.'

'Ice-cold, as well.'

'The *Feldkoch* fetched a block of ice from Bad Meinberg today,' said Dietrich.

'The village is five kilometres from here. You sent the cook in a tramp and pony all that way just for ice?'

He shrugged.

Elle knew it wasn't true. Dietrich was sending word to Berlin, and this was him just buttering her up. She didn't let on — there was sometimes more power in withholding knowledge.

'How did you know about the entrance down there?'

'A hunch.'

'*Was ist ein* "hunch"?'

'A guess,' she explained. 'My Aunt Anna brought me here a bunch when I was a kid. One morning, I ditched my cousins while they were having their morning swim and climbed one of the fissures in the tors.' She looked up from the pit towards the darkening towers.

'It was *verboten*, of course, but that made it all the more fun for a curious eleven-year-old. I found a tiny blocked-off alter chamber and managed to squeeze into it through a little hole, just as a single ray of morning sun pierced the darkness. It fell upon a beastly seraph chiselled onto the side of an empty sarcophagus. The Germanic god Hel.'

Turning to him, she continued, 'That was it. I was hooked. I wanted to know what I didn't understand. I've spent my career trying to know what I didn't understand. There was just something about that sarcophagus in that tiny chamber within the tor. It seemed like a red herring.'

'A red herring?'

'A distraction,' she said and smiled. 'Everyone looks for clues *in* the tors. Maybe the answers are beneath it.'

Dietrich looked to the jagged rock towers. 'What shall we do now?'

She looked back at the entrance of the passageway. Twelve steps led to an impassable dead-end. 'How long have you been the acting foreman at this site?'

'Seven months with you. Before that, I was here for perhaps two years with Herr Doktor Wirth. Another four years with other expeditions. I regard myself as something of an expert on the Externsteine.'

'An expert on the Externsteine'. Germany was full of experts.

'Witch stones,' he replied. 'This place is important in Germanic folklore. A mountain hollow is a place of pagan worship by early Teutonic tribes.'

'Teutonic tribes fleeing Carpathia.'

'A German flees no-one.'

She looked at him. 'A couple million doughboys would disagree with you.' She watched his brow furrow. Before he could reply, she threw him a bone. 'This tribe fled from Wilderzeichen.'

'Wilderzeichen? This is nothing but old Saxon gibberish.'

'Wild signs were omens of a coming revenant,' said Elle.

'Revenant? Like a witch?' he asked.

'Not really a witch. More like a banshee anthropophagous.'

'Eater of human flesh?'

Elle nodded. 'I think whatever these Teuton tribes fled from, followed them here.'

'Mystical hogwash,' he said, dismissing the idea. 'Germans depend on science, not folklore. The Externsteine is an important place for National Socialists.'

'Science, it's a helluva thing isn't it?' She winked. 'When the facts don't fit the science, make the science fit the facts.' She did so find pleasure in keeping the little Nazi and his nationalistic bilge in check.

Before he could reply, the labourers appeared from the passage. The day's work at its end, they filed along the trench and out the shallow end, singing.

'*Auf der Heide blüht ein kleines Blümelein.*'

Elle liked the song. A flower blooming on a heath. The flower, a girl named Erika. Probably she was a large German countrywoman with huge bosoms. The men were happy to have discovered something at long last, after so many months of work. Happy to have work. Happy the day was done.

They began the arduous climb up the switchbacks, and when they reached the top, they would march to the upper pond for their evening ablutions.

'What now?' asked Dietrich again.

'*Sekr.*'

'The runes we have discovered chiselled above the blockade? What does it mean?'

She nodded. 'It means Guilty.'

'Guilty of what?'

'Good question,' she replied thoughtfully, her mind on the end of the passage they had uncovered, and the runes chiselled above the massive solid rock blockade. No amount of digging would get round it.

'You have any gelignite?' she asked.

'In the stores. Left behind from Herr Doktor Wirth's expedition.'

'Let's wire that blockade and blow it.'

Dietrich stood, smiling. Clearly, the idea of blowing something up excited him. Putting down his emptied Vernors bottle, he went to fetch the explosives.

'Dietrich?'

He turned.

'This *is* science. Not politics. Do me a favour and don't organise a parade yet.'

He nodded his reply, and was gone.

Draining her own Vernors bottle now, Elle noticed how dirty her hands were. She had toiled alongside the labourers all day, and her wet clothes and hair were matted with dirt. Climbing from the pit, she returned to the *Reichsarbeitsdienst Lager* for a wash before the evening meal.

Germans fancied giving the most mundane of things grandiose names. Even the man who picked up the horse crap after a parade had an impressive title in the Third Reich: *Scheisshaufen Kommando*. The *Lager*, set in a grove of pines and birches, was nothing more than a bunch of mildewy canvas tents, interspersed with battered wooden tables and benches where the labour korps took their meals *al fresco*.

Elle's *Lager* was separate from the worker's encampment by a copse of trees, giving her a modicum of privacy. Winding the gramophone outside her tent, she lowered the needle on a quarter-inch Diamond Disc she'd brought from the States. "Gold Digger Stomp" by the Goldkete Orchestra warbled from the tired speaker. Despite Hitler labelling Harlem swing vile, the Germans were secretly mad on it.

Beside her tent stood a small water butt. Lifting its lid, she found a melting block of ice floating in it, left for her by the kitchen staff.

'God bless you, Dietrich,' she said, dipping a pitcher into the butt and pouring cold water into an enamel basin before stripping bare and washing as best she could, in lieu of the proper bath she really needed.

Changing into clean dungarees and a checked cotton shirt, she sat down heavily on her bunk. The old tennis balls fell from her rucksack and she picked them up. She had long-since forgotten which one had floated up to her when Titanic broke apart, and which was left by her late-night visitants.

She gazed idly out of the tent flap, a summer moon shining brightly through the branches of the tall pines. She looked at the dirty Detroit Tigers baseball cap sitting on her bunk and thought about Michigan in summer, with crickets chirping through the balmy evenings. She missed home.

A motorcar approached. Standing, she pushed the tent flap back further. Headlamps bore down upon her. A *Kübelwagen*—a dark-grey, tin can Volkswagen, open-topped with stamped metal sides. To her surprise, Dr Mauss sat in the back seat. He waved as the car creaked to a halt.

Returning his wave, Elle pulled on her cap and went to greet him. 'I must be close,' she said with a smile, as the driver, a fresh-faced young man in uniform, helped Mauss out. She had not seen him for a year. In that time, he had aged significantly, and was hunched over, walking with the aid of a stick.

'I must be *very* close for you to come out of your library.'

Mauss thanked the driver, who crunched the *Kübelwagen* into gear and drove towards the worker's encampment.

'Bonjour, Eleanor,' he said, doffing his Panama hat before kissing her on both cheeks, his warmth and decency in stark, welcome contrast to the cold precision of Germany, where even a compliment sounded like verbal stabbing. 'I bring you a delicious summer wine from the Languedoc.' He raised the bottle he carried in his other hand. 'Afraid it's *étouffant*. I've been on the train all day.'

Taking it from him, she opened the ice barrel and tossed it inside. 'Ice, I got. Chesterfields, I don't.'

Reaching into the pocket of his summer suit he retrieved a packet of American cigarettes. 'I remembered.'

Almost snatching them from his hands in eagerness, she tore open the pack, giving a cigarette a good sniff. She hadn't any decent tobacco for ages. Dr Mauss clicked his lighter for her, and she inhaled gratefully, the Chesterfields working their magic.

She welcomed him to sit in the folding campaign chair she had taken with her in the field for twenty years. Struggling to lower himself into it, he removed a polka-dot handkerchief from the breast pocket in his coat and mopped his brow.

'I never once imagined Germany to be so hot.'

'They call it Führer weather,' said Elle.

'Does Herr Hitler enjoy sunbathing?'

She sat on a wooden bench across from him, wafting away the smoke from the small campfire she kept alight to ward off mosquitoes, before putting up her feet. 'Whenever the sun's out, the National Socialists organise ballyhoos.'

Mauss looked at her feet. 'You look nearly like a member of the hard-working *Volk*. Except, of course, for your cap. Unmistakably American. Less formal out here in the provinces than Berlin, are we?'

She didn't disagree. 'Have a look around, Dr Mauss. What do you see?'

'I see trees and tors.'

'What do you *not see*?'

'Nazis.' He laughed at her playful pun. 'Just because there are no swastikas and goose-stepping, do not think for a moment that they are not here.' He eyed the water butt where Elle had left the bottle minutes before. 'Might we uncork that wine? It's been a long day's travel and I'm ever so parched.'

Retrieving a corkscrew from her tent, Elle took the bottle from the ice barrel. It was very slightly chilled. The cork popped easily, and she poured wine into two grubby enamel cups, offering one to him before sitting down.

'We're three hundred kilometres from Berlin,' she said. 'There's no Nazi pedantry out here.'

'The Nazis have a flair for the dramatic, do they not?'

'When I first got here, I made the mistake of agreeing to free labour from the local Hitler Youth battalion.' She took a gulp of wine. With hints of apple and fig, it was delightful. 'Useless malingerers. Sitting about listening to high-pitched squeals from that blatherskite with the ridiculous moustache on the wireless. All they were good for was goose-stepping and singing nationalistic songs. After a week, I sent 'em back to their commanding officer. I need less Sieg-Heiling and more digging. I won't have politics here. Just science.'

'There's a wireless here?' Mauss asked.

She nodded.

'Then you know perfectly what is happening?'

'Always the same nonsense. The latest plebiscite. Jews. The big finish and — wait for it— blame everything on the Jews. Again.'

She stood. Crossing to her phonograph, she took another record from its sleeve and gave the phonograph a wind before dropping the needle. 'Flat Foot Floogie' hissed and popped through the speaker.

'Swing,' she said. 'The labourers eat it up. This is their favourite one. They have no idea it's about a prostitute with the floy-floy.'

He offered a confused look. 'Floy-floy?'

'A hepcat's way of saying she's got the clap.' Elle sat down and sparked another cigarette. 'Like I said, no politics.'

'Maybe you don't see a *Putsch* or any black-uniformed goons burning books, but, again, it does not mean they are not here,' Mauss reminded her.

'Not like I sit round the campfire regaling the *Reich Labourer Korps* with tales of my mother's rabbi.'

'Trust in me when I say they already know,' said Mauss. He took a sip of his wine, adding, 'It's chilled enough.'

Elle shrugged, both at the temperature of the wine and at the presence of National Socialists.

'I'm half Jewish, Dr Mauss. And I know it's just a matter of time before I'm chucked out. But I'm reassured my bank account buys me some security.'

'Ah, the complacency of democracy. Eleanor, you suffer from reckless naiveté. The time comes soon when there is no difference between rich or poor. Only Jews and non-Jews.'

She couldn't argue with him. Much as she distracted herself from the realities of Germany with her beloved science, she knew that beyond the tors and trees of the Teutoburg Wald, Jews were having their homes and businesses confiscated. If they were wealthy, they paid for self-deportation. The unlucky ones… she tried to not think about it.

'My foreman, Herr Dietrich, sent out for ice blocks this afternoon. There's a telephone in the Bürgermeister's office in Bad Meinberg. I'm pretty sure he tittle-tattled to Berlin.'

'Dietrich didn't send word to Berlin.' Mauss chuckled.

She didn't see the humour. Another sip from his cup, and he presented it to her for a refill. She topped him up. 'No?'

'No.' He drank. 'Dietrich sent word to *me*.'

'Why would he do that? He's a Party member.'

'Everyone who's anyone in Germany is a Party member. Dietrich is no Nazi. Like you, he's a believer in science, not politics.'

'I'll be damned.'

Taking a long drag, she put her feet up again. The fire crackled. She looked up to the night sky, dense with stars. For the moment, the weight of the world was off her shoulders.

'Have you found it?' Mauss asked. She looked to him as he lit a cigar. 'Have you found your Pit of Hel?'

'*And* the Virgin,' she replied, lowering her feet before leaning in close. 'The mine I've spent seven months digging up, it isn't there. It's at the bottom of Lake Wiembecke.'

'Unfortunate for you.'

'Maybe I don't need to drain the lake, though.'

'Oh?'

'I found steps at the bottom of the dig site,' she said, taking a fresh drag. 'The steps lead down to a passage. And at the end of the passage, I found runes chiselled into the rock.'

'Sekr?'

She nodded.

'And where does this passage lead?'

'I don't know,' she replied, disappointed. 'It's blocked up. I'll find a way. If I'm right, on the other side of it is a back door to the Pit of Hel. And the Virgin.'

'All this,' said Mauss, looking around the extensive encampment. 'A grandiose expedition in the hope of answers.'

Perplexed by his obfuscation, she gave him a sour look. 'If anyone should understand, I expected it would be you.'

'You should not have come, Eleanor,' he said, voice patient but crystalline. 'Not now. Jews who can are *leaving* Germany, not entering.'

'I'm merely half a Jew,' she replied, put out by his comment. 'My Austrian *Großmutter* was Jewish.'

'In the new Germany nothing is done by half. You either are. Or you are not. Which makes you a second-degree *Mischlinge*,' he replied, his kindly eyes piercing. 'It will not be safe for you here much longer.'

'My predicament left me few options, Dr Mauss. Nobody in the States is funding digs on this scale. Not so soon after the Depression.'

'So you burnished your career with Boche austerity?'

'There's more to it than that,' said Elle.

'The Germans do all things on a grand scale these days. First, in Austria. Now, they occupy Czechoslovakia.'

'I left the States in the midst of a depression. Families didn't have roofs over their heads, let alone money to send their children to posh private schools. St Dunstan's didn't have enough students to fill their classrooms, or enough money from tuition to pay its teaching staff. Professors were dismissed. I was dismissed. Unemployed. Unemployable. I wouldn't even have been appointed to a school or museum as a janitor, thanks to my esoteric theories.'

He nodded. 'You got a rum deal, Eleanor.'

'What was I meant to do? Before Hitler became Chancellor, there were a handful of ethnology professorships in Germany. Now there are hundreds.'

'All of them tasked with bolstering the claptrap of Teutonic superiority through the most cloying and disingenuous methods,' added Mauss.

Elle smiled. She once described her own methods the very same way. 'But not on my dig.'

'No.' It was Mauss's turn to smile. 'On your dig, you depend upon feminine intuition.' It appeared that he remembered their conversation back in 1929 as well as she did.

'That was then,' she said. 'This is now. A time when everyone's bankrupt.'

'Yet Germany is flush.'

'And I'm fully funded,' she said.

'Where do you think your funding comes from, Eleanor?'

She shrugged. 'From *der Klassische Archäologie Institut*.'

'Correct. And from where do they get it?'

'Where all museums get funding: from the generosity of benefactors,' answered Elle.

Face wooden, he replied, 'The Ahnenerbe.'

'No,' she muttered in disbelief.

'*Studiengesellschaft für Geistesurgeschichte, Deutsches Ahnenerbe,*' he continued.

'I know what it means,' she said, shaking her head at her own stupidity. 'Study of the heritage and spiritual history of the German people. It's a load of old shit as well. An Ersatz think tank, formulated four years ago to promote bullshit Aryan doctrine espoused by Hitler.'

'Shall I explain how the Ahnenerbe gathers *its* funding?'

She could have guessed, but said nothing.

'Himmler. Head of the SS.'

'I also know who he is,' Elle replied.

'Then you know of his fascination with Teutonic paganism and the occult. He's the Ahnenerbe's patron. You needed funding; he tapped into his private piggy bank.'

'Jews?'

Mauss nodded. 'Jews.'

She stood. Examining the dirt on her hands, she frowned incredulously, realising with horror that she had Jewish blood on them as well.

'All this time, and I never realised the funding was being stolen from my own people.' She felt her face grow hot. 'I deracinated myself from everything I had accomplished. And for what? For Chrissake, I'm working for Nazis.'

Across the encampment, the labourers were returning from their ablutions, marching in rows of two to the cookhouse for late supper. The Externsteine thrust up beyond like a ruined wall built by giants.

'There is something magnetic about this place,' she said, staring up at the tors. 'I wasted time scrounging around the passages and chambers like all the others. I think the alter chamber above was a ploy to keep us away from looking at what lies beneath.'

Mauss pulled an unconvinced face. 'The Anasazi Indians had similar chambers, high on the cliff faces in Arizona. They were not a ploy. They were for resistance.' Finishing his wine, he put down the empty cup. 'Of course, there is another possibility to consider.'

She turned away from the Externsteine, facing Mauss. Before she could ask, he replied.

'What you have uncovered is no mine.' He said it as statement of fact, not supposition.

'You base this theory on…?'

'Agisterstein.'

'Gesundheit,' she replied sarcastically, perplexed by Mauss's cryptic comment.

'Very amusing. Agisterstein, from the most ancient of Saxon writings of this place means…'

'Stone with the dragon cave,' she interrupted as she began to realise what it meant.

He nodded. 'You learnt well. "Stone", meaning?'

'Jungfräu?'

He nodded. '"Dragon cave?"'

She shrugged. 'I don't know. You got me.'

'A Crimen hollow.'

'They're *here*?' she muttered.

He nodded.

'Now?'

He nodded again.

'How could I have missed it?'

It was Mauss's turn to shrug. 'When we stare too long at a tree, we forget about the rest of the forest. You look without seeing.'

Taking a breathe before replying, she finally said, 'Twenty-seven years has got behind me,' she said, whispering now. 'Not a day passes without thought of Balthasar.' She looked to him. 'But I can't remember his face any more,' she said, sounding uncharacteristically sentimental.

Without meaning to, she suddenly found a tear in her eyes. Lowering her ball cap, she tried to hide it behind the brim.

'I'll never forget the darkness of his eyes though. In them. Deep in the black of them. There I saw flecks of melancholy.' She took another deep breathe. The scent of forest at dusk.

'I'll never stop,' she said to him. 'Never. Not until I find Balthasar and get to the bottom of everything I saw that night. And I'm so close. So very close.'

'You said that here, there is only science.'

'I did say that.'

'Science will never define love.'

She smiled. It wasn't a smile of happiness, only consolation. 'I half expected you to understand.'

'We share experience with a wild sign only.'

'Balthasar Toule and I had a connection. He pulled me out of a flooding hold and saved me from drowning. And as he carried me out of harm's way, he told me: "You've a long road ahead of you." After everything that's happened; the ruin of my career, of my reputation, I feel for the first time I'm near the end of the road.'

'Possibly, you have taken the wrong road, Eleanor.'

'What other road can there be?'

Mauss sighed, almost as if he were disappointed with her.

'Surely you have not forsaken the most elementary tenet of *The Gift*?'

She stared at him for the longest time while the cogs in her head turned. Then a dark understanding arose not from her mind, but from the pit of her stomach. '*Angebinde*.'

'*Angebinde*,' he repeated. 'Binds created through gifting.'

'And gifts are seldom free,' she admitted, unhappily now.

'Seldom, if ever.'

'I'm bound to the Ahnenerbe?'

'It is worse than that,' he said. 'You're bound to the Nazis.'

She nodded, solemnly, so much suddenly becoming clear to her. 'They gave me a gift.'

'*Angebinde*. The Nazis do nothing without compensation.'

She cursed quietly to herself. 'What a fool I am.'

They sat in silence for a time.

'Something terrible happened here a long time ago, Eleanor,' Mauss spoke up, looking to the tors, lit by a new moon. 'Something best left undisturbed.'

❖ ❖ ❖

Elle awoke, elbow on the arm of her campaign chair, palm of her hand resting on the side of her face, propping up her chin. In the small hours of the night, the unattended fire had reduced to hot embers and was now giving off a sallow glow. Neck stiff, she stretched out.

Dr Mauss slumbered on her bunk, shoes still on. It was warm that night, and she hadn't minded sleeping outside. A flash lit the sky beyond the dark forest and a second backlit the Externsteine, the tors jutting up like a dragon's spine. Heat lightning. Gaining her feet, she opened the lid of the water butt and dipped a tin cup into the ice water. She drank, the cold liquid soothing her parched throat.

Another silent flash of lightning came, before she heard something. Something she'd not heard for a long time. It frightened her. Returning the cup to the barrel, careful not to make a sound as she closed the lid, she moved away from the fire's glow, and strained her eyes into the darkness. Again she heard it. A faint dissonance, far off. Taking up an iron fire poker for defence, she looked about the clearing, set apart from the greater Lager by a copse of tall firs.

The next closest tent was Dietrich's. It was dark, with the tent flap down. A parked-up *Kübelwagen* sat beside it, the heavy morning dew covering the hood.

She stood stock-still. No light came from the nearby labourer encampment, the night-watch nowhere to be seen. The camp strays, to whom the men fed their scraps, barked in the distance. Two steps more from the glow of the fire and a cloak of darkness enveloped her. The low morning mist obscured the terrain ahead.

A distant flash lit the sky again, momentarily illuminating her surroundings. She stood at the edge of the Lager, the high trees of the forest towering over her, August crickets gone quiet. The sound came again, from deep in the forest. An adolescent note from a boys' choir. It brought with it a sudden shudder. A memory of when she first heard it. Belowdecks on Titanic. In a blood smeared cabin.

Curiosity propelled her forward. She had no control over her feet. Already fifty paces from her tent, the blackness of the forest pulled her into its limbs. Straining her ears, desperate to pick out the direction of the curious sound, she heard nothing now but the distant barking of the dogs.

Suddenly, the dogs went quiet. Then, it came again. Closer. Different. The sweet refrain of a boys' choir, replaced by a desperate gull's trill. Something lurked in shadow. She squinted. There was movement at the edge of her vision. Then she saw them: faint circles aglow in the distant embers of her fire.

A pair of eyes. Wild signs.

The single set of eyes became many, as a flash of lightning lit the treeline. Her heart froze, feet turned to cement, body rigid. The trees looked to be alive — lithe seraphs, naked, skin porcelain, vermiculated among the high limbs of the beech trees. A lovely little thing crept along a branch towards her. It stopped, caressing its taught breasts as it looked down upon her. Another moved in close, shaft distended, taking the seraph from behind. It shuddered, mouth agape. Elle's body had an involuntary, almost primal, hedonic reaction to the seraph's brutal copulation.

Another flash of lightning and the seraphs turned hideous, faces elongating, noses burst, exposing knotted inner leafs while stickle-backed spines parted, sprouting membranous wings.

They took flight, swooping down from the beech trees towards her. Elle tried to scream, but her voice abandoned her. She turned to run. Hot breath prickled the back of her neck. An unholy banshee howl before she was struck.

She cried out as she launched upright in her campaign chair.

'Dr Annenberg?'

Her eyes focused. Dietrich was before her, a steadying hand on her shoulder. It was dawn, the heavy morning mist lingering, and distant hums of conversation could be heard from the labourers as they gathered at the long benches for breakfast.

'You are all right?'

'I'm fine.' She felt rough. Looking to the forest behind her tent, she saw nothing out of the ordinary and heard only birdsong welcoming the new day. 'I need a coffee.'

'Dr Annenberg has had night terrors,' said a dishevelled Dr Mauss, emerging from Elle's tent, pulling the arms of his wire-rimmed glasses over his ears.

'Dr Mauss. You are here?'

'Oui, Herr Dietrich. I received your telegram and came at once.' Pinching the bridge of his nose, he squinted at the morning sun. 'And if I could have a cup of tea to relieve this *mal aux cheveux*,' he said showing Dietrich the empty wine bottle upside down in Elle's water butt. 'I would be most grateful.'

Dietrich nodded. 'We have breakfast prepared. I will arrange for an additional guest, Herr Doktor.'

'Dietrich,' said Elle, shaking off her all-too-real nightmare. 'The gelignite?'

'All is prepared. But I think you should reconsider.'

❖ ❖ ❖

They stood in the narrow passage. Five gelignite charges hung from the massive slab of stone barring the way. Battery-operated lights replaced the oil lamps: open flames and explosives a happy ending did not make.

'*Mon Dieu*,' muttered Dr Mauss.

'What is sealed behind it must be important, to emplace such a massive blocking stone,' said Dietrich.

'They sure didn't want anyone getting in,' Elle remarked.

Dr Mauss moved closer to the stone, hands touching the inscriptions. 'Or getting out.'

Reaching into her trousers, Elle fished out the old compass Corky O'Shea had given her years ago.

'What d'you want to bet this passage leads due south-east, right under the Externsteine?'

Unsnapping its worn leather case, she looked at the compass. 'That's a helluva thing,' she said, showing it to Dr Mauss. The dial was spinning like a whirling dervish.

He looked up to her. 'This is not a way into a mine.'

'What then?' asked Dietrich.

'You know what this is,' said Elle.

'Oui,' Mauss replied, hand tracing the disembowelled human form chiselled into the stone, death's head eliciting a warning familiar to them both.

'*Expecto resurrectionem mortuorum.*'

'A *Totenkopf,*' said Dietrich.

They looked to him.

'Christ. That's exactly what it is,' said Elle. She'd spent so many years wondering what Balthasar's talisman meant to her, she'd completely overlooked what it meant to others.

'*Totenkopf*?' asked Mauss.

'The symbol of the Death's Head Division of the SS.' Dietrich turned to Elle.

She nodded, understanding. The Nazi Division had adopted Balthasar's death's head as their unit symbol.

'Until now, I half found your theory of the Externsteine utterly false,' continued Dietrich.

'I didn't possess evidence to prove predation until…'

Dr Mauss looked at the elaborate wiring leading away from the gelignite and back up the passage to the plunger at the surface. 'You must not open this.'

'But it was you who brought me to this point,' she replied in dismay. 'I need to know what's behind it.'

'Once you open this door, there is no closing it.'

Caution and prudence battled it out with determination, but it was no real fight. Elle knew she had to find her answer.

The gelignite was detonated, and the hollow breached.

A hand gripped the collar of her shirt, spinning her around. She caught a glimpse of coal-scuttle helmets and black uniforms before everything went sideways.

It would have been better, perhaps, had she chosen prudence after all.

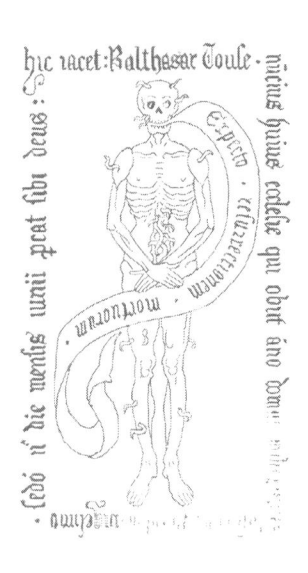

29 AUGUST 1939.
THE STRAIT OF DOVER

The wagons-lits carriage shunted onto the *Ferry Boat de Nuit*. It had just gone two in the morning and Elle couldn't sleep. She hadn't for three days already, and probably wouldn't until the night ferry crossed the English Channel and landed in Dover, England.

She was heading back to the States with her tail between her legs.

Raising the window blind in her compartment, she just glimpsed the *Quai des Monitors* before her sleeper carriage disappeared into the gaping gangway of Twickenham Ferry's train-deck. The port of Dunkirk was Elle's last stop on the Continent before crossing the Channel.

She watched from her window as a conductor waved his carbide lamp, directing the train onto one of the ferry's four tracks loaded with blue-and-gold accented sleeper carriages and baggage fourgons. The lights lining the train deck's riveted ceiling were dimmed, so as not to disturb First-Class passengers asleep in their berths.

A grinding clang echoed along the walls of the deck. A pair of labourers manhandled large, oily chains, while others busily jacked up the uncoupled sleeper to take the weight off its springs. The chains were attached to mooring rings on the underside of the carriage and tightened with screw-eyes. There was a carnival atmosphere to the loading of the carriages, the racket unnerving. Elle wondered if the French labourers took some kind of perverse pleasure in awakening the passengers.

Crossing the compartment, she raised a small folding table in the corner, revealing a tiny washbasin beneath. Turning on the taps, she moistened a wash-cloth and then looked at herself in the mirror. She dabbed the stitched wound at the back of her head, hardly recognising herself, her brown eyes hollow and surrounded by dark rings from lack of sleep. The rough dressing wrapped about her head had ceased weeping, but what she needed was a proper bath to wash out the dried blood caked in her hair. Tossing the cloth into the basin, she reached for her baseball cap sitting on the brass rack above her bunk and positioned it to cover her bandage. She would have to make do with a jaunty tilt.

'Marlene Dietrich you ain't.'

As if she didn't already look cuckoo enough in her soiled dungarees, clunky work boots, Shepherd's check shirt and moth-eaten grey sweatshirt with "St. Dunstan's" scrawled across the front of it in green and white chenille lettering.

Sliding back the berth's door, she guardedly looked both ways along the narrow corridor. Coast clear, she made her way aft; type F carriages were accessed at the rear. An attendant stood from his flip-up chair at the end of the carriage.

'Madam, can I help?' he asked quietly. She took a step back, his dark blue uniform too similar in the dark to the getup worn by the SS thugs.

'I'm going to deck,' she responded, opening the outer door at the rear of the sleeper.

'Do you not wish to sleep?'

'With that racket?' she said, jabbing a thumb in the direction of the ferry workers. 'I need to take some air.'

'Very well,' he replied graciously. 'Your carriage number is 3805. Please do mind your step as you alight.'

She smiled. Manners were a nice change.

With rainwater dripping from wet carriages onto the iron decking already slippery with rail grease, the hobnails on the bottom of her boots made negotiating the train-deck a thorny business. Even so, the dock labourers spared her nary a glance as they hurried over a slab of tracked gangway folding upwards as the ferry prepared to make way.

With the sleepers secured and the labourers now gone, the deck grew quiet. Flat-footing her way forward, she came to a stairway. A sign in English read: *First-Class Dining Saloon & Deck.*

After making her way up into a cloud of tobacco smoke hanging lazily in a companionway, she passed by a set of open double-doors to the First-Class bar. Ice clinked in glasses. A woman giggled. Apparently, Elle wasn't the only passenger unable to sleep. She could use a drink but didn't fancy the mindless banter that went with it. An open hatch led up to deck. Making her way amidships, she stopped below the ferry's red and black tipped funnels. Save for the sound of herring gulls and the distant *thrum-thrum-thrum* from the propellers, the night was peaceful, the air keen. Threatening clouds that had hounded her since Antwerp came apart and moonbeams patinated great swathes of the Channel.

Steadying herself against a lifeboat, Elle removed a crumpled packet of cigarettes from her pocket. *Enver Bey*. In her final, confusing minutes at the Externsteine, the Chesterfields Dr Mauss gave her went missing. She tossed the shit German *Zigaretten* overboard. Fluttering down the dark hull of the ferry, they landed in the waters of Dunkirk Harbour, disappearing into the bilge outflow.

She raised the collar of her shirt, pulling her St Dunstan's sweatshirt taut about her neck as she closed her eyes, taking in the briny night air. Although it was August, the Strait of Dover had a nip to it. The last three days had been torturously long. Bad Meinberg to Essen, and then on to Antwerp and from there to Dunkirk, where she had boarded the night train. In a few hours more, she would be safely in England.

Slipping a hand underneath her ball cap, she felt for the wound. It throbbed. If being butted in the head by a Schmeisser machine gun wasn't bad enough, having seventeen stitches hurriedly applied by Dietrich's shaking hands was worse still.

She had been tossed into the back of an Opel Blitz truck, followed closely by her hastily packed field trunk and driven to the train station in Bad Meinberg. Kept under guard by the SS, she was then unceremoniously booted off the train at the Belgian frontier — and still that wasn't the worst of it. Coming so close to validating everything she spent the last twenty-seven years trying to prove, but being unable to see it through, was the worst trauma imaginable. She had touched the blocking stone at the end of the passage, a familiar death symbol grimacing back at her, carved into the stone, the apothegm: *Expecto resurrectionem mortuorum.*

Balthasar Toule had been there.

Elle had detonated the gelignite and breached the hollow. But she never got a look within. She sighed, now wishing she hadn't tossed her cigarettes into the Channel.

A man in a wrinkled linen suit appeared through the hatch leading to the saloon. He lit a cigarette.

'Sorry to bother,' she said.

He nodded, his features becoming clear in the light from the companionway. Although his face showed signs of age, his grey hair was filled with waves, making him look younger. 'No bother, *mijn schatje*.'

He produced a packet of Gauloises and offered her one. She accepted. Clicking open his gold lighter he held out a flame for her. She took in a drag, her exhalation filling the night air with smoke. 'Looks as though you needed it.'

'That obvious?'

'You have the look of the vagabond.'

She stared at him in the darkness; something about the man gave her a curious feeling of déjà vu.

'Difficult journey, ja?' he asked.

She nodded.

'It would be impossible to fail to notice a lady dressed in such attire.'

Elle realised she looked a mess. 'I've had a rotten couple of days.'

'Ja. I should think you have, *mijn schatje.*'

He was speaking Flemish. Belgian. His manner suggested he held a lady in esteem, and not as an object of desire. Yet, something about his demeanour conveyed a rakish streak. Like an Eton drunk.

'I'm not much of a conversationalist just now, I'm afraid.' She put a hand out. 'Eleanor Annenberg.'

Even in the dim light of the saloon's windows, she saw the Belgian's face blanch. A long, uncomfortable moment of silence followed. She saw schemes hatch in his shrewd, blue eyes. When he spoke, his tone was changed.

'This ferry will not terminate at Dover in the morning.'

'Sorry?'

'It will call into Folkestone.'

'Folkestone?'

He nodded, eyes narrowing. 'Lovely in summer. I recommend a visit to the Parish of St Emiliana. It's quite *a meeting place.*'

With that, he dropped his cigarette end on the deck.

Elle watched as he turned from her and, without another word, disappeared through the companionway leading to the saloon. She had no idea what had changed in the man so abruptly, but after the thrashing she took in Germany, she wasn't keen to remain in the open.

249

Another cloud burst sent sheets of rain down onto the ferry. Elle scurried from deck. There were cabins and a dining room on the ferry for First-Class passengers, but after the odd behaviour of the Belgian, she wanted only to be safely back in her sleeper compartment. Returning to the train deck, she squeezed around the carriages, nervously looking around for the first sign of trouble, catching Dunkirk as it faded from view through the open aft deck.

'*Au revoir*, Continent.'

She made her way forward along the carriage's corridor, a tannoy crackling to life just as she reached her berth.

'Please excuse the interruption,' a subdued and all-too British voice announced. 'Due to heavy fog at Dover Marine, this ferry will divert to Folkestone. Please accept our apologies.'

Sliding the door closed behind her, she slumped onto the banquette, the ferry gently pitching as it changed course.

251

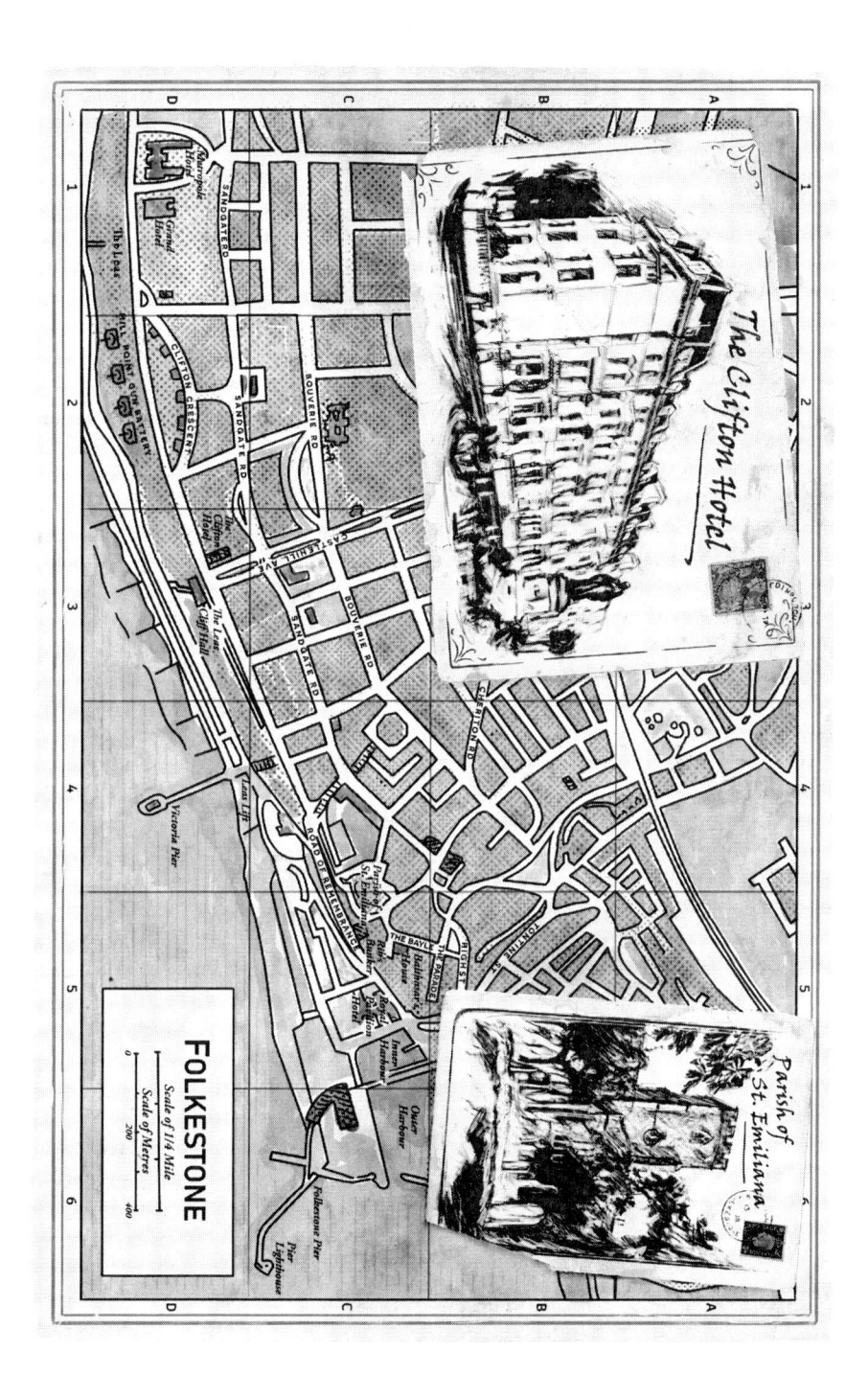

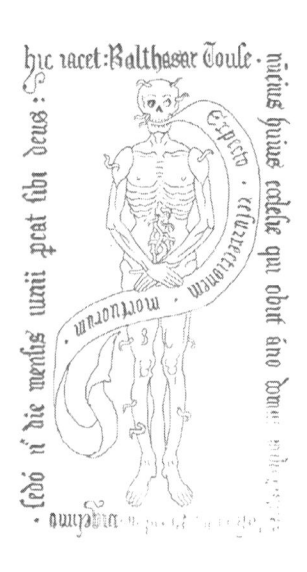

29 AUGUST 1939.
FOLKESTONE, KENT

The first hint of the new day arrived in glorious pink and red. It was half past four and Elle had still not slept. The chalky White Cliffs of Dover showed themselves in the distance, lights from the harbour winking to the east. So much for fog.

Eight miles down coast, she made out the lights of Folkestone. Had the paling Belgian merely informed her of a change in destination, or was she now seeing conspiracies everywhere?

By half past six, the early summertime sun began to show itself, and Elle was able to take the air just in her Shepherd check shirt. Features of the English coastline grew clear. Although not as vast as the port of Dover, Folkestone's harbour was humming. Packet boats preparing for the morning's sail to Boulogne jostled in the high tide with nimble fishing luggers. Down the coast from the harbour's fish sheds, the seafront became a place of amusement. A whitewashed pier jutted into the Channel, the pavilion's zinc roof glistening in the morning sunshine. At the top of the beach stood a long, undulating switchback roller coaster. Rows of yellow and white trimmed changing tents opened for bathers on the shingled west beaches, while porters set out wood and canvas chairs along the high-water mark. A few early bathers were taking their morning plunge in an open-air swimming pool.

While the Germans threatened their neighbours, Britain was on holiday.

On the cliffs above the beach stood a long row of stately Regency homes and hotels. Just showing itself over a copse of poplar and ash was a church tower.

❖ ❖ ❖

Twickenham Ferry made Folkestone's outer harbour in a scant fifteen minutes. Lines were tossed to dockhands, who pulled them over bollards, securing the ferry to the pier.

No sooner had Elle returned to her carriage than vibrations began to rattle her window. Lowering it, she leaned out and watched as the chains securing her carriage to the deck were drawn away. Darkness gave way to drenching sunshine as her sleeper rolled onto an iron gantry. The wagons-lits carriages marshalled along a siding, where a pair of Stirling locomotives waited to double-head the train up a steeply graded rail spur. As the carriage began inching forward, Elle retrieved from her rucksack one of the old tennis balls, *RF Downey & Co* still just visible in the worn felt.

Settling into her banquette for the two-hour trip up to London, she tossed the ball against the wall of her berth and caught it as it bounced back. The sun dazzled her though the open windows. Seagulls cawed overhead, and in the distance, she heard children laughing. A Union Jack fluttered outside the harbour master's office. She was safe.

As the locomotives crawled forward, Elle closed her eyes, the slow, drawn-out tugs of the Stirlings pulling the carriages across the viaduct, lullabying her. She was just dozing off when she was roused by the hoot from a steam whistle.

Opening her eyes as a signal shed passed by, she caught sight of a white sign below the signalman's window. In black letters: *Folkestone Harbour*.

Black letters on a white background.

A light clicked in her head as the carriage jarred, the pitch of the room changing as the train began climbing the incline towards the upper town. She opened the lid of her travel trunk, digging through a jumble of personal effects until she found the ledger Dougie Beedham had given her on Utila Island, ten years before.

The incline steepened. Elle tumbled onto the upholstered banquette, morning sun illuminating faint, gold lettering pressed into the ledger's cover: *US Commerce Committee Investigation into RMS Titanic.*

Inside it was Titanic's closet: White Star Line's cargo manifests. Transatlantic cargo was traceable — where it was heading and where it came from. Titanic's cargo manifests should have contained a record of the skeletons in Balthasar Toule's closet. She had pored endlessly over the manifests, from stem to stern. Keel to crow's nest, but there was nothing so extraordinary as a pair of sarcophagi. Nothing linked to Toule. Nothing in No. 2 Hold or any other on the ship.

Quickly flipping through the pages, her finger slid down the rows of cargo: forty-three mink coats from Russia, twenty-eight crates of leaded crystal from Venice, seventeen rugs from Persia, a 1912 Renault motorcar from Paris, eight dozen tennis balls.

No. No. And no.

Then, on page eighty-nine, an addition. Not written neatly with a biro, but scribbled in with a pencil. Last-minute. Her finger slid across the details:

27061965QI.
Item description: 1 Large Crate, Roentgen secretary.
Notation: Excess weight. Charge levied.
Destination: New York.
Port of Origin: Folkestone.

'Folkestone,' she said.

Black letters on a white background.

'I'll be damned.' Struggling to her feet in the cock-eyed cabin, she leaned out of the window. The locomotives had made the top of the incline. Although her sleeper remained on the slope, already she felt an increase in speed.

Folkestone. She didn't believe in coincidences. She was meant to end up there. If the night ferry had landed her in Dover, she would have zipped on by Folkestone without giving it more thought.

Rummaging through her trunk, she grabbed Corky's compass, shoving the tennis balls and the ledger into her rucksack, along with her Tigers ball cap. Sliding back the berth's door, she stumbled into the companionway.

'Madam,' the startled attendant called from his seat at the rear of the carriage. 'Please return to your cabin. It's dangerous in the companionway.'

'I'm alighting,' she replied, half charging, half-falling down angle towards the rear of the carriage.

'You mustn't,' the attendant said, alarm in his voice. 'The train will not be stopping. Please, you must return to your cabin.'

Elle hadn't felt such courage since the night she descended into Titanic's flooding holds. Twisting the handle to the outer door, it flew open, the sound of steel trucks below her screeching along the rails like nails across a chalkboard. She stood there, momentarily frozen by the rush of air that greeted her. The attendant tripped on the wool carpet as he made his way to stop her, crashing against the ornate wood panelling. With renewed vigour, she slung her bag onto her shoulders and leapt from the carriage, just as the attendant grabbed hold of her sweatshirt.

'Madam!' he shouted as she slipped from his grasp. Tumbling amidst the grease-soaked cinders at the side of the rails, she rolled clear from the rake of sleepers, kitchen carriages and fourgon vans. The attendant stared back at her in horror. 'Have you lost your mind?'

Laughing nervously as she staggered to her feet, knees wobbly, head spinning, even she was surprised by her bravado.

'Nope,' she hollered over the screech of the train, wiping off the oily ballast stones sticking to her sweatshirt. Uninjured, she made her way down the incline, pulling off her sweatshirt and rolling back her shirtsleeves before picking up her ruck and shouldering it, she added, 'I believe I have found it.'

❖ ❖ ❖

A porter in burgundy livery stood before the Royal Pavilion Hotel's entrance, adjusting his spotless white gloves.

'Could you tell me, do you have any vacancies?' Elle asked.

The porter gave her bedraggled appearance a not-so-kind looking over.

'Sorry, ma'am. You've arrived dab in the midst of our high season. We're bursting. You may have better luck at a hotel atop The Leas.'

'The Leas?'

'Up the Road of Remembrance.'

He pointed towards a steep road and the Heights above.

'Folkestone's grass promenade is quite notable.'

A hoot from his whistle attracted the attention of a taxi driver collecting his breakfast from a vendor hawking whelks and jellied eels.

'Don't bother,' Elle replied. 'I'll hoof it.'

'Up to The Leas?' he said. 'A lady does not walk up the Road of Remembrance. That sort of thing just isn't done in Folkestone.'

Elle turned without reply, heading towards the steep road. Beautiful day it might very well have been, but the fact was she didn't have a single penny to pay the driver. And considering the state of her, she couldn't blame the porter for wanting her to push off.

A footpath edged with rosemary ran along the side of the narrow road. Beginning the climb, she heard a howl from the harbour below. She looked back, saw steam billowing from the twin funnels of Twickenham Ferry as she prepared for her return journey to France. Continuing up the road, she saw what looked like roadworks ahead. As she got closer, she thought it wasn't roadworks after all but rather earthworks burrowing into the tree-covered hillside. With mere inches to spare between the entrance and the road, it seemed a precarious location. Workmen in overalls came and went from under Hessian netting which concealed a concrete bulwark.

It turned out not to be earthworks either; it was a bunker in preparation. A soldier stood guard beside another entrance, unconcerned by anyone happening by and having a good look. Another soldier appeared from the principle entrance, rifle slung, sipping a mug of tea.

'Hello darlin',' one of them called out, tipping his Tommy helmet back for a better look at her. 'Cor, blimey. Had a rough night of it then?'

'What you, then? A refugee? Fancy a cuppa?' said the other, lifting his tin cup.

Elle gave them a brief glance back before going on her way. She didn't fancy small talk. She wanted a bathtub and a bed. As she walked away, she heard one of them call her a rude name.

Reaching the Road of Remembrance's height, she passed a forlorn statue of victory. Facing France, her open arms held a cross in one hand and a laurel wreath in the other — a memorial to those killed in the Great War. Glancing back to the bunker being prepared, Elle wondered if it foretold the coming of another.

To her surprise, a trap pulled by a llama passed her by with a half-dozen well-dressed children in sun hats all giggling at her attire.

Llamas and a bunker. Folkestone was at odds with itself.

Following behind the llama as it made its way along a promenade fringed with manicured grass and flowerbeds bursting in late-summer splendour, Elle realised that even at seven in the morning, Folkestone was alive with holiday-makers. School girls played shuttlecock on flawlessly clipped grass, the matron shooting Elle a disapproving scowl as she passed, attesting to the state of her: grubby dungarees, shirt smeared with rail grease, bandaged head not well hidden under a Tigers baseball cap. Probably she niffed as well. Passing one Regency-style hotel after another without a vacancy, she began losing hope of finding a room, much less a bath.

An elderly Wall's ice cream man parked up his tandem bicycle, Warrick box mounted at the front, filled with frozen tubs and bricks of ice creams. He looked a bit of a lunatic in his polished Sam Browne belt and white officers cap, yet it was he who gave Elle a perplexed look.

'Cripes. Where have you came from?'

'The Continent.' She indicated to the Channel.

The Wall's man *humphed*. 'That what they're sporting over there these days?'

'Long few days of travel.'

He nodded, looking her over. 'Yank, are you?'

'Detroit,' she said. 'Eleanor.'

'Dagenham. Wally.' He put a finger to his neatly groomed moustache before asking, 'That clobber you've got on don't especially blend in with Snobbington-by-the-Seaside.'

'So it seems. If only I could find a hotel.'

'Hotel, you say? Well, the Clifton is just behind old Harvey there.' He pointed beyond a statue across the road. 'A fine establishment as well.'

'I'd have an ice cream if you accepted Reichsmarks.'

'Ho ho, you is lost. I'd have Hong Kong dollars and Indian cents, English pounds and Eskimo pence over Hitler money.'

Opening the lid of his Warrick box, Dagenham Wally handed her a raspberry and orange snofrute.

'Call it charity,' he said with a wink. 'The brats round here only want choco bars and wafer biscuits anyway.'

She thanked him before crossing the street and making her way to the hotel, pausing for a moment before the statue.

'Discovered the circulation of the blood, our Dr Harvey did,' shouted Dagenham Wally. 'From Folkestone as well.'

Opening the paper wrapper of the snofrute she bit off an ice cold chunk of frozen fruit. It went down a treat. Taking another bight, she read the bronze plaque on a plinth at the statue's feet: *Dr William Harvey. 1 April 1578 – 3 June 1657. Physician in Ordinary. His Majesty Charles I.*

She stopped chewing. 'Not Dr Harvey Folcanstan,' she said looking up to the statue's face. It was he who had travelled to the Tor Externsteine's cwicseolfor mine and led her to the Crimen hollow.

'Not Dr William Harvey Folcanstan,' she repeated, having to remind herself there was no such thing as coincidence. 'Dr Harvey *of* Folcanstan.' Suddenly, her failure at the Externsteine and the beating she took at the hands of the Nazis were forgotten.

Looking towards the hotel, she let slip a Michigan holler in front of the holiday-makers in their morning suits and flower-print summer dresses on the terrace. 'Yahoo!'

They replied with sharp glances over their morning tea.

'Eleanor,' she told herself, finishing the snofrute and hitting her stride as she ascended the terrace steps, 'you are exactly where you're meant to be.'

A porter intercepted her, a cross look on his face. 'Oi! Go off. Gypsies not welcome here.'

'I beg your pardon?'

'We won't have your lot disturbing guests,' he tut-tutted. 'No charity to be had here, miss.'

'I am not a "miss", you impertinent little twirp,' she barked at him. 'I have a PhD in ethnology, and you'll address me as Doctor.'

The terrace fell silent. A teaspoon clattered to the ground, and a lady drinking tea at a table nearby gasped loudly.

'I'm dirty. I'm tired. And I'm vexed. Now, wipe that stupid look from your mug and step aside.' Brushing by the shrinking porter, she mounted a second step to the entrance of the hotel before turning to rearrange her baseball cap. 'And, I'm an American.'

Entering the lobby, she took stock. Ahead, double doors led to a dining room, glorious white tablecloths spread across them. To her right, a small sitting area with a grandfather clock ticking way. To her left, a clerk in a dark-blue suit stood behind a reception counter. No greeting was forthcoming.

Her best American smile before she spoke up. 'I would like a guest-room, please.'

'We're quite booked,' the clerk replied politely, when really he was saying: *piss off.*

'Young man,' she interrupted, leaning across the counter. 'Before you inform me you don't want the likes of me in your lovely hotel, hear me through. I'm Eleanor Annenberg. Three days ago, I was boshed in the head by a pair of Nazi thugs and thrown out of Germany on my backside. I've spent the days since on God only knows how many trains.'

The clerk laughed. 'Nazis? That's fantastic. Best whopper I've heard in ages. What have you really done to yourself? Fallen from a fun fair ride down by the pier have we?'

'Nazis?' A voice repeated from behind an open door. The hotel manager, sleeve folded back where his left arm once was, joined his subordinate at the reception counter. He threw Elle a fixing glance as only an old Englishman could. Then, he smiled. 'The Hun can be cheeky can't they?'

'Did you lose that in the war?' Elle asked.

'This?' He turned his shoulder, showing her where his left arm had been. 'It went to the bottom with Titanic.' He smiled.

Then she did too, remembering him. 'First-Class Steward Swinburne.'

'Miss Annenberg. Or is it Missus?'

'It's Doctor. But by now you should call me Eleanor,' she replied.

'And by now you should call me Tony.'

He gave his subordinate a little thump on the shoulder. 'Only this one addresses me as Mister Swinburne.'

Turning, he addressed the clerk directly. 'A long time ago, Eleanor saved my life. Least we can do is offer her a superior room at one pound ten.' Turning his attention back to her, he continued, 'Afraid it hasn't an *ensuite*, but there's a nicely sorted bath down the hall. Shall I send a maid to launder your things?'

'Thank you,' she replied.

'Portmanteau?'

'I travel light,' she replied, showing him the rucksack on her shoulder.

'You really were tossed out of Germany.'

'I'm organising a counter-attack.'

Swinburne offered an amused nod. 'I shouldn't expect anything less.' Taking the oval key chain and room ticket off his clerk, he presented them to her. 'Welcome to the Hotel Clifton, Eleanor.'

❖ ❖ ❖

Max and Moritz, as she named them, cawed from the ledge. The herring gulls and Elle were becoming fast friends, and they crouched outside her bay windows, preening their feathers. After room service delivered her cheese and cucumber sandwiches, the cheeky birds, like the two terrible boys in Wilhelm Busch's *A Story of Seven Boyish Pranks*, made such a racket that she surrendered her crusts to them. It kept the birds quiet. For a while.

After a hot bath, she curled up in a comfy armchair by the window, succumbing to exhaustion both physical and mental. Every muscle. Every bone. Every last joint ached. The avalanche of events that brought her to Folkestone caught up with her and despite doing her level best to sort the lot of it out she could hardly keep her eyes open.

❖ ❖ ❖

She awoke to the terrible twosome making a racket, their big, webbed feet padding back and forth outside her opened windows. Rubbing her eyes, she squinted at her watch. It was near five in the afternoon. She had slept for nine hours.

Remaining in her armchair as her lethargy slowly melted away, she watched the world outside her window. Despite the time, the sun remained high. The Leas lay below, chock-a-block with parading holiday-makers. Children's laughter waned in the breeze. A Punch and Judy show was in progress. Porters in blue boiler suits lined folding chairs up around a bandstand, their supervisor adjusting the distance between them with a measuring stick.

Elle felt the taut corners of her mouth turn upwards into a smile. If Germany was ominous and austere, Britain overflowed with cheer and hope, lazy summer days at the seaside a reminder there was plenty of good in the world yet. She had a good few things to put straight in her head before she quite understood what brought her to this place. How did all of this bring her closer to Balthasar?

A hotel maid took pity on her attire and brought her a laundered blouse, left behind by a guest. A box outside Elle's door contained her sponged-clean dungarees and brown work boots, polished up and strung with new laces. Letting her robe fall to the floor, she stood naked in front of the mirror hanging in a wardrobe door, examining herself. It felt like a long time since she had such a luxury.

She was rested if not bruised. The dark circles, surrounding her eyes, were — like them — not brown nor green but something in between, began to disappear after a good rest. But not the smile lines around her eyes. They weren't smile lines, really.

Her bobbed brown hair had nary a grey strand. She was still slim and her legs strong from the endless climbing up and down the excavation site's switchbacks. Even her breasts had yet to go south like a snowbird in winter.

'You held up pretty good for a forty-five-year-old broad who took a beating from the Nazis.'

Sliding into her dungarees and the second-hand, peach linen blouse, she left her baseball cap on a hook behind the door. Giving herself a last looking over, she had to admit she managed to pull off *quite pretty* effortlessly.

Descending to the lobby, she was met with hushed tut-tuts from ladies and lingering glances from gents. Tony Swinburne stood at reception, thumb in pocket of his waistcoat, his patient smile welcoming. 'You are feeling rested?'

'Hot water and tea do wonders, Tony.'

'Noggin on the mend?'

'Yes, thank you,' she replied, touching the stitches on the back of her head. 'Feeling more like myself.'

'A scrub and a pot of tea can do that,' he replied with a nod. 'I am in receipt of a wire from your Stateside banker. It is quite in excess of your stay. Are you in need of a few Pounds Sterling for the pocket?'

She raised her arms, showing off her dodgy attire. 'Are you suggesting I'm inappropriately dressed for Folkestone?'

'I am happy to recommend several fashionable dress shops on the high street. They can arrange for a selection to be brought to the hotel, if you'd like.'

She smiled. 'I'd like. Just nothing too frilly.'

'Clearly.'

'I was wondering…' she started.

'How can I help?' he asked, with a little smile that reinforced to Elle she was safe now.

'… Might you direct me to a local church?'

'Any denomination especially?'

'The Parish of St Emiliana?'

'On The Bayle.'

'The Bayle?'

'Folkestone's oldest street. Just down The Leas from here. You can hoof it in under five minutes.'

Thanking Tony, she turned for the entrance. Five minutes? She'd be there in three.

❖ ❖ ❖

Leaving The Leas behind, Elle passed the war memorial, finding a narrow lane Tony had directed her to, shaded by poplar and ash. Down a steep slope to her right, hidden among the trees, she picked out sounds of the bunker worksite on the Road of Remembrance. To her left stood the Parish of St Emiliana, its Gothic ragstone tower stained by centuries of Channel wind and rain.

Turning off the lane, she strode through the parish grounds, the feather-shaped leaves of an ancient, weeping ash welcoming her as she passed rows of askew headstones. A plump woman with her hair in a bun pulled weeds from between flower-laden rose bushes along the cemetery walls. She wiped her hands on her apron, acknowledging Elle with a smile.

Following the parish path, Elle turned a corner and arrived at the front porch. The hinges of the heavy wooden door creaked as she pushed it in, the heat of the day vanishing in the coolness of the chancel arcade as she entered. She inhaled. She hadn't breathed so easily in a long while. There was calm in the old parish which soothed her. Defused light filtered through painted glass windows in the high chancel, falling upon a gilded altar. To its left, a small brass hatch was set within the wall. The vestry door opposite swung in, and a thin, but hardly frail, vicar stood before her.

'Hello, ma child.'

Still skittish from the last days' trauma, Elle had to fight off her instinct to step back. 'Oh. I'm sorry. Just came in for a look round.'

'It's God's house. His door is never locked to they who wish to have a look round.' The vicar stepped away from the vestry door, leaving it open. 'American?'

'Detroit.'

'Henry Ford?'

'Ty Cobb.'

The vicar had a little chuckle. Elle smelled whiskey. With an "e". Irish.

'Not seen many of you round about here since war's end.'

Elle looked over his shoulder into the vestry. A narrow, gated archway in the corner led into darkness. 'Folkestone wasn't on my travel plans. Just passing through.'

'That was what them doughboys done: passed through. Down the Road of Remembrance by the thousands. Off to France to fight the Hun. Was a long time ago, so it was.' He sighed. 'I'm Vicar Duigan. This 'ere is my parish.'

'Dr Eleanor Annenberg.' There was something familiar about the vicar, but she couldn't quite place him from her memory. 'Have we met before?'

'Oh I don't expect so. You've a face I wouldn't soon forget.'

She nodded and didn't say any more about it.

'You was looking at that, was you?' he asked, resting a hand on the brass hatch set in the wall. 'Within be the relics of our patron saint.'

'Relics?'

'Aye. Behind that hatch is a hollow containing the reliquary of St Emiliana.'

'A hollow?'

The mention of it sparked her interest.

'Rare, so it is. She rests within a simple stone coffin. Done so for hundreds of years.'

'Who was she?'

'Who was she?' The vicar looked aghast. 'You mean to say you don't know the story of St Emiliana?'

Elle shook her head. 'Dopey Americans.'

'Emiliana was incorruptible, so she was. A princess who did sacrifice all worldly splendour, providin' relief to unfortunate souls.'

'How did she come to be in there?'

'Came to the aid of one unworthy soul in particular,' he said, voice tinged with bitterness. 'A soul giving her cause to sacrifice her life.'

'Sad,' Elle replied, with condolence. 'It's a dear story.'

'A truer one I never spoke. May the Lord smite me if it not be.'

'A poignant way to remember her, I'm sure.' Elle's eye wandered, drawn to a recumbent effigy upon an altar-tomb set in a niche. 'Who's that?'

'Him?' Duigan asked. 'Deception.'

Elle detected disdain in Duigan's voice.

'Placed in that niche in 1643 for keepin' Cromwell's iconoclasts from discovering the crypts.'

'There are crypts here too?'

'Aye. There be an entrance through the vestry. Don't go down there much these days. Keep losing the infernal keys, you see.'

Moving closer to the recumbent noble, feet resting upon a lamb, she swallowed a gasp. Hands clasped, eyes closed, was the face she thought she had forgotten. 'Who was he?' she was just able to force out.

'Balthasar Toule.'

A shiver like lightning rode down her spine. She reached out, her fingers coming to rest on his cheek, the marble cold. She could barely breathe.

'Here you are,' she whispered.

'What's that you say?' The vicar's eyes narrowed, his voice now less welcoming and friendly. Accusatory, almost. 'Just happened upon our little parish, did you?' he continued.

She pulled her hand back, feeling suddenly distrustful.

'Comin' in here asking all sorts of questions. I remember who you is. And I know who you're after. You ain't fooling me.'

The vicar was either mad or spot on.

'Think you had better be leaving.'

'But—'

'*Now*,' he said, voice thundering through the parish.

She nodded, backing quickly away, making for the door.

❖   ❖   ❖

Lights from Victoria Pier blinked and flickered through the trees below, the merry sound of a ragtime band playing on the pier head, ebbing and flowing in the mild night breeze. Silently, she crossed the parish cemetery, the headstones trailing long shadows, the once-friendly weeping ash now reaching menacingly for her as she ducked under its branches.

Darkness changed everything. It always did. She was spooked. But determined. Confidence was winning the battle over prudence today.

Approaching the parish porch as she had a few hours earlier in daylight, she reached for the door's handle, recalling how it creaked. Inhaling, as if it would somehow deaden the noise, she slowly turned the handle and pushed the door in. Quite as she anticipated, it creaked loudly, echoing within the church. She opened the door enough to squeeze through. It was near pitch black inside. A stark contrast from the calming atmosphere from earlier that day.

At the far end of the chapel, candles beside the altar flickered in their stands. It was almost too theatrical. Like a Lon Chaney horror film. Distant lights from the pier filtered through painted glass windows, creating motion in every shadowy nook and cranny. Fishing through the pockets of her dungarees she retrieved the cigarette lighter the Belgian had given her the night before, her compass coming along with it. It clattered to the stone floor. Elle quickly scooped it up, holding it tightly in her hand, hushing herself.

Assuring herself she hadn't raised attention, she approached the altar cautiously, eyeing a box poking out from under the velvet alter cloth, illuminated by the lighter's flame. Rummaging through it, she discovered an open box of candles. They were only inches long, but better than bumbling about in the darkness with only a cigarette lighter. Lighting a candle wick cast a sombre pool of light around her. Passing the hatch where the remains of St Emiliana lay, she fumbled with her compass, catching its face in the glow of the candles. Its dial spun wildly.

Just as it had in the passage under the Externsteine.

'Damn thing,' she cursed quietly.

The vestry door opened. Hastily snuffing out her candle, she ducked behind the altar, heart hammering. There came a distant moaning. Not wailing, but proper vexing and muttering. The door slammed shut again, the bang echoing all around. Erratic footfall could be heard across the stone floor.

She peeked out from her concealment. Dressed in a night-shirt, Vicar Duigan fumbled across the high chancel, carbide lamp in his hand, its waning beam falling upon the effigy of Balthasar.

'God curse you, Toule.'

An empty bottle clattered to the floor, rolling to within inches of Elle. Redbreast whiskey.

'Where are you, scoundrel? The Lord don't want you in His house. I don't want you in His house, neither.' He stumbled. 'Where are you, then?' He glared at the recumbent noble, sniggering. 'You ain't in there, so you're not. But I knows where you is. Down there, ain't ya? Ain't ya?'

Elle watched the inebriated vicar put his weight against the vestry door. Once inside, she heard the sound of jingling keys, followed by more effing and blinding. 'For God's sakes, which key is ya?'

Crawling forwards, Elle moved as close as she dared. The vicar wobbled at the gate in the corner of the vestry, a large ring cluttered with keys in his hands.

'Bugger,' he grumbled, lazily trying one after another in a padlock securing the gate. Eventually, there was a click, and the lock fell to the floor with a loud clang. Elle leapt back as if the sound had given her away. She heard the gate swing open, followed by tottering footfalls. Waiting until they grew distant, she peered into the vestry. Dimming light and descending footfalls echoed through the open gate.

She looked in. Worn steps sank through an arched brick passageway. Relighting her candle she grasped the opened gate, steadying herself. Somewhere below, Vicar Duigan continued his whinging. Quietly, she followed his sounds.

The entrance to the crypt reeked of damp. Following the steps' course, she paused at a narrow landing from which the stairs lead into darkness. Torches sat in stanchions, the brick above blackened from centuries of use. Nineteenth-century oil lamps replaced others.

Removing one such lamp from its rusty hook on the wall, she opened the glass pane. The strong smell of oil suggested it was full. She held her candle to its wick and the lamp began to glow. Snuffing her redundant candle, she dropped it to the ground, adjusting the wick of the lamp. It offered considerably more light. Remembering her compass, she removed it from her pocket, opened its leather case and looked to the dial. It showed magnetic north. It wasn't broken after all.

Although she could no longer see the light from the vicar's lamp, she could hear distant muttering. Tucking away her compass, she swallowed dryly. No sense kidding herself, her mind already envisioned Spring-heeled Jack leaping out at her from the darkness. But Vicar Duigan had said he knew where Balthasar was.

Courage now.

When she reached the bottom of the stairs, a vast, arched crypt appeared from the dreary shadows cast by her lantern. Within the vaults lay sarcophagi covered in centuries of dust, hardened into a clay-like substance. The vicar was nowhere to be seen. Then, from the far end of the crypt, came a shuffle. Crossing the chamber, her lamp illuminated another stairway leading down, a distant glow indicating where Duigan had gone. The immensity of the crypt, particularly one with multiple levels, was unusual for a small parish.

From somewhere below came the sound of the vicar grousing over his keys, followed by the now-familiar creak of rusty hinges. Reaching the bottom of the stairs, Elle dimmed her lantern. They led to another crypt. At the far end, she picked out the glow from the vicar's lamp once more.

He unlocked a vault, swung back the gate and ventured inside. Hugging the near wall, Elle pressed on, tucking herself behind the pillars of each vault she passed. Nearing now, she heard Duigan messing about with something and, by his cursing, she reckoned he was failing at it. There came a slight click, followed by what sounded to her like gears winding and a distinctive grating sound. Only a single pillar separated her from him now.

'Ya loathsome urchin,' cursed Duigan. 'Are you down there?'

Elle inched closer. Carved into the stone above the vault was the surname: "Toule". All air left her lungs. Just as she was about to confront the vicar, she heard something slide heavily away, followed by a loud *thunk*. Taking a shallow breath, she slid around the pillar, peering as far into the vault as her eyes allowed. It was deep, and choked with cobwebs. Its position at the very end of the lowest crypt made it quite possibly the oldest vault in the church. Inside rested six sarcophagi, darkened by age. They were unexceptional. Like many to be found in England. No death symbol. No "*Expecto resurrectionem mortuorum.*" Not the sort of thing she linked to Balthasar Toule.

One, however, stood apart from the rest and not only for its resemblance to a Roentgen wardrobe with highly polished, inlaid wood and ornate brass fittings. It was also open. She raised her lantern to look inside. Within the imposing, but otherwise empty sarcophagus, lay the vicar, spindly legs flailing about his hiked-up nightshirt.

Apparently it was the same for Irish with their nightshirts as it was for Scots and their kilts. Fortunately, his kicking legs righted his nightshirt quickly.

Duigan had tumbled a good five feet to the sarcophagus' bottom. It was very odd — a sarcophagus partially sunk into the floor. Getting the old drunk out was going to be a challenge. Swinging a leg over the edge of the sarcophagus, she attempted to reach him. He was too far down. Balancing her lantern on the edge of the sarcophagus, she hopped in to join him. The vicar lay prostrate, mumbling something or other about catacombs. Blearily, he glared up at her.

'I bumped my noggin.'

'You've got yourself into a proper pickle, Vicar,' she whispered.

'Is it you Emiliana?'

'Yeah, it's me,' she replied. 'Boo!'

'Give me strength to cast him out. To let you be. To let you rest.'

'We've got to cast you out of here first, Vicar.'

'God give me a little boot up the behind.'

'What did you say?' she replied, her mind running a mile a minute.

'I don't remember.'

'*God give me a little boot up the behind*, you said.'

'Did I?'

'Yeah. You did.' And just like that she remembered. Cleric collar and soaking wet pyjamas. 'I'll be damned.'

'So you shall.'

'*God gave me a boot up the behind*,' she repeated again, nodding. 'You said it when we pulled you soaking wet from the North Atlantic in 1912.'

He squinted at her. 'Lifeboat 4?'

A moment of clarity?

'You was in it? You was on Titanic?'

'I was.'

'You didn't just happen upon me little parish, did you?'

'I did not.'

'No, you did not.'

The vicar's legs began kicking up a fuss again, and in doing so his heel came down on an inconspicuous iron lever.

'Be *still*. I'm trying to help you,' Elle said.

Mechanics whirred under her. An instant later, the lid above jarred, slowly rotating. 'What are you doing?' she shouted, grasping for the lid above. It was too heavy. She couldn't stop it. In another moment it sealed over them, clicking into place with an ominous *thud*.

'Oh Christ,' she muttered. Righting her lamp, she tried not to panic. All sorts of horrific ends crossed her mind, not least of which was being trapped forever with a drunken vicar.

The sound of mechanics came again. Elle's fears were immediately forgotten as the floor fell away.

❖ ❖ ❖

Reaching for her throbbing head, Elle felt the stickiness of fresh blood. Her wound must have reopened in the fall. She rolled to the side and inhaled what turned out to be a mouthful of dirt. Spitting, she fumbled for the upturned oil lantern, its flame still flickering. Sitting up caused her head to spin, and her hands fell to her side to steady herself. Her right hand landed on a canvas sack, which came apart in her hand. Folding over what remained, she held it to her head. When she pulled it away to inspect it, she saw fresh blood, though not enough to cause real concern. The vicar lay nearby. They had taken a good fall, landing on a pile of earth and loose brick.

Pulling herself to Duigan, she checked his pulse. He wasn't dead. Just dead drunk. Either the fall or the whiskey had knocked him cold. Adjusting the flame on her lantern, she looked around them. They had fallen some twenty feet into a high-vaulted chamber, tree roots growing through cracks in the arched, brick ceiling.

It was too large to be an undercroft. Up the side of a wall ran a treacherously narrow stair, terminating at a sealed, rectangular hatch in the ceiling, where the bottom of the sarcophagus purposefully fell in. Enormous, rusty hinges and cogs secured the other, controlled by a maze of cords and counterweights. Someone had built a highly elaborate mechanism for entering the chamber.

The vicar knew the way in. He must surely know a way out. She gave him a poke, but he was evidently done for the night.

Regaining her wind, she got to her feet. She was sore, but at least she was in. Wherever *in* was. Climbing down the pile of loose earth and bricks, she shone her lamp ahead. Criss-crossing cobwebs covered all manner of maritime detritus: old ship masts, torn sails, dry-rotted fishing nets, splintering wood barrels, piles of oars. There was even an old cannon, its wooden carriage rotted to bits. Nobody had gone that way for ages. Still, none of the old tot had got where it lay through the trapdoor in the sarcophagus. There had to be another way in — and out.

A hollow, distant thumping drew her attention. She followed it towards the opposite end of the chamber. Every passage radiating from the chamber was bricked over, but at its far end she discovered a high-arched corridor continuing into darkness.

She made her way along it as it narrowed, the bricks sweating with damp. Shallow recesses held lanterns covered in cobwebs. Wandering in the darkness she stumbled past low vaults filled with rotting wood casks and even a discarded grand piano, its legs long since collapsed.

The distant thumping continued steadily as she found even more gated vaults, these piled high with crates of French champagne and Turkish tobacco. Further along, she saw a gate ajar. Passing through it to enter the vault, she found crates stamped: "Product of Ireland".

She reached inside a loose lid and took hold of a bottle. Redbreast whiskey. Vicar Duigan was raiding the spirits cabinet. Cracking the cap, she took a drink. It was pure, liquid courage.

'Product of Ireland, indeed,' she said, before another nip.

Then it dawned on her. 'Smuggler vaults.'

None of the crates were crusted with solidified dust or cobwebs; they must have been in recent use.

Continuing on, her lantern illuminated vault upon vault overflowing with contraband. Crates marked: ".303" were stacked along a wall of the passage, suggesting they were only recently delivered. She looked closer. Ammunition. Thousands of rounds.

Beyond, long wooden crates were piled shoulder high, and stamped: "Lee-Enfield Rifles. 20 Lot". Still other crates marked: "Mk IV B Type C Mine. Property of HMS British Army".

'Not just smuggling,' she said out loud. 'Someone's pilfering from the British Army.'

The thumping grew louder still as she came to another intersection. Four low tunnels twisted off in opposing directions, two blocked by cave-ins. She turned to a passage on her right. Masses of cobwebs and teardrop-shaped egg sacs hung from the arched ceiling. She dared not venture that way. She was left with only one way to go.

More vaults followed, but unlike the others, these ones were secured by solid wood doors, and padlocks. At the end of the passage stood an arched vault, its entrance also barred by a strong door and padlock. At the top of the arch, just visible in the bricks were runes.

ᛁᚱᛉ

'Sekr,' she whispered, heart racing. 'Gotcha.'

She grasped the lock. It was recently oiled. She gave it a good tug, but its securing was bolt tight.

Before she could mull over what to do next, her lantern began to dim. The oil reservoir empty.

'Damn,' she whispered. 'Shouldn't have left the candle behind, dingbat.'

She wondered how long the lighter could last, and looked about for anything to replace it. A hefty mariner's lantern hung in a niche. She lifted it - it was full. She breathed a sigh of relief. Clicking her lighter, the lantern's wick immediately ignited just as the other huffed and extinguished itself. Adjusting the flame bathed the passage in undulating light, revealing a hand-hammered key behind the lantern.

'Can I really be this lucky?' she asked herself. Slipping the key into the lock, she gave it a turn. It clicked.

'Yes, I can.'

She dropped the lock to the floor and pushed the door in, its well-oiled hinges making no sound. Bracing for the unknown, she was just about to enter the vault, when somewhere off in the passages, a door with considerably less well-oiled hinges creaked loudly. An unintelligible voice echoed. Then, a second joined it.

It was not the vicar. Fear leached into her again, but she refused to cower. Not when she was so close. Extinguishing her lamp, Elle shuffled into the blackness of the vault, a smell like dry-rotted cloth, heavy in the air. The voices grew closer. A conversation she could not discern ensued. She gritted her teeth, fighting off the memory of being bludgeoned by a pair of SS goons at the Externsteine.

Fortunately, no alarm was raised by her intrusion.

Mustering up her courage, she left the lantern in the vault, stealthily making her way back up the dark passage, retracing the way she had come. Near the end, she saw a flickering light in the darkness. Sidling up to the intersecting passages blocked by a recent cave-in, the voices became distinctive.

'Look at this mess.'

British accent.

'I'll 'ave that next-to-useless Commodore put paid to if he don't stop that fuckin' drilling.' British *and* foul-mouthed.

'Second time in as many days, ja?' The second voice was neither British nor common. And Elle recognised it.

She stole a peek around the corner. Ahead stood two men, silhouetted by the glow of their electric torches. They inspected the cave-in. One was a giant of a man, his bulk practically consuming the entire passage. The other displayed a controlled demeanour. It was the Belgian from the night ferry.

The large man bent over as best he could. 'Bugger.'

'What is it?'

'Nuffin,' he replied, his torch scanning the ground of the collapsed passage. 'I popped a button on me strides. Help me find it.'

'Wait. Do you hear?'

They listened. Elle listened as well. The thumping sound. It was very close now.

'It's them, innit?' the large Brit said.

'We must have the Royal Navy reroute their tunnelling again.'

'I'll have words with the useless bellend. Costing me a packet every time I gotta pay him to move his digging.'

Without warning, the hotspur began to hoot and jump about like a man gone barmy. 'Fucking 'ell. Get off. Get it bleedin' off me!'

The Belgian raised his torch. Hulking hands slapped away at huge gangly spiders. Their long legs broke away from their torsos as the great wall of a man crushed them.

'You are quite all right, Cubby?'

'Horrible cave spiders. Give me the frights,' he groused, turning his torch on the broken ceiling, dozens of the creepy-crawlies scattering. 'Get yer torch up in there. Them bastards don't like the light.'

'We ought not linger,' said the Belgian. 'We risk having the entire passage down upon us if we do not stop them digging.'

'Pain in me arse, interfering with business,' Cubby jawed on. 'What's wrong with them Royal Navy engineers?'

They turned, making their way into the maze of passageways. Elle waited until their footsteps faded and she heard the distant door creak shut. The thumping continued, unabated. It was the engineers she had seen digging into the hillside along the Road of Remembrance. They must have been getting close to the smugglers' passages.

Clicking her cigarette lighter, she retreated as she had come, returning to the vault and raising the lantern's flame for a better look inside. There were dozens of sturdy brick columns supporting a cavernous ceiling. What lay below surprised even her.

She expected to find sarcophagi containing Crimen. Instead, there were row upon row of piled-up trunks. It looked like the baggage holding room at a port. No two trunks were the same. Some were wardrobes, others steamers. Still others looked like motoring trunks. None were large enough to contain anything like the beast she had witnessed in Titanic's hold.

Cautiously making her away through the rows, Elle began examining the names stamped into them. On a dome-lidded half-trunk: *B. Ambrose*. A wood and leather flat-topped steamer: *Major B Hadley*. There were hundreds of them.

Stopping before a barrel-stave chest, its oak slats worm-worn and metal banding rusted, she found the name she sought: *B Toule*.

'Balthasar Toule,' she said quietly, resting a hand on the rotting trunk's lid. 'You were here.'

One man in his time plays many parts, Dougie Beedham's voice resonated in her head strongly. She looked around at the piled trunks. 'Balthasar,' she said quietly, as if whispering to him. 'You have played all these many parts.' Resting her lantern on an adjoining trunk, she undid the barrel-stave chest's clasps, keen to see what skeletons were kept within. 'These are all yours.'

Slowly, she lifted the lid, its contents bathing her in sombre light. The trunk was tightly packed with rough-hewn ingots of a most peculiar golden aubergine, each stamped with Toule's death symbol. Moving to the next trunk, she opened its lid too. It was also full to the brim with ingots. And the next trunk. And the next.

She looked down the length of the vault at hundreds of trunks. 'Is this the haul of cwicseolfor Dr Harvey mined and brought back from the Externsteine?' she asked herself. 'Maybe this is what twelve thousand bushels of Jungfräu looks like?' Without thought, she reached in to pick up an ingot.

Suddenly, she somersaulted into darkness, her body striking a pillar with such force it crumbled the mortar. As she sank to the floor amid loosened bricks, her head wound began pouring blood anew.

A towering shadow moved in on her.

'What you doin' muckin' about in me business?' Cubby moved into the light of her lantern. He was even more massive up close. She was lifted from the floor by the scruff of her collar, the toes of her boots just scraping along. 'You picked the wrong fuckin' time to trespass, luv.'

Elle reached for his throat, but he had no discernible neck, just shoulders of thick muscle and a head like a bulldog chewing a wasp. 'Wait, wait!' she pleaded. 'I'm looking for Balthasar Toule.'

The name gave the brute pause. But instead of granting her reprieve, it seemed only to enrage him all the more.

'Why you lookin' for him?' Lifting her clear of the floor, he drew her close. He stank of fried tripe and tobacco. Squirming, she sank her teeth into his earlobe. He pulled her away roughly, howling in pain. She tasted blood, spitting out a gristly chunk of his ear. He heaved her against an iron anvil — Elle felt her ribs crack as she caught its edge.

Blood rolled down his neck as he approached.

'You're a spry one, I'll grant you that, but you ain't gonna find him here.' He rolled back his shirtsleeves, revealing strong, tattooed forearms.

She tried to crawl away as he reached down to grasp her. As she turned, her hand fell upon an iron poker. She swung at him with all her worldly might. Blocking it with one huge fist, he belted her in her ribs with the other. She doubled over on the stone floor, unable to breathe.

'Sorry, luv. I don't fancy slottin' a bird.'

Brandishing a shiv from the small of his back, he moved towards her. She tried to make it to her feet but was defeated. Closing her eyes she awaited her end.

Instead, she heard a loud thud, and then silence. She cautiously opened her eyes and watched in surprise as Cubby lurched forward and collapsed.

Another figure arose from the darkness.

'You do find the trouble, *mijn schatje*,' said the Belgian as he stepped into the light of her lantern, a benign grin on his face. He gazed at his colleague on the floor, tossing aside the coal shovel he'd just used to brain him. 'Forgive me, my friend.'

There was no reply from the huge, unconscious form.

'I simply cannot have you killing Dr Annenberg. No, no. That would be most inopportune.'

❖ ❖ ❖

'I'll have your bollocks for conkers, you cheeky foreign bastard.'

Elle's eyes slowly focused on Cubby. He rested on a stool against a long bar, tea towel to his ear, a second one held to the back of his head by the plump woman Elle had seen earlier, pulling weeds in the parish cemetery.

'There, there you big oaf, enough with your moaning,' the woman said, stitching his head with needle and thread. 'Impossible to stave your head in with that thick skull of yours.'

Elle leaned over a wooden table, bundled towels tucked under her head, hair sticky with coagulating blood. Groggily, she looked about. She was in a public house's taproom. When she breathed in, her ribs pressed against a dressing. Someone had trussed her up tight. Sitting up, she felt a stabbing pain.

'Don't mess it about, darling,' said the woman in the apron. Putting Cubby's hand to the reddening towel on the back of his head, she patted his shoulder. 'Hang on to that, dopey.'

Cubby turned, giving Elle a glare as if he were about to put her arse on the curb selling apples. 'Let her whinge, Mabel. She bit half me ear off.'

'There now.' Mabel stood over her, gently rubbing her back. 'You just be still. He didn't know who you was.'

'I *did* know who she bloody was,' he scowled.

'You'll forgive Cubby. I'll sort him out.'

'He tried to kill me,' said Elle.

'Actually…'

Turning, she saw the Belgian sitting in a chair, half-pint glass and an open bottle of Redbreast whiskey on a table next to him. She closed her eyes, wincing at the pain shooting through her ribs with every breath. When she opened them again, the Belgian was standing beside her, lambent blue eyes twinkling.

'He quite possibly saved your life. Had you touched one of those ingots of cinnabar, you would be dead by now, instead of enjoying a twelve-year-old single pot whiskey.'

Putting another glass on the table, he poured her a drink.

'I'm hacked off enough and you're fuckin' giving her drinks? You wants to be giving her the pillow from me bed next. Look at what she done!' Cubby complained to the Belgian, lowering the tea towel covering his damaged ear lobe.

'I must apologise; I found it necessary to bludgeon you. I could not permit you to do harm to the good doctor.'

'She's a doctor? Have her over here and look at me head, then.'

'Oi,' Mable scolded. 'Enough of your talking twenty to the dozen. You've had worse from me.'

Sulking over a pint, Cubby shrugged his consent.

'I'm not that sort of a doctor,' said Elle.

'Cubby Smyth is not that sort of a publican. This pub, the Priory Arms, is his,' the Belgian explained, helping Elle sit up so she could have at her whiskey. 'He is a smuggler of some note.'

'Redbreast,' she said after emptying her glass. 'This rot gut is from the vaults.' She looked up at the Belgian. 'Oh dear. I left the vicar down there.'

'That flinty old geezer,' said Cubby.

'Sleeping comfortably as we speak,' said Mabel. 'Back in his bed at the vicarage.'

Elle winced again as she breathed. The Belgian poured her another glass. 'I find whiskey to be an ideal sedative. You have cracked your ribs. You will find if you breathe shallow, the pain will subside. Cubby's wife Mabel has done a very fine job of stitching your head.'

Elle managed a nod of gratitude, despite the pain. 'Thank you, Mabel.'

'You are welcome, luv. Dunno who done them stitches before. They was dodgy.'

'A German fellow with shaking hands.'

'I ain't surprised they come loose.'

The Belgian held his hand out to Elle, introducing himself properly at last. 'I am Jean-René Gaele.'

Elle nodded. 'Yes. We met on Twickenham Ferry.'

'We met the first time on Titanic.'

She stared at him. Through waves of grey hair and weathered skin from hard living she remembered him. 'It was you?'

He nodded.

Her injuries forgotten, she smiled. 'You carried me up to the Boat Deck from Scotland Road.'

'Ja,' he replied, tipping back his glass. 'I was a young, idealistic man then. A Great War and too many hard years in the Belgian Congo have left what you see now.'

Inhaling gently, she looked away from him, her mind taking her beyond the walls of the pub. 'I was convinced everything leads back to Titanic,' she muttered.

Gaele nodded, suggesting he'd heard her.

Returning her gaze to him, she continued, 'I realise now I was wrong. All roads lead me to Folkestone. There are no coincidences.'

'Hardly, if ever.'

Dr Mauss had replied in precisely the same way.

'I'm pleased you discovered St Emiliana's secret. Even I did not expect you in Balthasar's vault.'

'You know him?'

Holding a cigarette to his lip, Gaele searched his pockets for a lighter. Elle fished out the one he had given her from her dungarees.

'You were right. This did come in handy,' she said, returning his lighter.

He tucked it away and then nodded. 'Yes, I know him.'

'Shut your gob, you dopey foreigner,' Cubby bristled, his face reddening. 'Ours ain't no social club.'

Gaele smiled. 'Mabel, is it not Cubby's bedtime?'

'Upstairs to bed, you.'

Although not half his size, his wife handled Cubby like a naughty boy sent to bed without his pudding. 'The all of us will be better come the morning.'

'Hang on, Mabel, I ain't finished me pint.'

'You can take your beer with you, my love,' she said, helping him to his feet. 'Chop, chop.'

Wobbling as he stood, Cubby tossed a displeased look in Elle's direction.

'You're in trouble,' he blustered, as he was guided to stairs at the back of the pub. 'Both of you.'

Gaele sniggered imperturbably. 'He is not a bad sort, our Cubby. He does not know you.'

'And you do?'

'Ja. I know you, Eleanor.'

Sitting back in his chair, he fired up a cigarette. 'Buster Hadley. He spoke of you at length.'

'I know nobody by that name.'

'You do know him. But as Balthasar Toule.'

Elle's whole countenance changed upon hearing his name spoken.

She looked at Gaele, eyes pleading.

'Please,' she begged. 'Tell me. Tell me everything.'

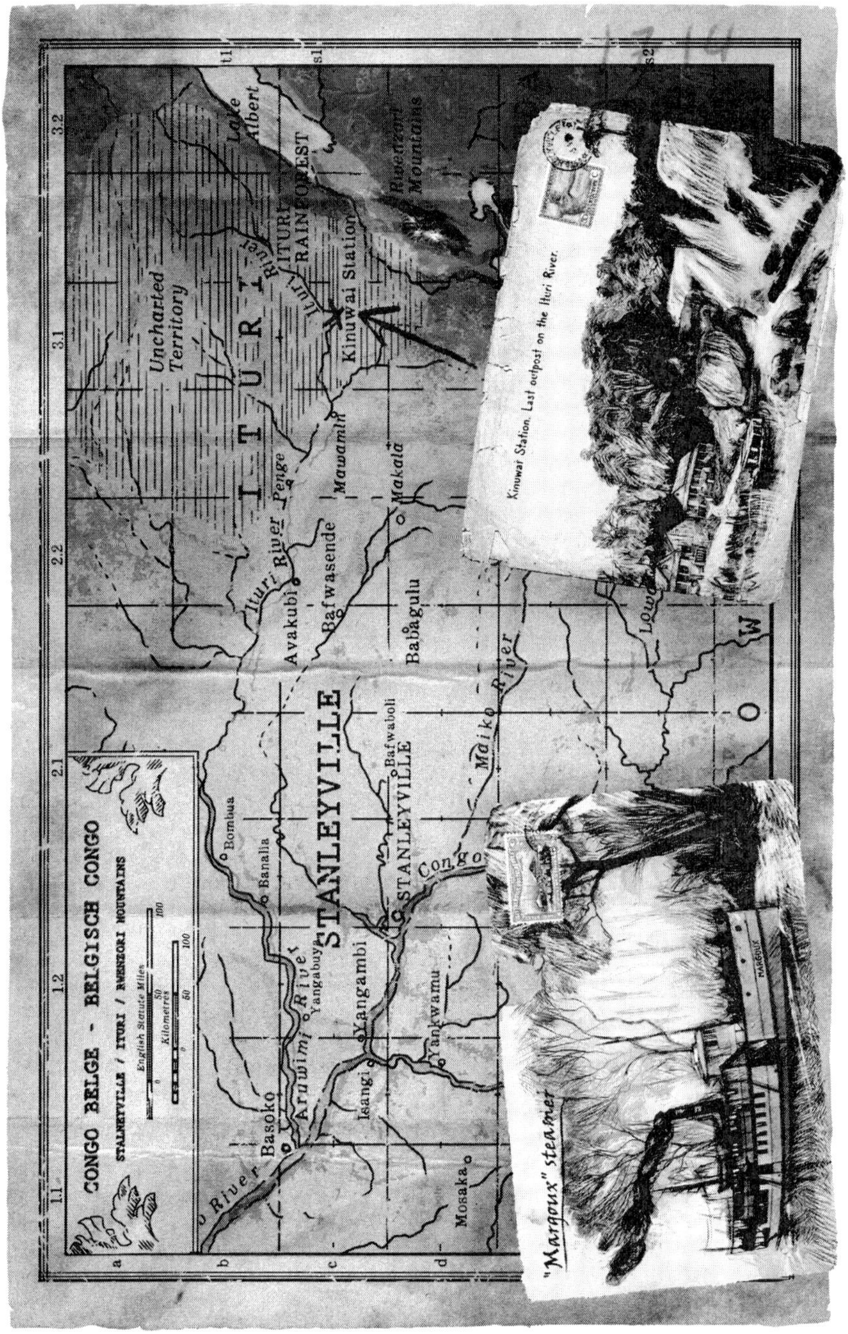
CONGO BELGE - BELGISCH CONGO
English Statute Miles
Kilometres
STANLEYVILLE
ITURI
Uncharted Territory
ITURI RAINFOREST
Kinuwai Station
Lake Albert
Rwenzori Mountains
Ituri River
Penge
Mawambi
Makala
Avakubi
Bafwasende
Babagulu
Bafwaboli
Maiko River
Congo
STANLEYVILLE
Yangambi
Yangabuya
Aruwimi River
Basoko
Banalla
Isangi
Kinuwai Station. Last outpost on the Ituri River.
"Margoux" steamer

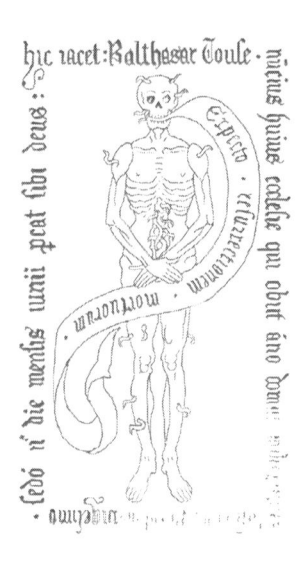

10 APRIL 1921.

KINUWAI, BELGIAN CONGO

*... 'gift' and 'food' are not mutually exclusive,
since, at least in theory, the essential form
of the 'total service' relates to nourishment.*

—Notes, 'The Gift'

Rainwater streamed off the back of Gaele's pith helmet, draining down the inside of his collar. Using the brim to shield his eyes from the deluge, he looked to the riverbank.

Swamped canoes were strewn about the trading station's landing stage. Beyond, a river steamer had run aground, stern submerged. The zinc roof of the station annex had collapsed, and the eaves over the director's villa were severely damaged.

Whatever had occurred at the last station on the River Ituri must have been sudden and violent. Shouldering the Winchester rifle he'd nicknamed Henry, Gaele climbed from Margoux's deck to the narrow aft platform, beside the steamer's steadily turning paddles.

'Private?' he shouted to a grenadier from the platoon, already disembarked from the steamer.

'Aye, Mssr Gaele?' the British soldier shouted above the rain's din.

'Do you see a name on the hull of that beached steamer?'

Moving closer to the ship, the soldier squinted in the pelting rain. 'Clémentine.'

The mystery was revealed. Chartered by a mapping expedition from the Royal Geographical Society, Clémentine had ventured up the Ituri to the last trading station on the river months before. There had been no word from either the expedition or Kinuwai Station since.

Taking up the port side mooring line, Gaele cast it towards the grenadier with a 'ready, steady, go'. As the soldier lifted his hands to catch the hawser, a peculiar *whomp* of wings filled the air. Before the private could catch the mooring line, he was hoisted into the air and heaved against a grouping of oil palms, the small of his back striking a spiny trunk with a sickening *crack*. An otherworldly shadow, obscured by the downpour, chased after the mortally wounded soldier as he crashed to the ground.

It bit into the grenadier's torso, savagely pulling him open.

Drawing Henry off his shoulder, Gaele quickly dropped the trigger guard and prepared a round. He fired. Dropping the guard, he ejected the spent cartridge and slid a fresh round into the chamber from the tubular magazine below the barrel. Despite the rain still pouring off his helmet, he managed to group three .44 rounds into the wraith's torso.

Unleashing a hyena-like howl, it dropped the gored soldier, and rushed at Gaele. Bipedal in form, and unpleasantly anaemic, the beast's brindle-coloured skin was devoid of hair. Membranous wings poking from its stickle-back spine pounded the air. Face gaunt, its jawbone oddly distended, serrated carnassials protruded from swollen gums.

Gaele had never witnessed such a beast. Not in Congo or anywhere else. Not even in his nightmares — and he had many.

Toggling the trigger guard, he chambered another round, raising the repeater. With the coolness of a hunter who'd earned his chops staring down the muzzle at charging predators, he sighted Henry just left of the beast's sternum. The Winchester squealed. A hot, rim-fire bullet zipped through the teeming rain, tearing through its chest. Striking bone, the bullet's trajectory changed, spinning out of the demon's back at a forty-five-degree angle before splashing into the water. As if hitting a brick wall, the beast twisted sideways, its wings flopping limply as it skidded into the river before Margoux's churning paddles.

A single .44 round from his Winchester could drop a charging rhino. He'd pumped four into the demon and still it wasn't finished. Drawn into the suction of the steamer's paddles, it brayed once before being torn to bits, the river's green shallows becoming inky black.

Turning towards the bow, Gaele felt the steamer drawn from the protection of the station's landing towards rough, impassable cataracts upriver.

'*Bordel de* merde,' he muttered, realising he had left the wheelhouse unmanned for too long.

Running along the port-side deck towards the wheelhouse stairs, he heard a crackle of rifle fire from shore, and the unmistakable *brum-brum-brum* from a thirty-aught-six Lewis gun.

Continuing amidships, he interrupted more of the fiends. Hunched on the deck in the belting rain, their sticky, webbed wings batting furiously as they butchered the regimental surgeon, his face crumpling like a wet cloak, stony eyes staring indifferently.

A beast looked up from its messing, hissing a spittle of human meat from its mouth. Abandoning the surgeon's corpse, the runty beast began to creep menacingly towards Gaele. Raising Henry again, he fired into it, momentarily slowing the seraph down. It was then he realised with horror that he'd expended the last of his fifteen rounds.

The seraph rushed him, wings buffeting the rain as it negotiated the confines of the deck, long, blood-stained talons steadying it on the riverboat's railings. It was naked save for the remnants of a *pagne* loin cloth. Gaele was struck with a shocking realisation; the fiends were once human.

Scurrying behind the steamer's funnel, the Belgian made for his berth. Throwing back the door, he took hold of a pair of leather bandoliers containing his extra cartridges and pulled them over his head. Quickly, he chambered fifteen .44 rounds into his repeater. As he grasped the belt containing his holstered Colt revolvers, he heard a ruckus coming from the berth opposite.

Major Balthasar Hadley's quarters. 'Buster? Is it you there?'

No sooner had he buckled the pistol belt about his waist than a powerful crash caused the wall dividing the berths to tremble, followed by a shuddering shriek like nothing he'd heard before.

As he was about to leave his berth, gun freshly loaded, the drifting steamer came to a jarring halt, the room pitching to starboard. Struggling through the doorway, he stumbled along the deck. Unmanned, the steamer had been drawn out into unprotected waters by the circular eddies boiling up from the cataracts that prevented further navigation up river. Gaele gritted his teeth as Margoux was sucked towards the swirling cauldron. He had moments to make another decision: attempt to reach the pilothouse and increase steam in the hope of keeping the riverboat from being torn apart in the cataracts, or abandon ship altogether. The latter would spell certain death for anyone remaining onboard. His only real option was to try saving her.

As Gaele grasped the rail to the wheelhouse stairs, the steamer shunted sideways, floundering in the bubbling whirlpool at the bottom of the cataracts. With that, Margoux was doomed. Even if he could muster full power, the old riverboat wouldn't be able to make enough steam to extricate itself. Twisting in the torrent, the steamer slammed bow-first into an outcrop of massive boulders, churning torrents shearing away her bow. Instantly, the shallow hull began to flood. The only thing left now for Gaele was to abandon the ship.

Struggling to the port side, he found Balthasar wearing thick leather gloves. He was hefting heavy trunks over the side of the foundering riverboat, onto a spit of boulders separating the waterfalls from the station landing.

Grasping the sleeve of the major's serge jacket, Gaele shouted over the roar of the cascades, 'For God's sake, Buster, what have you done?'

Feral eyes stared back at him. 'Disembark with all haste!'

'You knew something terrible had happened here!'

'I knew before we set sail from England, Mssr Gaele,' he hollered back, heaving another trunk from the shuddering steamer as the waters ground the boat to pieces. 'If you stay here another moment, it won't matter.'

Bristling, the Belgian pulled the rifle sling over his head. Securing Henry across his back, he leapt from the steamer just as it was dragged from under his feet. Stern-wheel flopping, Margoux was pulled into the swirling whirlpool and torn asunder, taking anyone remaining onboard to their deaths. Gaele, bounding across the slippery boulders to the riverbank, was on dry ground in seconds.

The deluge intensified — and with it came a swarm of wicked seraphs. Not ten yards in from the riverbank, a beast collided with a pair of grenadiers who had also managed to escape the sinking steamer before she went down. Taking one of the men roughly to the ground, it tore open his stomach with frenzied strikes. The soldier beat upon the beast's head with his fists, screaming as his sweetbreads were devoured.

Unholstering one of his revolvers, Gaele put a bullet in the soldier's head. There was nothing he could do to save him. Disturbed from its goring, the fiend reared up, chewing grotesquely, its ashen skin bubbling. He fired again, putting a .45 calibre slug between the beast's eyes. At such close range, the heavy round took its head off, leaving behind indistinguishable pulp, the fiend's emaciated body quivering as it collapsed into the mud.

The surviving grenadier, young and bare-headed, dashed towards him, crying out, 'Monsieur, I've lost my section. Let me stay with you.'

Brum-brum-brum. Brum-brum. The Belgian turned towards the station director's villa.

Under cover of the veranda's partially collapsed eaves, a Lewis gun emplacement poured fire into the sky. Grasping the grenadier by his webbing, he pulled the boy towards the building. As they made the veranda steps, a *whooshing* gust ripped the grenadier from his grasp. Taking him in its spindly arms, a seraph took flight. The Lewis gunner unleashed a stream of thirty-aught-six rounds into it, causing the beast to drop the soldier back to the ground. Khaki drill jacket torn by the beast's talons, the young grenadier tried to keep crawling forward.

'For God's sake, help me!'

The Belgian lowered a hand before the Lewis crew, watching the wounded seraph spinning in the mud like a crazed dervish.

'Do not fire. Our lad is too close.'

He took careful aim with his pistol, slamming a bullet through the beast's head in a spray of skull shards and curdled brains.

'Come along, *jeune homme*,' he shouted, hand outstretched. He had just got hold of the soldier's fingertips when the boy was ripped away by yet another fiend, vanishing into the rain-filled sky with a yelp.

Gaele removed his helmet and looked out from under the safety of the veranda's eave. A seraph fluttered towards him, its movement deranged, confused even. The Lewis gunner opened fire, the barrel's cooling shroud hissing as raindrops struck it. Knocked from the air, the beast released a hyena-like howl. Even riddled with thirty-aught-six bullets, its talons reached for him. Gaele had only seen such unrelenting attacks from river predators. A hungry crocodile, having tasted human flesh, ignored even mortal wounds just to taste it again. The seraphs exhibited disturbingly similar behaviour.

Gaele's rescue party was being hunted.

'In the name of God, what are they?' the corporal at the Lewis gun bellowed, emptying the ninety-seven-round ammunition drum into the beast. Flailing about in the mud, it continued to drag itself towards them. The loader's hands shook as he fumbled to insert a fresh ammunition drum into the gun. 'Get that bloody drum in!'

Drawing Henry from his back, Gaele cycled the lever action, raising the repeater. The rifle bucked; a .44 round squealed as it left the barrel. Crashing into the seraph, the bullet opened its stomach, maggots belching out from within.

'*Verdomme*,' the Belgian cursed in horror, watching the fiend twist and cringe in a seizure. 'What must be done to kill them?'

'Off with its head,' shouted Buster Hadley, climbing over the veranda railing from the deluge, a peculiar spike in his gloved hand. 'It's merely a Huntian. Lop its head off.'

Unsheathing his machete, the Belgian moved guardedly from under his protective shelter. Rain pelting his face, he pushed the Huntian to the ground with his boot and hacked through the puckered flesh of its neck. The beast shuddered, purging a viscous gunge as the blade struck its spine. A few more whacks and its head rolled away.

The beast was finally dead.

Turning back, Gaele quickly climbed the railing and retreated, soaked to the skin, into the protection of the veranda.

'They attack like *Stoßtruppen*,' he said.

'When did you fight off stormtroopers?' asked Balthasar.

'In France. In the Great War.'

'These are not *Stoßtrupp*. They are Crimen. And they're swarming. Hungry,' Balthasar said.

'For what?'

'Your flesh.' Looking towards the station annex, Balthasar said, 'I need to have a look in there.'

'Them ghouls will tear you to bits,' said a frightened grenadier, huddled on the veranda.

'That's not in the plan.' Then, jumping from the veranda Balthasar disappeared into the blinding rain.

A seraph flew helter-skelter through the crashing down rain. The Lewis opened fire, but the gunner couldn't get a bead on it.

'What is your name?' Gaele asked him, calmly.

'Lathbury, sir.'

'Lead them, Corporal Lathbury. Allow these Crimen to fly into your fire, not your fire into them.'

'Aye, sir,' the corporal acknowledged. Aiming again, he let loose. Colliding with the wall of bullets the fiend howled as it fluttered to the ground, Lathbury finishing it off with another spray of thirty-aught pulping its head.

'What in hell are they?' the loader asked, inserting a fresh drum into the gun.

'They are Crimen,' Gaele replied, taking aim. A powerful boom from Henry and a wraith's head dissolved in a puff of gore. 'And they *can* be killed.'

Through the mess of the beast's carcass, he recognised the tattered remnants of a khaki drill serge tunic. Then he understood: the beast was once part of the mapping expedition Gaele was sent to find. He didn't have time to think about what he was witnessing. Instinct and adrenaline took over. It kept him alive. Across the parade ground, he saw Buster on the station annex veranda.

'Major,' he shouted. He could not raise his attention over the peals of thunder.

Making a dash across the open killing ground, a crackle of rifles drew Gaele to the side of the customs shed. Catching movement from the corner of his eye, he was just able to raise his machete as a beast came down upon him. Knocking the fiend to the ground, the machete's sharpened blade split it open from chest to groin, a twisting pile of innards bubbling from the wound. Sliding undercover of the shed's drooping roof, the Belgian shouted to the expedition's Sergeant-Major, 'Clarke. Finish it.'

'Right, lads, kill me something,' the Sergeant-Major ordered. Sixteen rifles fired as one, Crimen bucking as .303 bullets inflicted ghastly wounds upon them.

'Get your men to the Lewis emplacement.'

'Mssr Gaele, I've fifteen lads left. They're all that's left of the Royal West Kent Regiment's 5th Battalion. You expect me to order them to break cover?' protested Clarke.

'Have you seen Barasa and Adongo?' the Belgian asked.

The Sergeant-Major shook his head. 'Who?'

'My adopted sons. Have you seen them?'

'No,' Clarke affirmed. 'I got fifteen adopted sons of my own here to look out for.'

Gaele had kept his adopted native sons with him since rescuing them as children. They were Loango. Fierce warriors. His odds of survival were better with them than the British.

'The Lewis gun will cover you,' he told Clarke, pulling on his helmet. Turning his attention to a Crimen writhing in the mud, he stepped forward and fired a bullet from his pistol into its brain. It went rigid, legs and arms curling up and stiffening like a dead cockroach.

'These beasts can be killed, Sergeant-Major.'

Moving along the station's perimeter, concealed by the encroaching jungle canopy, Gaele looked across the parade ground to the derelict station annex, where he had last seen Buster Hadley. Typical of most colonial annexes, it contained a series of offices set along an inner hall, with a larger open reception at the opposite end used by station staff. Most of its shutters were drawn, and like the villa across the parade ground, a veranda encompassed the entire annex protected by broad, zinc eaves.

There was no cover for fifty yards between the jungle fringe and the annex, except a flagstaff and pile of wood sleepers. Breaking from the treeline, he charged through the puddles of mud. Keeping low, he crossed the parade ground without incident, climbing over the annex's splintered, wooden railing.

Smashed Lloyd Loom chairs were strewn across the veranda, amidst them an eviscerated grenadier. Looking closer, he recognised the frightened face of the boy he had tried to pull to the safety of the director's villa.

'Poor fellow,' he said, trying so hard not to think of his own boys out there as night approached.

Arterial spray along the wall of the annex led to a door ripped from its hinges. Gaele peered inside its empty frame.

It was a small ransacked office within, fragments of soiled clothing hung over an upturned table. Slipping inside, he put his back against the inside wall, waiting for his eyes to adjust to the murky interior. He crossed the room cautiously, a stench from the hallway beyond causing him to retch. Eyes adjusting, he saw an abattoir. Blood and excrement were smeared along the walls, pieces of decaying bodies littering the floor. At the far end of the hallway was another open doorway, devoid of perceivable light. An unexpected cooing sound, given the situation, came from the darkness, almost a note from a boys' choir.

Raising his repeater, he advanced.

There was movement. He fired, the flash from Henry's muzzle revealing Crimen. Greasy from a feeding frenzy, they choked the narrow hallway. A .44 round slammed into the lead beast, throwing it sideways, the others clawing their way over it in the confined space, hurling themselves at him as he retreated over rotting corpses. He just made it into the wrecked office before taloned hands grasped the doorframe. A gaunt beast in soiled British uniform pulled itself round the door, mouth gobbing a fetid slime. Before Gaele could take aim, the beast was violently pulled back into darkness. A racket of savage violence ensued. Unintelligible shrieks, followed by cursing he understood perfectly.

No sooner had the Belgian retreated to the veranda than a wraith crashed through a shuttered window, landing in a heap amid broken window frame and glass shards. Captain Hamish Taggart, his khaki drill splattered with gore, climbed over the sill after it, rifle slung across his back. In his gloved hand, he held an engineer's hatchet soaked with feculence. He glanced at Gaele without acknowledgment.

Taggart was gone. Now there was only the Mohawk.

The wounded Crimen regained its feet. Unlike the malnourished beasts Gaele had witnessed before, this was robust, coal-black, over six feet tall and strapping, with a head full of woolly hair. The Mohawk closed with it, satisfaction marking his face. The seraph snarled, powerful wings splintering the veranda's floorboards.

'You need to wash your teeth,' the Mohawk ridiculed, launching his hatchet into the fiend's skull, cracking it open from hairline to tip of its nose. Howling, the ferocious creature attempted to advance, but its wings became entangled in the eaves' supports. Grasping the handle of his hatchet, the Mohawk wrenched it out in a spray of mottled brain matter. Hacking at the wraith's neck like a lunatic lumberjack chopping down a tree, his hatchet divided the seraph's ashen skin, exposing decaying tissue underneath. It shuddered, wings going berserk. Another strike from the hatchet severed its spine, and the beast collapsed upon itself. A final blow and its head rolled free, obsidian blood jetting from the severed arteries of the stump.

The Mohawk looked to Gaele now with a flash of recognition.

'Hello, me old china. Scrappy, ain't they?'

'However did you know that taking the head off silences the beast?'

Wiping the spillage on his face away with his sleeve, the Mohawk replied, 'Taking the head always kills the Guilty.'

His response suggested to the Belgian this was not his first encounter with the beasts. Raising his repeater, Gaele leaned forward, looking through the smashed shutters of the window, expecting another strike.

'Dark as Satan's arsehole in there,' said the Mohawk, regaining his puff. 'Never seen so many goblins.'

Looking over the muck fouling the Mohawk's khaki drill, Gaele realised he had gone barking mad.

'You have seen this before?'

'Oh yes,' the Mohawk said, his reply disturbingly jolly.

Brum-brum-brum. Brum-brum. He looked through the deluge to the director's villa. The gunfire opened up with the failing light of day.

'We do not have much time,' Gaele told him. 'We're losing the light.'

'It will be ever so sporting round here, then.'

Brum-brum-brum. Brum-brum. A pair of grenadiers broke cover, rushing across the parade ground, towards the villa. Crimen pounced, swooping in on them. The first soldier managed to duck out of the way. The second not so lucky. He was lifted free of the ground, legs kicking wildly. A volley of rifle fire. The guardsmen's aim was spot on; the beast crashed into the villa's roof and rolled down its side, releasing the soldier. More terrified than injured, the soldier crawled up into the safety of the veranda.

'What is there to do? Try holding out until the morning?' asked the Belgian.

'I've been unleashed, Monsieur,' the Mohawk said with a snigger, tucking his hatchet into his belt. 'By morning, there won't be a Crimen I haven't chopped to pieces.'

Gaele smelled smoke. He turned to see flames licking at the shuttered windows of the annex. 'Have you set the building alight?'

Before the Mohawk could reply, Balthasar Hadley burst through a closed door, black smoke trailing behind.

'Here they come,' he said, and an instant later, a mass of entwined wraiths thrashed their way from the burning structure. Feet tipped with curving talons tore into Balthasar's shoulders. He pivoted as he fell down the veranda steps, and a beast's claws raked off strips of his flesh.

Without even registering his grievous wound, Balthasar took hold of the seraph by its leg, heaving it against a mahogany tree with such magnificent savagery that the fiend came apart. Colliding with another, he grasped it by its forearm and snapped it in two. The beast yowled. Rage seethed in Buster's eyes as he tore its membranous wings away. Drawing a slab of rock from the muddy parade ground, he stoved its head in with a single smack. It whimpered.

In that moment, Gaele actually pitied the seraph. They were prey to an even more formidable beast.

Producing a burnished spike from the thigh pocket of his khaki-drill jacket, Balthasar poniarded the beast, holding tight even as its sloughing skin came away in handfuls. A final push and it sank into the mud, body haemorrhaging black ooze. Gaele watched the vile perfection with which Balthasar took the fiends to pieces. There was something horrifically noble in his bloodletting.

'Ah ha, Buster!' the Mohawk shouted to Balthasar with glee. 'I see it now. I'm not the only one whose primeval instincts are thinly buried.'

From the flames of the burning annex came a horde of Crimen.

'Wigs on the green now,' Balthasar shouted back, kicking aside the dispatched beast as he prepared to engage them head on.

The Mohawk leapt from the veranda onto a Crimen, an untameable Native American on a bucking bronco. Unholstering his Webley, he thrust the pistol's barrel against the beast's temple, firing. The side of its head blew out as it collapsed in the mud and went still, the Mohawk howling with rapture, 'Huzzah!'

With two killers beside him, Gaele took the moment to pull cartridges from his bandoliers and reload Henry.

'Where are your sons?' asked Balthasar.

'I don't know,' Gaele replied, dropping the trigger guard to inject a round into the chamber. 'It's chaos out there.'

'These Crimen, they have received stimulus,' said Buster, tossing a beast against the side of the annex. 'It's going to get very messy.'

A wraith lunged at Gaele, knocking his gun from his hands. Shifting his body, he managed to twist sideways as its weight smothered him. Gaele pummelled the beast under its chin, greasy suppurations sliding from its unhinged jaw. Slipping his machete from its sheath, he momentarily relaxed, allowing the beast's sore encrusted mouth to draw close, carnassials gnashing at his ear. With the machete to its neck, he sawed back and forth, the sharp teeth of the blade severing the seraph's spine, a painful howl cutting short as it fell limp. Then he heard a shot, and the fiend's head vanished in a spray of foul ooze.

Buster helped him to his feet before ejecting an empty cartridge from his rifle.

'How many can there be?' Gaele asked, exhausted from the endless skirmishing.

'Two missing expeditions. The inhabitants of the station,' said Buster, slamming the rifle bolt home and injecting a fresh .303 round into the chamber, before dropping another wraith with a head shot. 'A Crimen hive can be more than a hundred.'

'We cannot fight them all off,' Gaele replied. Tearing his pistol from its holster, he pumped four rounds into a pair of immolated beasts staggering from within the annex. 'No matter how many we dispatch, Sergeant-Major Clarke will have lost all of the West Kent Regiment to attrition.'

'We have the Mohawk.'

Grasping a pair of burning seraphs, Balthasar crashed their heads together repeatedly until they were an indistinguishable mess. He killed with an elegance that even a professional hunter such as Gaele admired.

'It's an even fight.'

'Even?' the Mohawk replied, striking with his hatchet, disembowelling a beast with barbarism bordering on obscene. A stew of intestines coiled out at his feet as he kicked the beast aside. 'I'll kill all of them.'

Balthasar nodded, his normally expressionless eyes piercing and alive. In that moment, Gaele could find little difference between the two men. Climbing over the veranda rail, Balthasar leapt to the parade ground, purposefully exposing himself.

'Kill anything you see, Mssr Gaele.'

'Where are you going, Buster?'

'To have a look in there,' he said pointing out a customs shed on the edge of the parade ground. Moving away from the light of the burning annex he called back, 'If you can survive the night, you've a chance.'

'Best of luck,' the Mohawk said, creeping off in the opposite direction. 'There's plenty of mutilation for us all.'

Gaele felt exposed and alone. If only he could find his sons; with their long spears, they could easily fend off the marauding wraiths. He decided his odds would be considerably improved within the Lewis gun position. Taking a half a dozen long strides though the ceaseless deluge, while avoiding a tangle of carcasses, he mounted the steps to the villa, hands pulling him under the eaves. Eleven grenadiers fired continuously at the frenzied beasts, while Corporal Lathbury poured fire from the Lewis into the darkening sky.

'For God's sakes,' Sergeant-Major Clarke shouted, helping Gaele upright. 'Where in hell has Major Hadley gone?'

'To the customs shed.'

'The customs shed?' Clarke dropped a beast with two rounds to its head. 'It's full of them devils.'

Inserting a stripper clip of .303 into the chamber of his Enfield, he turned to the men who remained, now not much more than a platoon.

'Aim for the head. Anything less is a waste of ammunition.'

The grenadiers unleashed a hail of rifle fire. All around, Crimen fell to their marksmanship.

'I'm starting to believe we just might make it through the night,' Clarke told the Belgian before the Lewis fell silent, ammunition drum spent. 'Reload,' Clarke ordered.

With shaking hands, the loader attempted to replace the ammunition drum as quickly as he could. A beast landed in their midst, pounding wings knocking the loader, splintering the railing. Tumbling from the veranda, the loader was set upon by the frenzied hive and quickly devoured.

'Give us another drum, for fuck's sake,' Lathbury stormed.

A grenadier lifted a loose drum amid the spent cartridges. Snatching it from his hands, the gunner slammed it into the receiver. As he chambered the first round, yet another Crimen pushed its way under the eave. Before anyone could get a shot off, it dashed Lathbury's head against the wall of the villa, cracking it open like an egg and sucked out the fluffy brain matter bubbling from inside. Using his Enfield as a cudgel, Clarke crashed the butt against the back of its head. It turned, an inhuman rattle bellowing from its flesh-clogged mouth. Jabbing with the rifle butt, Clarke struck its mandibles, shattering them. The creature wrenched the Enfield from Clarke's hands, and then set upon him.

Gaele fired, the Winchester barrel mere inches away from the fiend's head, blowing most of the top the beast's head off and killing it. With a nod of thanks, the Sergeant-Major took up the Lewis gun, bringing it to bear on the attacking horde illuminated by the flames of the burning annex.

'Christ,' he shouted, knocking down the wraiths with controlled bursts. 'There's no end to them.'

Moving from the cover of the veranda now, he positioned himself on the steps leading to the parade ground. From this exposed position, he widened his field of fire, sowing the hordes of beasts. *Brum-brum-brum. Brum-brum.* Knocked from their perch amongst the trees, three seraphs tumbled through the branches, landing on the ground. A volley of grouped .303 rounds from the rifles of the grenadiers finished them off. *Brum-brum-brum. Brum-brum.* Another one knocked from the night sky. *Brum-brum-brum. Brum-brum.* Yet another dropped as it attempted to climb into the veranda. A grenadier sighted in his Enfield, taking away the top of the beast's head.

Gaele watched Clarke fend off the marauding wraiths, expending the ammunition drum in five-round bursts. The station compound suddenly brightened as the customs shed went up in flames, revealing scores of wounded Crimen clawing their way over increasing piles of carcasses. *Brum-brum-brum. Brum-brum.* They were finished off.

A banshee howl pierced the night, and a wraith emerged from the torched shed, unlike anything Gaele had yet seen. A flash of lightning illuminated the beautiful seraph before peals of thunder drowned out its shrieks. It was swathed in a full-length, native kitenge, lush black hair surrounding a captivating face. A woman. Burning Crimen escaped from the shed behind it, wings alight.

'God's teeth,' said Clarke, checking his fire.

Gaele lowered his rifle, mesmerised. By the light of the burning shed, the woman appeared so pale as to be luminescent, and utterly flawless. She was different than the others, gliding as if on glass, escaping the flames calmly, the pelting rain bouncing away from her as the other beasts encircled her. The Belgian raised his rifle to put the fiend down. As he sighted in the seraph through the cordon of immolated Crimen surrounding her, their eyes met. Something inexplicable happened. He felt a jolt within so captivating, that it took away his breathe and he could not fire upon her.

'Clear them wretched ghouls away,' Clarke ordered.

A volley of Enfield fire grounded the burning seraphs moving around her.

Clarke's shouted orders brought Gaele back to the reality of the situation they were in. Realising what he gazed upon, he shouted, 'Shoot her. Kill her!' But his voice was lost in the deafening gunfire.

An enormous seraph appeared out of the burning shed, its humanoid body well-muscled and branded with exotic tattoos. Its elongated lower jaw and protruding mandibles more Goliath beetle than human. A thundering screech echoed across the station from its jaws, immense wings unfolding from its back, propelling it into the air as it darted towards the banshee. Buster emerged from the customs shed close behind the giant, his drill jacket smouldering. Leaping on it, the two of them tumbled into the morass of mud and carcasses.

The Sergeant-Major continued laying fire upon the beasts. With each wraith taken down, the grenadiers put a .303 round into their heads. *Brum-brum-brum. Brum-click.*

The Lewis gun fell silent.

'Come on, you bastard,' Clarke shouted, madly working its action, attempting to clear the jam. A clutch of Crimen fell upon him, goring him before Gaele could bring his rifle to bear.

'For God's sake,' Clarke cried out before he was pulled apart, the seraphs feeding on him, their malnourished bodies bubbling, then instantly growing robust. Corpse drained of nourishment, they cast the Sergeant-Major aside, turning on the horrified grenadiers.

The Belgian brought Henry to the fight, blowing one of the beasts off the veranda before another's pulsating wings knocked him over a pile of broken wicker chairs. His luck seemed to have run out on him.

Brum-brum-brum. Brum-brum. The Lewis fired again. Expended brass casings showered down upon Gaele, Crimen cut down like harvest wheat.

Much to his surprise, his son Barasa stood above him, laying a curtain of fire down on the beasts, while his other son, Adongo, ran through another with his spear.

'*Adongo – sa tête. Le coup de hache, le coup de hache,*' yelled Gaele, telling his eldest son to cut off the seraph's head.

'Ja, *bwana Mkuba*,' Adongo replied. Unsheathing his dagger, he lopped off the beast's head with a single pass.

Taking the Lewis off Barasa, Gaele shoved it into the hands of a grenadier. 'Keep up the fire.'

Scooping up the unused ammunition drums, he pushed them into the hands of still another soldier.

'If the Lewis gun falls silent, all of us are dead. You understand, ja?' The wide-eyed soldiers nodded. Looking to the ten remaining grenadiers he said, 'I'll go with my sons.'

'Where are you going, sir?'

'My boys and I will lure the beasts away from the swarm. Singling them out, we will exterminate them one at a time.'

'Out there? It's pure terror,' said another grenadier, directing his rifle across the killing field clogged with carcasses.

The Belgian was not frightened. Not with his sons in the fight.

'What are our orders?' the grenadier asked, catching his wind during a lull in the attack. Gaele realised that with his warrior sons fighting alongside him, he could be the hunter at last, and not the hunted.

'Keep those winged devils off this veranda,' he said. 'Conserve your ammunition. Short bursts.'

A wounded wraith lay at the bottom of the steps, wings broken, chest peppered with bullets. It hissed menacingly. Removing his pistol, Gaele blew its brains out. 'And make very certain they are dead. *Bonne chance*.'

Descending the steps, Gaele and his sons moved cautiously, past heaped Crimen bodies towards the cover of the jungle fringe, the canopy above alive with movement. Between the crashes of thunder, he heard the terrible howls of the wraiths. Silently, he made his way to the customs shed with his sons.

Crouching behind a felled Ulumbu tree, Gaele drew his sons' attention to the shed now fully engulfed in flames. Using hand gestures, he indicated they should flank it and meet around the front. The three of them together were too tasty a target, but individually, they could slip one by one through the cordon, protecting the banshee.

He watched as his sons silently crept away, waiting until they were out of sight before slipping out from under the canopy. He hadn't gone four paces before he felt the air above in flux, and sudden weight on his shoulders.

Twisting, he parried with his Winchester, fending a little imp off him. It tumbled into a pile of discarded pirogues. As it regained its feet, Gaele realised the imp was once a small boy, a pair of oversized shorts still clinging to his moulting frame. No more than twelve years of age, the imp retained more human features than the others. Even with a mouth of razor-like cuspids, its face remained childlike. Hissing, it beat its runty wings, charging at Gaele with incredible agility. He managed to fend it off with his rifle stock. In the light of the burning shed, he watched the boy's face transform into a ghoulish mask, carnassials snapping at him, hands clawing maddeningly at his serge jacket.

Then he understood; the small prig was after the fresh blood pounding through his heart. Wings thrashing, the little beggar screeched with rage. Suddenly, he was pulled away, hurled into the flames of the customs shed.

'Cheeky little nipper,' said the Mohawk as he appeared from the darkness, saturated in gore from the slaughter, eyes like a rabid hyena.

The imp reemerged from the annex, smouldering. It darted towards the Mohawk, sinking its teeth into his shoulder.

'Be off, brat.'

Gripping the hatchet from his belt, he buried it in the little fiend's head. It wobbled, before collapsing in a pile.

The customs shed exploded, fire burning hot through the zinc roof.

'Have you seen her?'

Gaele nodded.

'Come then. Let us run her to ground and cut her up proper.'

'Your mind is ravaged, Lieutenant Taggart.'

The Mohawk drew close, taking hold of the Belgian's arm tightly. 'Eaten away, Monsieur,' he said, eyes wild with mania. 'I know how to treat them. Bastards, the lot. Only question is, do *you*?'

Gaele slipped his grip. 'Is there not slaughter enough here to feed your urges?'

'I'm where I belong,' replied the Mohawk. 'Sod off and let me have my fun.'

A burnt Crimen crashed down between the two of them, its thrashing wings sending Gaele through the air. He landed hard, Henry slipping from his grip. The Mohawk went berserk, flaying the beast wide open from neck to groin.

Gaele raised the Winchester to his eye. It wasn't the seraph he aimed for — if he squeezed the trigger, he would end the Mohawk. But the night was not yet over. He fired. A.44 rim-fire crashed into the burnt Crimen's head, showering the Mohawk in brain matter.

'That's the spirit,' he yelled back gleefully.

Toggling the repeater's lever action, Gaele's attention was drawn to the *brum-brum-brum* of the Lewis gun again, knocking down the waves of swarming beasts. Balthasar continued skirmishing with the mighty wraith, anticipating each strike before the beast could make any counter-strike. With a rake of his hand, he tore away the seraph's mandibles, exposing a waxy facia underneath. It shrieked, bucking as it tried to break Balthasar's grip.

Sapphire flames erupted into bright orange as the customs shed burned hot, turning the night to day. Gaele watched a ghostly figure moving effortlessly within the hive, Crimen forming a cordon around it.

The banshee was exquisite as a Duchesse of Brabant rose rising from Congo's red earth. Gaele reloaded, his reaction visceral. Though beautiful, she had a blackness in her eyes more horrific than all the atrocities soaking Congo's earth with blood. Hunting predators was Gaele's profession, and experience taught him to keep eye contact at all times. But *La Reine Blanche* was a predator like none other. To make eye contact with her was to look too long into the midday African sun.

'Balthasar!' he shouted in warning over the peals of thunder.

The banshee stopped, flawless face still as the rain slackened. From her delicate mouth, she hissed, 'Balthasar Toule.'

At once, the earth went still, the hive docile.

Buster's ferociousness ceded too. Frozen to the spot, he released the beast he was fighting off. 'Siobhan.'

'Thy flesh,' said the banshee, her enchanting voice hushing Crimen susurruses. 'I remember your taste.'

Brushing aside her guardians, she lingered mere feet from him.

'Your flesh is frail,' she said.

The Belgian recognised fear in Balthasar's face. But rather than cower, he slowly brandished a spike from the waist pocket of his khaki drill jacket.

'𝔍ungfräu,' she spat, her voice a glottal snarl as her beauty shed, head elongating, eyes sinking into their pallid sockets as her nose leaf burst, exposing knotted inner cartilage. Fuscous eruptions wept on her spiny back as membranous wings forced their way out from within. Where words of velvet sprouted, now mandibles snapped a banshee's howl. 'Your filth shall not touch me.'

Balthasar hesitated, clearly entranced and yet terrified by her presence. Drawing back a clawed talon, the banshee smacked him across the face. Sent flying, he crashed through the side of the fully engulfed customs shed.

'Oi, luv.' Sinewy legs pivoted, talons digging into the mud as she turned. The Mohawk scooped up Buster's spike. 'Fancy a go, you ugly witch?'

Crimen quickly surrounded the Mohawk. Siobhan hissed unintelligible lexemes at them. They stayed back. Seeing the spike in the Mohawk's hand, she howled menacingly.

'That's right, darling,' he said, moving closer to her. 'My boss can't peg you, but there's nothing stopping *me*.'

Siobhan slithered back.

'You got no idea the spite I must get out of my head.' Raising the spike, he advanced.

Before he could reach the banshee, her horrific form sloughed. Clumped hair grew thick and luxuriant again, the ghastly wings protruding from her back curling up. Reabsorbed. Siobhan's exquisite *kitenge* fell to her feet. She stood disrobed, her flesh pale without imperfection once more. Sensual. Hips narrow and wanting, her shoulders lean and delicate, breasts firm and desirable. Siobhan was cunning. Even the Mohawk was seduced. Hands dropping to his side, the spike fell into the muddy earth. '𝔍ungfräu is useless upon me.'

She laughed, but too soon. Her chest exploded in a spray of spoiled cruor as a hot rim-fire round tore through her.

'No!' cried out the Mohawk, turning to Gaele as he lowered the trigger guard, ejecting the empty cartridge he had just fired into Siobhan. The wounded wraith Balthasar had released roared in anger, throwing itself before the banshee to shield her. Sighting his repeater, the Belgian had to decide between the beast and Siobhan. He fired, the energy from the bullet blowing further apart the already wounded Crimen's chest, black batter coursing from within.

Balthasar emerged from the shed's inferno. Tearing off his immolated serge jacket, he ignored his grievously charred body, scooping up the spike from the mud and leaping on the seraph. It flapped its wings madly, spiralling into the night sky. Balthasar, clinging to the fiend, buried the spike into it with such savagery his forearm vanished into its chest cavity. Releasing a primal knell the beast tumbled to the earth, Buster holding true as it thrashed madly in the mud. With a trembling hand, it reached for Siobhan. Showing no interest in its misery, the banshee retreated towards the jungle fringe.

Before Gaele could put a bullet into her head, he felt sudden pain in his side.

'I'll have you playing Victoria and fucking Albert,' snarled the Mohawk. Looking down, he saw blood sprouting from a gash in his KD jacket. 'You will not have her.'

He bashed Gaele across the face, and sent him tumbling into the mud. As the Mohawk reared back to strike him with his hatchet, the weapon was knocked out of his hand. He turned as a hurtling fist crashed into his face, sending him reeling away. The Mohawk drew a pistol from the holster on his belt, but before he would fire, his arm was wrenched back with a loud *snap*. He stumbled back screaming, right arm dangling grotesquely. Adongo grasped him by his throat, hurling him aside as he came to his father's aid.

Adongo held out a hand to Gaele. But the Belgian could only watch in horror as the Mohawk appeared like a demon from the rain, burying his hatchet in Adongo's back. Crying out, his son slumped atop him, the Mohawk continuing to hack at Adongo's back, opening mortal wounds. With his eyes meeting his son's, Gaele tried to ask for forgiveness, but under his son's weight he couldn't breathe.

'*Je t'aime, mon père,*' Adongo managed, just before he died.

Fumbling to retrieve his Colt revolver, Gaele got a shot off. The Mohawk knocked the gun away, leaving the bullet to ping off harmlessly into the night.

'I'll open you up and have Siobhan feast on your guts,' he sniggered, raising his hatchet with his good arm.

Gaele closed his eyes, awaiting the strike that would kill him.

But something struck the Mohawk first. He fell forward against Gaele, eyes wide with mania.

'Not now,' the Mohawk burbled, blood dripping from his mouth as he struggled to gain his feet. He turned unsteadily, a length of spear handle protruding from his back, pointing across the parade ground to the Belgian's younger son, whose arm was still extended from the throw.

Squirming out from under his eldest boy, Gaele climbed to his feet, grasping the bleeding wound in his side. By the light of the burning shed, he watched as the Mohawk stumbled to the jungle fringe, Barasa's spear still impaling him.

A few yards into the shadow hovered Siobhan. She watched Balthasar as he fought off her wraiths. A banshee shriek, and she was gone. The Mohawk attempted to pursue her.

Gaele raised his gun once more; it felt a tonne in his hands. He had lost too much blood. Vision growing fuzzy, he sighted in on the back of the Mohawk's head. He was a hundred yards distant, at the fringe of the jungle where the light from the fires began to fail. He aimed low, at the base of the Mohawk's neck, before squeezing the trigger. A bead of stinging sweat dropped into his eye causing him to quaver.

Henry squealed. The bullet zipped through the rain. The Mohawk yelped as the bullet carved out an enormous hole in his back. Lurching forward, he tumbled over a creeper vine, disappearing from view.

Gaele collapsed. The night grew quiet as the glow from the fires faded.

❖ ❖ ❖

An owl hooted somewhere nearby. The Belgian's eyes cracked. The morning sun percolated through the leaves of an apa tree. His eyes slowly met the long-eared owl's unblinking stare, unmoved by the night's horrific events. A fragrant tree-orchid growing from a limb dripped sweet water onto his lips. Beyond the spit of boulders forming the station's landing, he heard the distant roar of cataracts.

Slowly, he propped himself up. The wound to his side ached. He was not dead. He lay amid a pile of abandoned Congolese pirogues under the canopy of the jungle fringe. Someone had moved him. He raised his arm. His wristwatch was broken, the crystal cracked, hands frozen at 11.40 the night before. He gazed across the parade ground. The remains of the station annex smouldered and the customs shed still burned. The pitched eaves of the director's villa had fallen in, and the Lewis gun lay unattended on the veranda. There was not a carcass to be seen — neither Crimen nor grenadier — but a fetid odour of burning flesh told him where they were.

Major Hadley squatted at the edge of the River Ituri, washing crusted filth from his body. Only cicatrices remained as evidence of the horrific burns he had suffered. Repeatedly, he scrubbed his arms and hands, as if no amount of lather would take away the blood he permitted to be shed. Raising his head from the river, he shouted over the distant roar of cataracts, 'God in heaven, show no mercy to me.'

As he turned towards the Belgian, Gaele saw the disturbing savagery in his eyes had gone. After a wash-up, he looked young — dare, Gaele say — innocent even. Skin luminescent. Slight in build. Face without flaw of age.

Then joining him in the shade of the apa, Balthasar said, 'You're alive, then?'

'I am,' he croaked.

'Happy to see you survived.' Balthasar presented him with an old glass bottle.

Gaele struggled to pull the cork from the neck. He gave it a sniff. Uchema. A native wine fermented from Goma fruit. He sipped, but his throat wasn't having it and he coughed it up. He tried again. It went down the second go. It wasn't medicinal, but it would do.

'How long have I been down?'

'Two days.'

'Two days?' he forced down another gulp of the soured wine.

'You've been in a bad way.'

'Bilious fever,' Gaele said. 'Congo takes its toll.'

Balthasar nodded. 'Either in lump sum or by instalment.'

Gaele agreed, as he stiffly arose to his feet.

'I have experienced the barbarity of Congo's interior for more years than I wish to remember.'

Slowly, he made his way from the shade, lifting his face to the sun. In that moment, it was better to be alive. Turning, he looked to the still burning customs shed, a pyre stacked high with carcasses. Black smoke drifted into the cloudless sky.

'What I saw, those beasts, this is the fruit of your plague?'

'It's not *my* fruit.'

'Yet here you are, disposing of the evidence?'

Balthasar took the bottle off him, drank a mouthful. 'In a month, the jungle will reclaim this place. A few charred scraps of wood and rusted zinc, evidence Kinuwai Station ever existed.'

'You burn them?'

Balthasar nodded. 'The banshee Siobhan created a hive in the station annex.'

Gaele did not understand.

'Crimen. This is what they do.'

'Hive?'

'The hive remains close to her, creating a hollow. They swarm, consuming everything until the food source is exhausted. Then, Siobhan abandons the hive and moves on.'

'Your *Reine Blanche* has fled?'

He nodded. 'It's been a decade since my White Queen has shown herself. Now, she has vanished. Abandoning her Sentinels.'

'Sentinels?' the Belgian asked, slowly climbing the steps to the villa. Turning an undamaged wicker chair upright, Gaele sat down heavily. 'I understand these words, but not their meaning.'

'Crimen exist in a hierarchy. The lowest caste is a by-product of Siobhan's feeding. These are Huntians.'

'The mapping expedition and the search party who came after were her food source?'

Balthasar nodded before motioning towards the smouldering pyre. 'Those not devoured outright are infected and become Guilty. As you witnessed, these Huntians are sluggish, confused and weak. They are votaries, mindlessly striking for no other reason than to consume flesh, and easily dealt with by decapitation.'

The Belgian gazed from the pyre to the jumble of trunks Balthasar had recovered from Margoux. 'There are others?'

Balthasar left the veranda. Pulling on a pair of leather gloves, he lifted a metallic spike of a most extraordinary golden, aubergine hue.

'Jungfräu. Tool of my trade.'

'You must wear gloves when holding it?'

'It's mercury. One which can be made solid.'

'It is for these Sentinels?'

Balthasar nodded. 'The banshee fatigues and must rest during periods of brumation. She will become decrepit and retire to a hollow where she will go dormant in her sarcophagus. To mind her, she keeps a Sentinel.'

Gaele understood. 'Those great strapping beasts protect her?'

'Yes. In exchange for their servitude, she accedes to their predation.'

'Her blood flows freely within them?'

'Freely? No. She does nothing freely, Monsieur. She offers specious gifts. *Dosis*.'

'*Dosis*?' he asked. 'You mean a dose?'

Balthasar nodded.

'Dose of what?'

'A dose of her blood makes a Sentinel godlike. Their infatuation makes them the ideal tutelary.'

'On them, you use the spikes, Buster?'

'Yes, but as you've witnessed, engaging them is difficult. Killing them more so.'

'But not on Siobhan?'

'No.' He sighed. 'The banshee cannot be killed with this spike. Her wickedness is far too great. However, raw 𝔍ungfräu ingots can keep her in a state of brumation.'

'There is a way to kill her, ja?'

'With ℜisineum.'

'This, you do not have?'

'I do not.' Balthasar sounded tired

'And how is it you know so much?'

'A long time ago, the banshee gave me her gift.'

Gaele sighed, exhausted himself, and perhaps a little bit shocked by the things he witnessed. Looking to the pyre within the customs shed, he remembered that his sons were amongst the ashes of the dead. 'Once you obliterate all traces of this place, there will be no witness to your revolting legacy, save I. Will I be rewarded an equally merciless death?'

'You are not the only witness, Mssr Gaele.'

He looked at Balthasar, confused.

'Barasa is alive.'

The welcome news that his youngest boy had survived gave him renewed hope. 'Where is he?'

Balthasar tossed the spike back into his trunk, kicking the lid closed with his boot. Turning, he drew the Belgian's attention to snow-capped mountains many miles to the East.

'The Ruwenzori Mountains?' asked Gaele

Balthasar nodded.

'No one dare venture there.'

'He's gone on an errand for me,' said Balthasar. 'I expect his return at any time.'

The Belgian exhaled, nodding without really knowing what he was nodding about.

'What then?'

'I'll reduce Kinuwai Station to ashes, and disappear.'

'Go on,' begged the Belgian. 'Go on.'

'Away from here.' Balthasar gazed about at the sacked station. 'Where is your home, Mssr Gaele?'

'Oostende.'

'Do you wish to die in your bed there?'

Gaele shook his head, looking across the Ituri at the impenetrable jungle and the mountains beyond.

'There is nothing in Belgium for me.'

'Well, have you ever visited Folkestone?'

313

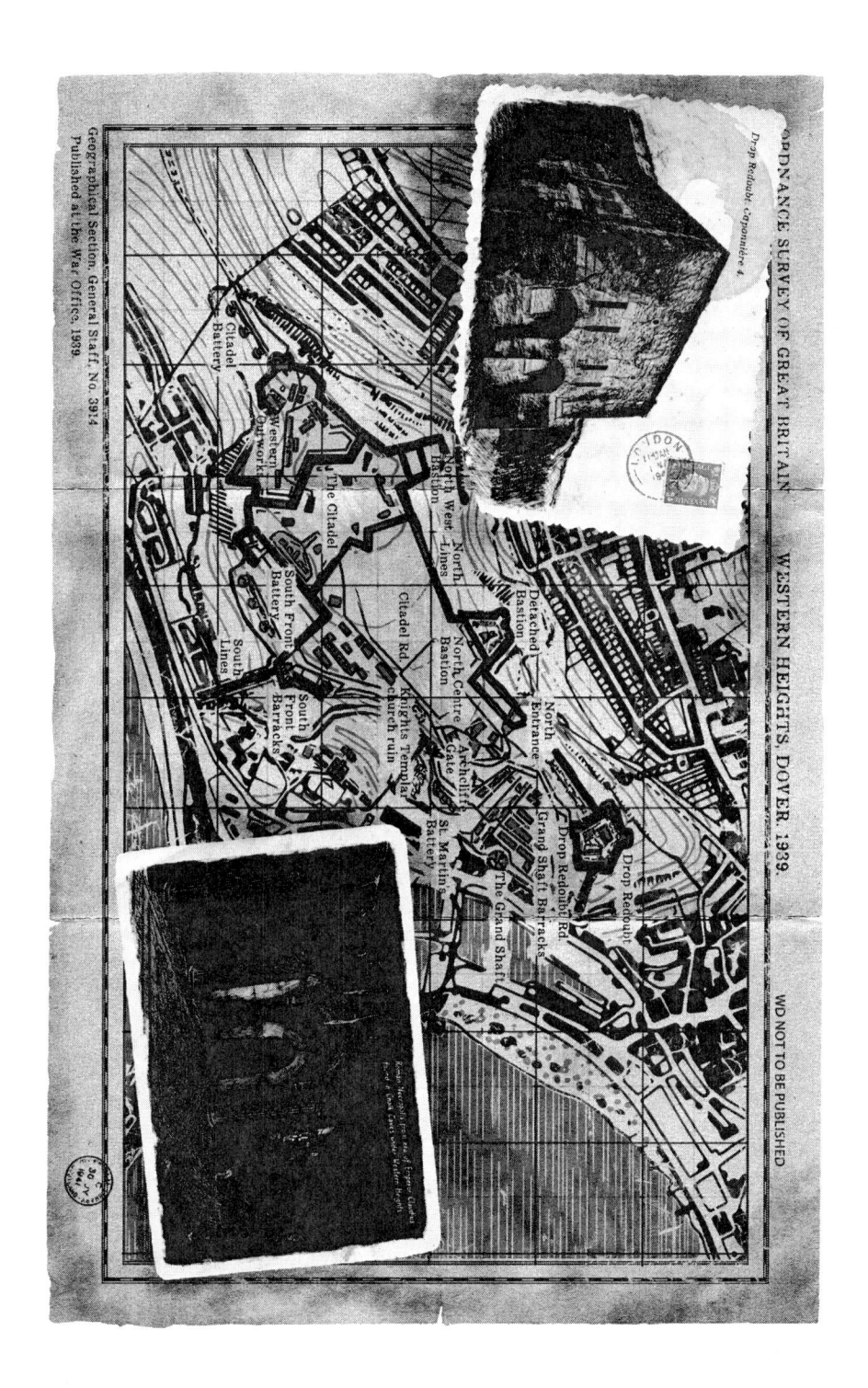

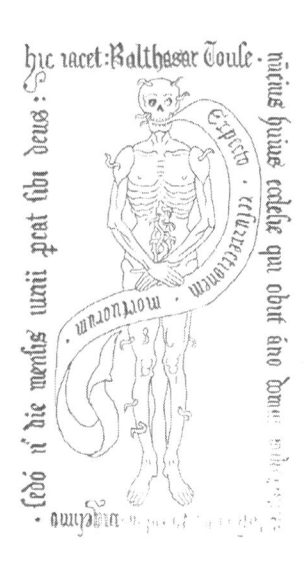

30 August 1939.
Folkestone, Kent

'For it is only given you on
condition you make use of it
for another or pass it on.'

—Mauss, 'The Gift.'

'*Expecto resurrectionem mortuorum.*'

They were the first words she'd spoken for hours. The Belgian's story was shocking, but she didn't for an instant doubt a word of it. Not after he mentioned the banshee's howl; remembering how Balthasar turned to her in Titanic's flooding hold, alerted by the unholy banshee howl. Elle realised then, she had been that close to the *Reine Blanche*. To the banshee Siobhan.

'What you were witness to,' she told him. 'It was a predation event.'

'I do not know what is a "predation event". But surely you will tell me.'

'An event when one species annihilates another. This attack you describe. I have heard of it before. Many times, actually. I've just never met anyone who witnessed such an event.'

'You have witnessed such an event?' Gaele asked.

Not exactly. But, I have witnessed a Crimen feeding.

'Then you have some understanding of their brutality.'

'I do.'

'The *Reine Blanche*,' Gaele reached for the whiskey bottle. It was empty. 'The banshee named Siobhan. What she offers, few can refuse.'

'*Dosis*.'

'*Dosis*,' repeated the Belgian. 'A simple dose of her blood brings out savagery as I have never witnessed before.'

'Including in Balthasar Toule.'

'Including in Buster Hadley.'

Tipping the bottle, he coaxed out its last drops; no sooner had they landed in the bottom of his glass than he tipped it back and returned it to the table. He sighed, wistfully.

'There was a time when I believed in man's decency. I was a man of faith, and faith alone.'

'What changed you?' she asked.

'Titanic,' he replied. 'The suffering of innocence shattered my faith. Congo. It extinguished my faith entirely. I could not return to Belgium. What use had civility for me? I remained in Africa. I thought I could save Congo from the brutality of the bourgeoisie colonials by taking so much as to make it worthless.'

'You don't strike me as a bitter man, Mssr Gaele. In fact, I would say the opposite were true. If you hadn't any faith, why did you take such a risk on me?'

'Because of Buster Hadley.'

It was not the answer she expected.

'After the obscene butchery I witnessed,' he paused, correcting himself, 'in which I *partook*, I was convinced he was no better than the Mohawk. It was not until later I realised I was wrong.'

'Later?'

'When I watched a young man turn to dust before my eyes. I knew nothing before then. You might say Buster saved me from the ennui that was my life.'

'You have a higher purpose now?'

'No more do I spend my days feeling old and useless. Although my task is a dangerous one and I have no desire to be eaten, I have a sense of purpose beyond fiduciary gain.'

Rapping his fingers on the old bar counter, he reached for a fresh bottle of spirits, and then pushed it aside.

'Despite his failings, your Balthasar Toule is worthy of redemption. Sadly, I cannot be the one to do it.'

'Not that I doubt you, Mssr Gaele, but you said something I don't understand.'

'What is it, *mijn liefste*?'

'About your faith being renewed. That it didn't happen until you watched Balthasar turn to dust before your eyes.'

He smiled sadly. 'You travelled a long way to arrive at this moment, Dr Annenberg. And you exceed even my expectations in picking up on clues.'

'Picking up clues is what I do,' she replied, feeling more confident that moment her long road was nearing its end.

'Good. Then I do dearly hope you will have a bit of faith in me, and travel a bit farther.'

'The incident at Kinuwai Station was nearly twenty years ago, Mssr Gaele. Nothing can possibly remain. And anyway, at this moment, I don't have the strength to book a passage to Congo.'

Reaching behind the counter, he retrieved the Winchester she had heard so much about.

'He's not so far as that.'

❖ ❖ ❖

Gaele turned off Old Folkestone Road and onto a dirt track, ill-suited for a Ford Anglia. Although new, the motorcar had been sprayed in khaki, giving it a nondescript, War Department look. He switched the headlamps off. Guided by the moon, the motorcar wound its way up a steep hill, branches whipping against the doors.

Elle dared not question him since he'd retrieved Henry from behind the long bar, but she could read road signs: Dover. They were headed up-coast from Folkestone. Not a long drive; nine miles paralleling chalk cliffs for most of it.

The car creaked to a halt. Switching off the motor, Gaele took his gun and a dinged thermos from the back seat before quietly closing the door.

'We've entered the Western Heights.'

'Sounds spooky. All right, I give up. What's that?' she asked looking around, only seeing hawthorn shrubs.

'A lot of old ditches built to defend Dover from Napoleon.'

'Call me daft, but I don't remember Napoleon ever invading England.'

'You are correct, dear Doctor. And so, during the reign of Queen Victoria, the army added barracks, transforming the Heights from a bastion into a proper military camp.'

Elle frowned. 'Don't you think the British Army's going to be suspicious of a couple of foreigners, one carrying an elephant gun?'

'The Heights is not currently garrisoned. There might be five guards on sentry duty at this moment,' he said, climbing a dirt trail along a gently sweeping hillside. A dark shape loomed above them. Three artillery emplacements emerged from the gorse, tresses of ivy creeping across the concrete barbette, the guns long gone. Bypassing them, the trail rambled through unattended grass and copses of trees and they passed a wide but shallow ditch. At its bottom lay the flint remains of a round, stone foundation. A rectangular chamber sticking out at the back gave the ruin a curious keyhole shape.

'I'm reliably informed it's the ruin of a Knights Templar preceptory,' whispered the Belgian, 'from the twelfth century.'

'*Here*?'

'These Heights…their secrets are often hidden in plain sight.'

As they made their way through a stand of sycamore saplings, Elle wondered what else was hidden in plain sight. She suddenly felt ill at ease as she realised that any semblance of civilisation was a long way off.

Crossing a tarmacked road, they descended a scrub-covered hill, ending at a sheer cliff edge. The lights of Dover's Western Docks twinkled in the night air below. In the distance, she saw a couple walking hand in hand along a beachfront boardwalk in the balmy evening air.

Jitters dissipating, she decided to follow on. Ahead, lamplight filtered through the leaves of the trees, the trees growing sparse as the trail came to an end. On a terraced hillside loomed austere barrack blocks with pitched slate roofs.

Steadily and quietly, she followed Gaele, climbing narrow flights of stairs linking the terraces, passing cook houses, ablutions blocks and even a gymnasium, all modernised with electric lamplights.

Through a lit window, she saw a guard sipping a cup of tea and puffing away on a cigarette. At such an hour, the mere crack of a twig underfoot would shatter the stillness, giving them away. It occurred to her the Belgian seemed more interested in the Thermos in his hand than being discovered by a British sentry.

'Strange,' he whispered. 'There's more activity since I was last here.'

'How long ago was that?' Elle asked.

'A fortnight,' he replied, looking to the eastern sky. Following his gaze, she saw the first blushes of morning. 'We must press on.'

'I've had enough of this,' she said. 'It'll be dawn soon and I still have no clue where your little stroll is taking us.'

He turned. '*Caponnière* 1, of course.'

'*Caponnière*? You're taking me to a chicken coop?'

He nodded, brushing by her, the Thermos in his hand grazing her sore ribs.

'That's what it means doesn't it?' she pressed.

'No chickens where we're going.' The Belgian came to a halt as they arrived at a point above the barracks. 'It's through there,' he whispered, pointing across the open ground to a high embankment covered with scrub. At its base sat a low tunnel entrance. 'That is where your chicken is kept.'

A soldier stood beside a piquet house outside the tunnel.

Elle gestured towards him.

Gaele had a long look. 'Private Jones. Don't you worry about him.'

'Either Private Jones is nine feet tall, or the tunnel entrance was built for the Seven Dwarfs.' As they moved closer, she saw that the guard was no taller than she.

'Who's that?' he challenged, displaying even less discipline than Elle expected of a soldier.

'Quiet,' hushed Gaele. 'You'll have the entire British Army awake.'

'That you, Flemi?' he said, and pushed the sling of his rifle back on his shoulder. 'Why didn't you send word you was coming?'

Producing a pair of women's silk stockings from his jacket pocket, Gaele handed them over to Jones.

'Do not think I neglected your request.'

Accepting them without hesitation, Jones gave them a sniff. 'Nice, ain't they?'

'Only two days ago, they were in a Paris hosiery.'

The soldier tucked them away inside his tunic. 'Me missus'll be well pleased with them.'

'She won't be the only one, I suspect.'

Jones offered a cheeky grin in reply, his teeth a row of bombed-out houses. He gave Elle a suspicious looking over.

'Ah, Private Jones, this is Dr Annenberg. An American.'

'A Yank? Nobody but you meant to pass through the engineer's tunnel. Cubby Smyth was quite clear about that.'

'Dr Annenberg is Mr Smyth's guest and as such shall be afforded equal discretion.'

The Tommy didn't mull it over for long. 'It'll cost you, Monsieur.'

'Everything does,' replied the Belgian.

'Bottle of fancy smells them proper ladies in Paris wear.'

'Toilette water or *eau de parfum*?'

'Wot me missus want with water from the bog?'

'*Eau de parfum* then,' Elle cut in, trying hard to remember the last time she had had a conversation about perfume.

The Belgian's eyes darted to her before he smiled at Private Jones. 'Without delay.'

'Get on with it, Mssr Gaele. You lot won't be welcome round here much longer, even if you was in with the king himself.'

'Oh?'

'They don't tell a screw like me nuffin' much, but I does know another brigade is boots-up here since your last visit. Another regiment arrives tomorrow.' Jones looked around. 'Best I shut me gob before I go on report.'

'Be a good boy now and look the other way,' said Gaele to the private as he motioned for Elle to enter the tunnel.

She ducked inside. Unlike the rest of the Heights, the tunnel was newly dug. Not more than shoulder width, the squared-off walls were barely four feet high. Fortunately, it was blessedly short, opening into a dry moat, its brown brick-and-flint revetments rising fifty feet. A polygon-shaped redoubt arose before her, trestles of ivy dripping down the brickwork, imposing bastions guarding the corners. Whilst the barracks they passed displayed a sense of order, the redoubt looked dilapidated. More overgrown Mayan temple than Victorian fortification.

'Imposing, no?'

'Very.' She stared down the sharp edge of the bastion, the brooding curtain walls of which was an endless expanse of brick and stone. 'It's immense.'

'The redoubt walls are twelve feet thick. If Napoleon had come, his men would have been scythed by enfilade musket and cannon fire from four *caponnières*.'

'And... Balthasar Toule is here?' Elle asked tentatively.

'He is.'

She studied the *caponnière*, the sills of the gun embrasures too narrow to crawl through. And in any case, out of reach.

'How do we go in?'

'Through the chicken coop.'

Crossing the moat, they stopped before a jutting corner. Five steps receded into a break in the brickwork. At its top an iron postern was secured by a keyhole. Producing a skeleton key from his pocket, Gaele slipped it in. The lock clicked gently, just like the doors in the smugglers' passage under the parish.

'Greasing doors a hobby of yours, is it?' Elle asked.

'Of Cubby's. Smugglers are nothing if not quiet,' he said as they went through.

It was pitch black inside. Gaele closed the door behind and locked them in.

A match was struck. She smelled sulphur. For an instant, the Belgian was illuminated by a wavering orange glow, dimming to blue as phosphorus ignited potassium chlorate.

Leaning forward, Gaele took hold of a dinged-up brass lamp. Holding the match to the opened lamp, it burst to light. Handing it to Elle, he lit another for himself.

Elle took the moment to have a look around. They stood at the base of a stair. Climbing them, she came to a landing made of slate.

'Posh, for a bastion.'

'Welsh slate,' the Belgian remarked.

'Opulent.'

'It doesn't spark.'

'That's a problem?' She reminded him he'd just lit two lamps using matches.

'Not any more,' he replied, joining her at the landing before ducking through a low-arched passageway into a cavernous casemate. 'But not long ago, these redoubts were filled with barrels of gunpowder. A spark could create a very nasty surprise.'

The vaulted interior of the caponnière was entirely lime-washed. Moonbeams filtered in through the loopholes of a musketry gallery above. The ceiling, a study in masonry skill, was supported by courses of finely joined brickwork, meeting at a spine wall. But the chickens had flown the coop, and from the amount of dust and bird droppings crusting the creaky wood floors, it was clearly abandoned long ago.

'It's empty.'

'Is it?' Gaele asked suggestively, turning to a passage ascending into darkness. Grasping a wrought-iron handrail, he disturbed a gaggle of slumbering pigeons, their wings flapping in the darkness. He reeled back as they fluttered up into the musketry gallery, settling in the loopholes. Something about them seemed to spook him.

'Jitters?' Elle asked.

He took a long breath. 'The sound of their wings brings unpleasant memories, that's all.'

Climbing the wide steps to the musketry gallery, they passed empty expense magazines. Tucked inconspicuously under a stairway was a small room, empty except for a peculiar raised ledge, reinforced with a glazed porcelain backsplash. An enamel bucket sat atop, its handle rusty.

'*Thuisken*,' he said before she could ask. 'For the men to relieve themselves. It is clever, no?'

'If shitting in a bucket is clever.'

'Very clever, as you shall see.'

Reaching through the cobwebs clogging a slit vent in the low ceiling, he fished about before a hollow *click* emanated from within. He continued fiddling. Another *click*. A third, and Elle heard the now-familiar sound of whirring gears. A final *click* and the entire loo popped forward an inch.

'Not so sophisticated a mechanism as that sarcophagus under the parish, but no doubt clever, *ja*?'

Handing her his lamp, he put his shoulder against the bucket. A firm nudge, and the assembly shifted. The porcelain backsplash, bucket and all, rotated sideways, balanced on a pinion.

'I have become well practiced in shifting these silly conjurer cabinets,' he explained. 'Come on.'

He ducked back into the darkness. Elle followed.

Their lamps bathed the arched passage of decaying bricks and crumbling masonry in an ominous glow. Stalactites leached from the arched ceiling.

'Lime,' he explained, catching her gaze.

'Balthasar is down here?' Elle's optimism battled with caution. Clever contraptions were all well and good, but she was not here for them.

'He is,' he said, beckoning for her to make the way down a newel staircase, spiralling into a dark void. The darkness receded before her as she descended, the stair coming to an end in a vault that smelled of damp, the remains of old barrels and smashed crates scattered about the chalky floor.

'A forgotten champagne vault,' said Gaele, lifting a scrap of crate. '*Heidsieck cuvée*. 1907. Ah, that was an exquisite vintage. Cubby tells me a lot of French champagne came through here.'

Elle shone her lamp down the length of the vault as it faded into blackness.

The Belgian continued, 'Behind the brick walls is chalk, mined for the lime. The Western Heights are honeycombed with tunnels, bored all the way from Dover Harbour. This one long ago caved in and was abandoned.'

Shining her lamp towards him, she replied, 'Not by everyone.'

'Precisely. These tunnels served many masters: stores awaiting payment of tax, cheese vaults, truffle growing. Even an air-raid shelter in the Great

War. Never mind smuggling.' Elle watched as Gaele removed a rusty lantern hanging from the brick wall. 'Cubby's ancestors made much use of this place over the years.'

His lamplight revealed a keyhole that had been hidden behind the lantern. From his pocket appeared a hand-hammered key. He inserted it into the keyhole and gave it a twist.

A *whirr* of gears. From somewhere deep in the tunnel rolled a deep grating sound. His lamp lit the way down a jaggedly cut chalk passageway, its walls dripping with calcifying lime.

Cautious again, Elle unsnapped the leather cover of her compass, checking the dial.

'Is it wobbly?' he asked.

She nodded. 'It took a fit in the Parish of St Emiliana's earlier as well.'

'Crimen.'

She looked at him, now even more ill at ease.

'Yes. When they are near, a compass loses its magnetic north.'

She remembered the reaction of her compass in the passage under the Externsteine. 'And if it spins like a whirling Dervish?'

'Pray.'

She was about to turn tail when she saw them: parallel gouges in the chalk floor.

The warning was forgotten as she followed the grooves, an anxious shiver running down her spine. They came to an end before an enormous blocking stone.

'*Expecto resurrectionem mortuorum*,' she said, staring at the familiar death symbol chiselled into the stone, its *Totenkopf* spitting an all to familiar apothegm, identical to the Externsteine.

Almost identical.

'It's open,' she said. 'Did the keyhole behind the lantern activate a mechanism?'

'An elaborate one, as well,' said Gaele with a nod. 'And easily missed.'

'That's the idea though, isn't it? To be easily missed.'

Had she, in her haste, missed such a keyhole in the passage under the Externsteine? Putting a shoulder against the boulder, the Belgian rotated it into the wall with surprising ease.

'What an ingenious pocket door,' she marvelled, pulse quickening as she awaited the reveal.

Inside was another chalk passage leading to descending stairs, precisely set with ornate tiles, and opening to a long chamber lined with fluted, Doric columns.

'What is all this?' she whispered in awe, her shoes crunching over a layer of calcified lime obscuring intricate mosaics. She twisted her neck to look at them better. A goddess, but upside down. They must have entered the chamber from the opposite direction. Turning around, she lowered her lamp to look again at the mosaics.

'Morta.' She looked up to Gaele. 'The goddess of death?'

He nodded. 'The *Roman* goddess of death.'

'Roman?' she repeated.

'The Heights have long been important,' he explained, seemingly not bothered by the subterranean chamber's importance. He had clearly come this way many times over. 'Before Normans, Saxons and Templars, there were the Legions of Rome, invading Britain through *Dobris*.'

'Of course—Dover.'

'The key to England.'

She heard his words, but her eyes found something more fascinating still. In the niches between the columns, under centuries of calcified lime, were bones. Thousands of them: femurs and tibiae, skulls topped with bronze helmets, now green from a millennium of oxidation.

'This is a necropolis,' she said.

'*Ja*. From the reign of Emperor Claudius,' Gaele replied.

She watched him lift a galea from the pile, the helmet falling to bits in his hands.

'That must be two thousand years old.'

'Centurions killed in Britain's outposts were brought here and comforted by the goddess Morta, whilst awaiting a ship of the Roman fleet to return their earthly remains to Rome. The chalk was ideal: it absorbs moisture, drying the bodies.'

He placed the bits of helmet back onto the old bones.

'Morta,' she mused, looking along the chamber's length, niches overflowing with the dead. 'Roman goddess of death.' Then a realisation. 'Camazotz, to a Maya. Hel, to a Germanic Pagan.' Turning to him, she said, 'This is a Crimen hollow.'

Gaele stood before an archway, darkness giving no hint as to what lay beyond. 'This way.'

She followed, caution gone, her lamplight revealing fluted Corinthian columns topped with acanthus-leaved capitals. If the previous chamber was suitable for centurions, this was fit for an Imperial legate. Between each column lay a recumbent emissary, surrounded by statues, vases and terra-cotta urns encrusted with calcified lime. Intricate mosaics underfoot reflected her lamplight.

Someone had tidied up, although not very recently. In the newly forming lime crystals, she saw footprints, leading to a strong door, not Roman, but a match to the one securing Balthasar's vault beneath the Parish of St Emiliana.

A padlock hung loose from the door. Lifting the latch, Gaele swung it open.

From within came sudden and violent movement. He was lifted from his feet and tossed against a column, his rifle, Henry, clattering to the floor.

Fumbling to lift the heavy Winchester, Elle recognised a familiar face glaring back at her. Bowler hat, small round spectacles, an air of abstruseness on a gaunt face.

'*You.*'

'You.' A slight smile crept across his face as he stared at Elle before fixing his gaze upon Gaele, Tommy gun gripped in his right hand. Releasing a disapproving sigh, he helped the Belgian to his feet.

'You ought not to have brought her here.'

Brushing lime dust from himself, Gaele lifted the Thermos from the floor of the narrow passage.

'I've brought your tea, Mahmoud. And I found some of those shortbreads you like.'

'It's not all you've brought,' Mahmoud replied discordantly, taking the Thermos off Gaele, before glancing at her again. He remained inexplicably donnish, unscathed by the years.

'It was you, wasn't it? Across the lake at St Dunstan's,' said Elle.

'It was.'

'And on Titanic, in the hold.'

'Have you got my tennis ball?' he asked.

'Have you got my talisman?'

'It wasn't yours to have.' There was nothing warm in his reply.

Taking Henry off her, Gaele said, 'Dr Annenberg, this is Mahmoud Hajian.' She leaned against the wall of the passage, a heavy exhalation disguising her nervous laugh as all the loose ends came together.

'What is she doing here?' he asked.

'You know perfectly well,' the Belgian replied.

Unscrewing the top of the Thermos, Mahmoud examined the tea inside. 'Good, it's still hot.'

He looked momentarily pleased. Blocking them from the door to another chamber, he added, '*He* wouldn't want her here.'

'It's not for you to decide,' Gaele shot back.

'Neither is it for you.'

'It's too late for this argument now.'

'I have naught interest in arguing, Monsieur. There is but one position. Mine,' Mahmoud stated.

'She's in it now,' Gaele told him.

'Up to her neck,' he rebuked, before turning towards her. 'A very pretty little neck it may well be, but don't think for one moment I wouldn't choke the life out of you.'

'In for a ha'penny, eh, Mahmoud?' said Gaele.

'In for a pound,' Elle blazed, fed up with being left out of the conversation. 'Stop Goddamn speaking like I'm not standing here.'

Mahmoud took a step back. 'I cannot possibly forget you are standing there, Dr Annenberg. Much as I *am* pleased to see you looking well, it would be better if you had not come.'

'But she is here,' Gaele interrupted. 'And you must let her see him.'

'Oh, must I?' Mahmoud's lips tightened.

'Can he be moved?'

By the look of his face, Mahmoud found the question odd. 'Why?'

'The British are mobilising.'

'I have been hearing increased activity above these last days.'

'It's time,' said Gaele.

'Neither you nor I make such a decision.' He glared at Elle now, but continued to direct his displeasure at the Belgian. 'What *have* you done bringing her here?'

After a painfully long pause, Mahmoud finally relented. He raised his Tommy gun to his shoulder, tipping the brim of his bowler with the barrel as he moved aside.

Elle brushed against him in passing, his woollen jumper itchy against her bare forearm. She looked into his spectacles. The eyes behind were empty. A little smile he tried best to stifle suggested that despite his outward objection to her presence, he was pleased she was there after all.

Gaele walked ahead of her through the open doorway at the end of the passageway and then turned.

'Follow me.'

The chamber beyond surprised her: the walls were cut from chalk, the bare floor lacking the bright mosaics of the previous chambers. A floral print armchair sat out of place by the entrance, a half-read novel lying open over an arm. *Vile Bodies* by Evelyn Waugh. A gramophone spun on an upended champagne crate, needle raised. An empty cup and saucer sat on a record sleeve. She looked at it closely. Andrew Sisters. *Rum and Coca-Cola.*

Oil lanterns sat beside the chair, one lit, flame low. A dartboard hung from a rusty nail pounded into the chalk wall. 'Necropolis kitted out by grandmum?'

Placing the Thermos on the record sleeve, Mahmoud tucked his Tommy gun under his left arm, unwrapping the wax paper around the shortbread Gaele had brought him. It didn't go unnoticed by Elle that neither man relinquished their weapons.

'Where is Balthasar?' she asked, her disquiet scarcely more thinly veiled than her impatience.

'He is there,' Mahmoud replied, directing her to another strong door at the far end of the humble chamber.

They walked towards it and she followed. Another chamber. Mahmoud turned the flame up on an oil lamp on the wall. A low-ceilinged crypt held four sarcophagi, none of them ornate, their sealed lids displaying Balthasar's death symbol and crusted over with lime. The fourth was made of limestone and appeared well looked after. She touched it. Only stone now separated her from Balthasar Toule.

'Why is his not chalk?'

'Chalk is an excellent desiccation agent. We can't have our old man drying out,' said Gaele.

Elle was so close to him now, yet she felt oddly empty; the realisation the best part of her life was now surrendered to a memory, hitting her. Now that she found him, she felt nothing. No electrical charge rising up through the limestone, passing through her. Like the limestone itself, she felt cold.

Without looking up, she asked, 'In the other sarcophagi, are they Crimen?'

'Yes,' replied Mahmoud.

'Why would you let him be with them?'

'It's not a choice.'

She looked up at Mahmoud. 'Leaving him beside those beasts isn't a choice?'

'He did not leave Balthasar here,' corrected the Belgian. 'Balthasar left himself.'

'He *is* Crimen,' Mahmoud explained, his words sounding almost like charity.

'And you? What are you?' she asked him.

'His Sentinel.'

'You are Guilty as well?'

He said nothing in reply. Elle looked to Gaele.

Raising his hands, he said, 'I am as mortal as you.'

'Yes, Dr Annenberg, I am,' Mahmoud said, his stare penetrating. 'I cannot explain why we hunger for such terrible things. No more than I can tell you why we rest with others like ourselves. I can only tell you—'

'*Expecto resurrectionem mortuorum*,' she said, remembering his words from ten years before. It was all true. What she had witnessed. The things she'd kept inside for so many years. Her theories. Turning to the sarcophagus containing Balthasar, she said, 'I need to see him.'

'You cannot.'

'I must.'

'Mahmoud,' Gaele pleaded softly.

'No,' he bristled, blocking them from the sarcophagus. They had ruffled his feathers all right, but Balthasar's Sentinel was not yet engaging them with his Tommy gun.

Elle watched Gaele tap Henry's trigger. 'Whatever are you hoping to do, Mahmoud? Hit us with your shortbread?'

He lowered his hand, crushing the biscuit to dust. 'Don't make me kill you both.'

If his ruthlessness alarmed Elle, his look of woe-betide terrified her.

'Give your Gyppo mafia routine a rest. It neither suits you, nor does it intimidate me,' snapped back the Belgian, before cursing, '*J'en ai ras le cul.*'

'*Va te faire enculer,*' Mahmoud growled in reply.

Elle sniggered. It wasn't everyday she heard one man tell another he'd bugger his arse.

Her reaction seemed to break the tension. Gaele lowered his Winchester and leant it against the armchair. Laying a hand on the Persian's shoulder, he said, 'You *must* permit her to see him. And you know perfectly well why.'

Elle looked to him. *She* didn't know perfectly well why. Before she could ask, Mahmoud spoke up. 'Disturbing him could have dire consequences.'

'Or it could be what he has waited these many centuries for.'

The Persian's countenance eased. He stared at Gaele for a long time before turning to Elle.

'A word of warning,' he said, laying his hands upon the sarcophagus lid. 'You may find his appearance upsetting.'

She didn't have time to process what Mahmoud said before he slid the lid sideways. Crystallised lime flaked to the ground as it grated. Gaele grasped an end. Together, they leaned the lid against the side of the sarcophagus.

Raising her lamp, she hesitantly looked within. Her breath buried itself, as the odour of dry-rotted cloth rose up to her nose. An atrophied corpse lay before her, brindle skin tightly drawn around its petrified body, head thrust back, dross-encrusted eyes sealed up, mouth wide in despair. This wasn't her raffish, dark-haired enigma in a duffel coat. This was a sad, frail fiend. She wanted to run from the hollow and curl up with her memories. But her legs were having none of it. 'It isn't him.'

'This must be shocking,' said Mahmoud, resting a hand on her shoulder. 'He went too long without dormancy. Over-fatigued himself.'

'More than a year,' said Gaele.

'Nearly two,' Mahmoud corrected.

'How long?' she asked, looking up to Gaele. 'How long has he been in this state?'

'He went away the end of July.'

'Four weeks,' added the Persian. 'It's not long enough. Not nearly.'

She forced her eyes back to the remains and a face so withered and sad, seven centuries of misery in a single, agonising gasp.

She remembered now. The handsome-yet-gaunt face she had forgotten. Before she could do anything to stop them, tears began to well up in her eyes.

In that moment, she loathed herself. Loathed she mistook those sad remains for anyone *but* Balthasar Toule. She reached in, her fingertips touching his face. The Persian went to stop her.

Retracting her hand, she turned to him, eyes flushed with tears.

'I'm sorry.'

Mahmoud nodded solemnly.

'I've spent my life hoping for this moment. Hoping to find him.'

Turning back to Balthasar, she gently stroked his emaciated face, his skin cold like his marble effigy in the Parish of St Emiliana.

'I never once gave a thought to what I would do if I did.'

Her hand lingered on his brittle hair, hoping her touch would resurrect him. In his frozen scream, she searched for even a hint of life. There was none. A full tear left her eye. Running down her cheek, it dripped from her chin onto his mottled forehead. Instinctively, she placed her lips on the spot where it landed.

She stood, wiping her tears away. 'Rest.'

Eyes cracked open. His voice croaked, 'You've changed your hair.'

THE BAYLE
Scale of Meters
September – 1940

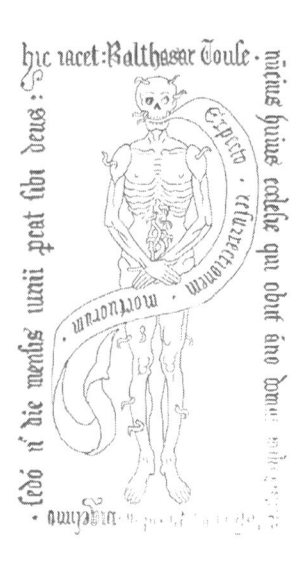

31 AUGUST 1939.
FOLKESTONE, KENT

No 1, The Bayle greyed with the years. Odd-coloured patches filled the crumbling mortar in the stonework, and its roof was a mishmash of slate tiles and shuttered dormers. The six street-facing windows were curtained. Hardy rose bushes grew from planter boxes on the ground floor, bursting with scarlet flowers. It was the only visible life to the house.

Gaele parked up the Anglia on Priory Gardens, a narrow side lane just outside the entrance to the house. He got out and quietly mounted the stoop, having a cautious look around before opening the front door. It was early. The Bayle was quiet. He turned to those still waiting in the car, and gave a nod.

The Persian bundled Balthasar in his arms, a worn, patchwork blanket covering him. 'You didn't lock the door behind you?'

'I have temporarily lost the key,' said the Belgian, closing the door and drawing the blind, blotting out the dawn.

'Bedroom or vaults?' Mahmoud asked.

'Take me upstairs,' a voice from under the blanket croaked.

'You're certain, Buster?'

A head underneath nodded. Mounting a narrow stair at the rear of a tiny lounge, Mahmoud flashed a look of daggers in Elle's direction. Choosing to remain in the entryway carrying Mahmoud's Thompson and Henry, she watched as he disappeared from view up the creaky stairs.

Gaele crossed the room. 'Shall I have them?'

Taking the weapons off her, he propped the Thompson against an armchair before lowering the trigger guard of his repeater, ejecting fifteen .44 rim-fire rounds, leaving them loose in a drawer by the entryway.

'What now?' Elle asked, restlessly wringing her hands.

'It's not as if he's going to die,' replied the Belgian, checking his wristwatch. 'Half five. I should like a coffee.'

'Shall I make some?'

He snorted. 'Good luck. You will find the larder bare. Only tea in this house. The Priory Arms is just a few doors down. Mabel keeps a bag of beans and a press.'

'The pub? Don't think I'm welcome there.'

'Cubby has already forgotten you biting his ear off.'

'Yeah? How long before he forgets you bludgeoned him?'

Gaele tossed his unloaded rifle onto a worn settee covered with yellowed newspapers, and was about to reply when an upstairs door creaked open. Footfalls crossed the floor above before Mahmoud appeared down the narrow stair.

'Get to the butcher,' he told Gaele.

The Belgian nodded.

'Buster's in need of victuals,' the Persian continued. 'On the high street. Make sure you see old Bill the Butcher about a freshly dressed sow. And buy all the sweetbreads you can.'

'Planning a meat pie?'

'Don't box clever with me, Mssr Gaele. This is on your head.' He glared at the both of them. 'Do you know what you've done? What harm you have caused?'

Elle's heart squirmed from guilt.

She was just about to apologise when the Persian started up again by holding his index finger and thumb hardly a hair apart. 'I'm this close to flaying the both of you alive,' he said.

Heading for the door, Gaele cocked a snoot behind the Persian's back. 'Someone needs a cuppa char,' he said, before closing the front door behind him.

Taking a long breath, Mahmoud looked angrily at Elle, before plunking down in the twin of the armchair in the hollow.

'He's right, actually. I *could* do with a cuppa.'

'I'll make it,' she volunteered, unsettled by the Persian's threat. 'If you tell me where the kitchen is?'

'Never mind,' he replied. He put his Tommy gun on his lap and removed the circular ammunition drum.

'What do *we* do now?' she asked, all butterflies, unable to stop herself thinking about what happened in the last hour and what was going on right now just above her head.

'*I* wait,' he replied coldly, ratcheting back the Thompson's bolt. A .45-calibre bullet sprang from the receiver and pinged about the floor, before rolling to Elle's feet. Crouching down to retrieve it, her cracked ribs protested. She winced.

'Whatever have you done to yourself?'

Tossing him the bullet, she pushed the pile of newspapers on the settee aside, gingerly sitting down.

'My ribs or my head?'

'Both.'

'My ribs are courtesy of Cubby Smyth. Discovered me in his smuggler's passages and gave me a hiding.'

'And the head?'

She felt the stitches. 'I was chucked out of Germany day before yesterday. Couple of Nazi goons clocked me in the head with their Schmeissers.'

'Then you were lucky.'

'Why's that?' she asked as she handed him the bullet.

'Normally, they use the other end of their machine guns.'

Taking the round, he inserted it into the drum magazine. It seated with a satisfying *click*.

'Where *do* you keep your tea things?' she asked.

He began to stand.

'Don't get up,' she told him. 'We can trade war wounds over a pot of tea.'

The Persian pointed her towards a narrow hallway beyond the front door. Following it, Elle came to a glass-panelled door leading into the kitchen. Like the rest of the house, it was painted eggshell-blue, and was horribly pokey. It smelled musty from disuse. Everything about the place suggested nobody special lived there.

She put her hand to an ascot on the wall beside the yellowed porcelain sink. 'Great. No hot water,' she whispered to herself. A dinged kettle sat on a cast-iron cooker. At least the Aga was hot - they always were. The tap spat at her, releasing a trickle of rusty water. As she waited for it to run clear, she pulled back the curtains above the sink, throwing open the windows to let in some fresh air. Across the narrow lane, the tower of St Emiliana peeked out from behind a high wall.

The water now cleared, she filled the kettle and set it on the cooker. Turning her back on it, she leaned against the counter and noticed two empty bottles of whisky on yet more yellowed newspapers. A tin of cigarettes poked out from underneath. Flipping the papers aside, she opened the tin. Only one remained. She didn't feel at all rotten taking someone's last gasper. Cracking a match from the box beside it, she lit it and took a deep drag before blowing the smoke out of the window. Still waiting on the kettle, she turned over one of the newspapers.

Le Petit Vingtième. A Belgian gazette.

She looked to the funnies. *Adventures of Tintin in the Congo.* She paused, looking up from the paper. Congo. Belgian. Was Gaele living there as well?

The front door opened and then closed with a crash, followed closely by a string of thick expletives. Heavy feet thumped into the lounge.

'Wot the fuck is going on with you lot?'

Cubby was back.

'Don't get shirty,' Mahmoud hushed.

'Don't order me about, you pompous Persian poof.'

'Cease your never-ending whinges and tidings, will you?' the Persian demanded.

'Me missus tells me Gaele come in asking for a coffee.'

'There's tragedy in that?'

'He tells her that Yank is here.'

Elle went to the kitchen door, gently pushing it open to better hear the conversation.

'She's not all that's here,' Mahmoud replied.

'Ah, his lordship up, is he?' Cubby asked, his voice lower. 'That was a short nap. I need words with him.'

'He's not seeing anyone today.'

'Wot?'

'He's poorly. His dormancy was interrupted.'

'Were it that Yank?'

'It was,' Elle replied, standing in the entryway. She watched the publican's head go purple.

'Wot she doing here?'

'She knows.'

'She knows? Knows *what*?'

'What would calm you?' Mahmoud asked.

'Her head on a fucking plate.'

'Didn't your mum ever teach you it isn't polite to crack a lady's ribs?' Elle asked, sarcasm biting.

'A lady didn't bite half me ear off.'

'Come now,' Mahmoud interjected. 'It was all cauliflower. You could hardly hear from it.'

'It's my ear, innit?'

'She left you the good one.'

Putting a hand to his bandaged earlobe, the publican turned to her. He was smiling now.

'Ah, sod it,' he said offering her his stout hand. 'Enough of all this. Mates call me Cubby.'

The enormity of his hand swallowed hers.

'My mates call me Elle.'

'Now that we're all mates,' said Mahmoud, 'perhaps you'll tell me what is so urgent you need to speak to Buster.'

'It's them engineers burrowing under the parish,' Cubby said.

'Close to our passages?'

'Close? If'n they fart I can smell it.'

'Need I have a word with the officer in charge of the engineers?'

'It ain't the barmy army I's worried over. I toss them a few coppers now and again. It's that Royal Navy Commodore overseeing the lot of them. Won't take a bribe.'

'The thumping in the passage,' said Elle. 'It's the bunker being built along the Road of Remembrance, isn't it?'

'Yeah,' Cubby replied. 'Them vaults been in me family for ages. And while the customs plonks is nosing about in the harbour, we're boots-up here. Six hundred years and the Bill never once cottoned on to what the Smyth family is up to.'

'Who's the officer in charge?' asked Mahmoud.

'A useless git he is. Commodore Wimbourne.'

'*Ribs* Wimbourne?' Elle asked, hubris showing in her smile.

'Yeah.' The publican turned to her, equally surprised. 'How you know that?'

'Let me have words with him.'

'You? Good luck,' Cubby scoffed. 'Bloke's so tight you could shove a lump o' coal up his bum, give him a boot up it and out pop a diamond. A crap one an' all.'

'The Commodore and I have history,' she said. 'He was on Titanic. You could say he owes *me* a favour.'

'So what? He's a strong swimmer.'

Elle nodded to Mahmoud. '*We* were on Titanic.'

Cubby scratched his head as the kettle began to whistle. Padding down the hall, Elle opened the swinging door to the kitchen to find steam pouring from its spout. As she pulled it from the cooker, whistling dying away, she heard the sounds of a discussion from the lounge she couldn't quite make out. By such time as she had assembled the tea service and made her way back along the hall, the publican was heading out the door.

'Come round the pub after you spoken to that plonk. I'll pull a pint for you.'

'Not staying for tea?' she asked.

'You're joking,' he said, daintily closing the door behind him.

She found Mahmoud standing at the window.

'I hope you didn't want your tea white,' she said. 'There's no milk in the icebox.'

'Modern conveniences.' He turned. 'I'm not accustomed to them. In the end, I leave the milk on top of the icebox rather than in it.'

A milkman, neatly dressed in a red-striped apron, his hair neatly side-parted and greased over, happened by the window, two bottles of milk in hand. She turned to Mahmoud. 'I tend not to believe in coincidences, but in this case…'

'Don't argue the toss?' replied the Persian.

She nodded before going to the door.

'Oh,' he said, surprised. 'Morning.'

'Morning,' she replied, wondering if he was more surprised by her attire, or a woman answering the door. 'I haven't any empties for you.'

'Never mind. Mssr Gaele puts them up on the back fence and shoots them.'

'There will be no more of that.'

'I've fresh eggs if you fancy?'

'Perhaps tomorrow. I'll plan omelettes.'

'Very well,' he replied with a smile. 'Not seen a lady round the old place before. Nice to see.'

So, it seemed there had never been a woman in the house. At least, not in the years the milkman was making rounds. Elle bid him farewell and returned to the lounge, prying the foil from the lid of a bottle.

'Please,' Mahmoud said, back in his chair and raising his hand towards one. 'Would you mind, terribly?'

She handed him the bottle. He drank the layer of cream off the top. Leaning back in the chair, he closed his eyes. 'Forgive my rubbish manners. British cream is the best part of my day.'

His eyes slowly parted. 'Been a month since I had any.'

Opening the second bottle, Elle dropped a dollop into both cups.

'Sugar?'

He shook his head, reaching for his cup and saucer. Settling into the settee across from him, she took a sip. After the night's happenings, it was divine.

'A man who indulges in sugar,' he noted, 'soon ceases finding satisfaction in it. Just as a hermitic man can never appreciate a life of toil and hardship.'

'You speak from experience?'

The Persian's gaze remained fixed on the street outside.

'Learnt the hard way,' he made mention, as if in passing.

'Shall I tell you something *I've* learnt?' she said, taking another sip of tea. 'You're Balthasar Toule's Sentinel.'

'Haven't heard that name for years and years.'

'Buster Hadley then. You're his Sentinel, yes? During his dormancy?'

'I'm his Sentinel *always*.'

'And you are Crimen. Like Siobhan?'

'Crimen?' he said, turning to her. 'Yes I am. Like Balthasar. To be Guilty is to once have been mortal. To be *us*, to refuse the one thing we find sweet, enrages her.'

'And you aren't talking about sugar.'

'I am not.' A cautionary smile. 'I do enjoy British cream, though.'

She smiled too, putting down her cup. 'I'm happy to see you again, Mahmoud.'

'I'm pleased to see you too, Dr Annenberg.'

Elle leaned forward, pouring him another cup of tea, ensuring he got an extra dollop of the thick stuff.

'Don't you think if the man whose ear I chewed half-off is willing to call me Elle, you might consider it too?'

'If you like.'

She sat back in the sofa, looking out the window as the day began, indulging in a moment's peace and quiet.

'How much has that daft Belgian let on?' Mahmoud asked her.

'He told me of the incident at Kinuwai Station,' she replied. 'I learnt about the Crimen many years ago.'

'And what is it you learnt?'

'*Sekr*,' she said, her eyes meeting his penetrating stare. 'I'm not just an ethnologist, Mahmoud. I also have a woman's intuition.'

'Is that so?' he said. 'Look at me, Elle. If what you see then is a man, then you see nothing. In your worst night terror you cannot imagine what it is to be Guilty.'

'I have an idea,' she replied, almost dismissively.

'Indeed, you have none.' His voice took on a menacing note. 'To protect Balthasar, I would crush your larynx before that tea cup reached your lips.

And as you lay gasping for your final breath, I would sit down and finish my tea.'

His face softened, if only slightly.

'For the moment, *Elle*, you are not a threat.'

'And for the moment, *Mahmoud*, I refuse to permit your very troubling words to deter me.' She sat in silence. As did he. Normally, she loved to bluff. The building tension. Normally, she won. There was nothing normal about the last few days. 'And Siobhan?' she blurted.

'I warn you not to blaspheme in Balthasar's company.'

'I'm not in his company.'

Her response gave him pause. Then he leaned forward.

'Unlike the banshee, *we* would not consume you.'

'You mean eat?' she asked, without batting an eye.

'I do mean eat. And, if I were you, I'd get as far away from here and him as you can,' he responded uncompromisingly. 'I am *his* Sentinel.'

Elle must have looked confused.

He went on to explain, 'His adjunct. You understand?'

'I think not.'

'An adjunct is not essential. I know what I am. A guardian. Nothing more. A bulwark during his time of dormancy. I'm subservient. When I am no longer useful, he'll be rid of me.'

'How long have you been his Sentinel?'

'Two centuries.'

She nodded slowly. 'You weren't subservient last night, letting me so close to him.'

'I was not.'

She nodded, in thought. 'Is Cubby Smyth subservient?'

'How do you mean?'

'If not for Gaele, I think the brute would have killed me.'

The Persian did not seem surprised by this. 'Cubby is a man of nil finesse.'

'Is that meant as some sort of reassurance?'

'He wasn't meant to kill you. He was meant to warn you off.'

'Who gave him the nod?'

'Curiosity is reckless,' he said, looking about the tea service.

'Curiosity is the most important prerequisite in my trade,' Elle responded. 'God, I fancy a shortbread.'

Without pause, she hammered home her inquiry. 'By whose order?'

'Whose do you think?' he answered, firmly.

'Balthasar?'

Mahmoud nodded reluctantly.

'Why?' she asked, voice betraying her shock.

'He worries.'

'Worries? What the hell has he to worry of me?'

'You haven't the faintest idea, have you?' he asked, narrowing his eyes.

She glared at him, at a loss for words.

'He worries you will get too close.'

'To what?'

It was the Persian's turn to keep schtum.

'Him?' she prompted.

He shook his head.

'If you were set upon by the banshee, she would cause you harm.' His eyes drilled through her. 'He would have to kill you.'

Her lips moved but there were no words.

The front door creaked open and the Belgian entered carrying a French press, the strong scent of coffee following him.

Mahmoud stood. 'Filled the butcher's bill?'

'Ja, ja,' he replied, disappearing to the kitchen. The Persian's eyes returned to Elle. Certainly there was more to say. Gaele returned moments later with a cup, and poured himself a coffee.

'The butcher was not yet open. I had them dress a swine while I waited.'

'Well, what have you done with it?'

'The butcher's boy will bring it, surely you did not expect I would carry a lot of guts and eyeballs up the hill?'

'I did.'

'Bah.' He gulped his coffee. 'At this very moment, Balthasar is resting upstairs in his bed. A far more comfortable alternative than that dreadful sarcophagus you seal him in.'

'The victuals?' asked Mahmoud with an unsettling snarl.

'The boy will be here with them at any moment. Why are you so impatient?'

'Do not make light of this, Gaele. It is you who are to blame for this.'

The Belgian *humphed*. 'Is it too early to drink?'

'Yes. It is too early for you to drink.'

'For me? No, no Mssr Hajian. It is *you* who could use the drink.'

The Persian climbed to his feet, confrontation escalating. A small knock at the front door broke the mounting tension.

'*Ja*, you see? Here is the lad now.'

Gaele emptied his cup and put it on the table as he stood to answer the door. Almost immediately, Mahmoud repositioned it on a pub coaster before following after him.

Elle looked out the front window. A barrow sat in the street. A lad, not yet ten, crouched inside, his flat cap tweaked to the side. She waved. He cocked a snoot in reply. A second boy, older, bounded down the front steps, followed by Gaele and the Persian. They stopped at the barrow, inspecting the contents. Gaele hefted a side of pork to his shoulder, Mahmoud gingerly lifting a pail by its handle. It knocked against the edge of the barrow and the dark red contents sloshed out. Fresh blood. The boys followed the men inside, carrying armfuls of brown-papered parcels. Elle arrived at the entryway as the Belgian came through the front door.

'In my country, it is tradition to salute an end to summer with a nice roast,' he told the boys as he made his way down the hallway. 'You may leave it here in the kitchen.'

As they mounted the steps, they greeted Elle with a tip of their brims.

'What you want all these sticky bits for?' the older boy asked, pointing out the greasy paper.

'Blood for the pudding,' Gaele explained. 'From *l'intestin* I make a nice sausage.'

'You *snotneus* eat them guts and eyeballs, don't ya?' the younger boy tossed in.

'Who taught you such a word at that?' asked the Belgian with an amused smile.

'Cubby Smyth calls you it all the day long,' replied the older boy.

'If I give you a shilling, you'll promise not to say it again.'

'Between us?' the boy asked, nearly unable to control his excitement.

Gaele produced two coins from his trouser pocket. 'Each.'

'Cor thanks, guv,' they replied simultaneously, snatching the coins away.

'Push off now. Be good.'

They scampered off, closing the door behind them.

'What's a *snotneus*?' Elle asked.

'An annoying little shit,' he replied. 'In Flemish.'

'Come and help me, you annoying little shit,' said Mahmoud, already opening the sticky brown paper to reveal its contents.

'Balthasar will have to eat *this*?' she asked.

'Had he not been disturbed,' Mahmoud said, 'Buster would have enjoyed a proper English breakfast when he awoke.' His stare did not linger. 'As things are, this is what he *wants* to eat now.'

'Let me come up with you.'

'No,' he replied emphatically.

Gaele agreed.

'Come, Eleanor. We'll have a coffee, *ja*?'

Grasped by the arm, she was shown back to the lounge. She watched Mahmoud disappear up the narrow stairs to the first floor, a dripping brown bundle in one arm, the pail in the other. Footfalls creaked along the upstairs hall. A door opened and then closed. Mad thumping pounded across the floor, followed by a jagged growl hardly recognisable as human.

Silence.

Nervously, she scanned the lounge, searching for a distraction. The Belgian calmly opened the front windows, filling the musty room with welcoming air.

'It will be all right,' he reassured her, as if it were the norm. She nodded, sitting anxiously on the edge of the settee and trying very hard not to imagine the things happening above her head.

'Coffee?' he asked.

'Got any Scotch?'

Producing a sterling silver flask, he unscrewed the top and poured a generous amount into both cups, topping them off with coffee. Elle gulped hers down.

Sitting in Mahmoud's armchair, Gaele lifted his Tommy gun.

'Like an American gangster, ja? Chicago? Al Capone?'

'Thompson. I know what it is,' she replied, her smile forced.

'The British call it a trench-broom. Personally, I believe the Winchester a superior weapon. You cannot engage a target at great range with a machine gun.'

'When we were in the hollow,' Elle interrupted, the whisky calming her, 'below the redoubt. Neither of you seemed eager to put your guns aside.'

'When Crimen are about, it's better to be armed. Never mind three of those ghouls in their sarcophagi.'

'But they're dead.'

The Belgian pulled a face.

'The difference between dead and undead is dependent entirely upon the Jungfräu.'

Elle slid her cup across the table.

'Refill please. And leave out the coffee.'

❖ ❖ ❖

Gaele's snoring sounded just as she imagined the noise of wildebeest mating. Whisky flask dry, he had dozed off mid-sentence in the sitting room armchair. Elle was wide awake after the night's revelations and had decided to return to her hotel for a bath and change of clothes. It was a glorious late-summer day. To the holiday-makers parading along The Leas, the world wasn't much different than the day before.

Elle nearly begrudged their serenity. How it must feel to go to bed the night before and awake to a new day as sunny and cheerful as the last? To crack an egg and dip sliced toast soldiers in it on the hotel terrace? To have nothing more to do than take a little swim in the seawater baths before Marine Crescent?

Yesterday she hadn't known if she would see Balthasar again. Today she had found him. Disturbed him. And for all she knew, he suffered, being force-fed the awful shit Mahmoud brought him. All down to her selfishness.

Mounting The Clifton's front steps, she entered the lobby. It hadn't changed: same old goats sitting about the lounge, sneering, same dunce at reception giving her the evils.

Yet everything felt different.

As Elle paused at reception to collect her key, Tony emerged from his office. 'Ah, Eleanor. Good morning.'

'Morning, Tony.'

'Rested, I see,' he said dryly, pointing out her soiled breeches and the spot of blood on her rolled-up sleeves.

She realised what a mess she looked. Again.

'I went riding. The horse reared. A dog, a little one, got under-foot,' she stumbled through her explanation on the fly. 'Took a fall. English saddle, you know. I'm really quite all right.'

'Quite all right,' he reassured her.

The clerk handed over her room key and Elle snatched it, retreating to the stairs across from reception, wanting nothing more than to be away from all eyes, and in a hot bath.

'Oh, Eleanor?'

She turned.

'A gentleman called round this morning for you.'

'A gentleman?'

'At just gone eight.'

'Did he leave a message?'

'No message. Suggested he would call again.'

'When you say "called",' she asked, 'do you mean called the hotel on the telephone or came calling?'

'Do beg your pardon. British English, not your American. I mean to say he stopped round to reception.'

'Thank you,' she replied, flummoxed. Retreating to the lift, she wondered who else could have known she was in Folkestone.

❖ ❖ ❖

Brrrinng-brrrinng. Brrrinng-brrrinng. Elle's eyes cracked. The telephone. On the desk in the corner.

Brrrinng-brrrinng. Brrrinng-brrrinng. She had fallen asleep and slept soundly. So warm was that last day of August, she had tossed aside her hotel robe and lain naked on the bed. Max and Moritz sat on the opened window raising a racket, even braving the interior of the windowsill to snatch biscuits from her tea service.

Brrrinng-brrrinng. Brrrinng-brrrinng. Reaching for the telephone handset, she knocked it from its cradle. It fell noisily to the floor. Tony's disembodied voice called at the other end. Grasping the cord, she pulled the handset towards her.

'Eleanor?' she heard again. 'Are you there?'

'Uh-huh,' she replied, hoarsely.

'I've awoken you.'

'What's the time?'

'Gone four.'

She had slept all day.

'Are you there?' Tony asked.

'Yup.'

'There is a gentleman in the lounge asking after you. Shall I inform him you are not receiving guests?'

'Who is it?' she asked, wiping the sleep from her eyes.

'Commodore Wimbourne.'

Jumping from the bed, the room spun as blood rushed from her head. She dropped the telephone and fell back onto the bed, fumbling for the handset.

'Down in five.'

❖ ❖ ❖

Elle tried to run down the stairs, but her new attire was not exactly ideal for speed.

A dress shop in town had left boxes of clothing at her door. In one, she found an unpretentious pair of cream linen flared trousers from Elsa Schiaparelli's *Le Sport* collection. They fit beautifully. Pairing them with a white blouse and coral summer weight jumper with brown pyramid-wedge sandals, she managed a playfully chic yet cosmopolitan look quite well. Far more acceptable in Folkestone than her *bärchen bulldagger* togs. Mother would *finally*, approve.

Passing reception, she caught the clerk's eye. He gave a double take, a lascivious smirk appearing on his face. Back to her, Tony Swinburne put messages into guest's key cubbies. Turning, his reading glasses fell from his forehead to the bridge of his nose. He smiled. Noticing the reception clerk's mouth agape, he cleared his throat. 'I believe you were about to tell Dr Annenberg how smashing she looks.'

'Oh, yes,' he nodded in agreement. 'Ever so lovely.'

If she had the nod from *him*, she felt confident she could blend in with Folkestone's summer society.

'Very glad we were able to sort out something to your liking,' said Tony.

'Yeah,' she replied, eager to be shown to Commodore Wimbourne. 'My unique sartorial style seems not to have gone down all that well in Folkestone so far. Schiaparelli is much more to my liking, anyway. I'm very grateful.'

'The Commodore requested afternoon tea. I've prepared it for two. I hope that's not presumptuous.'

'Not at all.' She looked to the lobby. 'Where is the lounge, exactly?'

She was shown through open French doors to the left of reception, and passed four ladies at a table playing Double Canfield. Shockingly, they offered her nods of approval. At the far end of the lounge in a bay window sat Ribs Wimbourne. A bit stouter in the tum, he was no less elegant in his naval blues, a row of gold braiding below a gold curl on his cuffs denoting his rank. Biscuit crumbs covered the front of his jacket, and a white officer's cap sat next to a tea service, one cup already half empty.

His face warmed as his eyes fell upon her.

'Hello, my dear,' he said, struggling up from the overstuffed armchair, wiping crumbs from his Kitchener moustache.

'Hello, Ribs,' she replied, crossing the lounge. He gave her a fatherly hug. He wasn't as tall as she remembered, and his hair had gone white. He smelled of ginger beer and cigars. Elle hadn't had a hug in a year. It made her feel vulnerable.

'Last time I saw you, you were in pig tails having an ice lolly,' he said, releasing her for a good looking over.

'Oh come now, Ribs. The last time you saw me I was twenty-five at the opening of St Dunstan's Science Museum. Neither was I in pig tails nor having an ice lolly.'

'Well, it's how I choose to remember you.'

Looking to Swinburne, he gave a nod. 'Thank you, Tony.'

'Sir,' Tony replied before retreating to reception.

Ribs offered her a seat. She chose the yellow and white floral chair across from him in the window, overlooking The Leas.

Wimbourne continued, 'Memory fails. This old battleship is overdue for the breakers.'

'Nonsense,' she replied, eyeing his commodore boards. 'Few more stripes on the shoulders.'

'Hmm,' he mused, 'I was about to retire. The navy, in their infinite wisdom, decided to keep me on the roster.'

He poured her a cup of tea from the silver teapot. She thanked him.

'I cannot imagine what I should do with myself anyway. Play golf? Tend the roses? Drop dead?'

'How did you know I was here?' she asked pointedly.

'A little bird.' He had a rascal's twinkle in his eyes. He held out a plate of biscuits. 'Digestive?'

She shook her head.

'When did you arrive in England?' he asked.

'Yesterday.'

'Yesterday,' he repeated. 'And in just one day you've fallen in with Folkestone's riffraff.'

'Presumably you are speaking of a certain publican?'

'If that were the blatherskite's only trade,' said Ribs, cracking a smile under his walrus moustache.

'His name is unmentionable within Folkestone's finer establishments, even as they procure their spirits from him.'

He sipped his tea.

'He was on the blower first thing this morning to my staff. I near dropped my morning cigar in my kippers when I heard your name mentioned.'

'You're at odds?'

'At odds? The scoundrel is an endless thorn in my side.'

'Put a few thorns in mine as well,' she said, rubbing her sore ribs.

'I was rather alarmed to learn of a lady of your standing associating with the likes of Cubby Smyth. I hope you'll forgive me, but I put a call through to your father. Awoke him in the middle of the night. Your family was not aware you had arrived in England.'

'Shit. I meant to send word. It's been a harrowing few days.'

Ribs nodded. 'You were wise to leave Germany when you did.'

The old navy man queered the pitch.

'How on earth did you know?'

He smirked. 'I wear the uniform of the Royal Navy, but Britain has me working on something hush-hush. It's my job to know who's coming and going these days. Especially from Adolf's neck of the woods.'

'Yet, you didn't know I'd arrived in Folkestone.'

'I didn't say that. I am, however, surprised by your associations.'

He looked out the opened bay window, cooling Channel breeze furrowing the curtains.

'Lovely afternoon, isn't it?'

'Folkestone is a dream,' she replied.

He leaned back in his armchair. 'I'm from Folkestone. I live on East Cliff. But I was born in the Durlocks.'

'I didn't know,' she replied, wondering then if there was more to this visit than tea.

'As a lad, I earned the odd shilling crewing a smack boat. My pop was a fisherman. His father, as well. You can't work a lugger nor ferry without having to deal with a Smyth.'

'I need a favour,' she interrupted.

'Oh?'

'That bunker being dug into the hillside.'

Ribs nodded slowly.

'It interferes with the unmentionable's trade.'

'The unmentionable's trade interferes with mine,' he replied, prudently. 'And his trade is rather less important than mine just now.'

'I know it must be important.'

'Every bunker being built is important. They well could mean the difference for Britain with what's coming.'

'The war you mean?'

He nodded. 'There's more at stake here than protecting a smuggler's booty.'

'How come they call you Ribs?' she asked, trying a different tack.

Removing a partially smoked cigar from his jacket pocket, he sparked it up, letting a few blue puffs of smoke rise.

'I learnt at an early age that the only way I should escape the drudgery of the working class was to serve at the pleasure of His Majesty. A uniform opened doors otherwise closed to a fisherman's son living in the Durlocks. I know the sea. I like the uniform. Unfortunately, as a young man, any uniform I put on was so generous of size, I was swimming in it. A stiff breeze would have blown me over, so ribby was I.'

'*Ribby*,' she said with a smile.

'By such time as Lieutenant-Commander pips were pinned on me, Ribs was left behind. Although I must admit to not having seen my ribs in many a year, the name persists amongst my close relations.'

'Do you still think about that night?' she asked as tactfully as she was able.

His face saddened. 'I've had three vessels go from under me. Two in the Great War alone. Titanic lingers in my mind the most.'

'I don't expect anyone who survived will ever forget.'

'Not my finest hour.'

'I knocked you into a lifeboat.' Elle laughed.

'Arse over kettle. Although a man of the sea, I admit to not being a strong swimmer.'

'Fortunately, you didn't have to test your stroke that night.'

Tipping his cigar ash into a teacup, his eyes narrowed.

'You were about to ask me to repay the debt for saving my life,' he said.

'I was about to ask for help.'

'How so?'

'Redirect your digging.'

He sighed. 'You do realise the sensitivity of such a request.'

'I'm sure it's a lovely bunker you're building, Ribs. Surely a little alteration wouldn't harm anyone?'

'Perhaps if I were to know why?'

'You're tunnelling under a parish with crypts beneath.'

'My engineers are not inexperienced, Eleanor. They did a thorough survey. I'm confident they're digging well below St Emiliana's crypts.'

'I'm sure they are respectful to the parish. But I don't imagine they, nor you, are aware of what might lie below the crypts.'

'Ah.' Ribs' head tilted with curiosity. 'I see.'

'Smugglers are a part of Folkestone further back than the laying of St Emiliana's foundation.'

'He's got vaults under there, hasn't he?'

'Not just Smyth.'

'The War Department's needs supersede the trade, illicit or otherwise, of a civilian. Particularly one as villainous as Cubby Smyth. If he were under my command, I'd frog march him into the choky and toss the key.'

'How about we do a deal?' she offered.

'What sort of deal?'

'A deal deal.'

'Ah, you mean an American deal?'

She nodded. 'Pretend you're a Republican.'

'Just for an instant, let's say I were to agree. What's in it for me?'

'You keep schtum about what may or may not be under the parish catacomb, and in return Cubby offers you one of his disused caves. Some of them are cavernous and brick-lined.'

'You mean to say you've seen them?'

'I have. It's a ready-made bunker. All you've got to do is link your existing digging with one of his caves. Your bunker is complete far ahead of schedule. Everyone is happy.'

'I doubt Smyth would be,' he scoffed.

'It would mean ever so much to me, Ribs.'

'The debt repaid?'

'Who came to see whom?' she replied, as genially as she could.

'What I cannot work out is why on earth would a respectable lady, such as yourself, want to help the likes of Cubby Smyth?'

'Considering my last employer, I think you'll find Smyth to be more respectable than I am.'

Ribs' mood lightened. 'Got yourself into a Horlicks, eh?'

She nodded.

'Nevertheless...'

'He's the right *sort* to have on your side,' Elle interrupted. 'Especially with what's apparently coming.'

He stared at her for a while in silence. 'Very well. I'll modify the direction of our tunnelling; you get me one of Smyth's smuggler's caves.' Finishing his cigar he asked, 'Are you planning to remain in Folkestone long?'

She replied with a smile. It was a very good question.

❖ ❖ ❖

Streaks of orange and red fought off the darkening hues of dusk. There was an end-of-summer feel to the air as she doubled her pace along The Leas. Having resolved one problem, Elle hurried to The Bayle to see about another.

Wally the Wall's man had shifted his tandem to the front of The Leas lift. Children broke from their parents' grasp as they came off the funicular atop the hillside.

'Mummy, Mummy,' a little girl in summer print dress and knee socks begged. 'It's the Wall's man. I ate all my peas, won't Daddy let me have a Snofrute?'

A weary father fished a two-pence from his trousers. Wally knew his trade, and where to get it.

In passing, Elle caught his eye. Wally gave her a double take before doffing his cap. 'Cor you clean up all right, Yank.'

She smiled.

Cutting across the grounds of St Emiliana's, she passed the oaken shrine listing the names of thirty-nine members of the parish who died in the Great War, before making for The Bayle. Mounting the steps to Balthasar's front door, she decided it was better not to enter unannounced. Gently, she knocked. The Persian peered through the curtain of the glazed door, eyes warming.

'Evening, Elle. Where did you run off to?' he asked, inviting her in.

'Went to the hotel for a wash and dozed off.'

'Bath and a rest do wonders, eh?'

By the look of his freshly pressed clothes and the odour of soap, she wasn't the only one who'd had a good scrub. Shown to the lounge, she noticed immediately the door at the far end of the room was open, an adjoining lounge on the other side.

'You live in the next house?'

'Good of Buster to offer me a bit of privacy. As you see,' he said, standing near the open door connecting their lounges, 'I'm never more than a few feet away.'

Elle went to the settee. The largest rose heads she'd ever seen sat in an old vase by the open windows. Still some life in the old place. Mahmoud's Tommy-gun remained by the armchair. The Belgian's Winchester had gone.

'Where is Mssr Gaele?'

'Gone home,' he replied, sinking into the chair.

'He doesn't live here?'

'Occasional guest when he's too pissed to stagger home. Mssr Gaele is an unapologetic arriviste, living in a smart residence at the West End of The Leas. Nine bedrooms, just. Cost a packet. Done all right in the diamond trade.'

'And yourself?' she asked. 'Number 1, The Bayle is quite humble.'

'I live at Number 2. Both belong to Buster.'

'Humble for him, as well.'

'Profligacy attracts attention. In the twelfth century, The Bayle was quite the swank street. As a matter of fact, all Folkestone was once held by the Toule manor.'

Elle peered about the lounge at the tatty Persian rug over worm-worn wood floors, at the eggshell blue walls, the yellowing floral print wallpaper around the fireplace and matching settee and chair ready for the tip. To suggest it was dated was an understatement. 'Did his grandmother decorate it?'

Mahmoud chortled. 'He's comfortable here.'

'Is he comfortable just now?' she asked, wringing her hands nervously.

'In better spirits.'

'That offal Gaele brought…'

'He required it.'

'Do *you*?'

'The very thing we must have, we deny. To taste the forbidden is to succumb. But, there are substitutes that quell the hunger. They don't diminish our desires, however.' Climbing to his feet, he made for the front door.

'You're leaving?'

Perching his billycock on his head, he said, 'Off to the pub. Fish and chips will quell my own hunger nicely.'

He was gone. And the house grew still. She turned to the stairs and crossed the lounge to stand at their foot, grasping the newel post. The stairs were narrow and far from plumb, and they ascended into darkness. She had waited twenty-seven years to be alone with Balthasar; she wasn't about to wait any longer.

Before she could climb the first riser, there came movement, a scraping, then footfalls above her head, and a sound like fluttering wings.

A door creaked in the hall above. Weak light illuminated the top of the stairs. Backing away, the heel of her wedge sandal caught on the Persian rug. She tripped backwards, landing hard in the floral armchair by the open window. Then, she felt wings buffeting her hair. Protecting her head with her hands, she awaited the strike.

Instead, a hand took hold of her shoulder. Slowly, she dared to look up. There he stood. The raffish, if not gaunt, face she had forgotten. It felt familiar, his bottomless eyes looking down at her.

'Balthasar,' she gasped, uncoiling.

'Eleanor.' His voice was calm and sure.

'You are,' uncharacteristically demure, she struggled to find words. 'You are okay?'

'I should ask you,' he said, helping her to her feet.

'I, I heard wings batting,' she said, struggling to compose herself, like a swooning teenager with a crush. Here was her ineradicable memory, fresh and vivid, his raw-boned face real, his unruly hair flopping over his forehead, obscuring his left eye.

He brushed it aside and studied her in return. So intense a look from him was too much. Her hard shell cracked at last, and she fell against him, arms wrapping around him tightly. She breathed him in. He smelled of summer in England. Of life.

Raising her head again, she looked to his face. He had shaved, the scruff on his chin gone, making him look even younger. Elle surprised herself by looking away again.

'Here you are, Balthasar Toule.'

'Been a long time since anyone called me that.'

'You are him, though?' she persisted.

'He is long dead.' He dropped his arms. 'Who you see is Buster Hadley.'

'I've had twenty-seven years to work out your hornswoggle.'

'Hornswoggle?' he repeated. 'You Americans. Your language is a mystery.' He looked to the window and smiled, albeit thinly. 'The Leas is lovely this time of evening. And I've been cooped up.' Fancy a stroll?'

'Let's go,' she said. 'I'll tell you all about it.'

'*It?*'

'Your hornswoggle.'

❖   ❖   ❖

A Union Jack fluttered above The Leas lift in the mild evening breeze. A step car hissed to a halt at the top, doors opening beside a queue of people waiting to pile in for the ride down the funicular to the boardwalk. A family with three children alighted, and made straight for the Wall's tandem to indulge in Choco Bars.

She and Balthasar sat on a bench facing the Channel, the lights of Victoria Pier winking to life below them. Distant voices cheered. Couples strolled along The Leas taking in the sea air, enjoying the last glimmer of summer. It was all so ordinary. Or perhaps, with all Elle had experienced in the last few days, Folkestone's patient and polite holiday-makers were extraordinary.

'Another summer at an end,' said Balthasar, gazing down towards a distant bandstand playing ragtime.

It was all she could do to concentrate on the Channel view, so badly did she want to take Balthasar in.

'Hard to imagine even a titch of trouble in the world just now.'

'I adore it here. Changed so much, this place. This world. When I was a child there was nothing more than wealds all the way to Dover.'

No matter how she tried to distract herself, Elle couldn't resist his profile. He had not aged a single day since 1912. He turned to her. Caught in the act of staring, she blushed.

'So…' she said, eager to move on. 'Hornswoggle.'

'You were going to explain.'

'You are Buster Hadley, yes?'

He nodded.

'As you were Balthasar Toule before.'

'You are perseverant,' he replied, tone neither here nor there.

'Your chicanery hoodwinked fate, as it did me, for quite some time. I was *hornswoggled*.'

'Hornswoggled,' he repeated. 'Clever Yank.'

'Clever I am,' she teased. 'That I am American is incidental.'

'It's not important. Never mind then,' he replied.

'You were my memory,' she told him without shame. 'I tried to hold on to you for twenty-seven years. I forgot your face. But not the bottomless twilight in your eyes. I could not forget that. And now, here you are. Here *we* are. And I realise I know nothing.'

He looked down to his white, summer brogues.

'A fragile façade.'

Was he talking about himself or her?

'Never mind.' She found she didn't have courage to say what she wanted to. Not yet. Seeing him now, feeling her relief in having found him, she also felt pained by his refusal to come to her in those lost years. She thought she might even carry an elusive bitterness within. Most women wanted to be pursued, not do the pursuing. Climbing to her feet, she turned.

'Fancy something from the Wall's man?'

'Can't say I've tried one.'

'You've never had a refreshing Snofrute? Not a wafer biscuit? Nor a frozen Choco Bar?'

He shook his head.

'Well. You haven't lived, Mr Buster Hadley.'

Leaving him at the bench, she approached Wally. He was just handing over a wafer biscuit to a little boy, his mum admonishing him to say thank you.

'You're welcome, me lad. Be good to your mum now,' Wally said, tucking a two pence into his pocket.

'Hi, Wally.'

'Ah, hello, Yank. Settled in have you? Looking smart.'

'I was out of sorts yesterday.'

Glancing in Balthasar's direction he quipped, 'In all sorts today.'

'Would you believe he's never tried a Wall's?'

'Blimey!' He rubbed his hands on the towel tucked into his belt. Opening the lid of his Warrick box, he asked, 'You're not still passing off Jerry Reichsmarks?'

'Pleased to say I've raided the Bank of England.'

'What shall it be, then?'

'Um,' she mused, looking through the fog of dry ice to the contents within. 'I fancy one of your lemon Snofrutes.'

She looked towards Balthasar. 'What do you give to a man who's never had the pleasure of a Wall's?'

Wally pushed the cap back on his head, scratching his neatly parted grey hair. 'I, myself, am mad on the wafer biscuits.'

He glanced to Balthasar too.

'A frozen chocolate bar never fails to bring a smile, though.'

'I couldn't agree more.'

'Snofrute and a Choco then,' Wally repeated, removing a triangular Snofrute for her and a frozen Choco Bar for Balthasar. 'Mixing with Folkestone society, are you? You look a proper English lady, you do,' he added, handing her the bars. 'Two pence, please.'

'Promise you'll keep *schtum*?'

'I'll never let on.'

'God bless,' she said, producing a pound note. 'Afraid I'm short of coins.'

'Hang on then,' he replied, fishing into his waistcoat pocket.

'No,' she said, gripping his hand. 'You've been so kind. Give your missus a nice bundle of flowers. Besides, I haven't a pocket to keep coins in.'

'I couldn't,' he replied. 'It's far in excess.'

Putting her hand on his she said, 'Look at like a downpayment against future ice cream treats.'

'Planing to stay on in Folkestone, then?'

Elle did not reply, but parted with a smile. Returning to the bench, she handed Balthasar the frozen Choco Bar. She sat. Closer. Unwrapping the end of the Snofrutes, she pushed at the other end, forcing the frozen fruit out. The sugared lemon juice was closer to Heaven than Folkestone.

She watched him unwrap his Choco, curiously looking over the frozen chocolate pressed between two wafers.

'Go on then. Tuck in.'

Hesitantly, he took a nibble. After a brief chew and a larger bite, his hard exterior melted.

'I saw that,' said Elle.

'Hmm?'

'No use hiding it. I saw you smile.'

'I never,' he replied, going at the melting chocolate.

'It wouldn't be scandalous, you know.'

'It's not at all bad; I'll give you that.'

'When I was a kid in Detroit, I'd go mad for Snofrutes. Eat five at a go,' she said, savouring every divine lick. 'I directly attribute my bitterness in life to consuming so many lemon Snofrutes.'

Her comment elicited a genuine smile out of him.

'There you go. See what you've been missing out on for seven centuries?'

They sat quietly for a time, enjoying the evening and their Wall's treats.

'The place you found me,' said Balthasar, breaking the silence, 'where I lay dormant.'

'I know,' she replied. 'The necropolis.'

'That the hollow is within a Roman necropolis is incidental.' He bit off a great chunk of the chocolate bar. 'I know I am old. Just not *that* old.'

He turned then to the Channel. And then so did she, watching the last shades of orange glinting off the calm dark blue waters.

'You were telling me you fancied those lemon Snofrutes when you were a child?'

'Yeah. I adored them. Still do. Summers in Michigan can be stifling hot. When I was a kid, I'd lay in bed at night, my bedroom windows wide open and I'd listen to the freight trains on the other side of Woodward Avenue, wondering where they were off to as I waited for the morning.'

'When I was a child, I fancied hunting deer with my father on the very Heights you crossed to reach the Drop Redoubt. It was different then, covered in hawthorn. In summer, orchids bloom across the slopes.'

His voice was different. Gentler; almost romantic.

'It's a nice memory,' he added. 'I have few.'

Leaning back, he rested an arm on the back of the bench. Probably without even thinking, he'd placed his arm behind her. Elle, however, was acutely aware of it.

'On the highest point of the Heights, was once a pharos.'

'Pharos?'

'A lighthouse. Romans built it. It went centuries ago, but when I was a boy, it was a hundred feet tall. My father told me tales of Roman legions camping on the hillside. They built an earthwork up there to defend Dover. My father had no knowledge of a necropolis. By his time, it had already been lost for eight hundred years.'

'How does a Roman necropolis become a hollow?'

'The banshee came for me,' he said laconically. Lowering the remains of the Wall's bar, he averted his gaze.

'Siobhan?'

He turned to her, a hint of surprise on his otherwise stoic face.

'I'm an ethnologist, Buster. I discovered your calling card.'

His look of surprise became curiosity.

'Sekr.'

'Expect you know what Sentinels are as well?'

'Like Mahmoud.'

'Yes. But it was the banshee's Sentinel that led me to the hollow. By the time I arrived there, she had gone.'

'Why do you slumber with them during dormancy?' she asked, the memory of his desiccated face just hours before still fresh in her mind. How could it be the same person?

'It's not borne of choice,' he replied, as if the statement had been rehearsed a hundred times over. 'When poorly, I'm drawn to them. I find comfort with them.'

'But you're not like them.'

'Oh?'

'No,' she replied confidently. 'You are different.'

'The only difference is that I am not strong enough. The very thing to make me stronger, I must deny.'

'Rest?'

'No,' he said, turning to her, his arm sliding away. 'The flesh of man.'

The notion of what he said made her feel sick. 'You need it?'

'Need?' he countered, pointedly. 'I *need* it, yes. But I reject what I need. And for that, I am outcast. For rejecting it, I am spared the banshee's most vile hex. And, as a consequence, I become as sickly as to be unable to prop myself up. My hunger is greatest then.'

'Dormancy renews you though?'

'Unrighteousness is sin. And there is a sin not unto death.'

Elle wondered what exactly his statement meant.

'My dormancy is nothing less than a period of brumation. And there is consequence to it. Enough to be worth fighting it off.'

She laid her hand on his. His skin was deathly cold. Neither spoke. Instead, they watched people go about their lives: strolling along The Leas, children playing. Elle realised how ordinary she and Balthasar must look. Just another gentleman and lady taking the evening air. Even if the moment was illusionary, her heart was content.

But something was nagging at her, and she couldn't let it go.

'Cubby Smyth,' she blurted, not without malice. Balthasar withdrew his hand. 'Strange you should have such a colleague.'

'I wouldn't describe him as a colleague,' he replied, unconvincingly. 'We serve the needs of one another.'

'Oh? So, what need did he serve when he was given the order to beat the hell out of me?' Elle snapped back, loud enough for Wally to raise an eyebrow. Even she was surprised by her sudden lack of restraint.

Balthasar crushed the empty chocolate bar wrapper in his hand, 'He was not meant to harm you, Eleanor.'

'I'd say your directive was not properly heeded.'

He said nothing in reply. No shrug. No pursing of the lips. Nothing.

'That publican gave me a damn good beating for someone who was "not meant to harm me". If not for Mssr Gaele, I believe your *colleague* would have killed me.'

'He was meant to dissuade you.'

'Dissuade?' Her voice trembled now, such was her disappointment in Balthasar. 'Something was lost in translation, clearly.'

He took a cautionary look round. A man enjoying a cigar on a nearby bench looked away.

'I don't want you hurt, Eleanor,' he said, voice hushed.

'You were with Mahmoud that night, weren't you?' she said.

'What? Which night?'

'At St Dunstan's. Ten years ago. The night you came for your phylactery.'

He said nothing in reply, his eyes empty of remorse.

'You came for your phylactery, but you didn't come for me.'

'I did come for you,' he replied tonelessly. 'Clearly, you didn't understand the message I left.'

'Oh, I got the message all right. The night you saved my life. On Titanic. Why would you tell me I had a long road ahead of me only to return years later and take away the sign post?'

Balthasar rose from the bench and took a step away from her, tossing his wrapper into a wrought-iron bin. He turned to her, eyes clear if not dark. 'There are many ways to butter a parsnip,' he said enigmatically.

'For Chrissake,' she cursed, rankled by his avoidance of the obvious. 'Do you know what a half-truth is?'

He shrugged.

'A half-lie.'

After an uncomfortably long silence he said, 'Follow me.'

❖ ❖ ❖

Leaving The Leas, they walked along the secluded towpath above the Road of Remembrance, his pace giving no hint as to where they were going. Distant music and laughter lingered in the trees. Turning onto the parish grounds, they ducked under a willow tree, its wispy branches scattering the moonlight on the grass. Bypassing the vicarage, they paused under the parish porch.

'Crimen are here,' she remarked, more statement than query. 'Last night my compass dial went barmy. It's them, isn't it?'

He nodded, unhinging the parish front door. It swung inward with a creak. 'He's never sorted that.'

'What?'

'The vicar,' Balthasar clarified. 'Rusty as these hinges.'

'And Irish as Redbreast whiskey.'

'Crossed paths with Vicar Duigan, have you?'

'I have.'

'He didn't land such a plum calling by chance,' he said, closing the door slowly behind them. Elle could not help but notice Balthasar slid the bolt across the door jam, locking them in. She followed him towards the chancel, lit candles showing the way. At the end of a row of pews sat a candle altar, a tatty donations tin beside it. Fishing a bundle of notes from his trouser pocket, he stuffed the lot into the tin. Then, he took hold of an unlit candle and lit the wick off another, adding it to the altar. Taking a step back he lowered his head, clasping his hands together.

'Won't you let her rest?' he whispered. A moment later he raised his head. 'It's this way.'

Following him to the main altar, they paused before the grilled brass hatch containing the remains of the parish's patron saint.

'She is here.'

'Emiliana?'

'Yes.' Sadness tainted his voice.

Grasping the grill, he gave it a tug. It came away with a grating sound that echoed across the parish's cavernous ceiling. Gently laying the hatch on the floor like a new-born baby wrapped in a blanket, he retrieved two altar candles from their stanchions, handing one to her. Holding a candle to the gaping hole behind the grate, he invited her to go in.

Elle peered into the void. An old, dusty vault. Crouching, she warily climbed in. Balthasar followed.

'This was part of the chancel ages ago,' he said, raising his candle to reveal pillar foundations supporting the upper arches of the chantry. The floor underfoot was dirt, the vault closed off a long time before. They turned a corner. At its end rested a rough-cut, chalk sarcophagus. It was not elaborate, and certainly not befitting a patron saint.

'Your compass was drawn to her wild signs.'

'She is Crimen?'

He said nothing in reply.

'The Vicar,' she said working something out. 'He cursed your name up and down this parish.'

'He drinks.'

'There is oft truth to a drunkard's rantings. He told me to get out. I didn't understand then. I do now. He didn't want me to leave this parish. He wanted to keep me away from *you*.'

'I tried to warn you away, Eleanor,' he said. 'I tried.' All at once, he shifted the sarcophagus lid. It slid off, landing on its side in the dirt with a deep thud.

Hesitantly, Elle stepped closer, the now-familiar smell of dry-rotted fabric filling her nostrils as a desiccated creature was revealed in her candlelight. Tawny solidified skin shrunk around a skull devoid of tissue, mouth locked open in despair, shrieking eternal misery. Bony hands grasped for a dull spike protruding from its chest.

'Emiliana?' Elle whispered.

Balthasar tenderly adjusted the gold fillet holding her frazzled hair in place. 'Yes.'

Looking to him she asked, 'Siobhan did this?'

'No,' he whispered. 'I did this.'

He slowly raised his face to Elle, and she looked for the sadness in his eyes, the remorse.

There was nothing. It should have scared her. Instead, she felt pity, for both Emiliana and Balthasar.

'Emiliana did not deserve this fate,' she said.

'Nor do you.' His voice was a brooding whisper.

'This isn't going to happen to me.'

'This is what happens to anyone who gets close to me. I mustn't permit this to be your fate.'

'You mustn't *permit* it?' she snapped. 'I've been making my own decisions my entire life, thank you.' She stood closer to him. 'You're making a mistake, Buster, if you think you can decide *my* fate.'

He backed away, nudging the sarcophagus. Truth be told, she didn't believe her own words. Balthasar had determined her fate from the very night Titanic sank, but she wasn't about to admit it to him.

'You think I'll end up like her?'

He turned to the remains.

'I won't see this happen to you. If it did, I would have to put you down with a spike.'

Elle didn't question the truth of his statement. She knew perfectly well by the coldness of his eyes he was capable of it.

'This is why you must stay away from me.'

'I won't leave,' Elle replied, tonelessly. 'I won't.'

Tearing a strip of velvet lining from within the sarcophagus, he wrapped it around his hand.

Although every window in the Priory Arms was left open, it remained sweltering inside, the low ceiling trapping the fading day's heat. Mahmoud took in the evening air, awaiting a bench and table to clear on the street. He hadn't seen dusk for a month. Nor a cooked meal.

Raising a pint of Speckled Hen he drank off the head, mindful of a pair of porters from the Royal Pavilion Hotel counting out the day's tips. They dropped a few coppers beside their empty pint glasses before they headed off down The Bayle.

Mahmoud removed his bowler, hair an uncontrollable mess of black waves. He sat at the vacated table. Gently pulling away a scarlet bloom from a mature rose bush beside him, he remembered when he had planted them. He bought them as saplings a century before, from a merchant in London, back when Persian roses were rare and exotic. Taking in the new bud's fragrance brought back memories of home, and family long dead.

'Mssr Hajian.'

He turned. The Belgian was just coming along The Bayle, his summer suit looking as though he'd slept in it. Puffing on a cigarette, he sat on the bench across from him.

'Hello, me old china,' Mahmoud replied, tucking the rose bud into the buttonhole of his lapel. Squeezing his thumb against his forefinger, he watched a bead of blood form.

'Thorny little things, rose bushes,' said Gaele with a smirk.

'Hm,' he groused, watching the bead of blood getting reabsorbed into the puncture before it closed up, his flesh healing. 'The most beautiful of things are often the deadliest.'

'I cannot begin to explain to you how many times I have heard that,' replied Gaele. 'I called in at Number 1, The Bayle. No one was at home.'

'I expect Buster has gone off with Eleanor,' he said, rubbing his thumb across his fingers, almost disappointed the wound had healed up already. 'Beauty is perfection and a curse,' he added, taking a long, satisfying draw from his glass.

'You do not approve?'

'Of Eleanor?'

The Belgian nodded.

'Have I said as much?'

The Belgian shook his head. 'Ah, you are so very much like him. Neither of you share your thoughts.'

'Whilst it could be said you wear your heart on your sleeve.'

Gaele guffawed. 'I have an idea, Monsieur. I suggest we do not bash heads today, ja?'

'I think it a fine idea if you would cease being so bloody irresponsible.'

The Belgian shrugged. 'Are we eating?'

Mabel appeared from the pub carrying a portion of plaice and chips. Two pickled onions rolled precariously around the plate.

Mahmoud brightened. 'I am.'

''ello Mssr Gaele.' She plonked the plate down. 'You wants some supper, an' all?'

He eyed the plate. 'Fish and chips, please.'

Nodding, she did then ask Mahmoud, 'Sauces, darlin'?'

'Wouldn't mind vinegar.'

She nodded, pausing before she turned to go.

'I tried to give your roses a little drink now and again while you was away. I couldn't get at them planters in the upper windows. Hosepipe ban. We's desperate for rain.'

'Not to worry, Mabel. I dead-headed this afternoon and gave them a good soaking. Persian roses are hardy.'

'Bring me bottle of champagne,' Gaele butted in.

'There'll be no French bubbly for you. You're on restriction 'til you settle up,' said Mabel, casually brushing someone else's crumbs from the table with her tea towel. 'I got British bubbly on offer.'

'What is that, dare I ask?'

'Pints of Speckled Hen.' She had a laugh at him.

'God,' he sighed.

'Suit yourself,' she added, disappearing into the door of the pub.

'Pint,' he shouted after. 'And fish and chips, if you please'

Tucking a napkin into his collar, Mahmoud pulled his fish apart with his cutlery. 'You won't mind if I tuck in?'

Gaele pinched a chip from his plate. 'Why must we eat in this midden?'

'You don't think it a manure dump when you're pissed.'

'There are splendid restaurants and ladies of high breeding to dine with on The Leas.'

'Nobody asked you to come,' said Mahmoud.

'Yes, that is true. But I prefer not to dine alone.'

'I have been dining alone the last four weeks.'

Cubby's wife returned with a pint of bitter.

'Your meal will be ready right soon, Mssr Gaele,' she said.

'Thank you, dear lady.'

'You know what I like about you, Monsieur?' she asked, wiping her greasy hands on a towel tucked into her apron.

'What is that my dear lady?'

'Absolutely nuffin.' Mabel creased up, giving him a swat with her towel as she went.

The Belgian laughed as well.

'See that?' said Mahmoud. 'You won't get such personal service like that on The Leas.'

Gaele sipped his beer, wiping the foam from his lip with his sleeve. 'Why do you drink this piss?'

Mahmoud rested his knife and fork on his china plate. Removing the napkin from his collar, he politely dabbed his lip.

'Because it's everything I love about England.'

The Belgian didn't understand.

'The pints, the fish and chips, mushy peas, onions pickled in vinegar, sitting outside a pub on a wood bench like this with the fragrance of roses in the air on a delightful late-summer evening. This is what it is to be in Kent. This is what it is to be British.'

A pair of local scruffs staggered from the pub, rolled shags dangling from their mouths. One took a last drag before tossing it to the kerb.

'Come along, you beer-sodden bag of shite,' one said to the other.

'*That* is too often what it is to be British,' Gaele countered, giving the lads a look over his shoulder. 'Oiks, the pair of them.'

'And bless them an' all, for they are indeed part of the Britain I so love.'

Mabel appeared with Gaele's fish and chips, handing a bottle of vinegar to Mahmoud. He gave her a smile of thanks as she left, dousing the opened batter with vinegar before returning to his meal.

Gaele prodded his own. 'I suspect there is a fish in here somewhere?'

'So then,' Mahmoud continued. 'Tell me of your visit to Paris. What did you find?'

'Nothing. There is nil Crimen activity in the hollow there.'

'Good. Best we have a look in on the London hollow soonish. Expect it to be the same, but could do with a check.'

Gaele shook his head as he ate.

'I stopped in at Highgate Cemetery a month ago. All quiet there as well.'

'And the other matter?'

'I met Commodore Wimbourne's colleague in the French military. He claims France is well prepared for the Germans, should they come.'

'*When* they come.'

'Ja. When they come. The French have built a series of casemates and bunkers along their eastern border with Germany. They call it the Maginot Line. They say it is impossible for the Boche to breach it.'

'And what do you think?'

'I think it is not so different from those redoubts that the British you love so much built on the Western Heights: fixed defences. An obsolete form of warfare.'

'I don't know if having an association with the Commodore is wise,' Mahmoud said, finishing up his plate. 'It complicates matters.'

'At this moment, perhaps. But a year from now?' The Belgian continued poking about in his batter looking for a fish.

'Are there not military intelligence chaps for this sort of thing?'

'Is that not the whole point of military intelligence? To avoid letting your adversaries know you are preparing for them?'

Mahmoud had a think.

'What concerns me is the idea of the Commodore and, worse still, those he serves, connecting the dots leading to us.'

'Which is why I involve myself,' Gaele continued. 'I am expendable, am I not?'

'What you fail to realise is the all of us are expendable.'

'But I am an inconsequential Belgian civilian with a special gift for smuggling people to and from the Continent without raising attention.'

'France is not our adversary.'

'Indeed not. But they drink wine and eat cheese while our mutual enemies grow stronger.'

'You think Germany will knock right through them, don't you?' Mahmoud asked, crossing the knife and fork on his now empty plate.

'I don't think this, I *know* it. The question is: will they stop at the English Channel?'

'That is a good question.'

'Perhaps the Commodore can be found useful to us, ja?' Gaele asked.

'Perhaps,' the Persian conceded. 'Perhaps.'

'Even I admit to being uncomfortable with his bunker so close to our passages,' said Gaele.

'It's been sorted.'

'Sorted?'

'Eleanor.'

'Ah, I told you. I told you.' The Belgian smiled.

'She is more resourceful than even I could guess.'

'I like this woman. She is arrestingly open.'

Gaele pushed aside his plate, offered Mahmoud a cigarette before lighting his own.

'There is something I find curious, though.'

Mahmoud shrugged a reply.

'This morning in the hollow. Just after you asked for your tennis ball to be returned, Eleanor said…'

'"I got the message".'

'Ja. What message were you sending? If you really wanted to keep Eleanor far from Balthasar, why offer up such a plum clue?'

'For the same reason you did.'

Gaele leant back on the bench and stared at him. 'Do you think he has told her?'

'I don't know.' Mahmoud took a drag from his cigarette.

'What if she were to do as he wishes?'

'She might get herself buggered.'

There was no hint of remorse from Mahmoud.

'You realise Elle is no simple buck-tooth girl from Luxembourg,' said Gaele, but then did not continue.

'Ask me,' said the Persian. 'Ask me.'

The Belgian sighed, giving him a hard stare.

'Ask me,' he said yet again, wanting so, so much to answer.

Gaele finally continued, 'We must consider her refusing him.'

Mahmoud exhaled, watching his cigarette smoke mingle with the Belgian's as it drifted into the diamond-clear evening sky.

'She might get herself buggered,' he said again with just a hint of satisfaction.

Elle dropped the candle.

Its hot wax spilled out onto the hard-packed earthen floor, snuffing out the flame. Fumbling for the remaining candle still burning on the ledge, she squinted through the flickering shadows, picking out Balthasar's silhouette at the deep end of the void. In his arms, he held the wilted remains of Emiliana. Tenderly resting her in the sarcophagus, he pulled her mouldy cassock over her.

If Elle had not witnessed the aberration, she would not have believed it. Despite the warning, she wasn't prepared for what had just happened, let alone what she had done.

When Balthasar dislodged the spike, the Jungfräu — reconstituted as it was — released from the corpse's heart. No sooner was it out than the entombed remains lurched upright. Eyes encrusted with centuries of dross cracked open, as gnarled hands took hold of the edges of the sarcophagus, brittle forelimbs balancing. Balthasar retreated, small stones on the floor crunching under foot. Alerted, the fiend turned, a grimace cracking the petrified skin about its lips.

'Balthasar,' it croaked.

'Christ,' Elle muttered. Neither of them heard her, their eyes remaining fixed on one another.

'Emiliana,' he said, his voice wavering.

At the mention of its name, the fiend became self-aware. Looking downwards upon itself caused the dry-rotted wimple to fall from its dander-encrusted hair, exposing bare bone beneath.

'What has thou done?' it rasped, forlornly.

Balthasar remained still.

'I hear the banshee,' it uttered, struggling to climb from within the sarcophagus. 'Her suffering eternal.' It stood, atrophied tissue creaking. 'Thou brought upon me this curse.'

'Emiliana,' he repeated. 'Do not.'

'Thou defiled me. Turned me. I am Guilty.'

Elle's eyes darted from the beast to him, awaiting a response. Some reaction, at the least. But there was none.

Then Emiliana attacked.

Knocked hard against the wall, Balthasar lost his grip on the spike. It disappeared in a cloud of dust kicked up in the tussle.

'Thou does love me not,' Emiliana protested, hoarsely. 'Balthasar, you love Siobhan.'

Taking hold of its emaciated arms, he attempted to fend it off. Such a bag of old bones could not have been strong, but it pushed him back, talon-like fingernails slashing his cheeks. Wheezing at the sight of the blood sprouting from his wounds, Emiliana pounced, sucking furiously from his split flesh. A grotesque kiss.

Fissured skin instantly puckered and bubbled, Balthasar's blood reviving the fiend, causing its anaemic moans to become wretched screeches as its erupting flesh plumped and grew smooth. Rising robustly, Emiliana appeared suddenly less bestial, face feminine, lovely even. But from its delicate mouth came an unholy hiss. Spiny canines pierced swollen gums discharging a greasy ichor.

Still, Balthasar refused to restrain Emiliana.

Elle saw something glint at the very edge of her candlelight: the spike. As she reached towards it, Balthasar sharply warned, 'Don't touch it.'

The fiend turned, jaundiced eyes locking onto her. A frightful squawk filled Elle's ears, like gulls in distress.

'Thou shalt have him not,' Emiliana shrieked as it attacked.

Elle dithered. It proved to be a costly mistake. The fiend knocked her aside with a single swipe. Elle's cracked ribs protested as she was slammed against the wall. Slumping to the floor and unable to breathe, she watched the wicked seraph turn on Balthasar again. There came a frenzy of strikes. His shirt was torn and flesh slashed, blood flowing from it. Emiliana drew close, face gurning as it fed on him.

At that moment, the spike pierced Emiliana's back, just to the left of its stickle-backed spine and right of the scapula. As its tip embedded itself in Emiliana's heart, the beast went rigid, arms flailing as it hopelessly tried to twist round to pull the spike out. A melancholy howl filled the void as Elle shoved it ever deeper; her bare hands weltered with putrid discharge foaming from the wound. Throwing Emiliana to the floor, Elle watched the fiend convulse in a mad seizure, arms and legs beating against the earth, sending the gold fillet in its hair flying, slime spewing from Emiliana's mouth as it soured.

'Get away from her,' Balthasar spat, voice filled with rage. His powerful hands took hold of Elle, roughly casting her aside. Emiliana withered. Festering boils appeared and began to suppurate as it dragged itself towards Balthasar, leaving a trail of sick behind. Hands outstretched, the suffering fiend cried out. Taking one of Emiliana's withering hands in his, Balthasar witnessed its end silently. Cruor-filled tears streamed down Emiliana's face as it waned, choking out words, lost in its atrophying face.

A final twitch and Emiliana perished. Again.

Bundling the remains in his arms, Balthasar slowly returned Emiliana to the sarcophagus. Lifting the gold fillet from the earthen floor, he tucked it gently into a lock of its brittle hair.

It was all Elle could do to keep the bile from rising in her throat; such was the vulgarity of what she had just witnessed. Despite being cast aside with such malevolence as to knock the breath from her, she felt something else. Something shameful.

She felt arousal.

Balthasar stood, turning to her.

'What have you done?'

'What? What is it?' she asked.

'You grasped Jungfräu with your bare hands.'

❖ ❖ ❖

She sat in the armchair by the window, staring at him. Although his face was shadowed by the moon outside, she saw enough in it to know he struggled with a sorrow greater than the sad remains of St Emiliana. Stifled as he might be, the rigidity of his lips revealed how broken he was.

She looked at her hands. She had washed and scrubbed them until they were raw. Rubbing her thumbs and index fingers together she thought about what Jungfräu did to Emiliana. Perhaps she had just got lucky. But she didn't believe in luck any more than she believed in coincidences.

'Emiliana was innocent,' Balthasar said, breaking his silence. 'She tried to protect me.' Hanging his head low, he sat quiet for a little while before saying, 'And for that, I killed her.'

'After what I'd done to her, I returned to the Western Heights, to the banshee's vile hollow, praying for an end to my bereavement. I found the ancient crypts of the necropolis still. Siobhan gone.'

He continued gazing out the window of the house on The Bayle, his face a portrait of tired resignation.

It was clear Emiliana occupied the place where his mortality once lived.

'Why do you suppose Siobhan fled?' she asked.

'I can't say,' he replied, his expression ascetic now, any previous vulnerability suddenly vanishing. 'You cannot imagine what it's like to understand little more than loathing.'

Elle didn't reply, she wondered if he loathed Siobhan, or himself. She opened the leaded glass windows fronting the street. A gentle breeze brought some relief from the tension in the room. From the direction of the harbour, she heard the distant squawk of seagulls. She wondered if Max and Moritz would visit.

379

Balthasar recoiled from the sound. 'That noise disturbs me.'

She turned from the window.

'It's just seagulls, Balthasar,' she reassured him, sitting again. 'And you are home.'

'Home,' he repeated, leaning back in the old settee, looking about the lounge. 'From the night I murdered Emiliana seven centuries ago I lived alone here.'

'*You* didn't murder her. That was Siobhan's doing.'

'It's naïve of you to think there is a difference.'

Lifting his head, he settled his eyes on the humble fireplace, its mantel surrounded by plaster and whimsical wallpaper in spring hues.

'This house. So cold. Empty. Greying with the years.'

Rising to his feet, he moved away from her.

'I tried starving myself to death. I didn't eat nor take drink for months. I became a living skeleton.'

He stopped before the old fireplace, resting a hand upon the cracked wood mantelpiece.

'I threw myself from the cliffs. Landed on the rocks below Shakespeare Cliff. Shattered every bone in my body. The Channel waves washed me away. I couldn't swim, but neither could I drown.' He turned to her. 'All good men do die. It is truth. Yet, mortal death is not a right for me, Eleanor. You see, I'm the son and the heir of nothing in particular. My existence not worth a tuppence. Not until I came to terms with what I became. What I am.'

'You are Balthasar Toule?'

'He died the night I accepted Siobhan's gift.'

Crossing the lounge, he muttered something about tea, before disappearing down the back hall to the kitchen.

Elle followed him to the kitchen door, through which she heard the clink of china cups and saucers. Gently pushing the swinging door open, she found him standing at the sink, back to her, shirt sleeves rolled back. He turned on the tap. Old plumbing banged before water spat into the sink. A seven-hundred-year-old noble busying himself with domestic chores. The ordinary for a man anything but.

He opened the window above the sink, tossing a couple of butter biscuits onto the sill outside, which were immediately pounced upon by a pair of fat seagulls. Max and Moritz wolfed them down and then looked up to him, cooing.

'Naughty lads,' he muttered as the kettle on the AGA began to whistle, frightening them off. He turned to Elle at the door. Caught spying, she took an embarrassed step back.

'Tea is on,' he said, removing the kettle from the cooker. An uncomfortable silence followed as the whistle died away.

She watched him pour water through the tea strainer, the fragrance of herbs filling the tiny kitchen. 'Is that rosemary?' she asked.

'Mother's favourite.' He put the kettle down. 'A house redolent with ghosts.'

Elle took a step nearer to him. 'I pictured you living in a manor house with a library and staff bringing tea on polished silver.' She stopped just behind him. 'At the very least someone else to make the tea.'

'One lump or two?' he asked, holding a tarnished sugar bowl in his hand, his courtesy seeming purely perfunctory. Raising her chin, she rested it upon his shoulder. His neck smelled of shaving soap. Leaving her fears behind, she pushed the sugar bowl in his hand to the counter, laying her hand upon his. He looked down, his fingers hesitantly intertwining with hers.

'You grasped the spike with your bare hand,' he said.

'Yeah, you said.'

'Jungfräu is toxic.'

'Am I going to die?' she asked, her fingers tightening on his.

'Not today.' His response was subdued. 'Jungfräu would have killed you quick.'

'Dumb luck,' she ceded.

'I've not witnessed it before.'

'Is that significant?'

She drew close, her chest now pressing against his back.

'Perhaps you're right, Eleanor. Dumb luck.'

She didn't believe him.

He turned from the tea on the kitchen counter, his eyes meeting hers. She had not been this close to him since Titanic. At least not while he retained his former self.

'Can you stop?' she asked.

'Can I stop?'

His nonplussed response made him look vulnerable. She liked it.

'Can you stop,' she repeated again, 'calling me Eleanor.'

His austere eyes warmed. If only slightly.

'If that brute of a man Smyth can call me Elle, and Mssr Gaele, and Mahmoud, I'd say it's kosher for you to do the same.'

'Elle,' he began again. 'I have caused misery to everyone who cared about me. You ought to leave before I am the death of you.'

'Not even a sockdolager like that frightens me,' she replied, his warning having no effect upon her by now.

He humphed.

'First hornswoggle, now sockdolager. Another American anachronism.'

She gave him her best coquettish nod.

'I'm learning all sorts about you, Elle.'

'Then learn this. Not even a remark like "you'll be the death of me" is a sock in the guts. I learnt a long time ago that getting out of trouble is far more interesting to me than getting into it.' Confidence beat back prudence, her fingers tightening around his. Their faces were mere inches apart, and when she spoke, she barely had to raise her voice over a whisper.

'The time to take it on the arches has come and gone. It was too late the first moment I saw you,' she said, laying everything bare before him. 'For me. You're the only game in town.'

She turned the last card down. She didn't care. She felt powerful. Without giving him a moment to consider her words, she kissed him. Her indomitable longing burst into flames as she tasted his lips. He responded, cautionary at first, then accepting. Mouths parted. His arms pulled her tight, his touch the most divine tonic. Her heart raced from an ache borne not from desire, but safety. The years of insufferable loneliness dissolved. Together, they retreated into her memories.

❖ ❖ ❖

The night was hot. Even with the windows in the upstairs bedroom flung wide open, there was little relief from the heat. Quaint, hand-stitched quilts and odd clothes were strewn across a worn wooden floor, cotton bed sheets twisted around their bodies. Deep kisses. Hands exploring.

The cool touch of his fingers upon her warm flesh made her tingle. Naked except for her blouse, she sat astride him. Pondering the dignified line of his neck, she rested her hands on either side of his face, the deep pools of his eyes revealing nothing of his thoughts. His body spoke for him. Timidity exiled, she felt him against her. Firm. It set her alight. Overtaken by a want she had cloistered since Titanic, there was nothing to disturb them now.

Fumbling with her linen blouse, he pulled the last buttons open, revealing her tapered breasts beneath. Arching her back, she raised her chest to him. He feasted. Her hands became lost in his thick, hair as his mouth grew eager and was overcome with delectation. Grasping his back, muscles like stone, uninhibited lust took away her control. Parting her legs further she moved upon him, a curious release begging, heart awakening.

As he moved up to meet her, she wrapped her willowy legs about his thighs, gasping with pleasure as her most treasured space was occupied.

Although her mind spun, she remained aware. This was deeper than coitus. This was something she'd never known. They were no longer separated. Not by distance nor time. This complex man, in this moment uncomplicated. He was within her.

'Balthasar,' she whispered, lost in the whirligig of his seizing muscle exploring her, his movement raw yet strangely regal, the sensations reverberating in her arms. Her body was a cacophony of convulsions. She held him tightly. Never would she allow herself to be separated from him again.

Elle lay amid the damp cotton sheets, taking him in. He was so close; his cool skin against hers took away the night's heat, his cold touch heavenly. Pressed against him, his nakedness familiar now, she felt comfort in this blissful, post-coital unity. The decades of loneliness, the feelings of longing, of not belonging to anyone, all worthwhile for this moment.

'I hear your voice inside me. I see your face everywhere,' she said softly.

His head turned slightly, black eyes on her.

'On Carpathia. On the pier in Manhattan.' She reached out, her hand uncurling a lock of his hair. 'I found myself always looking through crowds, hoping to pick you out. University of Michigan football games. At Tiger stadium. Speed boat races at the Detroit Yacht Club. You know, I once thought I saw you in the reflection of a store front window in Birmingham.'

He said nothing.

'Birmingham, Michigan. It's a town near where I teach. I thought I caught your face. It was my mistake. I turned round and there was nobody.' She sighed, holding onto him now, remembering just how many years she looked for him. 'And even when I forgot what you looked like, I kept looking. I knew you were out there. You left me too many clues, Balthasar. I just needed time to find them all. And I have. And here you are.'

Drifting away beneath the moonlight flooding through the open windows, she saw his ever-present confidence and barriers of self-defence drain from his extraordinary face, a sanguine whisper on his lips.

'I'm so very tired.'

❖ ❖ ❖

Voices in the street awoke her.

Sunshine drenched the bedroom through the open windows. A new day. A new month. A gentle breeze caught in the curtains, carrying with it voices from below. She rolled over. The sheets where Balthasar had lain were thrown back. Rubbing the sleep from her eyes, she focused on the grand yet intricate cabinet at the far end of the room.

Pulling Balthasar's jacket over her naked body, she padded across the wooden floor to look more closely at it. In the light of day, she recognised the cabinet's intricate marquetry immediately. It was a Roentgen secretary. They were a delight of ingeniously placed mechanics of cables, pulleys and cogs which, when activated, revealed all manner of curiosities. They were also priceless.

A key stuck out from a fold-down writing desk within the cabinet. Turning it, she lowered the lid, the newly revealed cubbies inside stuffed with folded papers. A drawer in the centre contained another key. As she twisted it, internal mechanics whirred, and a music box began to play the *Lacrimosa* from Mozart's Requiem.

She smiled, Titanic's cargo manifests returning to her mind. *Item description: 1 Large Crate Roentgen secretary. Port of Origin: Folkestone.*

'Each and every clue leads back to Folkestone,' she said, watching the tiny mechanical ballerina spin atop the opened music box.

There was a commotion outside. She went to the window and looked out onto The Bayle. People carrying Union Jacks chattered excitedly over newspapers. Wally the Wall's man peddled slowly up the street wearing a Tommy helmet, his tandem covered with bunting. Schoolboys gave chase as he tossed them ice cream from his Warrick box. A pensioner in jacket and tie wore a dinged-up tin pot on his head. In fact, nearly everyone on the street had donned an old helmet or kitchen stewpot.

Had she forgotten a bank holiday?

From the direction of the pub, Mahmoud and Mssr Gaele minded their way through the crowd. Elle drew their attention with a wave. Gaele replied with a nod as they disappeared from view below the window.

Quickly dressing in her own clothes, she met the two of them at the bottom of the stairs, immediately recognising the chalk on Mahmoud's trousers.

'What's happened?'

'Germany,' said the Persian, closing the front door. 'They have invaded Poland.'

'Britain will be at war any day now,' added Gaele.

Without considering what they said, she asked, 'Where's Balthasar?'

THE END OF

THE GIFT, BOOK I.

ELEANOR.

Acknowledgment

For gifts I can never fully repay: Foremost my darling wife Daiana, for being at my side through the thick and thin. And for our little boy Tom Chunky—he is a light that never goes out. To mum, for teaching me to respect history, and for being an endless first-hand source of knowledge relating to wartime England. And to Dagenham Dave. Theirs really is the greatest generation.

To Professor Dennis Largey at BYU, for teaching me humility. For Doc Sima, who in those early years, recognised a cheeky boy could be something more. To my mate Bryan, for being my mate no matter what. To Cranbrook/Kingswood for its endless inspiration. To editors Liz Fraser, Kate Nascimento, and Candida Bradford, for making this thick writer an author. Thanks go to artists David Pickford, for his skill in reimagining Balthasar's death heraldry, and the tremendously talented Uroš Pajić, for his magnificent maps.

To the learned staff at the Royal Geographical Society, for their ceaseless patience with me whilst I spent too many hours at Kensington Gor, researching the obscure and forgotten. To guest services at the Clifton Hotel, for making me welcome these many years. To the Western Heights Preservation Society, particularly Phil Eyden, for their knowledge and dedication to preserving a marvellous bit of Dover history from vanishing under ivy. To the Friends of Highgate Cemetery, who preserve the Victorian Valhalla, and to the calming influence of the Parish Church of St Mary and St Eanswythe in Folkestone. To the boys at the Kent Battle of Britain Museum Trust, for the tireless preservation work, and the Battle of Britain Memorial at Capel-le-Ferne who keep the memory of The Few alive.

To the Baldwin Public Library in Birmingham, Michigan, the Powell Library at UCLA and Harold B Lee Library at BYU, for being temples of curiosity and knowledge. To Mark Holden, Jeanette Evert and Marjory Atwell, special thanks for your thoughts and historical accuracy.

READ AN EXCERPT FROM
THE GIFT, BOOK 2.
BALTHASAR.

---

9 SEPTEMBER 1940.
HIGHGATE CEMETERY

Inhaling the night's sweet air, Elle watched as Mahmoud slid the manhole cover back in place, relieved to leave the sewer's stink behind. The rain let up, but the sky above the city glowed scarlet. *Crump-crump-crumps* rolled along the heath from below, invading the quiet of Swain's Lane.

'Albert. Victoria. West India.' The Persian slowly counted off another dock with each detonation. 'Surrey Commercial. Millwall.'

'Docklands are catching a packet,' Gaele remarked, reloading Henry. 'Woolwich Arsenal and Beckton Gas Works are also inviting targets.'

Balthasar gazed down the tree-lined lane, his face lit by bomb flashes.

'Madness.'

'Madness?' repeated Elle, pointing to the manhole cover from where they all just emerged. 'What I saw down *there* is madness.'

He looked at her without reply.

'I need a minute to catch my breath,' she said.

'You can have your minute while we rid ourselves of our rucks.'

Removing spikes from his rucksack, he tucked them into the pockets of his anorak, tossing the bag over the high wall abutting the lane.

Removing her own spikes, Elle stuffed them into the back pockets of her RN utility trousers, keeping the Risineum at the ready in her thigh pocket.

'When are you going to explain to me what that was all about down there? The Sentinel. What it said. "He will rip you to pieces"? Who is "he"?' she asked.

Before Balthasar could reply, slits of light appeared from around the lane's bend. Elle looked for a place to hide, but the plastered walls bordering the lane were too high to climb. Swinging open a gate in the wall, Balthasar ushered the lot of them through. No sooner had he lowered the latch than the vehicle lurched to a halt.

Climbing onto a water butt, the Persian peered over the high wall. 'It's a removals van.'

Crouching beside Elle, Balthasar replied, 'At this hour?'

Doors creaked, followed by abrupt orders. Hob-nailed boots clattered.

'Scratch that,' Mahmoud whispered. 'It's Dad's Army.'

'Home Guard,' Elle said, turning to Balthasar. 'Grandads with broom handles.'

'This lot have rifles.'

'And not one of them can shoot straight,' Gaele reassured them.

Bracing herself with her hands as she slid down against the wall, Elle felt a sudden twinge of pain in her right hand. Blood seeped through a split seam in her glove. Pulling it off, she found a bead of red formed on the tip of her index finger.

'You've injured yourself,' Balthasar whispered.

'It's a slight cut. Must have caught it on a brick shard in the collapse.'

'Even a scratch can get infected with Weil's.'

Undoing a strap on her rucksack, she removed her orderlies bag.

'Have you sulphur powder?' asked the Belgian.

'I thought I did,' she said, rummaging through the kit, before shaking her head. 'I must have gone through it.'

He unscrewed his flask and poured Brandy over the cut. 'You don't want staph, ja?'

'Well aren't you a *meyven*?' she replied.

Gaele's forehead furrowed.

'Means you're a flipping expert.'

'Rat piss can infect your brain.' He shrugged. 'If cleaning your wound makes me an expert, *fiât*.'

'He's right,' said Balthasar as he wrapped a plaster about her finger. 'We can't have you going mad.'

'Oh, so what I just saw in the sewers isn't enough to send me into madness?'

The van's motor kicked over, clutch grinding before it drove off.

'Have they gone?' asked Balthasar.

'The van has,' Mahmoud replied. 'Couple of blokes standing about scratching their bums.'

Elle leaned back, the thorns from a wild rose bush prickling her shirt. Freeing herself, she nudged her rucksack. The wind-up toy inside began to clatter.

'*Fais taire ton bruit, putain*,' Gaele snapped, voice hushed but harsh, he told her to shut up the noise, although not as polite.

'For God's sake, what is that?' asked Balthasar, teeth gritting.

Opening the bag, she grasped hold of the tin litho. Felix the Cat rocked back and forth on the tricycle's handlebars. Quickly shoving a finger between the bobbing cat and tricycle, she silenced it.

'Were they alerted?'

Mahmoud shook his head. 'Standing about watching the action over the city.'

Balthasar turned to her, the moon revealing his cross face.

'Half a moment,' the Persian whispered.

Elle waited for him to say the guards were coming their way. Instead, he shook his head.

'Nah, don't worry, they're tucking into sausage rolls.'

'You nearly had us in a scrap with the Home Guard,' Balthasar sighed, giving her a sour look. 'What was that racket?'

Opening her hand, she showed him the tin wind-up toy.

'Why on earth have you brought *that*?'

'I didn't,' she explained. 'It was in the caldarium.'

'But why on earth have you kept it?' Gaele asked.

'You don't think it's odd, this being in a caldarium?'

'A child's toy? You could purchase one in any cinema.'

'Or fun fair,' Balthasar added.

'You still don't think it strange?' she repeated. 'A Sentinel with a child's toy?'

'Sometimes they keep mementos,' Balthasar reluctantly admitted.

'You really think that abomination kept a child's toy as a memento?'

'It's possible it consumed the child it belonged to,' Gaele suggested.

'Are you lot thick?'

'Keep your voice down,' Balthasar hushed.

'A memento of *what*?' she asked.

'Of their former lives,' replied the Persian, looking down from the wall at the wind-up toy in her hand. 'Reminds them of a time before they were Crimen.'

'Never been able to work out why,' said Balthasar. Elle eyed him suspiciously. He knew full well why.

Gazing back over the wall, Mahmoud changed the subject. 'Good, they've moving off now.'

'Let's wait a wee bit.' Balthasar clicked on the Thompson's safety. Glancing towards her, he added nothing more.

Looking at the toy in her hands, Elle felt unease. The Sentinel had purposefully held on to the toy as a reminder. Somewhere within, it dearly held on to a memory of its mortal self. She had watched the seraph plead with Balthasar, aware how dreadful its last moments would be. Still Balthasar killed it. Just as Elle had killed Emiliana.

She inspected the dinged paint, hoping her shame would linger. Her own memory of being human. Then, she noticed the stamped gold letters on Felix's foot.

Produkt von Deutschland.

'Right, they've gone.' Climbing from the water butt, Mahmoud cracked the gate.

'Leave your rucksacks,' Balthasar instructed. 'We got to get a move on.'

She tucked the memento into her bag and left it inside the gate. Returning to Swain's Lane, she had a look around. The Home Guard had moved off and aside from the distant sound of ack-ack, it was quiet. Across the lane stood a Gothic chapel, stone buttresses and parapets blackened by coal smoke. No light shone from its lancet windows.

'Nobody home?' she asked.

'The gateman, but he maintains blackout regulation,' replied Gaele as she beckoned them to follow him under a Tudor-arched gateway between the chapels.

'Is it me,' she asked, eyeing their weaponry, 'or do we look suspicious?'

394

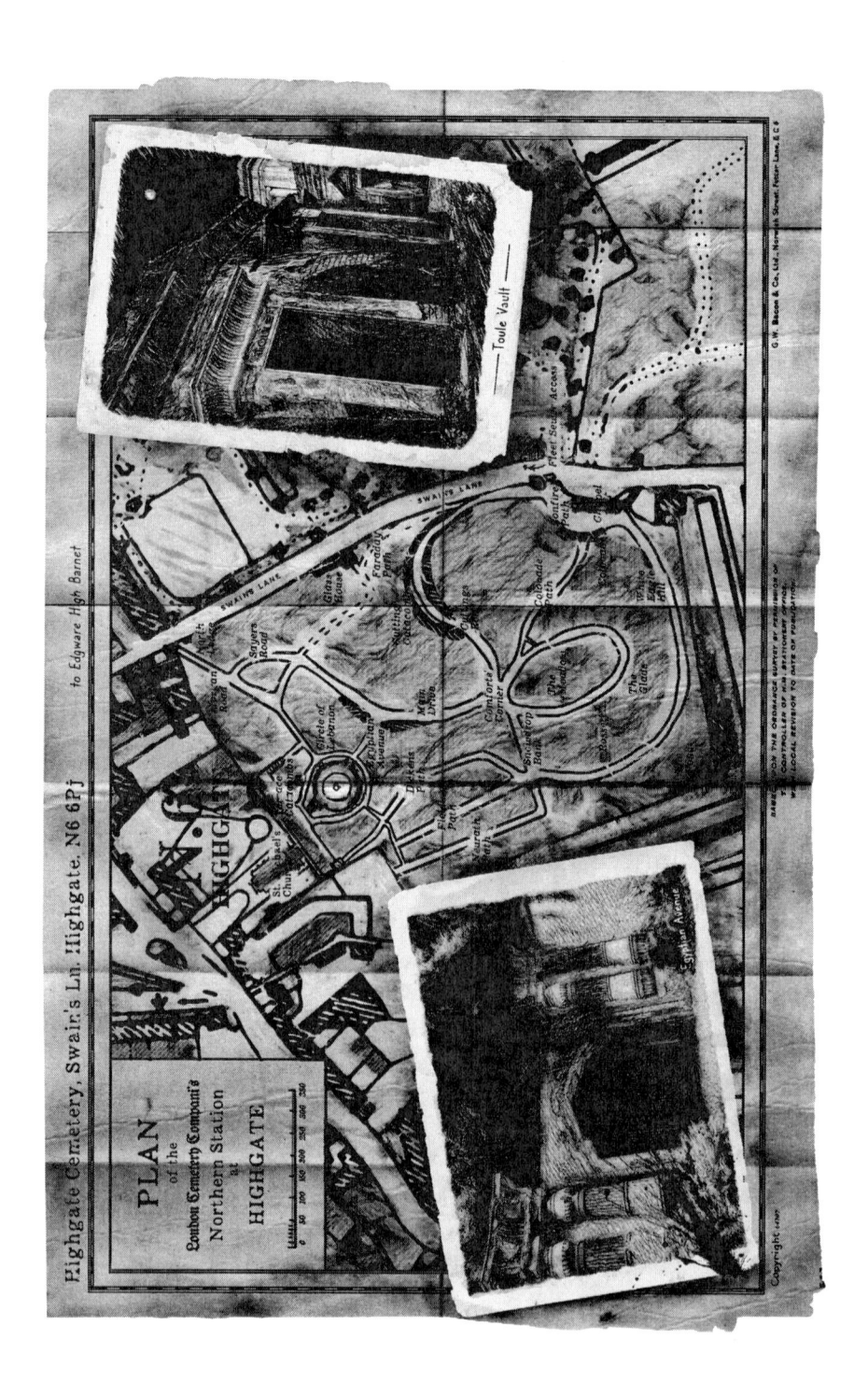

'Monsieur pays the gateman a few bob to look the other way,' Mahmoud explained.

Gaele pushed in a gate, hinges offering a familiar creak.

'I donate four litres of black market petrol a month for him to keep schtum.'

Closing the gate behind, he led them across a semi-circular courtyard, sinuous ivy vines disguising the arches of a crescent-shaped colonnade.

'The groundskeepers have joined up,' Gaele said, as if apologising for the neglected look of the grounds.

'Rubbish,' the Persian disagreed as they ascended a set of stairs. 'The West cemetery has been grotty for years.'

Making their way deeper into the cemetery, a path led them into a necropolis of headstones drunkenly leaning this way and that. Sinister shadows rose as the bombers' moon became partly banished above a canopy of yews and weeping willows. Terrible things lurked amidst sorrowing angels and draped urns. Flashes from the distant bombing lit a maze of rising terraces choked with forgotten tombs and vaults.

Despite the *crump-crump-crumps* rolling up the heath from the city below, Elle felt removed from the war. Passing a mausoleum, she noticed a weeping angel staring sadly back at her, protective wings lost amongst the brambles. She thought of Emiliana then, her own shame returning, reminding her of the terrible things in which she had already partaken.

She had strayed from who she thought she was. She couldn't have guessed it was possible to be so fearless. But the tapping of her finger on the trigger guard suggested otherwise, the adrenaline, which had kept her unafraid for a while, now subsiding. Her thoughts elsewhere, she stumbled over a tree root jutting out on the uneven path.

Balthasar caught her. 'Steady as you go.'

'Couldn't have picked a creepier place, could you?' she mocked anew, trying to shake off her nerves.

'Courage,' he said, 'is just fear holding on a moment longer.'

Was her fear so obvious?

'There's something else,' she blurted out without meaning to. Thankfully Balthasar didn't reply. She didn't want to say it. Underneath her fear was a frisson of pleasure. It worried her.

'Fancy humming that song again, Mahmoud?' she said instead.

He smiled thinly. 'You mean like whistling through a cemetery?'

'It wasn't always a cemetery,' Balthasar said, pausing at an intersecting avenue.

'Something more you've neglected to tell me?' she asked as she stopped in her tracks. 'If you expect me to lug about this useless peashooter, you can fill me in.'

Mahmoud and Balthasar looked at one another, resigned.

'Highgate is a *petit massif*,' Gaele said, returning from tabbing ahead. Casually shouldering Henry, he lit a cigarette. 'A little mountain,' he translated.

'Hampstead Heath is the other.'

They all looked at her.

'I'm well familiar with the lay of the land. I attended the Chiltham School for Young Ladies just down the road in Hampstead.'

'Then you know the city below is an enormous flood plain,' Balthasar continued. 'Over the centuries, the River Fleet, like all the others flowing down to the Thames, became open sewers.'

'An incubator for all manner of plague,' the Persian added, leaning against the edge of an overgrown tomb.

Sensing their more relaxed demeanour, she rested her weight on an old statue, fern sprouting from its cracked limestone. 'What does a river's source have to do with Crimen?'

'The ponds of Hampstead and Highgate, the Fleet's source, were a refuge,' Mahmoud continued.

'You have to understand: not all plague is bubonic by nature,' Balthasar said.

'Crimen,' she worked through it. 'They *are* plague?'

'Of a sort. Those with wealth fled London for Highgate's healing waters.'

'We've a Lord Mayor of London to thank,' replied Mahmoud, gazing down the path as a flash lit the sky. An instant later came a *whumpf* as a bomb exploded. 'That was close.'

'That's another miss-drop,' said Gaele.

'Sir William Ashhurst,' Balthasar continued to explain, disinterested in the bombing. 'Lord Mayor of London, was so taken by Highgate's healing waters, he built an estate here in the 17th Century.'

'Ashhurst House,' said the Persian.

'Never heard of it,' she answered.

'It wasn't always a cemetery,' Balthasar repeated. 'Highgate flourished.'

The breeze shifted, carrying the choking odour of cordite and smoke. 'Until a plague like none London had witnessed before.'

'Gruesome mutilations began to occur all along the river's course.'

'*Wilderzeichen*?' she asked.

'We tracked a Sentinel upstream,' Mahmoud explained.

'To Highgate?'

'We found the banshee. She consumed Sir William's heir.'

'And what, became Lady of the manor?'

The call of a night bird caused Balthasar to half cock an ear, and then he looked back at Elle. 'His valet became her Sentinel. Together, they fed on the household staff.'

'Collected your butcher's bill?' asked the Belgian, coolly.

Balthasar didn't bother turning to him. 'We scythed the lot of them.'

'But not Siobhan?' Elle asked, already knowing the answer.

The bird called again from the darkness. The Belgian panned the ivy-strangled tombs with his torchlight. Perhaps Elle's colleagues were not as at ease as she presumed.

'No, not Siobhan,' answered Balthasar. 'She abandoned the manor. It soon fell into decay.'

'Came as rather a surprise to us when the grounds became Highgate Cemetery,' said Mahmoud, his torchlight joining Gaele's.

'Desecrated before it could be consecrated,' she said.

'This hollow has been dormant a hundred years.'

'The murders in the newspapers,' she realised.

Mahmoud nodded. 'The mutilations, and where they occurred.'

'Along the course of the Fleet.'

Mahmoud got to his feet, alert. Torchlight leading, he inspected a Greek-revival tomb hidden beneath tentacles of ivy. Sliding Henry from his shoulder, Gaele joined him. The tomb's iron, double-leaf door was cracked. A blood-smeared handprint on the door.

Gaele looked to Balthasar, who gave him a nod.

'Take a butcher's at it,' he told the Belgian.

Turning, Gaele pushed the door in just enough to squeeze through, his voice echoing from deep within the tomb.

'Wild signs.'

Elle crouched for a look.

'Don't bother with it,' advised Mahmoud. 'A lot of dusty old bones.' Ignoring his caution, she went in. The smell of mortality greeted her, sweet and sticky. Distant bombing lit the subterranean vault through a skylight in the roof, revealing upturned caskets. On the ground of the tomb lay an eviscerated corpse, its chest cavity glistening. A fresh kill.

'Is that your man?' asked Balthasar.

'It is,' Gaele replied sadly, before slinging his Winchester.

'How recent?'

Crouching, he gave the corpse a knock. 'He's stiff.'

'Going in or coming out?'

'By the smell of him, I'd wager coming out of rigour.'

'Eight to twelve hours ago, then,' deduced Mahmoud.

Elle exited the confines of the tomb. The others followed. She watched Gaele have a long look around. An ethereal cantata broke the silence. High-pitched and pure.

'They are here,' the Belgian whispered.

Balthasar's eyes narrowed as he scanned the vine-choked trees. It came again. A distant, sweet melody of angelic voices. 'Indeed.'

'Siobhan?' asked Elle, instinctively patting the Ṙisineum in her thigh pocket.

'War provides the banshee fertile ground,' he replied, turning to the Belgian. 'There's nothing more to see here.'

Cautiously, they continued along the gravel path, making their way deeper into Highgate, the Belgian walking ahead. Balthasar followed, with Elle close behind. Mahmoud minded their flank.

On alert, Elle's senses came alive as grim statues rose and fell around her, the crunching of gravel under her boots thunderous to her ear. Ahead, from the encroaching mist, she picked out an enormous Pharaonic arch in all its gloomy splendour.

'We go through there,' directed Balthasar. 'Through the Egyptian Avenue.'

Elle shone her torch up at the ivy-entwined lotus pillars flanking the entrance. Victorian society had been mad on Egyptian symmetry. A wrought-iron gate hung by a single hinge. Passing between the pillars they entered a narrow, sloping avenue lined with vaults.

Gaele halted before a cast-iron door emblazoned with an inverted torch; symbol of the flame of life, extinguished.

'Toule,' Elle said, reading the familiar name engraved into the limestone above the door. 'You've a vault in Highgate as well?'

'Necessity,' Balthasar replied. 'I needed access to the wine cellar.'

'The cemetery has a wine cellar?'

'It wasn't always a cemetery, remember?'

While the other vault entrances were web-bound, the door to the Toule vault was clear. The Belgian pushed on the door. Inching it open, he thrust his torch inside. After a moment's hesitation, he turned to Balthasar.

'You go first.'

Mahmoud scoffed, opening the door further. Iron protested against stone. Raising his Thompson, he warily made his way in. Balthasar followed. Gaele raised his arm, blocking Elle until all was declared safe.

'Clear,' came the Persian's voice from within. They entered. The vault was unimpressive: a damp, brick-lined cell containing four lead coffins.

'The Sentinel didn't pass this way,' said Balthasar.

'How can you know?'

He tapped a web-smothered coffin, undisturbed.

'Who's inside?'

'A Marks and Sparks dummy,' Mahmoud replied.

Elle would have laughed, were she not so scared. Shouldering their guns, they shifted one of the lids, and true to his word, a plaster mannequin stared out at her, its painted smile macabre.

Gaele lifted it out and tossed it into the corner.

'So then,' said Balthasar, climbing inside. 'Into the rabbit hole I go.'

Elle watched as they reset the lid.

'What do we do now?' she asked.

A dull *thunk* set unseen mechanics in motion, the floor beneath her boots vibrating.

'We wait,' replied Mahmoud.

Gaele shifted on the lid of an adjoining coffin. 'We may find nothing out of the ordinary down there, Elle.'

'There's been nothing ordinary about this night thus far,' she replied, wiping years of dust away from the coffin's lid before sitting beside him.

He nodded. 'Or we shall have to deal with eleven things that go bump in the night.'

She sighed. 'Got any more of your giggle juice?'

Reaching for his flask, he took a swig before passing it to her. 'In a scrap, if you cannot finish off a Crimen with a spike, blow its brains out.'

Elle took a nip, the brandy steadying her nerves. 'I'll keep that in mind.'

'If inopportune, try to crush their spine,' he added. 'Huntians do not heal quickly unless they have fed.'

'These Crimen in this hollow,' she asked. 'They haven't fed?'

'Not for a century.'

Mahmoud shifted the coffin's lid, revealing it to be not only empty, but seemingly bottomless. Elle stood, looking inside. Narrow stairs spiralled into nothingness. The Persian called into the darkness. Balthasar's distant voice begged them to follow. Elle found him at the bottom, chopper pointing off into darkness. Her torchlight lit giant cogs and cords, identical to those beneath his vault in St Emiliana. Gaele gave an iron lever a tug, and the mechanics began to whirr anew.

'Ingenious, no?'

'Ingenious, yes,' Elle agreed.

'Roentgen's gizmos.'

She turned to Mahmoud. 'Abraham Roentgen? The cabinet maker?'

'David, actually. His son.'

'How?'

Cogs clinked, the thud of the false bottom of the coffin sealing itself in place unsettling.

'With the price of a Roentgen Secretary being close to that of a small estate, David threw in these conjurer's tricks for free.'

'It niffs down here,' Gaele said.

Elle sniffed, detecting only an earthy smell to the air.

'*They* have been released,' said Balthasar. 'Mssr Gaele, you will mind Elle?'

'Of course.'

'Good. Mahmoud and I shall tab ahead.'

'How do you know they've been released?' she asked nervously.

'By the odour,' said the Persian, simply.

'I've smelled it before. What is it?'

'Dry rot,' he added.

'Old fabric,' Balthasar explained, before making his way along a bricked undercroft.

The Persian followed after.

'Their clothing. The smell of it. It's a Crimen's dry-rotted clothing you are smelling.'

Raising her torch to the groined ceiling, intersecting arrises choked with spiders' busy work, she realised no one had ventured down there for ages.

'Is this Highgate?'

'No,' Balthasar said, pointing out a wide ascending stairway backfilled with spoil. 'When the manor was razed, the entrance to the undercroft was simply covered over.'

'Fortunately for us,' added Mahmoud.

'The wine cellar survives. A suitable hollow.'

'Heathens,' muttered the Belgian from the rear.

Their torches fell on row on row of load-bearing buttresses engraved with inverted doves, weeping willows and the usual skulls. Not even the cemetery matched the gloom of the undercroft.

'Buster,' Elle whispered, drawing his attention to her torchlight as it panned the packed earth, revealing a tangle of footprints, some soled, others barefoot. It was as if they just missed a ghoulish dance party. Although sweating cobs, Elle felt a sudden drop in temperature.

'Feel that?' she asked.

'Ja,' replied Gaele.

Balthasar halted, his torchlight picking something organic out of the darkness. Torches converging, a ghostly shape emerged. Turned away from them, against a buttress, it remained stock still. Elle squinted, discerning black breeches and long hose covered in grey dust.

'Oi,' the Persian whispered. 'You all right there?'

Slowly it turned, gaunt face glaring at them, mouth agape. It pushed out a raspy breath as though it needed a long drink of water. But it thirsted for something else.

Elle swallowed her fear. In the Fleet, she had not the time to process fright. Adrenaline propelled her on. But here, as they cautiously moved through the undercroft, her mind lingered on the awful beasts, and she was terrified.

'Huntian,' cautioned Balthasar, moving towards it. It was anaemic, with patches of scruffy hair clinging to its ashen head. It watched them approach. Curious but dumb, it raised its arms, not to reach out but to shield itself. Lifting his gun barrel, Balthasar prodded the fiend's shallow-tail livery, silver buttons torn open. The beast offered only a torporific snap.

'It has not fed,' Balthasar said, parting its waistcoat to expose a bruised puncture to the left of its sternum. 'Second Footman. From Ashhurst's household staff.'

'Where's its spike gone?' asked Mahmoud, pushing the fiend against the buttress.

'How many are there?' Elle asked, eyes darting to Balthasar.

'Ten,' he replied. 'Ten in this hollow.'

'How many Sentinels?'

'One. And we put him down in the Roman Bath,' replied Mahmoud, the beast lurching lethargically at him.

'It's docile,' said Elle.

'It's famished for flesh.'

Taking hold of her hand, Balthasar pulled off her glove. The plaster covering her cut finger now stained red with clotted blood. Even with eyes crazed by cataracts, the fiend zeroed in on the bloodied plaster, bolting towards her.

'Enough of that.' Mahmoud shoved the Huntian against the wall. It cooed, with hardly enough strength to protest. Removing a spike from the chest pocket of his anorak, Mahmoud plunged it into its chest. Unlike the Sentinel, the starved beast hardly gasped. Spindly legs buckling, it collapsed to the ground, foul gas hissing from its mouth as the Jungfräu transformed to its liquid state.

'These Huntians,' Elle asked, watching the pathetic beast's limbs curling, parched skin tightening against bone. 'All of them will be like this?'

Balthasar nodded, motioning towards the far end of the undercroft. 'So long as they haven't fed.'

Leaving the desiccated beast behind, they made their way to the far end of the undercroft, slowing as their torches picked something else out of the darkness.

A clutch of Crimen emerged. Huddled together, their heads bobbed rhythmically, their respiration laboured. Before Elle could withdraw a spike from her pocket, the others descended upon them, silently puncturing each Huntian. They collapsed without protest into a heap of reducing mush.

'Is this too easy?' she asked, watching the Jungfräu devouring the fiends. Nobody replied. She caught the Belgian's face in her torchlight. He nodded.

Beyond them, a narrow stairway led down. At its bottom, yet another Crimen. Too frail to stand, it scratched at the earthen floor. Disturbed by their torchlight, it turned to them, rotted lips parting as it released a croak. Elle could not help but pity it.

'First Footman?' asked the Persian. Balthasar knocked the Huntian over with his boot. Its torn shirt was covered with a century of shed dander, standing collar sprung. A wretched gasp spewed from its mouth as Balthasar thrust a spike into its chest, and its head quivered before falling slack.

'They've all lost their spikes,' said the Persian, watching as the Huntian burped up a foamy stew, mottled skin shrinking around its ribcage.

'Someone has removed them.'

Elle turned to Balthasar. 'How is that possible? The way we came was undisturbed?'

'It's not the only way in,' said Gaele.

Fear began to claw it way back into Elle's chest.

'There's another entrance,' replied the Persian. 'Just outside the cemetery back wall, through the crypt under St Michael's church.'

'Why the hell didn't we come in that way?'

'Not possible,' Balthasar told her, concentrating his torchlight on the narrowing passage ahead.

'The crypt is in use as a bomb shelter,' Gaele explained.

A whisper sowed the darkness.

'What was that?' Elle asked. A stifled snigger followed. It set her hair on end. 'What the hell is happening?'

Balthasar eagerly moved forward, his Tommy gun pointing into the blackness.

'Up ahead,' he whispered. Elle squinted through the disturbed dust. 'In the wine cellar.'

A few paces more and their torches struck upon another cluster of Crimen. Huddled morosely together, they appeared engaged in a household conference. Brushing her behind him, Gaele joined the others at the front. Quietly closing in on the Huntians, they felled them with butchers' efficiency. Stepping over the fiends withering at her feet, her torchlight picked out deep gouges in the packed earthen floor. Something heavy had been dragged that way.

The passage came to an end. Chiselled into the blocking stone was Balthasar's heraldry. Elle stared at the grimacing skull atop a human body. It was exactly the same as at the Externsteine.

Mahmoud looked back to Balthasar, unease on his face. 'It's sealed.'

'Who but we would open the hollow?' Gaele asked.

'Or could?' asked Elle.

'And close it up again after,' said Mahmoud.

Balthasar's torchlight illuminated the hulking slab of stone barring the way. 'Ten strong backs couldn't budge this.'

He struck the tips of his fingers into the seam of the massive stone. With a grunt he forced it back, the blocking stone rotating away with a grinding *thud*. The sticky odour of mortality wafted from within.

Mahmoud just managed to direct his torch into the passage beyond before he was set upon, the light revealing a Crimen, puffed up with rage. It threw itself on him, bony fingers grasping hold of his anorak. Confined by the narrow passage, he was able to raise the butt of his gun to fend off a bite. Balthasar was there in an instant, taking the feeder by the neck and heaving it against the opposite wall, shattering the mortar. Wild-eyed and flush-skinned, it shrieked in protest, the veins in its bare arms pulsing as it battered him.

'It has fed,' Balthasar said through gritted teeth, twisting as he thrust the Huntian against the wall of the passage again, vestiges of its rotted French-twill dress falling to bits. 'A household maid. Run it through.'

Brandishing a spike, the Belgian pushed his way towards the feeder. It shrieked in fright at the sight of the Jungfräu. Pushing its right arm back, he exposed its chest and thrust the spike in. It howled, putrescence exploding from the puncture. Unlike the starved Huntians, there was fight in it. Thrashing, it clobbered Gaele in the face. He reeled back, his rifle butt catching Elle in the stomach, causing her to double over. She rolled onto her side, trying to regain her breath and watched as another beast emerged from the cellar entrance and lunged at Balthasar. Raising her Sten, she fired off a burst. The discharge was deafening in the claustrophobic passage. Bullets caught the beast in its side, spinning it round, the tails of its lounge jacket flapping.

A valet.

Mahmoud slugged it in the face, crunching its nose as easily as dry leaves underfoot. Casting aside the maid's carcass, Balthasar took hold of the valet from behind, its jacket coming apart in his hands. Grasping its suspenders, he wrenched the beast off Mahmoud, pinning its arms back. The Huntian twisted, trying to break Balthasar's grip. Elle heard a distinctive ripping sound as the valet's sleeve tore at the shoulder and its entire arm came away like old rope breaking free. Tossing aside the limb, Balthasar put the feeder into a headlock, while Mahmoud punched a spike into its chest. Squirming in his grasp, the beast purged a viscid curd.

'Who have you eaten?' whispered Balthasar, thrusting the fiend into the wall of the passage with such spite its head went to mush.

Scooping his Thompson up by its sling, the Persian said, 'I'd say someone got themselves trapped inside.'

Gaele chambered a round into Henry as the beast fell into a raving fit, casting off a revolting stew of bodily fluids.

'And gobbled up.'

Balthasar pressed a finger to his lips, whispering for Elle to stay close to Gaele while he joined Mahmoud probing ahead. Before she could protest, the sticky stench of death filled her nose. She quickly put a gloved hand to her mouth, holding back the urge to be sick. Torchlight swept across web-bound wine racks set back between simple brick supports. Her boots crunched loudly on broken glass. Lowering her torch to the floor, she stopped to lift the remnants of an open wine bottle.

'Chateau Margaux,' Gaele said. 'I drank it last time I looked in.' He shrugged. 'Pity to let it spoil. Especially a Grand Vin Rouge.'

'Buster.'

Ahead, the Persian stood in the central arcade of the vault, probing the darkness with his torch. Lined up between the cellar's supports were ten sarcophagi, their lids all smashed open. They lay empty.

'How many Crimen have we put paid to?' asked Gaele.

'Eleven,' replied Balthasar, taking stock. 'I think.'

'Good,' replied the Belgian. He looked at his watch. 'We can just make a late dinner at The Ritz.'

'I wouldn't count on them holding a table.'

'Eleven?' Elle repeated, tossing the neck of the broken wine bottle into the darkness. 'And the Sentinel in the Roman Bath?'

Balthasar turned to Elle, his brow furrowed.

'Makes for twelve,' said Gaele.

'One too many,' realised Mahmoud.

The glass bounced off something metallic, shattering. Turning just in the nick of time, Elle side-stepped a beast stumbling from the murk. Gaele lashed it in the head with the butt of his rifle. A loud *prang* vibrated along the arcade. Shining her torch past him, the beam fell upon the tin helmet strapped to a Crimen's head.

'Bloody hell,' said Mahmoud, covering the Huntian with his chopper as it struggled to its feet. 'A suited and booted Tommy.'

Torches converging, it was plain to see why the beast had difficulty standing.

'Its arms have gone,' Gaele said unsympathetically.

With his gun barrel, Balthasar brushed aside the soldier's shredded battle jacket, the buttons of his shirt underneath torn away. On its chest, left of the sternum, over the heart, was a bite.

'*Putain*,' said the Belgian.

'What?' asked Elle.

'*Dosis*,' replied Balthasar.

'Dose?' she asked.

He nodded. 'He's been injected. If we'd arrived much later. we would have had another Sentinel to deal with.'

'How long does it take to turn?'

'Not long,' Balthasar replied.

'Not long at all.' Holding the beast down with his boot, Mahmoud thrust a spike into the Huntian. It heaved, its Tommy helmet flying from its head and rolling into the darkness. Booted feet dug furiously into the floor. Without arms, there was nothing it could do to defend itself.

As the mercury spread through the Huntian's internal organs, it shuddered violently, mouth forming silent words of despair before going still. Like an insect on its back, its legs curled up as life drained away.

'Poor bugger.' Gaele stared down at the withering beast. 'His mum won't be getting a notification from the War Office.'

Mahmoud rifled through the pockets of his battledress.

'Are you looking for loose coppers?'

The Persian removed the soldiers' ration book, flipping through its pages. 'His last ration stamp was on the eighth of September.'

'Yesterday,' said Balthasar.

'What in hell has gone on here?' Gaele asked.

Elle felt the hair on the back of her sweat-soaked neck stand on end. Instinctively, she turned to the darkness, her torch falling upon a heap of bleeding carrion.

'Black shit and buggery,' she gasped as her torch passed over the sprawled-out remains, picking out a schoolboy's cap, a single night slipper, a child's dummy, fox stole, and a blood-spattered apron.

Balthasar looked over the pile. 'What a jumble of sticky bits.'

'Civvies.' Mahmoud nudged a gas-mask bag with his boot. 'Seeking shelter from the air-raids?'

'This isn't a shelter,' replied Gaele. A sad-looking teddy lay nearby, its stuffing protruding from a missing leg. 'This is an abattoir.'

Elle swallowed, the bile rising in her throat again. 'How did they get down here?'

'They didn't,' said Balthasar. His torchlight fell upon a low passageway revealing a second blocking stone sealed in place.

Gaele nervously tapped Henry's trigger guard. 'They didn't what?'

'They didn't *get* down here,' he replied, eyes zeroing in on movement from the darkness. 'They were brought here.'

A fiend lurched its way into his torch beam; an old man, intestines unravelling from beneath spattered pyjamas.

The Persian pushed him into a wine rack, disturbing a millennium's worth of dust. Without pausing for thought, he spiked him.

'Nefarious *roué*.'

'Brought here?' asked Elle, watching the debauched old soul wither. 'Why?'

Before Balthasar could reply, the queer cantata broke the cellar's quiet once more. Not nearly as distant as before, it ended again in a curious fugue joined by a caw, like seagulls in distress.

'Mahmoud.' Balthasar stepped cautiously back as the singing died away. 'Circle the wagons.'

The Persian and Gaele closed with Elle, their backs brushing against her.

'So very clever,' Balthasar muttered, as he joined them in a defensive square around her. 'We've been baited.'

Raising the Sten, Elle swept her kill zone, focusing on a bottle vibrating in one of the wine racks.

'Balthasar,' she squealed, drawing his attention to the wine rack just as it toppled over in a cloud of dust and broken glass, the sweet scent of wine long gone off mingling with an odour of human decay. The others waited silently, all movement obscured by lingering dust.

'Can't see bugger all.'

Clipping his torch to a button on his anorak, Balthasar produced a fusée from his pocket, pulling its ignition cord. As it spat red flame, he tossed it into the fog. It bounced off something close by before rolling across the floor of the cellar. Flaring, it began to burn bright yellow.

'*Bordel de merde*,' the Belgian cursed quietly, pushing back against Elle. She jumped, unnerved, trying to force her courage to overtake her fear. A Crimen hive crept towards the fighting square. Ripped up and closing awfully fast, there were too many. Her instinct was to leg it, but there was nowhere now to go.

Nothing remained but to fight.